THE THREE GREAT SECRET THINGS

A Novel

by Anthony S. Abbott

MINT HILL BOOKS
MAIN STREET RAG PUBLISHING COMPANY
CHARLOTTE, NORTH CAROLINA

Author photo by David Crosby

Library of Congress Control Number: 2007931555

ISBN 13: 978-1-59948-077-0

Produced in the United States of America

Mint Hill Books
Main Street Rag Publishing Company
PO Box 690100
Charlotte, NC 28227-7001
www.MainStreetRag.com

*To the Members of the Class of 1953 at Kent School
and to the memory of John Oliver Patterson.*

ACKNOWLEDGEMENTS

LEAVING MAGGIE HOPE was published in 2003 by Novello Festival Press of Charlotte and was the winner of the Novello Award. The novel ended with fourteen-year-old David Lear graduating from Lowell School in Massachusetts, and virtually everyone I talked to about the novel asked me if I was writing a sequel. The answer was always "yes," and by the end of 2004 I was well into the book which became *The Three Great Secret Things*. Early on I knew what I wanted to call the novel, because John Updike's wonderful phrase from his memoir, *The Dogwood Tree: A Boyhood*, captured perfectly for me the three great passions which dominated David Lear's life between the ages of fourteen and nineteen: sex, religion, and art. And I am deeply grateful to Alfred Knopf/Random House for their permission to use this phrase as the title of my novel.

When I had completed a full draft of the novel, I sent it out to friends and former students to get a sense of how it was working. Cathy Landis, Ann Wicker, Sheri Reynolds, Ann Campanella, Bob Cumming, Rosa Shand, Jacquie Bussie, and Martin Clark all read and commented on this draft, and I thank them for their commitment and their friendship.

I revised the novel and sent it to Linda Whitney Hobson for editing. When I got it back from Linda, I realized both the novel's potential and how much further I had to go before it was finished. Her suggestions and corrections pushed me to see my characters more deeply, and to go places I had not been willing to go before. I did two more drafts, and sent them to Linda for her editing before I was satisfied that I had taken the novel where it needed to go. She is an astonishingly good editor, fervently enthusiastic and ruthlessly critical at the same time. Her belief in the book always supported me even as her criticism pushed me to make changes.

At some point in the process I sent the book to Lee Smith, who pushed me to "up the ante." With Linda's help I did, and I am grateful to Lee for her generous comments about the completed novel. I am also grateful to Fred Chappell and Josephine Humphreys for their support.

Finally let me thank Lisa Kline for proofreading the novel, and Scott Douglass the editor of Main Street Rag Publishing Company for taking on the project.

"Concerning the Three Great Secret Things:
(1) Sex (2) Religion (3) Art"

Chapter subtitle from John Updike,
The Dogwood Tree: A Boyhood

CHAPTER ONE

In the stifling heat of August and early September, 1948, at his sister Elizabeth's apartment in the Bronx, David dreamt of Maggie Hope. It was always the same. By the time he opened his eyes she had disappeared down the hall toward Elizabeth's bedroom. Sometimes he thought he saw her on the platform at the 167th Street Station, as he waited for the D train to take him downtown. He would walk toward her, and then she would vanish.

Maggie had died of cancer, and of drink, his sister said, almost a year ago, and though he had not known his mother very well, not seen much of her during his seventh and eighth grade years at Lowell School, David missed her. She was always Maggie Hope, even when she had married his father and become Maggie Hope Lear or married his stepfather and become Maggie Peterson.

He talked to her, mostly on the D train as it rattled back and forth between mid-town Manhattan and the Bronx. David thought the noise would cover his voice. "Who were you, Maggie?" he would ask, or "Tell me where you are now, Maggie Hope." Once a stranger sitting next to him caught him in the act. "You're talkin' to yourself, kid." David laughed. No point in explaining.

Now it was mid September, and David stood in the gigantic main concourse at Grand Central Station, looking up at the gold constellations in the blue sky painted on the ceiling. "There's Cancer, Maggie Hope," he whispered, "your sign," wondering if she had known even when she first showed it to him, that cancer would kill her. He wanted to tell her how he felt about starting at a new school, the strangeness of it, the uncertainty, the pain of having to make friends all over again.

He hoisted to his left shoulder her old leather bag with the faded gold letters M.H. on it, the same bag he had carried to Lowell School four years ago, and began walking down the long ramp to the new train and the car which carried the Wicker School sign. He took a seat by himself on the left-hand side so that he could silently salute the gigantic Life Savers over the factory entrance as they passed Port Chester. There was no Griff and no Terry to salute with him, no comrades-in-arms to share his thoughts and feelings with. Just David, alone. He was fourteen, no longer David Lear, the winner of the prestigious Founder's Medal at Lowell School, he was just a lowly ninth grader, a third former, a new boy.

No one talked to him. The other boys seemed busy with their friends, the older boys—fifth and sixth formers, he guessed—smoking, turning the air gray as the train gained speed through the tunnel and burst into the open. And then the Life Savers—huge rolls of green, blue, and red against the backdrop of the dirty brick. David thought of his friends and their club and how they had been lifesavers for each other. "Goodbye," he said, and closed his eyes. But he couldn't sleep, couldn't create the Maggie Hope dream. There was too much going on. With his eyes closed he could hear the talk around him, a blend of murmuring and snickers.

"But how far did you get? Second base? Third?"

"The Yankees in six games."

"You're full of it. They won't even win the pennant."

"She's got great tits."

"And then I barfed. . .right in the hotel room."

"Under the stairs. . ."

"Charlie's is the best. They never card you."

"Girls and baseball and beer," David thought to himself. "Girls and baseball and beer." He murmured it over and over, rocking his head quietly against the seat. "Well, Maggie Hope," he said, "this is going to be very different."

At Norwalk the Wicker car was switched to another track and they set off due north toward Danbury instead of northeast to New Haven and Lowell School beyond. At Wicker the boys placed their bags on the blue school truck, and David followed the others down the main street. They turned right at a blinking yellow light by a war memorial, crossed a swiftly flowing river, and then turned left into the school. David's first thought was that it was beautiful. He had never thought of Lowell as beautiful or not beautiful. It just was. But Wicker with its flowing river, its red-brick Georgian buildings framed in a valley against the mountain rising above them, was stunning.

At the first assembly in the auditorium that evening, he learned that the mountain was called Algo, that the river was Housatonic, and the valley Macedonia. Every new boy would be assigned a color, red for Mount Algo, blue for the Housatonic River, or green for the Macedonia Valley. He learned that he would have a job. Everyone had a job, because it saved the school thousands of dollars a year. Students cleaned toilets, washed dishes, raked leaves, shoveled snow, wiped down blackboards.

By his third day David had it figured out: the school was run by the sixth formers. They supervised jobs, inspected rooms, checked for lateness, sniffed for contraband. The masters turned up for classes and sports. You never saw a master in the dorms or in the dining room except for Saturday night dinner, when they were specially invited.

The school motto was "Temperantia, Fiducia, Constantia," which meant "simplicity of life, self-reliance, directness of purpose." It seemed much more complicated than Lowell's motto, "Poteris Modo Velis," "You Can If You Will." For Mr. Armbrister, the Headmaster of Lowell, life was a battle. If you fought hard enough you won. "God rewards those with the strongest will," the Headmaster had told the boys.

But for Father James Alexander Perkins, the Rector and Headmaster of Wicker School, such was not the case. Every Sunday morning he preached to them from the high stone pulpit in St. Matthew's Chapel, where the students worshiped six nights a week and twice on Sundays. But only on Sunday morning was there a sermon. The other services were short, mostly hymns and prayers, beautiful prayers with words that David learned easily. "O Lord, support us all the day long, until the shadows lengthen and the evening comes, and the busy world is hushed and the fever of life is over, and our work is done. Then in thy mercy, grant us a safe lodging, and a holy rest, and peace at the last."

The first time he heard Father Perkins speak those words, he felt his throat catch and his heart stir. He loved "shadows lengthen" and "busy world is hushed." The words sounded like what they said. He could see the shadows lengthening and feel the silence in the chapel at that moment just before dinner, when they paused to reflect on the events of the day. They were clean, showered, and newly dressed in their coats and ties for dinner after an afternoon of sports. The candles flickered on the altar, the light just enough to read the words by.

David sat near the front with the other third formers, only the twenty-odd second formers in front of them. The sixth formers sat in the pews along the side watching them. "No talking," a tall sixth former with short, cropped hair and thick glasses said to no one in particular almost every night. You learned quickly who was lenient and who was strict. You learned, when you crossed in front of the altar to kneel, to "genuflect," and to cross yourself. This, said Father Perkins, was to honor Christ.

And to explain Christ to the boys, Father Perkins preached every Sunday, first from the stone pulpit, and then walking up and down the center aisle, sometimes standing only inches from the boys in the closest seats, his deep voice echoing and resonating through the dark chapel with the flickering candles. "St. Matthew's Chapel is the center of this school," he told them. "Every evening here in this chapel we bring to God the concerns of the day. Every Sunday we bring to this chapel the work we have done during the week. We bring everything we have done during the week to Christ—our studies, our sports, our jobs—to remind ourselves that without His blessing there is no meaning to these activities. In the form of bread and wine, we carry these activities from the back of this chapel to the altar, where God blesses them and gives them back to us."

It made sense to David. You studied, you did sports, and you performed your job. Then you took it all to God. The best you could do was not good enough. "God," said Father Perkins, "gave His son, Jesus Christ, as a sacrifice. And the bread and the wine we carry to the altar is transformed symbolically into His body and blood—the bread, His body, the wine, His blood. We eat the bread and drink the wine, and we are made new, transformed, changed as we begin the next week. We carry forth from the chapel our best resolves, strengthened by the bread and wine. Sunday is both the last day of the week and the first, the day we bring our week to God, the day we march forth renewed."

After the service the boys walked to the dining room. They were hungry. "No human food until you've had God's food," one of the sixth formers said jokingly. It stuck. David was a little dizzy as he came out into the bright September sun. He was still in God's world, in the magical world the Headmaster had created in his sermon.

"JAP's a real asshole," said an older boy, walking in front of David, his hands thrust into his pockets. David remembered the boy from the train, the way he had smoked and talked out of the side of his mouth.

"Yeah," said his companion. "What a lot of bullshit. It's just a lot of ancient superstition. I mean what is this eating the body and blood. Christ! It's like we're cannibals or something."

David was angry. He knew the students called the Headmaster JAP, like Japan, the enemy, but he hated it. It was cheap. "You guys are wrong," he shouted suddenly, not knowing where the words had come from. It was not his voice, not his decision to speak.

The boys turned and looked at him.

"Who are you?" the first one said.

"David Lear."

"Well, I don't care if you're God almighty. JAP's a jerk, and you're nothing but a little dork. Don't you ever tell me I'm wrong."

The boy thrust his index finger into David's chest. David knocked it away. The boy grabbed David by the shoulders and shook him.

"Hold on there," came a deep voice from behind. "What's going on here?" It was the Headmaster himself, cigarette in hand, now dressed in his gray suit, the robes of the service locked away somewhere.

"Nothing, sir," said the older boy, reddening, backing away from David.

"Nothing, sir," said his companion.

"Then be on your way," said the Headmaster, turning to David. "Now, lad, what's this all about?"

"Nothing, sir."

"You can do better than that."

"Yes, sir."

"Well then?"

"They were. . . saying insulting things. . .about you."

"Indeed? And you were defending me?"

"Yes, sir."

"A brave thing to do, lad, but foolish. I don't need your defense, and you don't want to create enemies needlessly. I know about you, lad. You're a good one. You'll have enough trouble without looking for it." The Headmaster put his arm around David's shoulders, and then laughed. "Go get some human food," he said, "while I finish my cigarette."

David knew what the Headmaster meant. There was an air of trouble at Wicker. You could smell it in the halls at night in the bathrooms, you could sense it in the small groups of students whispering at they walked down to sports in the afternoon. At Lowell, everything had been open. Everybody knew what everyone else was doing. But at Wicker, things were secret. You never walked into anyone's room. You knocked. And if no one answered, you didn't go in. Maybe someone was in there, maybe not. If someone was in there and they didn't answer, it meant that you weren't wanted. Secrets hid everywhere, and boys spoke in whispers and muffled laughter as they walked from building to building David had floated above all that. He knew there were things he didn't understand, things about the teachers, about the parents, about the boys themselves, but he didn't want to know them. He liked the school for what it appeared to be—fresh, simple, and beautiful. The sun came up over the river in the morning and set behind the mountain in the afternoon, and the days were good. He had no trouble with his classes. Lowell had prepared him well. He was in Latin II with a lot of fourth formers reading Caesar's Gallic Wars. He was in French, which he'd had before, and math and history and English. He loved to study, and he loved the reward of doing well.

David's roommate was Jackie Callaghan. He was lean and tan with tousled blond hair. He wore striped shirts, khaki pants, and white buck shoes, and his jackets were Harris tweed. Jackie's parents, everyone said, had lots of money. During the first weeks of school the two boys saw little of each other. David was a Macedonian, Jackie a Housatonic. David was in the A section, Jackie in the C section. David got up at the rising bell in the morning, showered, and left for breakfast before Jackie was even awake. Jackie always waited for the warning bell, the five minute bell. He threw on his clothes, tying his tie and tucking in his shirt as he flew toward the dining hall, guarded by two sixth form monitors. If you were late you had to run the triangle—the triangular route from the dining hall out to the soccer field, then down the highway and back across the base of the mountain to the dining hall again. It took fifteen minutes. When you got back, you could eat unless the food was gone. Then you went hungry, unless a friend saved you something.

Jackie wasn't late every day, but he lived on the edge in everything, and he made David nervous. At night Jackie rushed into the room two minutes before lights out and changed into his pajamas in the dark. The bell rang, the sixth formers shined their flashlights in to be sure there was a body in each bed, and then they went to sleep.

At first Jackie teased David. "Come on," he would say in the dark after the sixth form bed check, "tell me something you've done that was bad. Come on, Mr. Goody-goody, let's hear about your exploits. Like how you got a B once, or something really terrible."

But when David didn't respond, Jackie got tired of the game. Then, one particular day in October, just after lights out, there was a furious pounding on all the doors.

"All right, you little stinkers, everyone out in the hall, on the double," came the voice of Harry Young, otherwise known as "Mighty Joe Young." He was a wrestler, he had hair on his chest and back, and he was the North Dorm prefect.

They stood in a line, each of them, backs to the wall, next to their own doors, David and Jackie, on their left Billy DuPont and Ricky Farrell, on their right Hugh Packard and his roommate, whose name David couldn't remember.

"Everybody down," said Mighty Joe Young.

Everybody squatted.

"Now duckwalk, down to the end of the hall and back to your rooms."

No one started.

"Move!" said the prefect. "Move!" echoed his assistants, a couple of lesser sixth formers.

The boys moved, down and back, then down and back again until their legs ached and Ricky Farrell fell over. Somebody laughed.

"No laughing!" said Mighty Joe.

They stood again against their doors.

"Now listen!" said the prefect. "This hall stinks. This hall smells. And this is what we do to stinkers, to smelly bastards who don't take showers."

He started at the end of the hall, closest to the river. He walked by David and Jackie, by Billy and Ricky, and then stopped. He touched Barry LeMaster on the shoulder. "You," he said. "Strip!"

They turned their heads, ever so slightly, to see what was happening. Barry didn't move. Mighty Joe's hands reached toward the boy. Each hand grasped a lapel of Barry's pajamas and yanked hard. The boy's pajama top burst apart, buttons clattering on the hard floor. Mighty Joe wrenched it off the boy's shoulders and down his arms, leaving him shivering.

"Now the bottom," he said.

It was cruel and therefore wrong, David knew, but there was something strangely exciting about it, too, something dark and dangerous like the secrets whispered on the way to sports. He watched as the boy dropped his pants and then ran for the shower room, holding his hands in front of his exposed genitals. The sixth formers followed him inside. When he came out, his skin was pink and his eyes had the glazed look of a steer being led to slaughter.

"Now, get in your rooms, all of you, and let this be a lesson," said Mighty Joe.

They turned and started into their rooms.

"Not you, Callaghan," said Mighty Joe. "You wait."

David climbed into bed and pulled the covers up. He was afraid of what they might do to Jackie. It began to make sense, Jackie's sleeping late in the morning, his undressing in the dark. Maybe he didn't want anybody to see him. The showers were public, three or four at a time. He had never seen Jackie in the showers either in the morning or after sports.

When Jackie came in, David turned to look at him across the room.

"What happened, Jackie?" he asked.

"Last warning," Jackie said softly. "Next time it's me."

"Then do it, Jackie. What's wrong with taking showers?"

"I won't let those bastards tell me what to do. That's why," he hissed. "It's fine for you. You like it here, I can tell. Mister fucking rise-and-shine. You like it, don't you? Mr. JAP's favorite. We know about you."

David didn't know what to say.

"You like it here, don't you?" Jackie continued. "I didn't want to be here in the first place. They can do what they want, but I'm damned if I'll kowtow to that hairy brute."

"It's just a shower," David said quietly.

"Just a shower! Just a shower! For Christ's sake, don't you stand for anything? You just do everything they say, and pretty soon, there's nothing left of you. You've got to draw a line somewhere, OK? This is mine."

It didn't make sense to David, to draw a line over a shower. Still Jackie's words echoed in his heart—"pretty soon, there's nothing left of you."

Two nights later they came for him. "Bring your towels," Harry Young shouted as he pounded on the doors.

David hesitated, then grabbed his towel and walked into the hall.

"You're a real bastard," Jackie Callaghan said to David as he passed.

David waited in the hall terrified. If Jackie didn't come out on his own, they would go in and drag him out. David didn't want to see that. He didn't want any part of the whole thing, but there was nothing to be done, nothing to be achieved by fighting. And then Jackie's words again, ". . .pretty soon there's nothing left of you," and Jackie being dragged down the hall, naked except for his white underpants, a sixth former shouldering each arm. They turned into the shower room, and David could see the limp legs disappearing behind the door.

After ten minutes Jackie came out, dripping wet, a towel around his middle, and he walked slowly down the hall toward David, as all the third formers started flicking their towels at him. That was the routine. If you had been warned and you did not comply, you got the towel treatment.

David couldn't stand it. He broke ranks, ran toward Jackie. The next thing he knew there was a hairy arm around his neck choking him.

"Look, buddy," growled Mighty Joe Young. "Don't you ever disobey me." And the prefect grabbed David with both hands, shoved him against the wall, then yanked him back and shoved again, yanked and shoved until David slumped to the floor. "And if you say anything about this, any of you, you're all dead meat. Now get to bed."

For a while Jackie and David just sat there on the floor outside their room, side by side, their backs against the wall. Then Jackie laughed. "Not bad for a goody-goody, not bad for a fucking sheep. I gotta hand it to you." They helped each other up and went to bed.

The next day Jackie Callaghan was gone. David came back to the room after morning classes and saw the bare mattress and the empty closet, the bureau drawers slightly ajar, the pictures gone, the wall on Jackie's side bare except for some odd pieces of tape. David put his books on his desk and joined the others who were walking to lunch.

"Jackie's gone," he said to Billy DuPont.

"His parents came to get him," said Billy. "I heard it from one of the sixth formers. They pulled him out of math class, packed his stuff, and put him in the car."

Two days later Father Perkins addressed the school at morning job assembly. "I am deeply disappointed," he said, "at the behavior of the sixth form. One of the things that makes Wicker stand out from other schools is the responsibility of the sixth form for the discipline of the school. That responsibility has been badly abused. I have met with the prefects to discuss the incidents in the North Dorm during the past two weeks, incidents that resulted in one of our students being forced to leave because of the cruelty he suffered. This kind of behavior cannot be allowed to continue."

The Headmaster paused and looked out over the student body, strangely still and silent in the auditorium. He began again, his voice deep and resonant, carrying easily to the back. The prefects sat on the stage behind him, all except Harry Young whose chair was empty. "I have taken the following actions. First, I have suspended the North Dorm prefect until after Christmas. In his absence, the Editor-in-Chief of the Wicker *Messenger*, Frank Harrington, will serve in his place."

There was a sudden buzz, as Frank Harrington walked down the length of the auditorium to the stage—tall, skinny Frank Harrington, whose horn-rimmed glasses and long hair marked him as something of an intellectual. He had talked to David on the first day, inviting him to come write for the *Messenger*.

"Quiet down," the Headmaster said. He waited patiently until he could feel the silence in the room. Then he began again. "Secondly, the practice of 'stinks,' of paddling and other harassment of underclassmen by the sixth form will cease immediately. To that end, I will meet with the entire sixth form in my study tonight after lights out to begin the process of finding other ways of maintaining order and discipline at Wicker School. Tomorrow night I will meet with the Student Council.

"To all of you, young and old, sixth formers and underclassmen, I say this. If this change is not implemented with passion and with vigor, then the entire Wicker way of life is endangered. Sixth form responsibility is the cornerstone of what we learn here. Through that responsibility sixth formers become adults, and they learn what it means to shape the lives of those for whom they are responsible. To simply terrorize is not to teach; to bully is not to shape. Let that be remembered."

Then he turned and walked down the steps, up the aisle and out the back door. Job assembly continued in hushed tones, classes continued, sports continued, but there was something different in the air. It was as if the underformers had taken on a new life, a new being. They were, for the first time, important.

On the following Sunday, during the Eucharist, Father Perkins spoke to the school once more. David watched him with intensity. He watched every gesture, listened to every word. His back hurt where the prefect had shoved him against the wall, but he didn't care.

"Touch your fingers to your eyes," the Headmaster said. "Touch your nose and mouth. Look down at your legs, which are so strong and enable you to run so fast. Hold your hand on your chest and feel the heart which beats so firmly, so evenly."

David touched his eyes, his nose and mouth. He looked at his legs and put his hand to his heart. It was beating rapidly.

"Now turn your heads," he continued, "and look at Father Hill, Father Edward Eugene Hill, whose heart and mind and soul carved this school out of the farmland of Macedonia Valley, whose strength of vision made a dream into a reality, this man whom we call 'Pater' to honor him as the father of this school. Look at the wreck which time has made of this brave and fearless man, and then think. He cannot hear my words or see my gestures, he cannot take a single step, or hold even a spoon in his hand. Those of you who tenderly care for him and bring him in his wheelchair each evening to chapel and each Sunday morning to this Eucharist know these things."

David could feel in his heart something he could not call by name, and he knew that those around him felt it, too. There was no smirking or yawning or stretching. You could almost hear the stones breathing.

"Look at the figure of our founder, my young friends, and know that some day soon he will die, and that you too will die, and nothing that science or medicine can do will save you. That is the reality upon which Wicker School is founded. That is the reality which ultimately must save you or condemn you. In Jesus Christ alone, we are saved. Jesus Christ alone has overcome death. In Jesus Christ alone is eternal life. He and He alone must become the cornerstone of your life, as this chapel is the cornerstone of this school. He alone can save you from the sure and final extinction of the body."

They filed out into the beautiful blue of late October, the last blue before November's winds and rains. Then came the cold of December like the chill of death. David could not get the Headmaster's sermon out of his head. After lunch he changed into his blue jeans and his Macedonian sweatee shirt, and he walked alone up the river to the place where the road curved to the left up Skiff Mountain. There he turned to the right and walked down to the rocks and watched the current. He thought of Maggie Hope, remembering the day he had seen her for the last time and how he had thought of eternal life, her life. He wondered where she was. "Maggie Hope," he whispered to the wind, "where are you? Are you alive somewhere? Can you hear me?"

He tried to figure it out. If you believed in Christ, you would never die. That's what Father Perkins had said. But Maggie Hope hadn't believed in Jesus, or if she had, David never heard her talk about it. She had given him his first Bible, the one he had taken to the cave with him when he was ten, but he never remembered her reading the Bible. "You're quite a religious little boy, Toots," she had said to him once. But why was he religious? Where had it come from? He couldn't remember. And now, suddenly, it seemed terribly important that he believe. The eyes of Father Perkins watched from behind the trees, from under the water. They reminded him that he must choose between life and death.

Then, surprisingly, he thought about Jackie. He wasn't really sorry that Jackie had gone home. David had enjoyed the time alone since Jackie's departure, enjoyed having the room to himself. It gave him time to think, though sometimes he did more worrying than thinking. In his mind he played over and over the record of those final hours. It wasn't his fault. He couldn't have done anything to save Jackie. That wasn't the point. Jackie was strange, he hated the school, he was self-destructive. It was as if he had willed his own departure. Jackie hadn't wanted to come to the school in the first place, and the only way he knew to get home was to get kicked out. What bothered David was his own cowardice, his own failure to stand up for his roommate. There was that desperate little gesture at the end, the running down the hall toward Jackie, but that was too little, too late. Jackie was his roommate, and David had made no effort to get to know him, to understand him, to support him.

Father Perkins was right. He had to change. If you ate the body of Jesus and drank his blood, you became a new person. But you couldn't take communion, you couldn't partake of the Eucharist until you were confirmed. That was the rule at Wicker, and so Father Perkins had asked all the third formers to consider joining the confirmation class. The Bishop would come in April and lay his hands on the heads of the boys who had decided to renew their baptismal vows, and they would become new people, they would be born again. And if he were born again, maybe he would be braver, more resolute, less worried about what other people thought.

When he got back to the room he wrote to Molly Ariel, his godmother and his benefactor in San Francisco: "Father Perkins thinks I should be confirmed. What do you think? I am signing up for the confirmation class, and they want to know if I have been baptized. If I haven't, then I will be baptized also." In the letter he said nothing about Jackie Callaghan. That was too complicated to deal with in a letter.

The week before Thanksgiving a reply came back from Molly Ariel on her familiar gray paper. She could testify that he had been baptized. "You cried like hell when the minister sprinkled the holy water on you," the letter said. Then it went on: "Go ahead with the confirmation. The Episcopal Church is a good one."

Something about the letter bothered him. He adored Molly Ariel. She was his favorite person in the world. He loved her wisdom, her straight-forward honesty. He could trust her. But there was something odd about that sentence: "The Episcopal Church is a good one." The question was: is it true? Is there really a heaven, and is it somehow reserved for those who believe in Jesus? Is there a hell where sinners will be tortured?

In English class they had been studying Greek mythology. A myth, said his teacher, was not a lie, but something which never happened. It was a symbol. Like the Eucharist. The bread stood for Jesus's body, the wine for his blood. Myths were stories that taught us something about how the world works, even though they might not have happened literally. There was a literal meaning and a symbolic meaning.

Tantalus had killed his only son, Pelops, cooked him in a pot and served him to the gods. But the gods were not fooled. They punished Tantalus by having him stand forever in a pool of water with luscious and beautiful fruit trees all around. The boughs of the trees hung low over the water, and each time Tantalus reached up to pick an apple or a pear, the bough drew back. Each time Tantalus bent over to take a drink of water, the water receded. It was a terrifying story. David could see it vividly. Forever and ever, Tantalus would be hungry and thirsty. His punishment fit his crime. "That is what hell is like, young gentlemen," his English teacher said. "That is what hell is like."

That is what David wanted to know. Was it true? On the last Sunday before Thanksgiving vacation, Father Perkins answered his question, or at least started to answer it. "Life," the Headmaster said, "is essentially mysterious. The world at large, what we call the secular world, does not believe that. It adopts as its religion what we call 'secular humanism,' the belief that man can solve his problems by himself without any outside help. There is nothing beyond this life. We live, we work, we age, we suffer, we die and that is the end of it. Our job, says the secular humanist, is to do the best we can with the time we are given.

"The Christian affirms that life is essentially mysterious, and that God came to this earth in the form of Jesus Christ to show us something of that mystery. All things have at least two meanings, a literal and a symbolic one. A sacrament, the Prayer Book tells us, 'is an outward and visible sign of an inward and spiritual grace.' The sign of baptism is water. It is real water, but it also stands for inward purity, for the inward cleansing which takes place when the child become a member of the church, a member of God's family.

"Life is essentially mysterious," said the Headmaster again. "Today is the First Sunday in Advent. Advent, from the Latin words 'ad venere' meaning 'to come toward.' We are coming toward, we are approaching the ultimate mystery, the mystery of the Incarnation, when God becomes man and lives among us. This is the time we prepare ourselves for that coming. We think about what that coming means to our lives. As you go home to celebrate Thanksgiving at the end of this week, think also of ways that you can prepare yourself for Christmas, for the coming of the Christ child into your lives. When you return, we will talk about this once more.

"In the name of the Father and of the Son and of the Holy Ghost," he said, and then he crossed himself. David crossed himself too.

Anthony S. Abbott

CHAPTER TWO

E ven though Jackie Callaghan was gone, his presence remained a powerful one in David's imagination. When he went back to the room after class he could still feel Jackie there, and he could hear Jackie's voice. Jackie liked to talk about sex. In fact every boy at Wicker School liked to talk about sex. David was sure of that. It was not exactly his most popular subject of conversation, because he didn't know anything about it, but he was a good listener. Of course, he knew the scientific names for things. He had learned those at Mr. Armbrister's lectures at Lowell, but his own experience was, in the words of Jackie Callaghan, "pathetic."

His only conversation about sex with Jackie had taken place during the second week of school. They hadn't seen much of each other, and with Jackie's strange bedtime habits, David didn't even see him during that thirty-minute free period before bed. Then one night, after lights out, he heard Jackie's voice from across the room.

"Have you ever jacked off?"

"What?"

"You heard me. Have you ever jacked off?"

"I don't know what you mean."

"You know what I mean. Do you beat the meat? It's a simple question. Yes or no?"

"I don't know what you mean."

"Christ, Lear, how old are you?"

"Fourteen."

David could hear Jackie's sigh of disgust from across the room. The beds weren't that far apart, but it was too dark to see, and so their voices drifted safely across the space between. David grew bolder.

"Do you, Jackie?"

"Damn right."

He wasn't sure what Jackie was talking about. This would be tricky. He couldn't let on that he was a complete fool. He'd have to ask the right questions. He'd learned that at Lowell from Terry and Griff. Whoever asked the questions controlled the conversation. If you didn't want to be made a fool of, then it was best to be the question-asker. Besides, people liked to talk about themselves.

David spoke again. "I guess there are different ways to do it."

"Oh yeah."

"What's your way, Jackie?"

"Well, I just think about a pretty girl, one with good tits, and keep thinking about her until my prick gets big. Then I just take it in my hand and start kind of slow, moving my hand up and down, and then I go faster and faster until I come."

"Come?"

"Jesus, Lear, you don't know anything. You know, what comes out. The sperm."

"Oh," said David. "And then what?"

"Then I go to sleep."

"What about the sperm? Where does it go?"

"On my pajamas, on the sheet. I don't know. Who cares?"

That was the end of the conversation about sex. Jackie didn't want to talk about it anymore, not with David. David didn't know anything. He didn't have anything to contribute to the conversation. That was that. So Jackie talked to anyone else he could find who would listen, anyone, that is, who knew something. And that included just about everyone else at Wicker School, except for the second formers, who, of course, knew nothing.

The dining room was a veritable hotbed of conversation about sex, except on Saturday nights when the teachers and their wives came for dinner, and the tables were lit by candles. Then they had conversations like the ones David remembered at Lowell. But the rest of the meals were free-for-alls—not breakfast, because nobody talked at breakfast. But at lunch and dinner sex bounced off the walls like a trapped bird that can't find an open window. There were two sixth formers and two fifth formers at every table, and David enjoyed listening to them.

"You know they put saltpeter in the milk," said Dickie Parker.

"Of course, they do," nodded Peter Berger. "You can't have a bunch of horny guys all over the place."

"But it doesn't work," Dickie said. "Shit, I'm horny all the time, especially when I get letters from Sally."

"And you smell the perfume," said Peter, "and the balloon blows up."

Big laughs at the table.

"So is Sally a good girl or a nice girl?" Peter asked.

"None of your business, buddy," said Dickie Parker.

David wasn't sure what the difference was, but he figured he'd find out if he kept his ears open. The thing was he really didn't know anything about girls. He had never had a date, never really been with girls except at the dances Lowell School had once or twice a term. Girls were completely strange, but the other great topic of conversation at Wicker was sports, and sports David could do.

Billy DuPont was a sports nut, and he was David's new friend. After Jackie had gone, Billy started to come down to David's room and visit. They began walking to meals together and to classes. Billy was a Dodger fan, and he liked to keep records. He got his mother and dad to send him the box scores of all the Dodger games right up until the end of the season. He kept track of the batting averages, the runs batted-in, the earned-run averages of the pitchers, and most important, the home runs. He was a walking encyclopedia. The sixth form monitor called him a flea in heat. He was short, wiry, and could talk a mile a minute.

"Hey, Dave," he would say, shoving an article into David's hands. "Look at this. It's about Jackie Robinson." Jackie Robinson was Billy DuPont's favorite player. "Look at this. It says how when the Dodgers go on the road the fans yell at him and call him 'nigger.' It says in some of the cities where the Dodgers play he has to stay in a different hotel because he's colored. Players on the other teams yelled at him too and even tried to hurt him. It was awful in St. Louis. Enos Slaughter tried to spike him, and Pee Wee Reese, the Dodger captain, you know, he put his arm around Jackie and said, 'This man is my friend.' Isn't that great, Dave? 'This man is my friend.'"

After Pee Wee had stood up for Jackie, a lot of the taunting stopped, David learned. Pee Wee was a Southerner, he was from Kentucky, and if a Southerner could stand up for Jackie, then, by God, everyone else could. That's what Billy DuPont said, and David agreed.

In the afternoons Billy DuPont and David and Hugh Packard walked down to soccer together. They were the only third formers on the team. They had never had soccer at Wicker before, except as a club sport. Now, for the first time, they had a varsity soccer team, coached by a Chemistry teacher the students called "Jumping John" because of his fondness for jumping jacks, and David had tried out for it because he had played soccer at Lowell for four years. His feet didn't really bother him any more. He ran in a funny way with tiny little steps, but he was fast and he was fearless and he made up in determination what he lacked in natural ability. He also knew how to play the game and where to be. Twice, in a scrimmage game, he had scored goals because the ball had come all the way across the goal mouth from the other side, and he was there to tap it in behind the surprised goalie. His biggest problem was blisters. He couldn't buy shoes small enough, and the size seven shoes rubbed up and down his Achilles tendons until they bled. He wrapped them every day in layers of bandages. But still they bled. He didn't mind as long as it didn't stop him from playing.

After practice David and Billy and Hugh would walk back to the North Dorm to take their showers. There was no locker room for soccer. They would take their shoes off outside the building.

"Gross," said Billy DuPont, when he saw David's bloody wrappings.

Hugh Packard just smiled. He was handsome, jet black hair, dark eyes, and a style so easy he didn't seem to be working.

"Every time I see my feet I think of DiMaggio," said David.

"You mean the bone spurs in the heel," said Billy.

"How it must have hurt him all the time to play," David continued.

They all loved DiMaggio, his grace, his power, his long strides.

"The 56-game hitting streak is the greatest achievement in baseball history," said Billy triumphantly.

"It'll never be broken," said Hugh.

"Never," echoed David.

In the shower David looked down at his legs. From the knee to the ankle there was little flesh. He had spent most of his first five years in casts, being operated on for bilateral club feet. His muscles had not developed. They had atrophied. David thought of his mother when he said the word "atrophied." She had taught him the word, and she had also taught him to be strong. He hadn't dreamt of her much at Wicker, not the way he had in New York at his sister's. Maybe her ghost only haunted the city.

One day in November on the way to class Billy surprised David by asking him where he was going for Thanksgiving.

"To my sister's in New York," David said.

"Where in New York?"

There was a slight pause. "In the Bronx," said David.

David could tell that Billy didn't know what to say. People didn't live in the Bronx.

"It's not bad," said David, "not what you think. It's only eight blocks from Yankee Stadium."

"But your parents," Billy asked, "where do they live?"

"My father lives in California, no I mean my father lives in Phoenix, Arizona. He just moved there. I forget. I've never been there."

"And your mother?"

"She's dead," said David abruptly.

It was a strange conversation. David realized that he had thought very little about his family since he had been at school, and no one at Wicker really knew what his situation was. In this way Wicker was a lot like Lowell. The boys just didn't talk about their families. David knew that he would go to Elizabeth's for Thanksgiving because that was the only place he could go. He had gone to his father's for the summer when he was twelve, and it hadn't worked out, so he didn't go back. His mother had died in New York the next year, and, really, Elizabeth was his only family, if you didn't count Molly Ariel, and of course you couldn't count Molly Ariel, even though she was the most important of all.

He adored Molly Ariel. She was his godmother and his mother's best friend in San Francisco. When the family broke up it was Molly Ariel who paid for David to go to boarding school. She was his mother and father combined; she was in charge of his life. After the fiasco with his father, she had let him spend the summer with her and her husband Jack on their ranch near Santa Cruz. He had felt at home.

"I live with my godmother on her ranch in California," he would say to himself, and when people asked where he was from, he would say, "I'm from California. I was born there. I live with my godmother on her ranch." But he couldn't say that any more. Molly wouldn't let him. The following summer, the summer after his graduation from Lowell, she had sent him to a camp in the mountains near Morgan Hill. He had loved it, and when he got back to Santa Cruz, he asked Molly if he could come back.

"I don't think so, chum," she said. "You'll be fifteen, and that's too old for camp. Fourteen is the oldest."

"Maybe I can be a junior counselor," said David. "Buck said he'd like to have me back. He said he would give me free room and board and even a small salary."

"Well," she said, "if you can pay your own way to California, then that's fine. But you'll have to be on your own. You'll have to find a way to work it out."

But now it was nearly Thanksgiving, and he hadn't done anything. He had been too absorbed with school, with classes, with soccer, with Jackie Callaghan, and, most of all with the words of Father Perkins. Well, even Father Perkins would have to wait, David thought, as he packed his bag on the last night before Thanksgiving break, until he could figure out how to get to California for the summer.

CHAPTER THREE

W hen David emerged from the ramp at Track 28 into the light of Grand Central Station, there were two people waiting for him. The first he recognized immediately as his Aunt Estelle, Miss Estelle Hamilton, his father's aunt, whom he had met on his return from California during the summer after his fourth form year at Lowell. She had taken him to lunch at the Plaza, and they had become great friends. It was Aunt Estelle who had helped him find a Christmas tree for Elizabeth that winter. The other woman David did not recognize, but she walked toward him smiling as if she had known him all his life. She was short, not as short as Aunt Estelle, but short and sturdy looking. She wore a gray skirt, a white blouse with a turquoise Indian brooch at the neck, and a blue blazer. She extended her hand, and took David's firmly.

"I'm your Aunt Louise, and your Aunt Estelle and I have come to welcome you home for Thanksgiving," she said. "Now put that valise of yours in a locker, and we shall proceed to luncheon."

Aunt Louise was his father's sister, which made her his aunt, and Aunt Estelle her aunt. They were very much alike, both referring to luncheon rather than lunch, and pronouncing "aunt" with the broad English *a*. They were clearly not "ants."

"Aunt Estelle was my chaperone in Paris in the 1920's," Aunt Louise said. "I had graduated from the University of Minnesota and wished to go to Paris to continue my study of French and of French art. In those days a young woman could not travel abroad without a chaperone. So Aunt Estelle took me."

"And it was quite delightful, I must say," said Aunt Estelle.

"And now, here we are together again," said Aunt Louise.

"A little older, perhaps," said Aunt Estelle.

"But much wiser," said Aunt Louise, and they both laughed.

Aunt Louise, after her trip to Paris, had come home to Minneapolis and earned an M.A. degree in French from the University. Then she had studied art at the Minneapolis Art Institute, and had begun doing her own painting, mostly water colors of animals. She loved animals and had always had at least two dogs, usually cocker spaniels. One of her teachers at the Institute was a Swedish American artist named August Swenson. He had taught in Minneapolis for a while, then moved to Santa Fe and come back to Minneapolis when the war broke out. He and Louise had become friends, and after the war they decided to marry. He left his first wife and moved to Lambertville, New Jersey, where he found an old farm with a barn on it. He bought the farm, and while he was rebuilding the barn, he lived in town at the Lambertville House. He invited her to join him in Lambertville, and she agreed.

"Until the house was finished," she said, "we lived in the studio, the old barn. We painted in the mornings, and worked on the house in the afternoons, along with the carpenters and electricians and plumbers. Swen loved it. The house was his own design. You'll see. We want you to come out for Christmas."

"What about Elizabeth and the children?"

"We want them, too."

"Where will we all sleep?"

"You'll see," she laughed.

"And I'll be there, too," said Aunt Estelle. "A regular family Christmas."

David told Elizabeth the story the next morning. She already knew. Aunt Louise had telephoned her and invited them the week before. She had asked when David was coming down for Thanksgiving. She wanted to meet him at the train.

"But have you seen the house? Have you been out there?" David asked.

"Nope," said Elizabeth. "We'll just all go together, you and me and the kids. Phil will have to stay here and work. Christmas is a busy time for him. He gets lots of playing engagements."

"Vroom, vroom," said Alex as he cruised by the kitchen with his racing car. "Come play, Unca Dave."

"In a minute, Alex," said David, collecting his thoughts.

Elizabeth smoked. It was morning nap time for Maggie, and Elizabeth was ready for David to take Alex out, but it was cold and gray and David wanted to talk. He was going to learn about his family.

"It was so weird," David said again. "I didn't know who she was. I didn't even know Daddy had a sister."

"Of course, you did, silly," said Elizabeth. "You just forgot. She came to visit us in Westport when you were little. She's wonderful. I think she's the only sane member of the family. She's a letter writer. You'll see."

He did. He got two letters from her between Thanksgiving and Christmas, newsy, interesting letters, describing the house, the surrounding area, and their lifestyle. "It's quiet here," she said in one of them. "It's not like living in New York where you can walk to the movies or visit museums. We are two miles from Lambertville, straight up hill, on a small country lane. We have neighbors, but we don't see them often. Swen gets up early, has his breakfast and goes to the studio to work. Every day. Sundays included. He doesn't go to church. I don't think he cares a bit about religion. Art is his religion. Don't expect us to entertain you. You will have to find your own resources. But then, you are a very resourceful young man, I understand."

And in the second letter: "You asked about your grandparents. Your grandfather was Allan Simpson Lear, a lawyer and judge. He taught law at the University of Minnesota. Your father always disappointed him. That was a great difficulty between them. He died in 1940 of a heart attack. Your grandmother, Emily Hamilton Lear, is a lovely woman. Aunt Estelle is her sister. After your grandfather died, I stayed at home to help take care of your grandmother, and when I told her that Swen and I wished to get married, she said, 'Don't stay here on my account. I'll be fine.' That was brave of her, and kind. We sold the house, and I found her a small apartment, where she lives today. A girl comes in to cook and clean."

David began to understand. She was what people at school called "a responsible party." When David signed out for vacation, he had to list a responsible party who was meeting him. Aunt Louise was responsible for her mother, she was responsible for Aunt Estelle. If something happened to them, then she would have to take care of them. And here she was taking care of him and Elizabeth, too, over Christmas. They would have their presents in New York on Christmas morning, and then take the train to Lambertville in the afternoon. They would stay over the weekend and go back to New York on Monday. Then David would go to work down the street from Elizabeth and Phil's delivering groceries. On New Year's Day he would deliver flowers. It was a way of saving money for his trip to California. It wasn't enough, but it was a start.

Christmas afternoon was cold and clear, but the radio said that a storm was coming from the West on Saturday. Snow was predicted.

"Thank God it didn't snow today," said Elizabeth as they trudged up the hill to the subway. They would take the D train to Rockefeller Center, then change to the E, which took them to Penn Station. Then the Pennsylvania Railroad to Trenton, where they changed to another train that took them up the Delaware River to Lambertville. Aunt Louise would meet them at the station.

David was in charge of directions. He liked that. He and Elizabeth each had a kid and a suitcase. They should have taken a taxi up the hill, but they couldn't afford it. That was always the way. So they struggled up the hill and then along the Grand Concourse for two blocks to the 167th St. Station, then down the stairs, and through the turnstiles.

"Don't let go of Alex, David," Elizabeth said. "He's like a comet once he gets loose."

"I know," David answered, being pulled along by Alex, who

slithered under the turnstile, while David was trying to manage him, the bag, and the money at the same time. The rest of the trip was easier except for the stairs. It seemed like everywhere they went, they had to go up and down stairs, and by the time they got on the train in Penn Station, Elizabeth was completely worn out, and so was Maggie. David found them two seats facing each other, and then, after the train started, he took Alex for a walk. They rattled like the train back and forth as they made their way from car to car. Everywhere there were people with piles of packages sticking out of shopping bags with the names of stores on them. David picked Alex up and carried him through to the next car. It was too risky to let him walk. Finally, they found the club car, where David bought them a Baby Ruth to share.

When they came back Elizabeth and Maggie were fast asleep. David put Alex in the seat next to the window and whispered to him. "Be real quiet, Alex, your mommy is sleeping."

"Shhh, be real quiet," Alex parroted. "Mommy seepin'. . ."

David laughed, and then, inexplicably, the train lurched to a stop, throwing Alex across into Maggie and his mother. The baby woke screaming. Packages tumbled from Lord and Taylor bags, from Macy's and Gimbel's bags, and the aisle was full of Christmas.

Elizabeth described it to Uncle Swen and Aunt Estelle at dinner. She had already told the story once to Aunt Louise in the car on the way up the hill from town, but now she had to tell it again to the others. They were seated at the table in the living room of the new house. There was no dining room, just a table set up in the living room, next to the stairs going up to Aunt Louise and Uncle Swen's bedroom. She was at one end of the table, and he at the other. David sat next to Alex, who was propped up by two New York telephone directories and was banging on the table with his spoon. Maggie was on Elizabeth's lap, sucking on a pink pacifier. Aunt Estelle, who had come out the day before, sat next to Elizabeth staring at the baby as if it were a creature from Mars.

"It was terrible, waking up to all that screaming. Not only Maggie, but every kid on the train. Why it stopped we still don't know. A signal light turned red, the conductor said."

"Yight turn red," repeated Alex, banging his spoon.

"Don't bang your spoon on the table, Alex," said Aunt Louise gently.

"Here were all these people on their way to grandparents' houses," said Elizabeth, "with all their presents, and suddenly they were dumped from the overhead racks right onto their heads or into the aisle. We were lucky."

"Look," said David, pointing to the window at the far end of the room, "it's snowing." And it was snowing, soft, large flakes coming down whitening the hard ground. By the time they finished dinner and got Alex ready for bed, the snow was coming down harder, covering the bushes and coating the cedar trees in the back yard. Aunt Estelle had retired to the bedroom at the front of the house where she would sleep with Elizabeth. The children would sleep in the small bedroom next to the kitchen, Maggie in the crib borrowed from the neighbors and Alex on a cot that was made up as a couch in the daytime. David would sleep in the studio, which was about thirty yards away. You went out the back door on to the porch which looked out over the woods behind the house. The studio was to the left and through a small gate that was closed to keep the dogs from getting out of the back yard.

Aunt Louise had taken David to the studio when they arrived. David had never been in a room like this before. It was huge. It had been a barn before Uncle Swen had remodeled it into a studio, and there was a window on the north side almost as large as the wall. "For the light," Aunt Louise said. "It's always best to have north light." Below the window were all of Uncle Swen's things, which David was not to touch—his paints, his brushes, his easels, set up with half-finished paintings on them. He always worked on more than one painting at a time. Against the east wall were frames and completed canvasses lined up in racks. If people came to look at the paintings, he could pull them out. On the east wall were two doors leading into smaller rooms, one a storage room for materials, the other the room where David would sleep, a small room with a bed, a bureau and a chair. "Swen would sleep here sometimes while the house was being built, when he didn't want to go back to town. Sometimes he would work into the night."

David was glad to get back to the studio that evening. He was not scared, and the emptiness of the studio gave him a chance to think. There were so many people in that little house. They were all in each other's way. After supper, while Elizabeth was giving Alex a bath, David took Maggie into the little bedroom and gave her a bottle. He sat on the bed and put his arm behind her neck, as Elizabeth had showed him. Her head fit right in the crook of his right arm. She lay across his lap, and he held the bottle up with his left hand. So far, so good. "If she starts to cry," Elizabeth had said, "then pick her up and put her over your shoulder. Pat her back gently. You've seen me doing it. It's called burping her. You'll know if she burps."

David talked to her while she drank, and even while he was burping her. "You'll never know your grandmother, Maggie," he said. "I didn't really know her very well. I just went off to school and never really thought about her. Then she was dead." He whispered the word "dead" almost so she wouldn't hear it. He didn't want to upset her. He could hear the voices of Aunt Louise and Aunt Estelle talking in the kitchen while they washed the dishes. Somehow he couldn't imagine Aunt Estelle doing dishes. That smart little lady in her black dress, holding up traffic with her umbrella as she crossed Park Avenue—she didn't seem at all like the dishwashing type. And Uncle Swen sitting in his favorite chair in the living room, next to the radio, smoking his pipe and listening to classical music. David could hear the music in the little room. It sounded familiar, like something he had listened to in Mrs. Rossiter's class at Lowell School. He missed her terribly, this beautiful woman who had taught him Beethoven and Brahms and how to sing Gilbert and Sullivan.

"Hey, David," came Elizabeth's voice. "Get that bottle out of Maggie's mouth. She's just sucking on air." He'd forgotten for a moment where he was. She was standing next to him, holding Alex wrapped in a white towel. She put Alex on the bed and then took the baby from David. "Now, why don't you help Alex get his pajamas on?"

And so the night had gone, one thing after another, the kids in bed, but not really in bed, Maggie crying a little, Alex jumping up and asking for water, and Uncle Swen trying to listen to his music and finally going upstairs, and Elizabeth and Aunt Louise and Aunt Estelle talking about cousins that David didn't know, all those Hamilton cousins in Delaware and Pennsylvania, until finally Aunt Louise took mercy on him and walked him to the studio to show him how to turn off the light by the front door, and how to turn the electric heater off when he went to sleep.

"Good night," she said, cheerfully. "You'll sleep better out here away from all the women."

He walked around the studio and looked at all the paintings, paintings everywhere, some of them finished, some of them just started. A bright rooster on one of the easels, white space all around it. Some of the paintings were of fish and rocks and waves, but they were not realistic. They were brightly colored and outlined in dark, black lines, the fish, the rocks stark, strong. David fought in his mind for words. He couldn't think how to describe these paintings. He really hadn't looked at that many paintings at school. He knew about Michelangelo and the Sistine Chapel and the Mona Lisa, but he had never thought about anything like this. His favorite painting was one on the east wall, leaning against a group of frames. It was of Jesus. He was sure of that. Jesus riding the donkey into Jerusalem on Palm Sunday, the disciples following, playing on little pipes, Jesus in white, the disciples in red and green and blue. They were outlined in black, almost like the stained glass windows in St. Matthew's Chapel at school. Their faces were not quite finished. You had to supply with your imagination what the paint only hinted it. David liked that.

He went into his little room and got ready for bed. It was cold, unless he stood right next to the electric heater. He put on his pajamas, but kept his socks on. Then he pulled a sweater over his pajamas and went to the bathroom. Aunt Louise had warned him it would be cold. But he could snuggle down under the blankets and the comforter, and then he could turn on the heater again when he woke up.

The next thing he heard was a rapping on his door. It was morning, and Aunt Louise was there. "Get dressed quickly, David," she said. "There's been a power outage, and we need your help. I'll meet you at the door. It's like Minnesota out there."

He reached to turn on the switch of the electric heater and then remembered. It was freezing, and there was no power. He quickly went to the bathroom, and slipped on his blue jeans and his heavy jacket, his hat and his gloves and his boots. Aunt Louise stood outside the door shoveling. The snow was up to her knees, and it was still coming down. She had shoveled off the steps, and was working her way back toward the house. "Here, David," she said. "You finish shoveling your way back. We're heating water in the fireplace for cooking and for the baby's bottle. It looks like we'll have to be pioneers."

She smiled and started moving toward the house. "I remember these snows from my childhood. Sometimes we were snowed in for days."

David shivered, not so much from the cold as from the thought of being snowed in for days, with Elizabeth and Alex and Maggie and Aunt Estelle. What on earth would they do? How would they keep warm? The whole house was electric, and as long as the power was off, all they had was the fireplace. At least there was plenty of wood, cut and piled neatly on the side porch. But what about food? Suppose they ran out? The nearest store was down in Lambertville two miles away. But he had forgotten. The stores would be closed, the streets empty, nothing out there but the plows and the trucks from the electric company trying to fix the lines.

He shoveled his way to the porch and came inside. Everyone was in the living room near the fireplace, Aunt Louise crouched over the fire cooking something in a pot, Aunt Estelle wrapped in a blanket and looking pale, Elizabeth rocking Maggie and instructing Alex not to get too close to the fire.

"David, thank God you're here. Take Maggie. I need to help Louise fix breakfast. We're starving."

So David rocked Maggie and whispered to her while he watched Elizabeth and Louise cook bacon and scrambled eggs in the big black frying pan, while Uncle Swen brought more wood in from the porch. Then he disappeared.

"Where's Uncle Swen going?" David asked.

"To the studio to paint," said Aunt Louise.

"But it's freezing out there."

"He has a wood stove in the studio," said Aunt Louise. "He'll warm it up enough to paint. He's used to it. When he first came out here there was no power. He's tough."

"What about his breakfast?"

"He's been up for hours. He started the fire and cooked his morning bowl of oatmeal before the rest of you woke up. Now, Elizabeth, why don't you get Alex started, and Aunt Estelle, take off that blanket and get some breakfast. Come on over here by the fire."

All day long she was cheerful. David couldn't figure out how she managed it. She disappeared into the bedroom where Aunt Estelle lay huddled under her blankets to keep warm and came out with a handful of children's books. "David," she said, "here are some books I read to Elizabeth when she came to visit in Minneapolis. I brought them with me when we moved here." One of them was *Ferdinand the Bull*. David couldn't believe it. He hadn't seen the book in years, but he remembered the cover and the drawings and the story, which he had memorized when he was small.

"Come on, Alex," he said, "Let's go read a story," and off they went into the little room. He read it over and over, and each time they got to the special words, Alex would say with him, "But Ferdinand just liked to sit and smell the flowers." Alex's "reading" sounded more like "smell a fowers," but David didn't correct him. It sounded better that way. After a while Aunt Louise came in with two empty pails.

"David," she said. "I've got a job for you. The pump is out, so we have no water. You will be the water brigade. There's a little stream out back. Fill these up and bring them in. We'll heat some of the water for cooking and washing, and some we'll use to flush the toilets." So David became the water brigade, trudging through the knee deep snow to the stream, filling buckets and trudging up again to the house to dump them in the toilets or in the big metal pots by the fireplace. Elizabeth and Alex went upstairs to rest in Louise and Swen's room. Maggie slept in the crib in the little yellow room, and Aunt Estelle whimpered in the guest bedroom. Uncle Swen painted in the studio as long as there was light.

The gray day turned into a black night. The snow had stopped, but there was still no power, and the room looked eerie with the flames flicking out from the fireplace. The only other light was the kerosene lantern which Aunt Louise kept with her when she went from room to room. If you went to the bathroom, you used the flashlight, but only for a moment or two. You didn't want to wear out the batteries. David thought about those pioneers, those people in the movies who lived in log cabins in the west. How did they do it? How did they get through each day? It wasn't so much the cold as the boredom. That was it. At school, there was always something to do, something to pass the time, to make the time fly by. But here, in this space, he couldn't read, couldn't think. Everyone was tired. Even Aunt Louise was worn down.

Then the miracle came. Just at the moment David thought they would all go crazy, the power came back on. Lights sparkled everywhere, the furnace whirred, the pump clicked on, Alex ran in circles shouting "Hooray, hooray!" It was as if Santa Claus had come again. "Praise God," David thought, and then he thought again. He'd never said "Praise God" before. It had just come out. It was as if God had just created the light. It was like the first chapter of Genesis that they'd studied in confirmation class. God created the light and the darkness. Without God there was no light.

When the children and Aunt Estelle were asleep, David and Elizabeth played Parcheesi with Aunt Louise and Uncle Swen, and they listened to the radio. The storm had dumped two feet of snow in northern New York State, and power was still out in the mountains of Pennsylvania, in Scranton and Wilkes-Barre. Elizabeth talked to Phil on the phone in the city. He was fine, but he had been worried about them. When were they coming home?

"When the road is clear," said Aunt Louise. And the road wasn't clear until Monday, which left them another day, a day to play and rest and eat and talk.

"Well, David," said Aunt Louise at dinner, "What do you think about the election?"

David didn't think anything about the election.

"You should take an interest, David," said Aunt Louise. "It's important to keep informed."

David knew that Truman was President, that he had become President when Roosevelt died. And he remembered how close the election was in November. The New York papers had gone to press announcing Governor Thomas Dewey as the winner, and they had posted one of these papers on the bulletin board in the library. It wasn't until the next morning that Truman found out that he had won. But David didn't know any more than that. They really hadn't talked about it at school, or at least the third formers hadn't talked about it.

"'Give-'em-hell-Harry,'" that's what they call Truman," said Aunt Louise smiling.

"He just out-campaigned Dewey. Dewey was overconfident. He was cold. Truman was the people's choice."

David realized how much he had to learn. There was the Cold War and the Berlin blockade and the Atomic bomb and J. Robert Oppenheimer right over there in Princeton a few miles away. Louise and Swen and Elizabeth talked about all those things. David thought about the Yankees and what they would have to do to beat Cleveland and the Red Sox next summer. He just couldn't seem to keep his mind on politics and science.

He was glad to get back to New York, back to the Bronx even. He was busy, working his old job as a delivery boy for the grocery store down the street. He was happier about it than he had been the year before. Maybe he was stronger, but carrying the bags of groceries up the hill didn't seem quite so hard, and he was getting better at the small talk. On New Year's Day he delivered flowers downtown and went to dinner with Aunt Estelle at Schrafft's. She smiled at him across the table.

"Well, my young friend, how did you enjoy your weekend in the country?"

"It certainly wasn't New York City."

"No, indeed, it certainly wasn't. I believe I shall decline the next invitation."

"And why might that be?" David asked slyly.

"I believe the city mouse does not fare so well in the country. I miss the sounds of taxis and the taste of good coffee."

"Here's to New York," said David, and they clinked coffee cups.

CHAPTER FOUR

When David got back to Wicker after Christmas he discovered that he had a new roommate. He walked into the room, and there it was, the other side of the room beautifully arranged, college banners and posters on the wall, bed made, pictures of the family on the bureau, rug down the middle of the floor. David looked at his own stuff. His bedspread was worn, his extra blanket, folded at the bottom of the bed, was frayed at the edges. Next to whoever this was, he was pretty shoddy.

He found out who it was soon enough. The door opened and there stood a tall, grinning blond, his hair neatly combed, his tie tied, his tweed coat glowing as if it had just come off the rack at Brooks Brothers.

"Hi, D.J.," a voice said, "I'm your new roommate, Wally Hinson, or if you like, Wallace B. Hinson, Jr." He extended a hand warmly.

"D.J.?" David gulped.

"Sure, why not? You're David Johnson Lear. You're smart as hell. I've been talking around. But you don't have a nickname. So why not D.J. to start with? Come on, let's go to dinner."

So they walked out the door together and down the covered walkway to the dining room. They were at the same table.

"So, how did you end up with me?" asked David.

"They said your roommate left in the middle of the term, and there was a free bed in your room. Sounded good to me. Hell, I don't have any brains. I need a smart roommate."

"I wonder why they didn't tell me," said David.

"Who knows," said Wally, "and who cares. Let's just enjoy it."

And they did. Wally had been sent to school because of his parents' divorce. His mother had moved to Princeton and his father had stayed in their apartment in New York City. His father was in advertising. Wally had lots of clothes and he wore them well. Everything always matched.

"That tie looks awful with that jacket, D.J.," he would say and then toss David the right color tie from the rack on the inside of his closet door. He was about six inches taller than David, so nothing else he had fit. Wally was easy. "Take whatever you need, D.J.," he said, "my stuff is yours."

David spent a lot of time in the room alone. He had earned the second highest average in the third form at the end of the fall term, and so he no longer had to go to study hall. During the morning, if he didn't have a class he could go back to the room and study, and at night, after supper, during evening study hall, he could use the room. The only other people around were the sixth formers and the third formers who made the honor roll, and there weren't many of them. He would often go for days without seeing anyone during these hours. Mostly he worked on his English. That was another way Wicker was like Lowell, David thought. At both schools English was the only subject that really made him think. The others were just memorization. He could do his homework quickly, get the answers right, and then move on to English.

His English teacher was Clark Jaworsky, the head basketball coach, but he wasn't like the dumb coaches in the movies who couldn't teach. He was young and handsome, and he loved the students. He made them feel special. "Listen," he said. "We don't have to read that old stuff all the time. There's some really exciting new work being done, and I think you guys are smart enough to read it." David liked being trusted. One day he brought them a new play called *The Glass Menagerie*.

"It's by Tennessee Williams," he said, "the next great American playwright. He just wrote *A Streetcar Named Desire,* which won the Pulitzer Prize for Drama, but that one may be too tough for you. This one's better for starters."

They read about thirty pages a day, and acted out scenes in class. Mr. Jaworsky would move the furniture around, and get different people to read. The narrator's name was Tom, and he lived with his mother and sister in a little apartment in St. Louis. He felt trapped there, and he went off to the movies as often as he could. It was eerie, David thought, how much he was like Tom, how much the little apartment in the play was like Elizabeth and Phil's apartment. The mother was like Maggie Hope, from the South, but trapped in a big city with no money. Tom wants to be a writer, but he can't be, because he has to work at a factory to help support the family. He writes at night in his room and in the bathroom at the factory. They call him "Shakespeare." David loved that.

The last part of the play was the most powerful. Laura, the sister, is crippled. She is self-conscious because of the way she walks, and she spends all her time playing with her glass animals. Tom brings home a friend from work, and the friend is kind to Laura, he makes her feel like she is pretty. He is very gentle with her, and she falls in love with him. But then he tells her he can't see her again, because he is engaged. He was really just coming over to meet Shakespeare's sister. He wasn't expecting her to fall in love with him. The whole thing broke David's heart. He found himself almost in tears. He was angry at the Gentleman Caller, really angry, but at the same time he knew that Jim didn't mean any harm. Jim only wanted Laura to be happy.

"They're not real people," said Wally Hinson. "They're just characters in a book, in a play, for Christ's sake."

"But then, what's the point in reading it?" David asked.

"I don't know," said Wally. "It's just stuff you have to do to get through school. Like Shakespeare."

"It's more than that. It's got to be more than that," said David, but he couldn't quite figure out how to say what he meant.

It stayed with him, on into February, when they began to study American poetry. They were reading Robert Frost and Edna St. Vincent Millay. "This week, you can write either an essay or a poem," said Mr. Jaworsky.

"How can you grade a poem?" asked Billy DuPont. "It's all subjective, isn't it?"

"Good question," said Mr. Jaworsky. "I'll tell you what. If anyone writes a poem, I'll read it to the class and let the class decide if it's any good."

"Does it have to rhyme?" asked Billy DuPont.

"No," said Mr. Jaworsky. "Remember Walt Whitman, who we read last fall? His best poems don't rhyme."

"O Captain my Captain," came a voice from the back.

"That's not one of his best poems," said Mr. Jaworsky.

David was excited. He liked the idea of writing a poem that didn't have to rhyme. "Mending Wall" didn't rhyme, and he loved that poem, the way the farmer (the narrator, Mr. Jaworsky called him) and his neighbor disagree about whether walls are good or bad. He would write a poem about Laura in *The Glass Menagerie.* That was it. He would pretend he was Laura, the way Frost pretended he was the farmer. He worked on it a long time, scratching out things in his notebook, tearing out pages, pacing up and down the room. It was hard, but it was fun.

"Laura," he wrote, "the sound of your footsteps echoes in my room. I hear them on the stone walkway. You are gentle and kind, fragile like the glass animals you play with. I would be better than the Gentleman Caller. I would not break your unicorn's horn. Laura, my sister, friend of my soul, I too am shy. I too hold something secret in my heart. I too wait for the unveiling."

He turned it in to Mr. Jaworsky, and asked him how to make it into a poem. "If it doesn't rhyme, how do you know where to end the line and start the next one?" he wrote to the teacher. Mr. Jaworsky asked him to stay after class. Since English was the last class of the morning, there was free time before lunch. They talked.

"It's like breathing," Mr. Jaworsky said. "You think of where you need to pause for emphasis, or where you need to breathe. It's natural. For example, the first line might be 'Laura, the sound of your footsteps' and the second might be—"

"Echoes in my room," said David. He was getting the idea.

"Right," said Mr. Jaworsky.

"And the next would be, 'I hear them on the stone walkway.'"

"Good," said Mr. Jaworsky. "Now you do the rest. Turn it in tomorrow for credit."

"But...." said David.

"But what?"

"I'm scared of reading to the class."

"Why?"

"They'll laugh at me. They'll tease me about it."

"So what? If you're going to be a writer, you have to take some teasing."

David thought about it that night as he worked on the poem in his room. "If you're going to be a writer," Mr. Jaworsky had said. That was interesting. He'd always loved English, but this was the first time anyone had called him a writer.

He read the poem in class the next day a little nervously at first, but stronger as he went along. There was a titter of laughter from the back, and then another, but somewhere in the middle of the poem the room went silent.

"Well," said Mr. Jaworsky, "is that a good poem?"

The room was silent. You could hear feet shuffling under the desks.

"No one wants to say bad things about a friend's poem," said Ralph Wisdom, who was as wise as his name. He was the son of the school carpenter, and lived at home somewhere in the town of Wicker. David didn't know where. He came to school every morning with his father and had been elected class president second form year. He was tall, quiet, and old. That was it, David thought. He looked older than his years. If you told him something or asked him something, he would think about it, he would put his hand on his chin and smile, and then answer.

"Good point, Mr. Wisdom," said Clark Jaworsky. "But suppose I were to say that I won't grade the poem until the class has had a chance to critique it. Let's say that the writer, not just Mr. Lear, but any writer in the class, can get his poem critiqued before receiving a grade."

"Perhaps the author would rather have his poem critiqued in private, not in front of the whole class," said Ralph Wisdom.

"Good point," said Billy DuPont. "I certainly would."

"But you'd never write a poem, DuPont," said Wally Hinson from the back.

Mr. Jaworsky waited for the laughter to subside. He waited a long time. Then he said, "Well, maybe we're not ready for this. Maybe it's too difficult, too complicated. Perhaps it would be better if I read the poems and critiqued them and then gave you a chance to revise them, at least for the time being."

David didn't know whether to feel relieved or disappointed. He was scared of what the class might say, but he also wondered what they would think. Now he would never find out.

As they walked to lunch, Ralph Wisdom came up beside David. "That was a fine poem, my friend," he said easily, sliding into step with David's. "But not a poem to throw to the wolves. They would eat you up. Jaworksy is fresh out of graduate school. He doesn't know how mean boys can be. But he's a good teacher. We need him here."

That was Ralph Wisdom. He knew just how much to say and not to say. They parted in the dining room, and David knew at once that he would like to be friends with Ralph Wisdom. But how? That was the question.

The next morning the senior prefect announced that Father Perkins wished to address the school. Always, when such an announcement was made, a collective shiver of fear ran through the student body. Someone had been caught drinking or stealing and had been suspended or kicked out. Students took risks that David would never have taken, often for the sheer excitement of it. One student had been caught in the chapel drinking the communion wine, the wine that had been consecrated and placed on the altar in case of need. A sixth former had been sent home for taking bets on college football games during the fall. He had a radio stashed away

　　　　　　　　　　　　　　　　Anthony S. Abbott

somewhere where he could get the odds and the scores. What was it this time?

Father Perkins looked pale. He didn't look angry as he did when he had spoken about sixth form abuse. He didn't look stern, or even intellectual. He looked sad. He walked to the podium, held the sides with his hands, bowed his head, then slowly raised it and spoke: "It is my sad duty to report to you that Mr. Clark Jaworsky was killed last night in an automobile accident on the way home from a basketball game in West Hartford. There were, thank God, no members of the team in his car. Team players had been driven back after the game in the school station wagons by the assistant coach and the trainer. Mr. Jaworsky had stayed on to have dinner with friends. When he left West Hartford visibility was very poor. On a country road, another car came around a curve at a speed well in excess of the speed limit and hit Mr. Jaworsky's car head on. He was killed instantly. We will dedicate the Sunday Eucharist to his memory."

David suddenly felt very cold, cold running up his arms and down into chest, down into his stomach, his groin. He felt weak. He looked down at his legs. They were shaking. He knew he wouldn't be able to stand.

"Let us pray," said Father Perkins. "Our Heavenly Father, we ask for your mercy upon the soul of Clark Jaworsky, which has been delivered to your care. We do not understand the reasons for such sudden and terrible tragedies, but we deliver our fears and doubts to you in the sure knowledge of your grace and heavenly wisdom. We ask your care for his family, especially for his wife, Melanie, and his son, Clark, Jr. Strengthen our faith in this difficult time, and use these sad events to draw us closer to you and to your son, Jesus Christ. Amen."

There was no sound as the Headmaster left the podium, no sound of voices as the Senior Prefect dismissed the school, only the sound of shoes scuffing the floor. Classes went on as usual, but only mechanically, and for the next few days there was little else on the minds of the three-hundred students at the Wicker School. Mr. Jaworsky's English classes, of course, did not meet, and students were sent to study hall or to their rooms during those periods.

David sat at his desk, his extra blanket wrapped around him. He tried and tried to sort it out. It was not in his nature to be sad. He had learned about pain and loss from his mother's life, and he had no expectation that life would be easy. But this was different from anything he had experienced before. He had just gotten to know Mr. Jaworsky. It was as if there was something private, something personal between them. He was going to become a writer, and Mr. Jaworsky was going to be his teacher, his mentor. He had written his first poem, and he was proud of it. They were a team. And then suddenly he was gone. David knew that it was selfish to feel that way. But he couldn't get beyond it. He simply couldn't imagine going on as a writer, going on in English without his teacher.

For three nights he dreamed of Maggie Hope. She was always far away, beckoning to him, as if there were something she wanted him to do, some place she wanted him to go. He knew it had some relation to Mr. Jaworsky, but he didn't know what. In one of the dreams she was standing in the river at the place where the road turned to go up the mountain. The water flowed around her. "Come," she seemed to say, though there was no sound from her lips.

At the Sunday Eucharist Father Perkins came down from the pulpit once again and walked among them. He read the scripture lesson from Job: "When the Lord had finished speaking to Job, he said to Eliphaz the Temanite, 'My anger is aroused against you and your two friends, because, unlike my servant Job, you have not spoken as you ought about me.'"

"You all know the story of Job," the headmaster said, pacing slowly up and down the stone aisle in his white cassock with the rope tied around his waist. "You know how Job suffered and how unjust that suffering seemed. You know how Job's three friends, his so-called comforters, came to talk to him—Eliphaz, Bildad, and Zophar—how these friends told him he suffered because of his sin, how God was punishing him for something he had done. What a crude and brutal way of thinking about God this is, and God himself tells the three friends so at the end of the story. What a powerful ending. Job is justified, Job's complaints against God, his

Anthony S. Abbott

cries for justice, are heard. The comforters are wrong. Job loses his wealth, his health, his children, not because he has deserved it in some way, but because that is the way life is. He is right to cry out to God, just as we are right to cry out to God in our loss. We do not understand why a man so young, so promising should suddenly be taken from us. Why does God let this happen, we ask?"

David could feel the goosebumps on his arms as the headmaster passed by. He could feel the headmaster's eyes on him, if only for a moment. Yes, Father Perkins was speaking to him. He needed to know the answer to this question.

"Think of the citizens of Hiroshima, the merchants standing in the doorways of their shops, the mothers at home with their young children, the lovers in the park, at the moment that the most terrifying weapon in human history was unleashed upon them. They shriveled in an instant, and their shadows were burned into the sidewalks. Those who survived did so in terrible agony. Or think, if you will of the Jews in the prison camps at Auschwitz being led into the gas chambers for their 'showers.' These are terrible things, and we do not do justice to God to say that any one of these people was being punished for his sinfulness. That would be the mistake of the so-called comforters, those worthless physicians, as the Bible calls them.

"So why, why do these things happen? It is a great mystery, and the first thing we must do is to recognize the mystery of creation, of a species we call man, created perfect yet free to fall away from that perfection, free to be what they choose to be rather than what God intended them to be. Why this should be so is itself part of the mystery, but because it is so, then God can never interfere with the freedom of the species he has created without turning that species into robots or puppets. Things happen because human beings make them happen. Clark Jaworsky died because a drunk driver came around a curve on a foggy road and hit him head on. He did not die because it was God's will."

You could hear an audible gasp in St. Matthew's Chapel, a gasp of astonishment that the headmaster could say such a thing. David looked around. He couldn't find him. He had lost the voice for a moment. Then he looked up. Father Perkins was back in the pulpit, looking down at them.

"Could God have stepped in at that moment? Could He have made the Germans stop persecuting the Jews? Could He have made the pilot of the Enola Gay turn back with his fearsome bomb and return to his home base? Of course He could have. But He could not do so without denying human beings their freedom. That is the terrible cost of being human. We are free, free to do good, free to do evil, free to perform acts of great kindness and sacrifice and generosity, free to be mean and selfish and petty. That, my young friends, is the price of our humanness, but it is also our dignity."

There was a pause, another of those deliberate silences, David thought. He looked around. There were no smirks, no shuffling of feet, only faces lifted up to the high pulpit in hope of an answer. Father Perkins continued.

"Next week we begin the Lenten season, the season of preparation for Easter. And as we do so, we will consider what the cross, the crucifixion of Jesus, has to do with what I just told you. In the name of the Father and of the Son and of the Holy Ghost, Amen."

On Monday they went back to English class and discovered that their teacher for the remaining months of the school year would be Daniel Armstrong Lee. David didn't know what to think. "General" Lee, as the students called him, was a powerful man, perhaps the most admired and feared faculty member at Wicker. He was in charge of the work details, and those students who received "hours" as punishment for sloppy rooms or sloppy jobs worked under his supervision. No one took him lightly. No one laughed at him, even behind his back. It was not so much fear as respect. All of the students who had come as second formers had learned from him the art of how to study. All those who had come as second formers had taken his Greek and Roman history class. He was a great teacher, pure and simple. He was also a remarkable person. He was short and compact with the body of a wrestler. Up on the hill north of the playing fields overlooking the river, he was building his own house, cutting the trees and sawing them for lumber, hauling stones up the steep driveway, lifting the rafters in place. He was, one of the sixth formers said, Henry David Thoreau in the twentieth century—builder, naturalist, philosopher, historian.

He taught them Shakespeare's *Julius Caesar* and almost made David forget Clark Jaworsky. He loved the Roman Republic, loved it the way Brutus did in the play. He made them understand what could happen to a people when they gave up their freedom. He talked about simplicity of life, directness of purpose and self-reliance without ever mentioning them directly. Here he was, a classical scholar building his own home on the rocky hillside, and at the same time teaching them how to read Shakespeare, how to say the lines as if they really meant it. They acted out scenes in class, they made togas from old sheets. Ralph Wisdom performed Mark Antony's funeral oration as if he had known it all his life, pretending not to praise Caesar, pretending to praise the conspirators as "honorable men." "That is how irony works, gentleman," said Mr. Lee, "through the voice, the subtle intonation of the voice. Too little and you can't hear it, too much and you give it away. Excellent work, Mr. Wisdom." Ralph Wisdom smiled his wry smile and looked at David. David understood.

Still he could not quite shake the sadness of the loss. The spring came, bit by bit, the forsythia near the chapel door bloomed, but the sadness did not go away. Then, Father Perkins gave his Easter Sermon, and the Bishop came to confirm the new class. "We have never needed Easter more than now," said the headmaster. "But our loss is nothing compared to that of the disciples, that hardy group of rebels willing to risk their lives for this extraordinary man, this Jesus. Think of it—how they felt that day He was taken from them, how Peter, the best of them supposedly, denied Him three times to save his own skin. Think of their confusion, their terror, their devastation when He was crucified like a common thief and laid to rest in a dark tomb. They had nothing."

David was transfixed. The words whirled in his head. His imagination seized them. He could see the scene, the cross on the hill, the disciples watching as it was raised and lowered into the hole, their leader, their friend, their master dying in front of them, the blood dripping from his palms, where the nails had bit through flesh and bone.

"They had nothing," the headmaster said again, "but then, in the depths of the night, in the depths of their grief, God answered. 'Here I am,' Jesus said on Easter morning. 'Here I am. The worst that men could do has not destroyed me. Even death itself has not destroyed me. I am here. I am with you always, even to the ends of the earth.'"

David thought of Clark Jaworsky, and he thought, suddenly, of his mother. Where was she? How odd, he had never asked, never thought to ask, never wanted to ask. Where was she buried? Where were her earthly remains? He didn't know. Or did it really matter? Was she alive and well somewhere the way Jesus was alive and could say to his disciples, "Here I am"? Ralph Wisdom reached over and touched him on the shoulder. "Kneel down," he said, "we're praying now."

How strange. David had never heard the end of the sermon, never heard, the "let us pray," never heard the sound of his classmates slipping to their knees on the cold floor. He listened to the prayers, and then he heard the sound of his name and of the others who were to be confirmed. He rose, in a daze, and walked forward to the front of the chapel where a kneeling rail had been placed across the chancel. They knelt down, each of them, and the Bishop rose from his chair, rose with his shepherd's crook and his high pointed hat and his gorgeous robe. The Bishop rose and put his hands on each boy's head, and spoke: "Defend O Lord, this thy child, with thy heavenly grace," and then, moving to the next boy, "that he may continue Thine forever."

David felt the bishop's fingers on his head, felt the power of the words, the depth and sonority of the voice. The words of the headmaster mingled with the words of the Bishop. "Here I am," said Jesus. "Here I am," thought David to himself, a new person in a new world.

"Do you feel different?" asked Ralph Wisdom, with his wry smile, as they walked to breakfast.

Anthony S. Abbott

"Yes," said David.

"Bullshit," said Wally Hinson, coming up beside them. "It's all a crock. They want us to believe this so we'll be good. It's just a way of keeping us under control." He didn't sound angry or bitter, just matter of fact. For Wally, that's just the way it was. Most of what went on at the school was bullshit according to him.

"You'll change your mind one day," said Ralph Wisdom calmly. "Experience will teach you the truth."

"What's that supposed to mean?" asked Wally Hinson.

"It's an emotion, a feeling," said David. "It doesn't make sense unless you feel it."

"Well, I sure didn't feel it. That Bishop is just an old fart dressed up in a funny costume. It's just words."

"It's poetry," said David.

"Jesus Christ, Lear," said Wally Hinson. "You are really weird."

"So was Jesus Christ," said Ralph Wisdom, as they went in the dining hall.

CHAPTER FIVE

It was hard to be different. The feeling David had during the confirmation didn't last. Life was the same. He went to class, to meals, to sports, he did his homework, he got good grades, but he felt like the same old person. Being confirmed didn't make him any better at baseball, and it didn't solve the problem of how he would pay his way to California for the summer.

He had had a discussion with Elizabeth about money during spring vacation, and it had come out badly. They were sitting at the kitchen table, her cigarette in the ashtray sending a narrow swirl of smoke toward the ceiling.

"David," she said, "we need to talk about money."

"OK." He hated conversations about money.

"When Mommy died," she said, "that entitled you as a minor to social security benefits, until your eighteenth birthday."

"Wow," he said, "that sounds terrific. I can save it and use it to pay my way to California next summer. I won't have to take the bus. I. . ."

"Slow down. Give me a chance."

"I'm sorry."

"I've written to Molly about it, and she thinks you should give the money to me."

"But why?"

"Food costs money, David. You're always hungry, remember? I want you to think of this as your home. I want you to feel you can always come here, but we just can't afford it. Phil doesn't make very much. We need the money just to be able to keep you."

She reached toward him and put her hand on his arm. "I have the first check," she said. "It was mailed to you here, at this address. All you need to do is endorse it, sign it on the back, and then we can cash it."

And that's the way it was, he thought in his room looking out the window at the river. They had discussed this in confirmation class, Father Perkins had preached about it, he had talked to Ralph Wisdom about it, and it always came out the same way. There were two things: what you wanted, and what was right. There were "wants" and "oughts." Why was it that you always had to give up what you wanted for what was right? Why couldn't what was right be what you wanted?

The spring wore on. Then one day he saw the book in Wally Hinson's bureau. It was in the second drawer, under the shirts. The drawer had been left slightly open, and David's eye caught the glitter of the gold clasp which held the leather-bound volume shut. He opened the drawer and pulled it out. The clasp was not locked. He opened it.

The book was full of pictures, pictures of girls in bathing suits and low cut dresses, some in bras and panties. As he looked at the pictures David could feel a swelling in his penis. His penis was growing. He remembered the conversation with Jackie Callaghan back in the fall. He sat on the bed, unzipped his pants, and holding the book in his left hand, began slowly to move his right hand up and down on his penis. It grew larger, and the pressure of his hand felt good. He looked again at the pictures and knew what Jackie had meant. Then, all at once, he heard footsteps in the hall. Quickly he pushed his penis back into his pants, zipped himself up, slipped the book into the drawer, and sat down at his desk. His heart was beating crazily. The footsteps went by, turned the corner, and faded. His heart slowed.

He thought it through. You couldn't just sit there and *do* it. Someone could come in and catch you. There were no locks on the doors, and sixth formers and masters were allowed in the room at any time. They could just knock and enter. He didn't have to worry about Wally; Wally was in study hall. But one of the other honor roll students might come by. Sometimes they did their homework together in one another's rooms. It saved time, especially with translation. They could knock off the Latin assignment in thirty minutes if three of them did it together. David laughed, imagining himself opening the door with a huge swelling in his pants. Then it occurred to him that everyone must have the same problem. He was just a third former, fifteen years old. What about all the older boys? What did they do? "Don't play with yourself, Toots," his mother had said to him. "Promise me you won't play with yourself." He had promised, not really knowing what she was talking about. Now he knew. But what he didn't know was why it was so bad. It didn't hurt anyone. It wasn't like cheating or stealing or lying. It wasn't as if the Bible said, "Don't play with yourself."

One day he figured out how to do it. If he lay on the bed facing the wall with his extra blanket over his legs, he could do it with his left hand and let the book rest on the bed. Then if someone came, he could just slip the book under the pillow, pull the blanket over him, close his eyes and pretend he was asleep. People took naps all the time. That was the best thing about studying in your room.

It worked. Twice someone knocked, opened the door, looked in, and then went out again. He enjoyed it, the excitement of the ritual, the book, the pictures, the growing flesh, the arousal, the final climax and release.

Then Wally burst into the room unexpectedly during study hall.

"Jesus Christ, Lear, what in hell are you doing with my book?"

David handed him the book, and turned away toward the wall, ashamed.

"God damn it, Lear," he said, shoving the book into the bureau drawer. "Don't you ever touch anything of mine again. Jesus Christ, what is this?" Then he started laughing.

"Damn it, Lear, you are a sight. Mr. Pure, Mr. Religion, you and oh-so-smart Mr. Wisdom. And here you are beating the meat to my book. Well, go ahead, beat the meat to your heart's content, but if you touch my stuff again, I'll kill you." Then he grabbed his math book and stormed out the door.

For days David walked on tiptoe. Wally had him over a barrel. All he had to do was tell one person, and that person would tell another one until everyone knew. But it never happened. Finally one day, Wally said, "Shit, D.J., I don't really care what you do. Hell, if you'd asked me, I'd of given you the goddamn book. It was just your taking it, and you being so religious and all. It just made me mad."

"I know," said David. "I'm sorry."

And that was the end of it, and also the end of David's rooming with Wally Hinson. Wally asked Ted Barber to room with him fourth form year. They rowed together in club crew and liked the same jokes. They were naturals. So David was on his own again, until Borden Smith came in and asked David to be his roommate. It was nice, being asked. David didn't really know Borden Smith very well, but he was quiet, neat, and a great reader. He worked in the library, cataloging books, magazines, and newspapers. He was from New York City. If David could have had any roommate in the third form it would have been Ralph Wisdom, but Ralph was a day student, living at home with his parents. So David said "yes" to Borden Smith.

At the Eucharist he prayed to God for forgiveness, then knelt at the altar and received the wafer on his tongue. He drank the strong wine, holding the bottom of the chalice with his right hand, tipping it upward to his lips. He promised God he would not "play with himself" any more. He started to study in the library instead of his room, just to keep out of temptation's way, and he planned his strategy for summer vacation.

He had $193 in his bank account in New York. He got his allowance four times a year from Molly Ariel in California, and he would not get another check until July. He had saved a little money from his grocery job over Christmas, but not much. He loved New

York, he loved the movies, he loved to go to baseball games and hockey games. All that cost money, but it was worth it. That was the problem. The minute he got to New York for spring vacation he had started reading the papers. Jane Wyman had won the Academy Award for her role as a deaf-mute in *Johnny Belinda*. He had to see that. And then Laurence Olivier had won the award for best actor in *Hamlet*. That was even more important than *Johnny Belinda*.

Mr. Lee had talked about it in class and had urged everyone who lived in New York to go see the film. He didn't say "movie," he said "film." He said that they would understand Shakespeare better if they saw the film, because they would hear the language spoken the way it was meant to be spoken. Mr. Lee was right. On the afternoon before they went back to school David had seen the film with a bunch of other Wicker students. Someone had arranged a group rate. The film was long, but not as long as the play, which they would read in the fifth form. Some of it had been cut to make it easier for movie audiences. The whole play would have lasted four and a half hours.

David liked Hamlet. He understood Hamlet's problem. In fact, he thought he was kind of like Hamlet, because he had trouble deciding what to do. It wasn't as if he couldn't make up his mind. It was just that he was different, that was it, he was different from everyone else in the play. And so the decisions were more difficult. You could see inside Hamlet's mind, you could see him struggling to figure out what was right, and you could see the trap closing against him at the end, the King and Laertes plotting against him so that no matter what he did he couldn't win. They stabbed him in the back with the poisoned sword. It was dirty, it was evil. It made you sick, and here was Hamlet dying for no reason. It seemed so unfair, David thought. He wrote a poem about it when he got back to school, and gave it to Mr. Lee, who told him it was a good poem and that he should put it in the school magazine. "Still, it is a little idealistic, Mr. Lear," said the teacher. "After all, Hamlet is hardly the paragon of virtue you make him out to be, but it's still a good poem, a fine poem."

David opened his English notebook and pulled out the poem:

HAMLET: THE DREAMING PRINCE
　　　Good night, sweet prince, Horatio says
　　　Good night, sweet prince, I say too.
　　　You're better than the rest, you're blessed.
　　　You care where the crown lies.
　　　You see the truth in your father's eyes
　　　But can't be sure if you're right
　　　If the ghost is true, so you wait
　　　To see Claudius's eyes, you surprise
　　　Him with the mousetrap play
　　　 Then you delay no longer
　　　—or do you? You can't stab him
　　　At his prayers. He might go to heaven.
　　　Then there's no chance until the end
　　　But too many are against you,
　　　Prince of dreams, too many to defend
　　　Yourself against. So, good night,
　　　Sweet Prince, I say, you're better
　　　Than all those dirty grownups
　　　Grovelling in their poison and their drink.

The magazine came out the week before final exams started, and Father Perkins sent David a note. "Fine work, lad. I particularly like the ending. We're all proud of your work." He went into exams with a fury, and ended the year with the second highest average in the class, a fraction behind Ralph Wisdom. That was all right, David thought. There was nothing wrong with being second to Ralph Wisdom.

Still, when he got to Elizabeth's, he hadn't solved the money problem. The ticket to San Francisco, meals along the way, clothes for the summer would take more than he had. He decided to ask Aunt Estelle about it, so he called her and arranged lunch.

She was funny. She kept talking about the country mouse and the city mouse and how she was never going to Lambertville again in the winter time, nor was she going to spend another night with crying children. "If I had wanted children, I should have married," she laughed. "That was quite a Christmas."

David agreed. He had enjoyed bringing the water in, being a pioneer and all, but he was really pretty much a city mouse too. They toasted to that just as they had at Shrafft's before, and then David asked her about the summer.

"I mean, Aunt Estelle, what should I do? I have to go, I couldn't stand being around here all summer. Besides, they will pay me, and then I can afford to come home. I just need enough for the trip out."

"Well," she said, "you could sell your stamp collection."

"Sell my stamp collection?"

"At that other school you collected stamps. You were in the stamp club. I remember you always talked about it."

"That's true."

"Now you don't talk about it."

"Well, there's no stamp club at Wicker."

"And what do you do with your stamps?"

"Nothing, I guess."

"Exactly. They no longer mean anything to you. So sell them."

"To whom?"

"Very nice. 'To whom' is quite correct."

"Thank you. But you didn't answer my question."

"To one of those stores over there on Broadway."

After lunch, he walked over to Broadway, and sure enough there were several stores with big signs saying "Stamps and Coins Bought and Sold." He knew he would get cheated. That was the way these stores worked, but there wasn't much choice, so the next time he came downtown he took the book to two of the stores and compared prices. One was ten dollars higher than the other. They gave him cash, five twenty-dollar bills and a ten. That was the end of it—all those years of saving money and trading stamps. It had been fun, but Aunt Estelle was right. They no longer meant that much to him. Still, it was like giving away a part of himself, and once the stamps were gone, then the memories the stamps brought back would be gone.

He thought suddenly, with a kind of lurch, of Terry and Griff. They had written back and forth and talked about meeting in New York and going to Port Chester to have their pictures taken under the Life Saver factory, but nothing had come of it. They got out of their schools on different days, and somehow it just never seemed like they could manage to be in the city at the same time. Terry was at Deerfield and Griff was at Groton, and they went to Boston to the airport to fly home. David missed them, and now that he was in New York he missed them even more. The rhythm, the business of school life kept him occupied, and the empty places in his heart were filled with activities. But here, in the city, he was on his own, and when the subway left him at Grand Central Station, and he came out into the huge central concourse with the clock and the constellations on the ceiling, he would sometimes walk to the information booth and wait, just in case, for the odd chance that one of them would be passing through. "Well, Maggie Hope," he would say to his mother, "here I am again at our favorite place. Talk to me. Tell me something. You never say anything in my dreams. You just stand there. I need a friend, Maggie Hope, I need someone to talk to."

Five days later he was on the way to California, packing his bag and saying goodbye to Alex and Maggie and Elizabeth. "You no go," said Alex as his uncle turned to walk down the steps. "You stay here."

"We'll miss you," said Elizabeth, with Maggie in her arms. Maggie only laughed.

He hauled his bags up the hill to the Concourse and was sweating by the time he got to the top. He wore blue jeans, sneakers, and a blue button-down shirt. He didn't want to look too dressy, but even the button-down shirt was dressy for Greyhound. The bus station was filled with travelers—all of them poor as far as David could see. It was a different world, a world full of Negroes and Puerto Ricans, Italians and Greeks, families with small children, all of them with too much luggage, all of them trying to get somewhere different, somewhere better, David thought, than New York City on a hot June day.

David got a window seat in the middle of the bus on the right-hand side. The right-hand side was better, because you could look at the scenery, if there was scenery. He was excited and scared both. For four and a half days no one would know where he was. He could be anywhere.

The bus rumbled through the Lincoln Tunnel and out across New Jersey to pick up the Pennsylvania Turnpike. They had a one-hour dinner stop in Pittsburgh, and then cruised on through Ohio and Indiana. The next day they reached Chicago and changed buses. "I'm halfway there," he thought, but he was wrong. The West was huge. He had forgotten how long it took to get from Chicago to San Francisco, he had forgotten the endless cornfields of Iowa and the prairies of Nebraska. He hadn't realized how long it would take to climb the winding highways up the Rocky Mountains and down again. On the fourth day they got to Salt Lake City, and he had a two hour break, time for a walk down the main street and then lunch. He counted his money. Three dollars left for one more night and another day. He'd be all right if he didn't eat too much.

He walked out the door of the bus station into the bright sunlight, and there in front of him was one of the most beautiful churches he'd ever seen. It towered above the rest of the city. Six spires reached into the blue sky. The massive granite walls glowed with some secret hidden within. It was like a medieval castle. He walked toward it, and the closer he got the grander it seemed. He could feel something coming, the same way he had when the Bishop touched him at school. He could feel the tingling. He approached the gigantic wooden doors, and opened one. Inside was a guide to the church—"The Salt Lake City Temple of the Church of the Latter Day Saints" it read.

Suddenly he looked at his watch. There was only five minutes before the bus was scheduled to leave. He turned and raced toward the entrance, then out the door, and down the street. He was out of breath when he boarded the bus, and very hungry. He had completely forgotten lunch.

At nightfall they stopped for dinner in Reno, Nevada. David was ravenous. He didn't care how much money he had left. He had to eat dinner. So he blew two dollars on steak and French fries. He had a dollar left to get him through the last day—that is— he would have had a dollar left had it not been for the slot machines. He watched mesmerized, as his fellow passengers fed nickels and dimes and quarters into the machines and pulled down the handles. His eyes were glued to the spinning reels as they stopped one by one, revealing cherries, oranges, bells and bars. He knew he shouldn't, but he couldn't help himself. He had to try. Maybe he'd win, maybe he'd actually make some money. So he went in tentatively, a nickel at a time, until finally there were no nickels left. "You never win if you have to win," the man next to him said. David turned away, ashamed, and returned to the bus.

Ray Cartwright and his mother met David in San Francisco. "You look terrible, David," she said. "Are you sick?"

He could hardly answer. "Yes, ma'am," he said politely.

She took him home and put him to bed and fed him chicken soup. He told her about the money and the slot machines. She laughed. "Well, better to lose your last dollar than your last hundred. It'll teach you a lesson." In two days he was himself again, and they set out in her green Buick for the camp.

David was glad to be back. Buck Dooley greeted both the boys heartily, and explained their duties. Each of them would be in charge of a tent. They were to get the boys up in the morning, supervise their activities, and get them to meals on time. At night they would get them to bed. The senior counselor, Jack Palermo, would also have a tent, and he would be their boss. There were no strict rules, no uniforms, no phony Indian stuff—just "common sense and good, clean fun," as Buck put it.

And he was right. David could not have been happier. The days were glorious, one after the other bright and sunny, but comfortable in the dry California air. In the morning when he heard the first bell from the cook shack up the hill, David jumped out of bed and went out back to wash his face and pee into the weedy bank behind the outhouse. Then he woke his boys and made sure they all got to breakfast on time. He loved them, Butch and Jack and Ernie, and Peter and little Finnegan, known as Finn. He hustled them up the hill, and made sure they were seated at the table before the second bell rang.

After breakfast they saddled the horses and went riding, before the sun got too hot, following well-marked trails up into the nearby hills. Buck supervised the riding. Then, when they had unsaddled the horses and turned them out, they grabbed their bathing suits and headed for the pool, where the icy creek had been dammed up enough to make deep water. The shock of entering the icy water never wore off, but it felt good in the noonday heat. Then lunch, and rest hour, when David and Ray could play ping pong outside the dining room while the campers napped. They could see the tents from the ping pong table. Then, after rest hour, team competition.

David and Ray had divided the campers into two groups—the Yankees and the Dodgers. David took his tent, Ray took his, and they divided Jack Palermo's tent in half. That gave them nine boys on each team. They competed in everything—soccer, archery, swimming, and softball, mostly softball. The teams were almost exactly even, and so were the leaders. Ray was taller, faster, and a little stronger. But David was smarter, more aggressive, more daring. He made up in effort what he lacked in skill. David was a better leader. He was more patient with his team, and when the smaller boys were batting, he urged them on, remembering his own struggles at Lowell. Ray got angry when his weaker boys did poorly, expecting of them the same high performance he always gave. Despite this, Ray's team began to win more and more. They were just a little bit better, just as Ray was a little bit better than David.

Six weeks into it the girls arrived, and everything changed. Buck Dooley had a blond daughter named Eloise. Everyone called her Ellie. She had spent the month of July at a camp in New Hampshire with Tracy Warren, who was both her best friend and also Butch's older sister. Now Tracy was coming to spend August with her at the ranch. The girls slept in a small bedroom at the end of the cook shack. They got up early in the morning to fix breakfast, and they helped with the clean up after meals. The rest of the day they were free to join in the activities. They loved to ride. That was their favorite thing. As soon as breakfast was over, they headed to the barn to start grooming and saddling the horses. They rode bareback frequently, and David found himself paying more attention to them than to his campers, as they rode in their blue jeans and halter tops with their hair flowing out behind when they galloped. Ellie was beautiful. Her blond hair glowed in the sun, and her blue eyes lit up when she smiled. You could see the tops of her breasts. Tracy was tall and slim, built more like a boy than Ellie, and she loved sports. And that was how she ended up on David's softball team.

The girls arrived one day, after rest period, and asked to play. Butch was on David's team and wanted his sister to play with him. Ray didn't object. He wanted Ellie on his team. David said nothing. He knew he had gotten the best of the deal. As the summer wore on, David's team started winning more often. Next to David, Tracy was the best batter on the team. She just stood up to the plate and whacked the ball into the outfield, while Ellie swung like a girl.

"It's because of her tits," said Mike Palermo. "She don't want to hit her tits with her elbow, so she just kinda punches at the ball."

One night after supper, David was cleaning up, putting the bases, the extra gloves, the bats and balls back in the big brown canvas bag. The kids had gone down to the tents for their free time before bed. When he was finished, he sat down on the wooden bench under the tree and pulled a letter from his pocket. It was from Aunt Louise.

"Dear David," she wrote. "You may wish to know that your grandmother Everett died last week. There was service for her at the same funeral home where they held your mother's service. She had been very ill with cancer and her release was a blessing. Your grandfather will go back to France, where he seems determined to live. Elizabeth looks terrible—very tired. The heat is dreadful, and I have invited her out here for a few days, but I don't know if she will come. She doesn't know if she can make the trip by herself with the two children. She misses you. 'I wish David was here.' She said that twice during our telephone conversation. Be thankful you are out there away from all this."

He folded the letter up and put it back in his pocket. That was Aunt Louise, he thought. She always gave it to you straight. He put his elbows on his knees and his face in his hands. Why did he feel so guilty?

A voice behind him said, "Hi." He looked around. It was Tracy Warren.

"Are you OK?" she asked. "You look like you need a friend."

David stood up, and pointed to the bench. "Would you like to sit down?"

"Thank you," she said. For a while they just sat in silence.

"Bad news?" she asked quietly.

"You might say. My grandmother died."

"I'm sorry. Were you close to her?"

David laughed. "Close? No, I wouldn't say so. I go to boarding school, so I hardly ever see her."

"Oh, where do you go?"

"Wicker. What about you?"

"Greenwich Country Day. I live at home. I know a guy who goes to Wicker. Pete Gallagher. He'd be a fifth former."

"I don't know him," David said.

"This is nice," she said.

"Yes," he answered.

"You know," she said. "This is the first time we've had the chance to talk, to just be ourselves without all the kids around."

"And without Ray," he added, then suddenly caught himself as if he had said more than he really intended. He liked Ray. Ray was his best friend, but somehow Ray and girls didn't mix.

"I don't like Ray," she said after a moment.

"Why not?"

"He's kind of stuck on himself. When he looks at me, I feel ugly. I feel like he thinks he's better than I am. You're much nicer."

"Thank you."

She put her hand on top of his. "Why don't you come up and visit after lights out, after the boys go to sleep? You can just run up the hill, slip in the door, and come talk to us in our room. We can get to know each other."

"What about Ray?"

"Wait'll he goes to bed."

"Ray and I play cards in the counselors' tent every night."

"Tell him you're sleepy and pretend to go to bed."

"I can't do that."

"Come on, David. It'll be neat fun. We can sit up in the dark and talk, the three of us. Ellie likes you, too."

"But what if Ellie's dad comes over? He'll kill me."

"No he won't. We aren't doing anything wrong, just talking."

"But I'm supposed to be in my tent. What if one of the boys wakes up?"

"What if, what if, what if," she said. "Have some guts, David."

She got up and started toward the cookhouse, tall and easy, and smiling, more like a young deer than a girl, David thought. It was terrible, and David knew it. Ray was his friend, his best friend, really his only friend at the camp. They had competed day after day, they had traded stories, and read the box scores of the major league games every day after lunch. They played ping pong during rest hour and gin rummy at night. He had never lied to Ray before, and he did not want to start lying now. He had really never wanted to be away from Ray before, but this was different. It wasn't something they could do together. It was different, and it was terrible, and his feelings toward Ray would never be quite the same.

At nine o'clock he tucked his boys in, and went down to the counselors' tent to play cards with Ray. At nine-thirty he feigned sleepiness, and said he was going to bed.

"What a wimp," said Ray. "You just don't want to get beat again."

"I'm really tired," said David uneasily. "See you in the morning."

At nine forty-five he cut out from the corner of his tent, dashed up the dark of the hill and entered the cook shack. He could hear laughter from the girls' room. He hesitated. He would go back down the hill and go to bed. He would forget the whole thing.

But the door opened and Tracy Warren came out in her blue pajamas and sat down at one of the tables. David sat across from her, and they talked. At first, Tracy asked questions, and David answered tentatively. He didn't know how much to say, how much to trust her with. Her told her about Molly Ariel and how she knew Buck Dooley. He told her about going to his father's ranch and how it didn't work out. He had never told so much to anyone.

"What about your mom?" she asked.

"She died last year, of cancer."

"What was her name?"

"Maggie," he said, "Maggie Hope."

"I like that name," she said. "My mom's name is Lisa."

"And your dad?"

"He's Ed. Pretty ordinary family. Ed and Lisa Warren with two kids—a boy and a girl."

"I think I'd like ordinary," David said.

Tracy laughed from deep in her throat. "Yeah, I can see that. There's sure nothing ordinary about you." Their hands touched in the middle of the table, just for a moment, and then the windows lit up. A car was coming from the big house.

"I've got to go," he said, and he bolted out the door and down the hill to the safety of his tent. He undressed silently in the dark and slipped under the covers. For a long time he lay awake, his heart thudding. It was so complicated. He did and he did not want this to happen again, this secret thing in which he had just taken part. It was like the Eucharist, the mystery of the bread and the wine—the moment of exhilaration when he felt seized by something bigger than himself. He loved being with Tracy, the secrecy of it, the sharing, the knowledge that he had told her about himself, trusted her with knowledge about himself. He loved that. He loved the small touch of Tracy Warren's fingers. We speak with our bodies as well as our mouths, David thought. He would have to write a poem about it.

But then there was the other side, the terrible side, the getting caught side. He vowed he would not go back, but his vow had no force. Slowly his head began to rock on his pillow, back and forth, back and forth, the way it had at Lowell when he was ten and eleven. Back and forth, yes and no, back and forth into an uneasy sleep. The next thing he knew, Butch Warren was shaking him.

"Hey stupid," said Butch, "you missed the bell."

David sat up with a start. The boys were getting dressed and laughing at him.

David smiled and shrugged his shoulders. "Well, we'll all be late together," he said, and they marched up to the dining room and walked inside to the stares of the other campers.

David looked at Tracy and Ellie at the stove flipping flapjacks and trying to hold back their laughter. "Mr. Lear," said Buck Dooley, "why is your tent late for breakfast?"

"I overslept, sir," said David, "and didn't hear the bell."

"Up too late last night, were you?" said Buck.

"Oh no, sir," said David sheepishly, "I went to bed early last night. I was really tired."

"Don't let it happen again, young man," said Buck, "or I'll have to dock your wages." Then he grinned his big Buck Dooley grin, and shook with laughter. "Mr. Perfect late for breakfast. That's a good one."

The next night David didn't go up to the house, or the night after that. He was too nervous. He didn't want Ray to catch him, and he didn't want to be late for breakfast again, but he could not get Tracy Warren out of his mind. On the third morning, she slipped him a note after breakfast. "Come up tonight," it said. "I'll be alone. Ellie's going to sleep in the big house with her Mom and Dad. She doesn't feel well."

So he did it again, dashing up the thirty yards to the cook shack and entering the dark dining room like a thief. The door to the bedroom was open, and Tracy was waiting for him.

"Take off your shoes," she said, "and come lie next to me."

He lay on his side, and turned toward her. She smiled, touched his face lightly with her free hand, and kissed him on the cheek. Then they began to talk He told her about school, about Jackie Callaghan and how they had hazed him.

"I wish I had stood up for him better," David said.

"Yes," she said. "I do too."

He could see her eyes smiling and listening as he talked. It was different from what he expected. He had felt himself growing large when he first lay on the bed, but the longer he talked the less he thought about sex.

"I really like you, David," she said. "I want you as a friend. I want you to come to see us in Greenwich, when you get back. Butch thinks you're great, and I know my mom and dad would like you. You can just come be part of our family."

She talked about her family and her school and how it was hard being so tall, because it made her feel awkward around boys. "Besides," she said, "boys only want one thing. But you, I don't know, you're different. You're sweet. We'll make a pact to be friends. OK?"

"OK," he said.

"Give me a hug," she said, and she took him in her arms and held him for a moment. "Now scoot," she said, and laughed as he searched for his shoes in the dark.

Back in the tent he thought again. He was glad camp was almost over. He couldn't take much more of this. He felt guilty about betraying Ray, he felt guilty about his sexual feelings. "You're different," Tracy had said to him, and he liked that. He liked the fact that she trusted him and wanted him for a friend. He wanted to go to her house and be part of her family. But he did have sexual feelings, and he did want the same things that other boys wanted. Why didn't Tracy feel that same stirring he felt? Did girls feel differently from boys about sex? Did they just spend their time fending boys off? Boys attacked. Girls defended. But that was stupid. What was the point of doing something unless you both enjoyed it? Touching a girl made no sense unless the girl enjoyed it too. It was so complicated it made David want to be back at school. At least there, choices were simple, and there were no girls.

On the last night of camp, David went up to say good-bye to Tracy and Ellie, and on his way down, he ran straight into Ray.

"You're a real bastard, Lear."

It was dark, and they couldn't see each other.

"Shh," said David. "Don't wake up the kids."

"Christ," said Ray, "How long you been doing this?"

"I don't want to talk about it now."

"Don't be such a damn coward. I caught you."

They walked down to the counselors' tent. It was empty and the light was out.

"I'm sorry," said David.

"No you're not. You been getting any?"

"No."

"Come on. Tell me the truth. Christ, we've been friends. You trying to keep it all for yourself?"

"Tracy and I are friends, Ray. We just wanted to talk. I'm going to visit her in Greenwich."

"And what about Ellie?"

"Ellie just let us talk. Sometimes she talked, too."

"You're telling me that you were in Ellie Dooley's bedroom, and all you did was talk? Hell, either you're queer or you're crazy. And anyway, anyway, oh shit, I don't know."

Ray looked at him, then got up and turned toward the door. "Keep your goddamn girls, I don't care. But don't think you're gonna get away with this. I bet Buck Dooley would like to know what's been going on up there with his daughter."

He turned and walked out into the night.

The next morning at breakfast the campers were happy and excited. They buzzed about plane schedules and train tickets and what they were going to do when they got home. Buck Dooley sent them down to the tents to pack and wait for their parents to arrive. David started to leave with his boys.

"Not you," said Buck Dooley to David and Ray. "We have a little issue to discuss." He sat David and Ray and the girls down at one of the dining room tables. He grabbed a chair and at sat the head. He was going to hold court.

"Well," he said to David, "what's been going on up here?"

David reddened. He knew that Ray had told Buck. He wanted to lie, to say that he had just come up the night before to say good-bye. That would be the easy way out. He would have to tell the truth and take his chances.

"Tracy and I are friends, Buck," he said. "I've come up two or three times to talk to her. Ellie can tell you."

"Is that right, Ellie?"

"Yes, Dad," she said. "David and Tracy are kind of like brother and sister. I think she wants to adopt him into her family."

"That right, Tracy?"

"Yes, sir. We just wanted to talk, because there was no other place to have some privacy. If we talked around the kids, they'd just make fun of us."

Buck Dooley shook his head. "Girls," he said. "I knew this wouldn't work. Once you have girls at a boys' camp, then everything gets screwed up."

CHAPTER SIX

"Well, that was quite a summer you had for yourself, chum," said Molly Ariel.

It was David's last night at the ranch, and they sat after dinner for their going-away talk in his favorite place on the patio. Bert and Jessie, her stepchildren by her husband, Jack, had left the day before for Washington, D.C., where they lived during the school year with their mother, and David had Molly Ariel all to himself.

"I never thought you'd really come," she said. "I couldn't believe you'd sell your stamp collection to pay for your bus ticket. I guess you must have wondered why I didn't pay your way."

"I did, a little," said David.

"It's not good to get things too easily," said Molly Ariel. "I don't want to spoil you. If you don't have to work for things, they're not worth it."

"I understand," said David, and he did understand. Whatever Molly Ariel did was all right with him. If she did it, then it was right, and he felt no bitterness.

"But I don't think we'll do this again," she said. "You won't go back to Buck's next summer."

"No," said David. "But it was worth it, I mean, everything was worth it. I'm sorry about getting into trouble, and I'm, sorry about Ray, but. . ."

"It was still worth it," Molly Ariel said, laughing.

"It was."

"But you should have been more honest about it."

"I was, at the end."

"Yes, but to Ray. Ray was your friend."

"But what could I tell him?"

"You could have told him how you felt about Tracy."

"But then he'd have wanted to come, too, and that would have spoiled everything. They didn't want him."

"You don't know that. Maybe he would have shrugged his shoulders and given you his blessing. But you went behind his back, and that made him angry. Now you've lost a friend forever."

David was silent. He watched her smoking her Fatima. She wasn't mad, she wasn't even "disappointed," that word adults always used. She just wanted to teach him something, tell him how it was.

"But. . ." David started.

"No 'buts,' chum," she laughed. "I'll pay your way back this time. You can take the train and eat your meals in the dining car. Enjoy it. It's my gift. But this is positively the last time. You'll be sixteen next summer. Get a job in the East. You can stay with Aunt Louise and Uncle Swen out in Lambertville. They have room. She can find you a job, a real job."

"Do you know them?" David asked.

"Of course, I do. I've known Louise forever. She is your dad's sister, after all, and she loves the California coast. So does Swen. They were out here this spring, painting up north of San Francisco and then down in Big Sur. They stopped here for the night. She's also a great letter writer, your Aunt Louise, and she writes me about you and Elizabeth and the family. I heard about last Christmas."

"That was something,"

"I'll save her letters. You'll enjoy them someday. Get to know her. Now that she's in the East, you can count on her to help you arrange things."

"What about you?"

"I'm here, chum. You know that. But family is important."

It was Aunt Louise who met the train in New York and took him to lunch, this time without Aunt Estelle.

"Your grandmother died this summer," she said during dessert.

"I know," said David. "You wrote me about it."

"Ah, but you didn't write me back," she said with a smile. "How would I know that you received my letter?"

David blushed.

"Manners are important," she said, lifting her dessert fork carefully to her mouth. "She died of cancer, like your mother, but it was the drinking that led to the cancer, I'm sure. That's why you saw so little of her. Your grandfather simply gave up on her, paid to have her hospitalized, and went off to France to live. He couldn't stand it. He came back for the funeral, and then left again a few weeks later. He's very proud of you, you know. We all are."

"Thank you," said David. "What a switch that was," David thought to himself. From the grandmother's death to the grandfather's pride. He tried to remember them, tried to make pictures of them in his mind, and all he could come up with was the old apartment on Central Park West, near the merry-go-round. He thought of the night he and Elizabeth had come knocking on their door, so many years ago. He thought of Thanksgiving and English marmalade and white linen napkins and good table manners. But he really knew nothing about them, about their lives. What did he know about anybody's life? What did his mother do every day before she died? What did Elizabeth do? Was every day just the same? Taking care of Alex and Maggie and making supper for Phil and doing the laundry and making the beds?

Aunt Louise brought him back. "Speaking of manners," she said, "the gentleman always pays the bill. She reached into her purse, pulled out a twenty-dollar bill, and handed it to David under the table.

"What do I do?" David whispered.

"Ask the waiter for the check. Then hand him the twenty. When he brings the change, leave a tip."

"How much?"

"It depends on the service. But usually ten percent. That's not so hard, is it?"

"No," David said, and he raised his hand to summon the waiter.

They walked up Madison Avenue to 57th Street and turned into the Passedoit Gallery. Aunt Louise greeted the owner by her first name, and then introduced David to her. "You're a lucky young man to have this lady for your aunt," said the owner. "I am Georgette Passedoit, and I represent your uncle's paintings. Go have a look at them."

Aunt Louise took him around. He could recognize Uncle Swen's work right away—the strong colors, the dark, outlined shapes, the straight lines. Still, you could always tell what he was painting. It was, Aunt Louise said, "the recognition element." His work was never totally abstract. There were lots of seascapes, rocks, mountains, waves—new work from his trip to the West Coast in the spring and work from the desert—from Arizona and New Mexico. There were fish, in a net, and underwater scenes. But his favorites were the religious paintings, some of which he had seen in the studio over Christmas. There was Jesus riding into Jerusalem on Palm Sunday, and another one like it of the last supper, the disciples outlined, sitting at the table waiting for some final word, some final truth, and then a huge one of Lazarus rising from the dead, unfolding from his tomb, uncurling almost.

"I really like these," he said to Aunt Louise.

"Well, when you are older and settled down, I'll give you one to hang in your living room. Would you like that?"

"Yes," he said, "I'd like that very much.

When he got up to Elizabeth's he told her all about his lunch with Aunt Louise and about the paintings. Elizabeth seemed to know everything already. That was the interesting thing about grown-ups, David thought. How they managed to know everything before you did. He was excited about learning new things, but they weren't really new, just new to him. Elizabeth had known about his grandmother's death, of course, but she had also been to the gallery.

It was nine o'clock in the evening, and the kids were in bed. He and Elizabeth and the kids had had dinner together. Phil had gone downtown to work on some arrangements. After dinner, David had given Alex and Maggie their baths, while Elizabeth did the dishes. He always loved his first day with the kids after he hadn't seen them for a long time, and Maggie was especially charming. She had learned to walk while he was in California, and she was racing all over the apartment. She kept throwing her yellow rubber duck out of the bathtub and screaming with delight when David threw it back. Kids were funny. When you told them they had to take a bath, they said, "No," but then once you got them in, you couldn't get them out. You had to trick them, make them forget that they'd said "No." You could bribe them with a treat, or promise them something special the next day. At least that worked for Alex. With Maggie, if you were wild enough, she'd do anything. If you swooped down on her like a bird with the towel, and wooshed her away into the air, she laughed and laughed and forgot that she didn't want the bath to be over.

Now, after stories and drinks of water and trips to the bathroom by Alex, they were finally asleep to the sounds of the fans whirring away in the hot back room, and David and Elizabeth were sitting at the dining room table playing gin rummy. She was smoking.

"Your grandmother really loved you," she said. "I wish you had seen more of her. She was determined to come to your graduation from Lowell last year, but when Mommy died, it just took the starch out of her. She just fell apart, and then the cancer got her. That's how it is with cancer. It always strikes when you're down."

"Gin," said David, spreading his cards out on the table.

"You sure got me," said Elizabeth. "I was thinking about Mommy and Grandma instead of the game."

"Yes, you were," said David. But he didn't want to take this subject any further. There was nowhere to go with it, nowhere good that is.

Elizabeth looked tired. She played the game listlessly and then excused herself to go to bed. David sat at the table alone, and thought about Tracy Warren. He remembered their last conversation under their favorite tree, the "baseball tree" they called it. Ray had left, scowling as he stepped into his mother's Cadillac, and most of the kids had gone. Tracy and Butch were waiting for Buck to drive them to the airport. They would fly back to New York.

"You wish I was Ellie, don't you?" she said softly.

"No, I don't."

"She's beautiful, I understand. Sometimes I look at myself in the mirror and shake my head. I feel kind of like a colt, all arms and legs."

It was true. David didn't know what to say. He, like everyone else, had fallen in love with Ellie Dooley. He had stared at her across the room, and thought of what it might be like to kiss her, and it was Ellie he fantasized about, it was Ellie whom he pictured in her nightgown. But Tracy was his friend. Ellie had no interest in him.

"I'm glad we're friends, Tracy," he said. "I really am. I don't know. I feel like I can tell you things I can't tell anyone else."

"I know," she said. "It's nice."

He tried to say something, but it wouldn't come. She reached out and put her hand on his knee. Quickly, before it was too late, he covered it with his own. Their fingers intertwined.

"It makes me so mad, Tracy," he said. "I try not to have feelings. I try to do what everyone wants me to do. I try to please my teachers and Molly Ariel and Buck Dooley and Ray and you and all the kids. I want you for a friend, but I hate the sneaking around. I just wish I could have you for a friend and not have to hide it."

"Well, you don't, not anymore," she said. "You can just come and visit me in Greenwich when we get back."

"I can't. I only have a few days before school starts. There's no time."

"Well, come at Christmas, then. We'll work it out, OK?"

She looked at him, then kissed him lightly, on the lips, like a friend. "I don't know anybody like you," she said. "I need you in my life. You don't understand that, but you will someday. Write me."

David heard a whistle behind him. It was Butch, laughing. David turned red.

Now he sat at the table trying to start a letter. He was not good at writing letters, and it was a strange thing. He loved writing, and he loved words, the sounds and shapes of words. But writing letters was tricky. It was really a question of honesty, of how much to say and not to say, or what was right or not right to say. It was those silly wants and oughts again. He wanted to say "I love you" to Tracy Warren. He'd thought about her all the way home on the train, and he'd written her a post card, which he'd given to the Pullman porter to mail for him. He'd signed it, "Your friend David," but that was too cold, he felt now.

"Tell me you love me, Toots," his mother used to say, and he had held back, afraid to say the words. He never said that word, but he wanted to, to Tracy. There was something about her that was different, something he trusted. She wouldn't hurt him or tell him he was wrong or stupid, but then he thought of her going back to her friends and her school and her life in Greenwich, and he thought maybe she was just being nice when she told him to come see her. Maybe it was just the emotion of the moment, the saying goodbye, the end of camp. Everybody got emotional at the end of summer camp. He crumpled up the paper and threw it in the waste basket. He'd write her from school, later on, closer to Christmas. Then he'd see if she really wanted him to come.

That night he dreamed of Maggie Hope. She was sitting in a coffee shop with her waitress uniform on, the one she had worn at the first hotel, the one on Madison Avenue. She kept stirring her coffee over and over and saying "Tell me you love me, Toots." David kept saying, "I can't, Mom, I can't, Mom," and when he spoke his teeth would come loose in his mouth and he would have to spit them into his hands to keep from swallowing them. He woke in a cold sweat in the dark living room.

The next day David took Alex to Yankee Stadium. It was Alex's first Major League ball game. "He's been talking about it all summer," said Elizabeth that morning. "He's so excited he can hardly stand it."

They had their gloves, the two of them, and they sauntered down Morris Avenue toward 161st Street like Huckleberry Finn and Tom Sawyer going for a stroll down the streets of Hannibal.

"Who's the best, Unca Dave?" Alex asked.

"The Yankees are best," said David.

"No, Unca Dave, I mean the name of the best."

"Oh, you mean the best player."

"Right, the best player."

"Joe DiMaggio, Alex, he's the best."

"Yeah," said Alex, "Joe. Go, Joe."

"Right," said David. "Go, Joe."

DiMaggio had had a difficult year. Elizabeth had sent David clippings from the New York papers. Half the time he couldn't play. First it was one thing, then another. He'd get sick, and when he got well, then the heel would start acting up again, that Achilles heel, which David understood so well. When he was healthy, he was a terror, slashing the ball wickedly at the infielders. He hit the ball so hard that he sometimes spun them around, or the ball would ricochet off their gloves into the outfield. The reporters loved him. But you never knew from day to day whether he would play. David loved his courage, his determination. If he could get out of bed, if he could walk without crutches, he would play. He never took himself out of the lineup. But the new Yankee manager, Casey Stengel, was a funny guy. He was unpredictable, and so you could never tell what might happen.

The Yankees were playing Detroit, and for some reason they had a harder time beating Detroit than any other team. The hated Red Sox they could always beat if they had to. Dimag would rise up to the occasion. But Detroit was a different story. They had George Kell, the best hitter in the league next to Ted Williams, and Vic Wertz, who hit more home runs against the Yankees than any other player.

David and Alex sat in the general admission seats high above home plate in the upper deck. It wasn't hard to get tickets during the week, and there were always seats up there, except if the Red Sox were playing. Then you had to get there really early. David bought a scorecard and a pencil, and he showed Alex how to keep score. In the clean-up spot for the Yankees, Alex wrote JOE in big capital letters, kind of squiggly. They bought hot dogs and Cokes and watched the players finishing their fielding practice. David looked out over the grass, and tears came to his eyes. Why was this? Why did the beauty of the grass move him so, and the sight of the monuments to Ruth and Gehrig out in center field? He turned to Alex. "Go, Yankees," he said, as the Yankees trotted out onto the field. "Go, Yankees!" shouted Alex, as Joe DiMaggio, number 5, emerged slowly from the dugout and ran easily to his position in his long, loping strides. "Go, Joe!" said Alex.

By the seventh inning Alex was tired and so were the Yankees. They were trailing, 4-2, but when the fans sang "Take me out to the ball game," Alex was revived, and so was the team. Yogi Berra, the new catcher, slapped a pitch off his shoe tops for a double, then Joe rifled one to left center for another double, and Doctor Bobby Brown, the third baseman, hit Joe home. Suddenly it was tied, and the fans were screaming. The eighth went by without a score, and the Yankees came to bat in the ninth. They called them the Bronx Bombers in the paper because of their late-inning home runs. "Bronx Bombers," said Alex. "Boom. Boom. Boom."

"That's what we need," said David. "Boom. Boom. Boom."

Jerry Coleman, the second baseman, singled, and Joe Page bunted him to second. Rizzuto grounded to short. Then came Old Reliable, Tommy Henrich, playing first base now, because his old legs couldn't manage the outfield any more. The Detroit pitcher walked him to set up a force, and everyone booed. Alex loved the booing. Then it was Yogi again. "Go, Yogi," said Alex. You could never tell with Yogi. He would swing at anything. The count went to 3 and 1, and the pitcher looked into the on deck circle. There was Joe, quietly kneeling on one knee, studying the pitcher's every move. There was no way the pitcher would walk Yogi and have to pitch to Joe. He threw a fastball chest high on the inside corner, and Yogi lofted it high into the right field stands. As he crossed the plate, everyone stood and cheered, and there were tears in David's eyes once again.

He bought Alex a pennant, and they walked home slowly with the other fans. No one wanted the day to be over.

And then it was time for school, blessed school. He felt like Brer Rabbit in the briar patch. How did the story go? "Oh, please, don't throw me in the briar patch," Brer Rabbit begged Brer Fox, really wanting to be thrown into his favorite place. "Do anything else to me, but DON'T THROW ME IN THE BRIAR PATCH." School was David's briar patch. He loved the ease and regularity of the days, and the blessed privacy of his room. At Wicker he had his own space, a closet in which to hang his clothes and a bureau and a desk and a wonderful, kind roommate who brought to the room a kind of elegance David had not experienced before. A little oriental rug lay between the beds, and art reproductions—prints of Picasso and Monet and Van Gogh—covered the bareness of the sterile walls. Borden Smith lived in Manhattan and bought prints at the Metropolitan or the Museum of Modern Art. He read the *New York Times* in the library, and went to the symphony and the opera with his parents. He was quiet and considerate, he was clean and neat, and always on time.

The fall was beautiful. The leaves turned purple and yellow and red on Mount Algo, and on the soccer field the team played with a new enthusiasm. It was David's joy, every practice, every game, just to be there, starting on the varsity team with Hugh Packard. They played together, Hugh at center forward, the best dribbler on the team, the one who could keep the ball away from anyone, the only one who could make a run all the way down the field by simply, as Wally Hinson said, "faking everyone out of their jocks." You thought he was slow, he was so easy, but he fooled you. David played left inside. He was a feeder for Hugh, and he played defense too, hustling back to help out the halfbacks, breaking up the opposition runs with his fearless tackles.

They had a new coach, a history teacher from England named James Whitfield, and he knew much more about soccer than Jumping John, who was very kind, but no more equipped to coach soccer than he had been the year before. So Wicker had invited Mr. Whitfield as an exchange teacher, someone who could bring their game to a higher level. At first, it was frustrating for the boys. They had to learn a completely new way of kicking, not with their toes but with their insteps. With the toe, Mr. Whitfield said, you had no control. You never knew where the ball would go. But with the instep, you had absolute control. You planted the opposite foot next to the ball, and snapped the kicking leg around like a whip. You could direct the ball perfectly. He did it for them, demonstrating it over and over with perfect patience and facility.

For a while the boys hated it, because they were not very good at it, but in time he made them believers. He taught them to pass the ball up the field, to execute plays and patterns instead of just kicking it down the field and following it. He taught them the science of the game and the importance of control, the value of the team over the individual. He taught them to head the ball "smartly," as he said so crisply in his English accent, "with a quick snap of the neck." He taught them to take the ball off their chests and drop it to their feet, and he taught them to kick with either foot, which delighted David no end, because before he'd been just a leftie. Walking back from practice with Hugh Packard and Wally Hinson, David was tired and dirty, but happier than he had ever been.

Wally roomed next door to David and had decided to play soccer instead of football because, in his inimitable words, he was tired of getting his "fucking butt turned to jello every time I turned around." He wasn't a very good soccer player, because he didn't know anything about the game, but he was tall and he could kick the ball a country mile, and he could entertain the entire team with his antics. When Jumping John insisted that everyone wear protective cups, Wally revolted. "Those goddamn things are worse than getting hit in the balls. If you get hit, at least the pain is over quickly. But, Christ, those cups, they chafe your groin like hell. You get rashes, you're just fucking sore all the time. You can't run with them on. They just rub and rub." David hated the cups too, and after a while they just quit wearing them and Jumping John didn't say anything.

The three of them were also in English class together, along with Ralph Wisdom and a new boy named Antonio Black who, it appeared, was smart as hell. "He's gonna bust your ass, D.J.," said Wally Hinson one day in November. Wait'll the grades come out. He's just a goddamn brain machine. You can see the little wheels going around. He doesn't think about anything except studying." Antonio Black was short, with tight dark, curly hair, and a lift of his eyebrow that gave fair warning he was for real. "He's the kiss of death," said Wally Hinson. "Osculum Mortis."

It was Mickey Saperstein all over again, David thought, Mickey Saperstein, the smart Jewish kid who had been his chief rival at Lowell, but he was not going to be drawn into a personal rivalry this time. He was not, as he had at Lowell, going to be suckered into making Antonio Black into an enemy. They would be friendly rivals, and besides there was Ralph Wisdom, who was probably the best student of them all, and no one considered Ralph Wisdom a rival. Whatever Ralph did, the others respected, and so the three of them now just accepted their roles and waited to see what would happen. What happened is that they made each other better. Ralph did better in history, because he knew more history; Antonio was a math and science whiz; David did best in French and English.

English was his salvation. His teacher was J.K. Richardson, who always signed his comments, JKR. He was a brisk man, a man of precision and great energy. He wore bow ties and button-down blue shirts and corduroy jackets and gray flannel trousers. He was a Princeton man and a great admirer of the *New York Times.* He was the adviser to *The Wicker Sentinel*, the school newspaper, and he would not let the paper go to press with a comma error in it. Nor would he let his students' essays slip by with sloppy mistakes. The weekly essays would come back absolutely bloody with red marks.

"Crucified by JKR" was Wally Hinson's favorite phrase.

David loved the order of it, the clarity of it. Things happened for reasons. If he had few red marks on his essays it was because he understood the reasons behind the rules. Semi-colons separated equals. A semi-colon was like a junior period. It served the same function. Commas separated main clauses and subordinate clauses. Commas separated two main clauses joined by a conjunction. You didn't just put a comma in when you paused. Punctuation told the reader something. You had to be consistent. It all made sense to David, and the reading made sense, too. They were studying Stephen Crane's *The Red Badge of Courage,* and it was full of symbolism. The hero is a young man fighting in the Civil War, and his best friend is named Jim Conklin. Jim Conklin gives his life for his friends, and at the end the reader sees his wound, the terrible wound in his side, like the wound made by the Roman soldier in Christ's side. Jim Conklin's initials are J.C., the same as Jesus Christ.

"What a lot of crap," said Wally Hinson after class. "They just make this stuff up to give teachers something to do. I mean is every goddamn character with the initials J.C. supposed to be some kind of Christ figure?"

"It makes sense," said David. "At least in this case it makes sense. Jim does give his life for his friends. He is crucified in the war. It's not just because of his initials."

"The red sun was pasted in the sky like a wafer," said Ralph Wisdom. "Now that's a line. That's a symbol. The sun looks like the communion wafer. It reinforces the symbolism of Jim Conklin's death."

Antonio Black smiled eerily. "Osculum Mortis," said Wally Hinson. "You guys are something else. You just think up all this stuff so you can get better grades than the rest of us. It's a game. It's just a game."

Maybe it was a game, but as far as David was concerned, it was a grand game, a game he loved, a game he was good at. It was nearing Christmas vacation, and Father Perkins was giving a series of sermons for Advent. The sermons were part of the same game. All the pieces fit together.

"Advent," said Father Perkins, "is the most important season of the church year, except for Easter itself. Advent comes from the Latin. It means 'coming toward,' *ad venire.* It is the time we prepare ourselves for the coming of Christ into the world. It is the end of autumn. The colorful leaves have fallen, the remaining leaves are brown. The sun sets earlier and earlier behind the mountain. The days shorten, and there is a grayness, a sterility in the earth. Nothing is growing. Winter is approaching, death is approaching. The joy we felt in September is replaced with a feeling of weariness. Then God intervenes. Into this darkness, this winter, comes Christ. That which was dying is now alive. Through Christ, we are given the gift of life."

He paused, and there was a silence in St. Matthew's Chapel, a silence strange because it was unexpected. Father Perkins looked up as if to the sky, and then brought his eyes back to the boys, the younger boys in front, the older boys in back ready for the sermon to be over, ready for Sunday breakfast, the sixth formers in the seats along the side, casting quick glances at one another. What did this silence mean?

David was mesmerized. He listened to his heart beat. Then the Headmaster resumed. "It struck me," he said, "at this very moment that we are not here at this school for Christmas, for the celebration of that gift of life. And I want to say something I had not planned to say."

That was the reason for the silence, thought David. He was thinking, thinking of something that he had not written down.

"I want each of you to make me a promise. I want you to bring this place, this school, this chapel into your homes this Christmas. I want you to bring Jesus Christ into Christmas. Not in some silly sentimental way, not through the mania of the stores, the ribbons, the paper, the gifts that no one can use, but in some way that will, perhaps, change you, change your families. For each of us must, in this advent season, prepare for the coming of the Christ, prepare for the opening of the door, the knocking of Jesus on our doors. He will say, 'Come, follow me,' and what will we do? Will we be ready? Will you say, 'Go away, I'm tired. I need my sleep?' Or will you say, 'Enter'? Jesus, the Christ, stands at your door, waiting to be invited in. He is the gift which God has given us, and it remains for us, each of us, to accept that gift and to be, in turn, made new by that acceptance. Let us pray."

Anthony S. Abbott

David bowed his head. He was trembling. He had not changed. He had not been made new. He went forward to receive the body and blood, the wafer and the wine. He thought of Jim Conklin, he thought of his own life and how little he had done, how little he had given. He thought of his mother, who had died two years before, and how little he had done to comfort her in her sickness. He thought of his grandparents whom he had hardly known, and of Elizabeth in the Bronx. He crossed himself, and walked back to his seat, head bowed. "I'm sorry, Maggie Hope," he said, and he knelt to pray and ask for strength. He would make a new beginning.

CHAPTER SEVEN

They were on the train to New York for Christmas vacation, and Wally Hinson was teaching David how to smoke. Most of the fifth and sixth formers smoked, and some of the fourth formers.

"It's like an initiation," said Wally Hinson, who was already sixteen. "An initiation into manhood."

Billy DuPont, who was sitting across the aisle, laughed. "I started when I was fourteen because my older brother smoked, so I wouldn't exactly call it manhood."

It amazed David where all the cigarettes came from. No one was supposed to have any, not even the sixth formers, but when they got on the train at the Wicker station, suddenly everyone lit up. Wally shook a Chesterfield out of his pack, and pointed it toward David. "Hold the cigarette in your left hand, between your first two fingers," he said.

"But I'm left handed."

"Then hold it in your right hand."

"OK," said David, and took the cigarette, tentatively. He smelled it. The tobacco smelled good—earthy and sweet.

Wally handed him a pack of matches. "Strike the match and hold it a little bit away from the tip of the cigarette. You can always

Anthony S. Abbott

tell an asshole that doesn't know how to smoke. He puts the match on the cigarette and burns the hell out of it. Girls are the worst."

Billy Dupont laughed again. "They want to seem so delicate, so smooth, and then they get the match halfway down the cigarette."

"OK," said David. "After I light the match, then what?"

"Then you draw," said Wally and Billy both together.

"Draw?" asked David.

"You know," said Wally. "You breathe in. You draw the smoke into your lungs."

"Into my lungs? You're kidding."

"What did you think happened to the smoke? It has to go somewhere. You don't just hold it in your mouth," said Wally.

"Try it," said Billy, trying not to laugh.

David lit the cigarette easily, then sucked smoke. He held it in his mouth, then let it out casually, as if he had done it all his life.

"Jesus Christ, D.J.," said Wally. "You just held the smoke in your mouth. You gotta breathe in, breathe it all the way into your lungs."

"Will it hurt?"

"Hell, no. Look at me," said Wally.

"And look at me," said Billy.

Each of them took their cigarettes, holding them between their index and middle fingers. Then, as if on cue, they raised the cigarettes to their lips and drew, slowly, taking the smoke all the way into their lungs. Then they blew the smoke out just as slowly.

"That was beautiful," said David.

"OK," said Billy. "Now you do it."

"Yeah, you do it," said Wally Hinson, winking at Billy.

David did it. It was horrible. He didn't know which surprised him more, the burning or the bitterness. His face turned red, he coughed, and ran for the end of the car to the water fountain. He came back, crying.

"It's like being a virgin," said Wally.

"It only hurts the first time," said Billy DuPont.

David was hardly interested.

In New York, they walked from Grand Central to Charley's bar on 43rd and Vanderbilt. It was full of prep school boys coming home for Christmas, suitcases everywhere, coats slung over one another, smoke filling the dark room. Everyone was excited.

"What you need is some lubrication," said Wally.

"I don't know if I can take all this in one day," said David.

"It's simple. You drink beer. You feel loose, it cools your throat. Then the cigarette doesn't burn. They kind of go together."

"Right," said Billy.

"But I don't know if I want to drink beer."

"Look, D.J., I'm just trying to help you. Do you wanta grow up and be one of the guys, or do you want to be a fucking Christer like Pittinger and Frothingham and the rest of those assholes? You're not gonna have any friends if you're so goddamn chicken."

David took the beer. At first it was bitter, like the cigarette, but Wally was right. It did make the cigarette cooler, and if he took little puffs, just a small amount of smoke at a time, he could do it.

At six o'clock they parted, headed their separate ways, Wally to his father's apartment, Billy back to Grand Central to catch the local to Bronxville. David went down the stairs to the subway. He took the shuttle to Times Square and the local to 59th Street, where he changed to the D train which would take him all the way to Elizabeth and Phil's. He breathed into his hands. His breath smelled of beer and cigarettes. He took out a stick of gum and began chewing. He tried to imagine what Elizabeth would say or Aunt Louise or even Aunt Estelle. They wouldn't want him to smoke, or especially to drink. "Look at what liquor did to Mommy," Elizabeth would say. "And to your grandmother," Aunt Louise would say.

Liquor could do terrible things to people, David knew that, but the boys at Charley's had seemed so happy, so free, so relaxed. Everybody did it. You just had to be careful. Anyway, David thought, it didn't matter for now. There would be no drinking or smoking at Elizabeth's or Aunt Louise's. He would just have to figure it out later.

"David, where have you been?" Elizabeth cried as he bumped his way into the apartment, bags in hand.

Smoking and drinking at Charley's bar, he thought to himself. "We just couldn't say goodbye," he said, "so a bunch of us went to Nedick's for an orange drink and a hot dog," he lied easily. He almost wished he had gone to Nedick's for the hot dog.

Alex and Maggie were all over him, Alex jumping up and down, and little Maggie hanging on to his ankle. "I really need you tonight," said Elizabeth. "Phil's out again, and the kids are crazy."

David put down his bags by the familiar couch in the living room, he took off his coat and tie, rolled up his sleeves, and dove in. He was home, and this is what home meant. It meant Alex and Maggie and Elizabeth, and if it wasn't always fun, it wasn't supposed to be fun. It was what you had to do, because it was right, and for the first couple of days, he was good, the way he had been at the end of the summer. They built blocks and knocked them down, and read books, and made strange creatures with Tinker Toys. They played hide and seek, and David and Alex took walks while Maggie was sleeping. He liked being good, and besides he was most at home with Alex and Maggie. It was almost as if he had become Elizabeth, and Alex had become him, and he was somehow giving Alex what she had given him.

But it didn't last. As each day went by, he longed more and more to see a movie, go downtown, do anything to get out of the house. Then he remembered Aunt Estelle. Was she all right, he wondered. He called her.

"Aunt Estelle," he said, "it's David."

"David who?" a strange voice answered.

"David, your nephew, your. . .great-nephew."

"Oh, you want Estelle," the voice said. Then there was a silence and the sound of rustling. "Yes?" a weak voice answered.

"Aunt Estelle?"

"Yes?"

"It's David."

"Oh, David," she answered. "How are you? How nice to hear your voice. I've been ill. This nice young woman has been helping me get dressed. Are you in New York?"

"Yes, I'm at Elizabeth's."

"Oh, up there in the Bronx. Do you need another Christmas tree?"

David laughed. It was wonderful to hear her speak. She was still herself; she remembered the time she had helped him find a tree for Elizabeth. She was weak, but she was still Estelle.

"Can you lunch at the Plaza tomorrow?"

"Oh yes, Aunt Estelle," said David. "I would like that very much."

"Well, then, we shall meet at twelve noon in the Oak Room."

David didn't know why he was so excited. Partly it was getting out of the apartment, partly it was his relief that Aunt Estelle was still herself, and partly it was a silly desire to get dressed up and go somewhere. "Don't let them take you in," his mother had said. "Don't let them fool you with their fancy clothes and their lunches at the Plaza." He remembered that vividly. She had wanted to make him feel guilty, and she had succeeded. He understood what she meant, but still he loved it, the dressing up, the going out. In the bathroom, he talked to her as he tied his red and black striped regimental tie. "I don't know, Maggie Hope. It's not so bad. You may be wrong about this."

He kissed Elizabeth on the cheek, hugged Alex and Maggie, and turned to walk out the door.

"Better not pout, Unca Dave," said Alex.

"Better not cry," said David back.

"I tellin' you why," said Alex.

And together, "Santa Claus is comin' to town."

He closed the door and sighed as he walked down the front steps. It was warm day for December, and the wind did not cut into him as it usually did when he walked up the hill to the Concourse. He was happy. He had no money, and he didn't know what he would do for Christmas presents, but still he was happy. He took the D train to Columbus Circle and walked the few blocks across Central Park South to the Plaza. It was a beautiful walk, past the other storied hotels, where the horses breathed easily as they waited to take tourists for a carriage ride in Central Park.

Aunt Estelle was there, sitting at her favorite table, when he arrived at the Oak Room. The headwaiter took his coat, and pulled out the chair for him.

"Just a moment," he said, and turned to kiss Aunt Estelle's leathery cheek before he sat down. She had shrunk, if that were possible. She seemed to disappear into herself, a very small woman in a black dress whose hands seemed like those of a very old doll. But her eyes were still bright, and her smile brought something like tears to David's eyes.

"My first outing since my illness," she said.

David raised his water glass and touched hers.

"I have something for you," she said, and she reached into her small black pocketbook for an envelope.

"Don't open it now," she said quietly, "but then again don't wait until Christmas."

"Thank you, Aunt Estelle," said David.

"I see that you have different shoes," she said, with the hint of a laugh.

"Oh yes," said David. "We don't wear white bucks in the winter time."

"I see," she said. "I thought your taste had improved, but it was only the season."

They talked easily over lunch, about David's school, about Aunt Louise and Uncle Swen and the art world, about Paris, the city Aunt Estelle had loved the most as a young woman. She seemed sad. Her voice rustled like leaves, and David could feel that she was leaving him, saying good-bye.

"Louise doesn't know," she said in a whisper.

"Doesn't know what?" asked David.

"What it's like."

"What what's like?"

"You know."

The conversation was so cryptic. It was as if they were in a play or a novel, saying dialogue written for them by some mysterious author who didn't want the audience to know what they were talking about.

"Oh," said David, "you mean leaving."

"Yes," she said. "One never wishes to leave. One never wishes something to be the last time. One always hopes to come back, to see this fine oak furniture, to feel the weight of the silver, to taste the soup slowly."

"Yes," said David. "I understand."

"Of course you don't," she answered, almost with a snap. "But you will. Indeed, you will. That is the whole point."

At the end they rose together, and he held out his arm so she could place her hand on it for support. The headwaiter helped them with their coats, and they walked slowly through the Palm Court and down the steps of the main entrance, where David assisted her into a taxi cab.

"Don't say anything," she said, looking up.

"Good-bye, Aunt Estelle," said David, and, "Merry Christmas."

"Ah yes, that," she said. "Now close the door and be off."

He closed the door and watched as the cab pulled away, then went back upstairs to the Palm Court, where he sat to read the letter. The writing was strained, the letters shaky. "Dear David," it read. "Here is something for your Christmas. I wish it could be more, but my funds, like my hours, are coming to an end. Bless you. And be sure to live your life. You are only young once, and there is no romance in old age. Estelle."

In the envelope were two tickets to *South Pacific* and a twenty-dollar bill.

He literally skipped down the carpeted stairs, through the revolving door, and out onto 59th Street. The joy he felt was unlike anything he had known, because it was so unexpected. He thought momentarily of Father Perkins and the idea of grace, how God's gifts to us come unearned. How could Aunt Estelle have known how badly he wanted to see *South Pacific*? It had opened in April, and even during the closing weeks of his third- form year, David had heard the Wicker boys singing "There is Nothing Like A Dame," usually with great gusto in the shower, and in the fall the Glee Club had presented "Some Enchanted Evening" and "Bloody Mary" to great raves as part of their concert. Everyone wanted to see *South*

Pacific, but David hadn't even thought about it seriously because of the money, and now, here, he held in his hand two tickets for December 27, 1949, two days after Christmas. Not one ticket, but two tickets. He stopped for a moment to catch his breath. This always happened to him, when he got really excited. He forgot to breathe.

Slowly he resumed his natural breathing pattern, and he smiled to himself. "Two tickets," he thought. He could invite anybody, and he had twenty dollars for dinner. How could he thank Aunt Estelle? He skipped along almost laughing to himself, not really looking where he was going, not really caring. Then he heard something like a cry, like a moan. He looked up. Approaching him, almost upon him, was a woman, the strangest woman he had ever seen. What he noticed first was the coat, the garish, checkered coat, black and green and white, and the legs below, bare in the cold, white, pasty white, with splotches of black and blue, bruises probably, and her stockings down around her ankles. On her head was a hat of sorts, raked at a wild angle, dark blue with fruit hanging over one eye, grapes and leaves. In her hand she swung a purple purse. She mumbled to herself, moaned, and then as they passed she suddenly swung the purse and hit him squarely on the head. David stopped, astonished.

"What are you so goddamn happy about?" she shouted, and stumbled on, mumbling once more in that half moan.

He looked after her. The blow had not hurt him really, only surprised him. Here he was, with his new theater tickets and his twenty dollars, and she, God only knows, she probably had nothing. She had shouted at him, stung him with the purple purse and moved on with her mottled coat and her pasty legs and her look of dark despair. She had broken his mood entirely.

He thought again of Father Perkins, and now it came to him for the first time what Father Perkins had meant when he asked them to think of Jesus at Christmas. Jesus came to help the poor, the lonely, the sick. Jesus didn't care for theater tickets. He walked down the stairs into the subway, an appropriate place for his new mood. He sat on the D train as it rumbled toward the Bronx, and he thought of Elizabeth and Phil and the children, and how little money they had, how they never went out it seemed. He could see Elizabeth sitting at the kitchen table smoking her cigarette and wondering how she would get through the next day. And then it came to him what he must do. The whole thing was a test. Maybe even Aunt Estelle had planned it that way, to see if he would know what to do, but regardless, he could see his way now only in one direction.

O n Christmas day, they exchanged presents in the apartment, the tree ceremoniously poised between the two windows that faced out on the street, the first thing the children would see when they came running down the hall so anxious to see what Santa had brought they almost forgot to wake David, who slept on the couch by the piano.

"Unca Dave," shouted Alex. "It's Christmas Day."

"Daaa," shouted Maggie, who didn't have many words yet, but always tried to sound like her older brother.

David sat up and rubbed his eyes. "Wow," he said. "Look at all that! Where did that come from?"

"Santa," said Alex knowingly.

"Oh," said David, "and how did he get in here? I don't see any chimney."

Alex looked puzzled for a moment. Then he said, "He no need chimney. He just go poof." He clapped his hands and threw them in the air.

"Poof?" asked David.

"He go poof and he here. Then he go poof again and he gone."

"That's good, Alex. I like that."

David went to wash his face while the kids sat on the rug and stared with wide eyes at the presents.

The morning was mostly theirs, mostly presents for Alex and Maggie from Santa and Mommy and Daddy and Aunt Louise, who liked to send books, and one from Grandpa in Arizona. At eleven Maggie went down for her nap, and Phil and Alex sat down on the rug to build castles with the multi-colored blocks that Santa had brought him. David took the silver envelope with the tickets from its place high up on the tree and handed it to Elizabeth. "Merry Christmas to you and Phil," he said proudly.

"Get me an ashtray from the kitchen, would you sweetheart?" she asked, as she took the envelope from him. "What a beautiful silver envelope."

"I picked it out myself," he said.

By the time he was back with the ashtray, she had opened the envelope and was staring at the tickets. "My God, David," she said, "How did you get these? They're so expensive. You don't have that kind of money."

"But aren't you happy to have them?" the boy said hesitantly. "Don't you and Phil want to go? I can watch Alex and Maggie. I'm old enough now."

She turned and hugged him, tears in her eyes. "Of course we want to go. Of course, you are old enough. I just couldn't believe it. It didn't seem possible."

He hesitated, then blurted out the truth. There was no point in lying. It would only make matters worse, and besides Aunt Estelle might have told her about the tickets. "I got them from Aunt Estelle," he said quietly. "I couldn't use two tickets, so I thought you and Phil would like them. It just seemed like the right thing to do."

Elizabeth started to cry, then stopped. "But, sweetie, these tickets were a Christmas present from Aunt Estelle to you, not to us."

"Yes, but she would want me to. . . " He searched for the words. ". . . to use them in the way that would make me happiest. That's it. And it makes me happiest to give them to you. You and Phil never get to go out, do you?"

"Well, no, we don't."

"Then, that's settled. The tickets are for you."

"OK," she smiled. "That's a deal. Right, Phil?"

Phil nodded his agreement, and rose to take a bright yellow envelope marked "David" from the tree. "Here," he said to David, "now it's our turn to surprise you."

Inside the envelope was a ticket to *Death of a Salesman* for December 27, 1949.

"We bought it for you last summer," said Elizabeth proudly. "Some people say it's the best American play ever written."

He had heard of the play, of course. They had talked about it at school, and B.N. Benson, the fifth-form English teacher, had taken a group of his students over Thanksgiving. One of the students had written an article about it in the student newspaper, and the idea of it had fascinated David. He looked down at the ticket.

"Oh my God," said David, laughing. "It's the same night. The exact same night. What a coincidence. We'll just have to get a baby sitter and all go out together."

Alex laughed and knocked over the castle. David switched places with Phil, and began to build it up again, with Alex's help. Phil and Elizabeth sat together on the couch.

She lit her cigarette, and blew smoke rings toward the ceiling.

"What gave you the idea?" Elizabeth asked.

"What idea?"

"You know, to give us the tickets."

"Father Perkins," he said.

"Who?"

"You know, the Headmaster at Wicker. Father Perkins. He told us to think about Jesus at Christmas."

"Jesus?"

"Yes. He wanted us to really think about what Christmas was, what Jesus being born really meant. You know, Jesus instead of Santa Claus."

"Why would Jesus want you to give us the tickets?"

David couldn't answer. Instead he just turned away and began to play with Alex. They piled blocks on blocks, red ones and blue ones, square ones, long ones, and rectangular ones with openings on one side where you could peep through. David thought about Jesus.

"I should have gone to church last night, to the midnight service," he said. "I forgot about it."

"I suppose Jesus would have wanted that, too," Elizabeth said. Phil laughed.

David felt uncomfortable with all this Jesus talk. It was the same way at school. If you brought Jesus into the conversation, people either got silly and started making bad jokes or they got quiet.

"Could I make a phone call?" David asked, getting up from the floor. "A long distance phone call?"

"To where, sweetie?" Elizabeth responded.

"To Greenwich, Connecticut," he said. "It's not far."

"Who do you know in Greenwich?"

"Just a friend I wanted to wish Merry Christmas."

"Why don't you write him a letter?"

"It's not a him, Elizabeth," said David, reddening.

"Well," said Elizabeth, tapping out her cigarette in the ashtray. "I guess you better call."

He picked his wallet up from the little table next to the couch, and walked down the hall to phone. He needed to talk to Tracy Warren. It had come to him at that moment of silence, that awkward Jesus moment—he needed a friend, and no one else would understand his need except Tracy. He had kept her number in his wallet all fall and he had meant to call her, but calling from school was impossible, and he couldn't call from Elizabeth's without asking. For David, asking was hard. Asking meant having to answer questions, and one answer always led to another question.

"Hello."

"Tracy?"

"Who is this?"

"Tracy, this is David, David Lear from last summer at the ranch. Do you remember me?"

"David Lear, my God, you sound like a ghost. Where have you been? Why haven't you called before? I thought you didn't care. I thought you'd forgotten about me."

"No," he said. "No, not at all."

There was a silence.

"I want to see you," he said. "I need to see you."

"Well, just come on up here. My parents would love to meet you. They've heard all about you, and Butch would just go wild if you came. Come for New Year's."

"How?"

"Just pack your bag and get on the train. We'll meet you at the station. Just let me know what train you're coming on."

"My sister will say I have to have an invitation from an adult."

"I'll get my mother."

He could hear her drop the phone and call her mother. He called Elizabeth and gave her the phone. "Mrs. Warren wants to talk to you," he said, and walked back to the living room. He didn't want to listen to their conversation.

CHAPTER EIGHT

Tracy Warren looked wonderful. This was not a subjective judgment. It was, quite simply, David thought, a fact. Her hair was longer and it fell to her shoulders, her skin was paler, and her lips seemed softer and redder. At the train she waved and waved when she saw him, she ran up to him and hugged him as if he were her oldest friend. He stood momentarily, the bag with Maggie Hope's initials in one hand and a gift for her parents in the other, unable to respond. He just smiled and said, "This is for your parents," and she took the box from his hand and put her arm through his, and together they walked to the car.

Her parents were glad to see him. Mr. Warren, tall, athletic, his skin still a little tan from the summer, in dark grey slacks, ski jacket and toboggan, had opened the car door and stepped out toward David. He took David's hand and shook it briskly. "So glad you could come, son," he said. "Get in the back seat there with your buddy. I'll put your bag in the trunk." And so he had opened the door and slipped in beside Butch who was smiling and laughing. They shook hands, awkwardly half-hugged, and talked about friends from camp. Somehow everything seemed so easy—the drive to the house from the station, Mrs. Warren standing at the front door to greet them, and David and Butch going up to the younger boy's room, where David would sleep, kind of like an older brother returning home from school.

And then suppertime, the family seated around the table, talking easily back and forth, telling tales about their friendship with Buck Dooley, how Buck and Ed Warren had been friends at Berkeley and how they'd both worked on ranches in Wyoming during the summer, how Ed had met Lisa at Eaton's Ranch and fallen in love, and how she'd lured him back East to get married and settle down, and how Buck had decided to buy a ranch of his own and turn it into a boys' camp. The children had maintained their friendships from the time they were babies.

They talked and ate, and Mr. and Mrs. Warren took turns serving the food. They all said "please" and "thank you' and David was allowed to drink a small glass of wine. It seemed quite magical, as if he was suddenly and inexplicably in a family, a family that seemed to want him. Why hadn't he called Tracy before? Why had he waited so long? He really didn't know, except it seemed in his nature to avoid things that were complicated, things that might come out badly. He had no confidence when it came to girls, because he had no experience.

After dinner Tracy took him to the playroom in the basement. In the middle of the room was a Ping-Pong table, and at the far end a blue couch and a side table with a radio on it. In the corner on the other side of the couch, a Monopoly game rested on a card table surrounded by four chairs. Banners on the walls announced the names of all the Ivy League Schools. They played ping pong first, round robin style, David against Butch, Butch against Tracy, then David against Tracy. She was good, good enough to beat David if he didn't play well, but he found himself not really caring if he won. It was as if her laughter, her smile, the bounce in her hair when she hit the ball were more important, more interesting than the game. He knew he wouldn't get mad if he lost, the way he had in the summer against Ray.

Then they played Monopoly until Mrs. Warren came down to send Butch off to bed.

"Good night, you two," said Mrs. Warren. "Don't forget to turn off the light when you come up."

"Good night, you two," said Butch with a wink and an echo of his mother's words.

"Good night, Butch." Tracy's and David's voices echoed together. For a moment there was silence, except for the low sound of music coming from the radio. Tracy got up from the table where they had spread out the Monopoly game and pushed her chair back against the rear wall. Then she walked over to the couch. David was still in his chair, counting his money.

"Shall I put the game away?" he asked.

"No, leave it up," she said. "We'll finish it in the morning. Butch'll be mad if we put it away. He was winning."

She got up and switched off the overhead light, then turned up the music on the radio, and sat back down on the couch. "Come on over here," she said softly. "I just want to sit and close my eyes. Come sit with me." She patted the space next to her with her left hand. Glenn Miller's "In the Mood" was playing.

David felt like he was in a movie. He got up and walked toward her, then slowly lowered himself onto the couch. He didn't know where to put his hands. She sat with her head back, her eyes closed, her long legs stretched out on the coffee table, ankles and feet bare.

She reached out and took David's hand. "Relax," she said. "You need to learn how to relax. Don't worry. Just close your eyes and feel the music." Her fingers gently squeezed his, then opened. She ran her fingers down his arm from his shoulders to his wrist and took his hand again.

"I thought you'd never call," she said. "I waited and waited and then just gave up."

"I'm sorry," he said.

"But why didn't you write or call? Didn't you care?"

"Of course I cared."

"It doesn't make any sense, David."

"No," he said, "it doesn't make any sense."

"Is it because of your family?"

"Maybe. I don't know."

"But I do." She sat up and turned toward him, her eyes fixed on his. "You're closed up, David. You're afraid of emotion. It makes you vulnerable. You're a little grown-up. You're careful. That's fine. That's good, but you don't have to be that way with me. Don't you see? We can be what we want to be. We don't have to be careful all the time. It's all right."

She took his hands in hers and leaned toward him. Then she moved her hands upward to his face, and placed a hand on each side of his face. Then she drew his face toward hers and kissed him softly. For a long time, neither one of them moved. Then she could feel with her hands the tears coming from David's eyes. He had not known except in dreams that anything like this was possible, and so he did not move for fear that he might spoil it.

She moved first, smiling at him, then kissing his cheeks and moving her hands back to his.

"I know," she said. "I know what we'll do. I'll be right back." Then she was up the stairs and gone. In a minute she returned, scampering down the stairs with great excitement. "Come on," she said. "Sit down on the floor opposite me."

She held a candle in one hand, which she set between them. Then she struck a match and lit the candle. With her other hand, she held a needle in the flame.

"Give me your thumb," she said, and David held out his thumb.

"Blood brother and sister," she said. "We will prick our thumbs and share blood and swear to be true to each other, to be honest and open and true, OK?"

David nodded. She took the needle and held it in the flame of the candle, then pricked his thumb. He could see the small bubble of blood rise from the tiny hole. "Now, you do me," she said, and he took the needle, heated it once more in the flame, and moved the needle toward her outstretched thumb. But something held him back. He looked up at her face outlined in the flame of the candle. She was smiling. She was waiting.

"Come on," she whispered. "Do it."

He hesitated, then took the thumb in his right hand, and pricked her hard. She didn't wince, didn't cry out, only looked down at the blood and smiled. Something scared him. She took his thumb and pressed it against hers.

"Blood brother and sister," she whispered.

"Blood brother and sister," he echoed back, mesmerized.

They put their arms around one another and held each other close for a long time. Then David pulled back and looked into her eyes.

"Well," he said softly, "now what do we do?"

She laughed. "We tell each other everything. We're blood brother and sister. We have no secrets."

"I've dreamed of this," he said.

"I know."

"How do you know?"

"Because I have, too. Because I was always the ugly ducking, the long-legged goose, the one who was nice, but you know. . .like Ellie was the beautiful one and I was the friend. You wanted her, didn't you?"

"I guess I did, at first."

"And when did it change?"

"The day we sat by the tree after the baseball game and talked."

"I know. Me too."

"You too, what?"

"I knew you were special, not like other boys. I knew I wanted you as a friend."

"Not as a boy friend, just a friend."

"Oh David, don't go spoiling it. Just let it be." Her face darkened, and the small scar under her eye shone white in the candlelight. She got up and walked away.

"What is it?" David asked.

"Nothing," she said. Then she came back toward him and sat down. She was different somehow. David didn't know what to make of her.

"This isn't going to work," she said coldly.

"What do you mean? What are you talking about?"

"David, I'm not what you think."

"I don't care what you are."

"I'm bad, David. You don't want to get involved with me."

"You're not bad. That's not true. I don't believe it."

"Come on," she said. She blew out the candle, and led him up the dark stairs to the kitchen and then to the second floor. She turned into her room. "We'll talk tomorrow," she said, and closed the door.

For a long time he lay in bed awake. What did she mean by "I'm bad"? How was she bad? What had she done? Why wasn't this going to work? "Maggie Hope," he whispered to himself, "I'm in way over my head. What do I do now?" He waited, but all he heard was the scratching of a tree branch against the window.

When David woke up, the sun was shining and it was ten o'clock. He dressed quickly and walked down the carpeted stairs to the front hall.

"Anybody home?" he called.

"In here, brother of mine," a voice called from the kitchen. David followed the sound of it down the hall to the back of the house, where he could see Butch outside shooting baskets. He could hear the thump thump thump of the ball and swish as it fell through the basket. He could see Butch, in his Princeton sweatshirt, dribble and shoot and then run toward the basket for the rebound. Tracy sat at the kitchen table drinking orange juice.

"Hi," she said to him. She smiled. It was the most beautiful smile David had ever seen. All the darkness of the night before had disappeared.

"Hi," he said, and smiled back. "Where are your parents?"

"I don't know. Dad's gone to work. Mom's at the grocery store or the beauty parlor or both. They're going out tonight. We're in charge of Butch. We get to be Mom and Dad."

"Just you and me and Butch? They'd let you be alone with me?"

"Sure, they love you. They trust you. Butch talks about you all the time – and the Dooleys have told them about you. They wouldn't let me stay alone with just any boy." She laughed again and raised her eyebrow. "You are trustworthy, aren't you?"

David blushed. "If I have to be," he said with a sudden boldness.

"Well, you better be, brother of mine," she said.

He bent over and kissed her on the lips. He could taste orange juice. Then he sat down in the chair next to hers and sighed.

"Big sigh," she said.

"Tracy," he said suddenly. "I'm confused about last night, about what you said. Everything was great, and then suddenly it got. . .I don't know. . .dark. You were so strange."

"That's a lot of words, mister."

"I feel brave right now. It won't last."

"Just forget about it, David. It didn't mean anything. Let it go. I have these moods. It's fine now. Everything is fine."

So they ate breakfast, cereal and toast with marmalade. He'd forgotten about marmalade. They never had it at school, and Elizabeth and Phil didn't like it. He used to have marmalade at his grandparents', he remembered, marmalade from England, not the sweet kind they made in America, but the real kind. Tracy's was real too—Scottish, bitter but perfect.

After breakfast he went outside and played basketball with Butch. They played "horse" for a while, and one-on-one, and then Tracy came out with her sweatshirt on and a red wool cap down over her ears. "It's going to snow tonight," she said. "I just heard it on the radio. Snow for the new year. A fresh beginning. I like that."

David loved listening to her. He couldn't figure out where her wisdom came from, her seeming to know things he didn't. He tossed her the ball, and she dribbled twice, then shot easily. The ball swished. Butch rebounded and passed it back to her. Swish again. David began to understand what she'd said the night before. She'd been a tomboy, she'd played with Butch, with other boys growing up, she was tall and athletic. She'd never thought of herself as beautiful.

"You're beautiful," he whispered to her as she drove by him toward the basket.

She missed the shot.

Mrs. Warren called them in for sandwiches and hot cocoa, and they sat around the table, cheeks red, flushed with the cold, chattering about nothing. They played ping-pong, and finished the Monopoly game, and listened to jazz on the record player. At five Ed Warren came home from work. "It's going to snow tonight," he said. "The roads will be slippery. I'm glad you three aren't going anywhere."

David looked at Tracy and knew what she was thinking. They ate dinner and then at eight o'clock the Warrens left for their party. "There's champagne in the ice box for you," said Mrs. Warren, "but don't let Butch have more than one glass. The number's next to the phone." She kissed Butch and Tracy, and gave David's hand a shake. "Happy New Year, kids, it's a new decade, a half century."

At midnight they huddled by the radio and listened to the crowd roar as the ball fell in Times Square. They sang Auld Lang Syne with their arms around each other. Then they drank their champagne, and sent Butch to bed, and because there was still some left in the bottle, Tracy and David each had another glass. David felt a little dizzy. He liked the champagne. It wasn't like the beer he had drunk at Charley's with Wally Hinson. The beer was bitter, but the champagne had a sweet aftertaste and went down easily. David took Tracy's hand, and for a while they just sat. Then David started laughing.

"It's so funny," he said. "I really like this feeling. I never understood, you know, about my mother drinking. It never made any sense. But now it does. Drinking makes you feel good, it makes you forget. All my teachers would say to me, 'David, you work too hard,' or 'David, you've got to learn how to relax,' and I didn't really understand what they meant. But now I do."

"I know," said Tracy, and then she turned to him, and kissed him, harder this time than she had before, and David could feel the passion rise in him, he could feel himself hardening, growing. They held each other close, and he pressed up against her. He knew she could feel him. Tracy closed her eyes and lay back on the couch, pulling David down on top of her. He moved against her, and they

Anthony S. Abbott

rocked together in a silent rhythm, touching only through their clothes. There was no unbuttoning, no groping, just the rhythm of their movement and David's sudden cry when it was over. Tracy opened her eyes and smiled at him. "Don't move," she said. "Just stay here next to me."

They lay on the couch side by side, and then Tracy said, "Oh my God, look, it's snowing," and they sat up and looked out the French doors to the outside, and sure enough it was snowing. "Let's go out," she said, and they put on their shoes and coats and hats, and went out into the yard and looked up into the sky, and stuck out their tongues and tasted the falling snow. "Happy New Year, David," Tracy said, and lay down in the falling snow, moving her arms up and down until she made a snow angel.

"You make one, too," she said, and David did the same.

They stood up and looked down at the companion figures. "It's so funny," Tracy said.

"What's funny?"

"Two angels," she laughed. "Well, one of them sure isn't."

Then they went back in and talked.

"Your parents trusted me," David said.

"It's OK," said Tracy. "We didn't do anything bad. It was beautiful. We just have to know where to stop and what we can't do. Do you understand?"

"Yes," he said, "but it's scary. It's like your body just takes over and you don't think any more."

"I do," she said. "Don't worry. I'll know what's OK and what isn't. We're brother and sister, we can trust each other."

"But brothers and sisters don't do what we just did."

"Of course not. We're a special kind of brother and sister. We're friends. We're honest."

"Have you ever done that before?" asked David.

"No," said Tracy quickly.

"Really?"

"OK, brother of mine, yes, the answer is yes, but this is private, just between you and me."

"We don't talk about it to anyone else."

"No."

"At school everyone talks about sex and what they did and didn't do."

"At my school they did more than talk."

"What do you mean?"

"My parents made me change schools. I was at Greenwich High. It was wild there."

"So they sent you to Country Day. It's safer."

"Yes."

"And they like you being with me, because I'm nice. I'm a big brother."

"Yes."

"And it doesn't matter what we do, as long as it's private."

"Yes."

There was a long silence. "Now," she said, "do you understand what happened last night?"

"Yes," he said, because he wanted to, but he really didn't.

They touched their thumbs and kissed again, and then they went upstairs, each to a different room, and went to sleep, because they did not want be up when Tracy's parents came home.

CHAPTER NINE

A t Schrafft's Restaurant he sat across from Aunt Louise. She looked pale and uncomfortable. Aunt Estelle had not come with her, and David knew immediately that something was wrong, very wrong.

"Aunt Estelle isn't well," she said. "I have been looking for a place for her."

"What kind of place?"

"A nursing home. That's the truth of it. Of course, we can't call it that. Aunt Estelle is a very independent woman. She's lived in New York most of her adult life. But she really can't take care of herself anymore. She loves you, David. She loves taking you to the Plaza for luncheon. I think she may have had a little stroke. Not enough that you can see it. But you can feel it when you talk to her. She forgets things."

"I'm sorry," David said. He couldn't imagine Aunt Estelle in a nursing home.

"I think I have found the right place," Aunt Louise continued, "in a very nice home near Philadelphia, about a forty-minute drive from Lambertville. I told her about it this morning, and she looked at me with that terrible stare she gets when she is angry. She will not hear of it, she says, but it simply must be done."

Aunt Louise was eminently practical and fair, and she would not do this unless it needed to be done. David understood that. But still, for Aunt Estelle, it was the end, or at least the beginning of the end. She had lived in New York most of her life, she had always been independent, she had always cared for herself. David could see her standing on Park Avenue raising her umbrella in the rain to stop the taxicabs as she was crossing. The fierce little lady in black would just be another old woman in a nursing home. It was terrible, but then what other choice was there?

"Her room is a shambles," said Aunt Louise. "She can't dress. She can't fix her hair, she can't be trusted out of the building. They're worried she might go out and not find her way back. So I shall move her down to Pennsylvania as soon as a space becomes available. When you get back from school in the spring, perhaps we can go down there and take her out to lunch. Perhaps she will be better. Well, enough of that. It's a sad business. What about you?"

David told her about Christmas and about the tickets.

"Yes," said Aunt Louise, "I knew about that. Have you written to Aunt Estelle to thank her?"

"No, I haven't."

"Well you must do that right away. It is very important, David, to remember to write. Just saying "thank you" is not enough. For Aunt Estelle especially. She will have few real pleasures, and hearing from you is important. You can write her in care of me, and I will take the letter to her. I will read it to her if she cannot read."

"Yes, Aunt Louise."

"I know you think all of this is silly, but manners are important. They show people that we care. Letter writing is a lost art."

"Do you think she'll be angry I gave the tickets to Elizabeth and Phil? Was it wrong to do that?" David asked.

"Not at all, but you must explain why you did it in the letter."

"Will she understand it?"

"It doesn't matter." She smiled at him. "It doesn't matter, does it? Do you see?"

He didn't see.

"Now," said Aunt Louise, "we need to talk about next summer. You'll be sixteen. You need to have a job, and you can't stay in New York all summer. There simply isn't room, and it isn't practical. So, you will come and spend the summer with Swen and me, and I will find you a job. How does that sound?"

He didn't know how that sounded.

"You can have the little room next to the kitchen all to yourself and your own bathroom downstairs. Much more privacy than in the Bronx."

"That would be wonderful, Aunt Louise," he said, but without enthusiasm.

Then they ate their lunch and talked about art for a while, and Aunt Louise told David more about her trip to Europe with Aunt Estelle in the 1920's, how she was too young to go to France alone and how her beloved Aunt Estelle volunteered to be her chaperone.

"And did she ever have any boyfriends?" David asked.

"Boyfriends? I don't think so. I certainly don't remember any."

"That was too bad," David said.

"Perhaps," said Aunt Louise, "but look at your parents. Look at all these people who get married and divorced and have a terrible time. Maybe she was better off away from all that. I just had a letter from your father from Phoenix. They are going to move back to California. He's given up the hotel supply business, and they will move to Carmel. Diane wants to open a gift shop now that the children are in school, and Carmel is the perfect place. I don't know what Allan will do. He's never quite found a place for himself. He's very intelligent, your father. He was always brighter than me, but he never applied himself."

After lunch, David walked Aunt Louise back to the hotel. "You run along now," she said, "and send my love to Elizabeth and the children."

In Grand Central Station, David picked up his suitcase and bought a pack of cigarettes. It had come to him suddenly on the way back from Greenwich that he wanted to smoke. School would be starting soon, and Wally Hinson and Billy DuPont would offer him a cigarette. And besides, he just felt like smoking. So he bought a pack of Pall Malls and sat in a coffee shop on the lower level, smoking and drinking coffee, just like Elizabeth. He wasn't ready to be in the Bronx just yet.

And then he thought of Tracy Warren, and his heart stirred. He had not said "love" to her at the station, but he had wanted to. He reached into his bag, and pulled out a small notebook, which Aunt Louise had given him for Christmas. "For your poetry," she had said on the card. He had not thanked her for it yet, but neither had he used it. He would write her when he got back to school. He would write her and Aunt Estelle and Mrs. Warren. Of course, he would write Molly Ariel and thank her for the Christmas check which came without fail in her card.

Now he sat and wrote in the notebook. "Willy Loman" were the first words that came to him. He and Tracy had talked about Willy and Linda and Biff again on the last night after she had finished the play. They had argued, not really argued, but discussed who was the most important character. She thought it was Biff. She liked Biff because he was honest, because he had the courage to go out West and leave all the bullshit behind. She had actually said the word. "Are you shocked, David?" she smiled. "Don't be. Girls think those things, too, you know. We're not little angels. Don't idealize us."

He started putting down lines, one after the other.
Willy Loman
little man, poor little man,
you think you're so big
you lie to save the image of yourself
you give stockings to the woman buyer
in return for sex while your wife
darns the old ones at home.
Willy Loman, so sad, you try
to pretend you're full of money
but even in Hartford they don't like you.
Don't like you, Willy, because you're so full
of hot air. Why can't you tell the truth
for once. Tell Biff you love him.
There was that love thing again. Willy can't say love to his son Biff.

Anthony S. Abbott

David thought about school, and he was excited about going back. He would write an essay about Willy Loman if he got the chance. He would finish the poem and copy it and send it to Tracy Warren. He stood up, a little dizzy from the cigarettes, and put the pack in his suitcase, under his socks. Elizabeth wouldn't look in there. His M.H. bag was private. Surely the cigarettes would be safe there.

On the train, he sat with Wally Hinson and Billy DuPont and they smoked all the way to Wicker. When the train neared the station, the sixth form prefects came through the train, collecting contraband in their baskets. David knew what the sixth formers did. They collected the cigarettes and took them up to the Headmaster's Study where they smoked them after the rest of the school had gone to sleep. He dropped the red package of Pall Malls into the basket as it went by, but Wally Hinson didn't drop his. It was a risk, a big risk. Things were better than they had been the year before, but there were still stinks, and if your room was searched and they found contraband, it was at least five hours, or even worse. If you were caught smoking, you could lose vacation days, or even be suspended.

In the room Borden Smith was busy unpacking. On his bed were cameras and camera cases for film and lenses. He was going to do photography for the yearbook and the newspaper, and his parents had given him new equipment for Christmas. He would get a key to the darkroom on the third floor of the auditorium building, and he would be able to develop his pictures during free time.

"You need a hobby," he said to David.

"I need money," David answered. He hadn't intended to say that, but it was true. Hobbies cost money. He liked to go to the movies, or the theater—that could be a hobby—but he never had the money.

"I know how you can make money," said Borden.

"How?"

"You can learn to type." On his desk was a Smith Corona typewriter. He pointed to it. "How many people in the class know how to type? Practically nobody. Typed papers look good. We can charge ten cents a page. A dollar for a ten-page paper. We could go into business, you and I, and while I'm out there taking pictures, you can type papers."

And so he began teaching himself to type on Borden's typewriter. You put your left hand on "asdf" and your right hand on "jkl" and semi-colon. Each finger had a row of letters it was responsible for. The little finger on the left hand was the hardest. David could never quite get his finger on the "q" or the "z." The numbers he simply had to look at. Borden said it was important to look at the text you were copying, not at the typewriter. Your fingers would remember where to go if you practiced long enough.

And so he began, day after day, night after night, hammering away at the typewriter whenever Borden wasn't using it. He liked it. He had never really liked his own handwriting, and now he could not only type papers for others, but type his own papers. He also liked the idea of typing poems. Somehow they looked more like real poems on the page. He could scribble his first drafts in the notebook, and then revise them on the typewriter. He'd turn them in to Mr. Richardson, who might give him credit for them or might not. But it didn't matter. David just liked writing them. That was good, he thought, not to care about credit, not to feel like getting the best grades was the most important thing. He knew it was a competition between Ralph Wisdom, Antonio Black, and himself— there was no one else close—but winning was less important than the game itself. He remembered *The Red Badge of Courage*. He had learned to like the game.

First he turned in the Willy Loman poem. Mr. Richardson read it in class and asked if anyone else had seen the play. It had won the Pulitzer Prize, he told them, and it was the best American play ever written, except maybe for *Streetcar Named Desire* by Tennessee Williams. David remembered *The Glass Menagerie*, but he didn't know about the other play. There was a new actor, Mr. Richardson said, named Marlon Brando, who was wonderful as the Polish factory worker, Stanley Kowalski. A Polish boy in the class named Henry Kosmalski laughed. "A Polish guy as a hero in a play? That's something new," he said.

"Miracles happen every day, Kosmo," said Wally Hinson. Mr. Richardson waited for the laughter to subside. He didn't seem to mind. He didn't need to say anything to Wally, David thought, because he could restore order whenever he wanted. A little laughter was a good break.

In February David wrote a poem about the woman in the checkered coat for Mr. Richardson. The teacher turned it back with the suggestion that David use rhyme. "Try rhyme and meter for a change, David. You don't want all your poems to sound like Carl Sandburg." For a while, the comment stumped him. He didn't use rhyme because he wasn't good at it. All the rhyming poems students wrote sounded kind of sappy or melodramatic, David thought, so he stayed away from it. Then he realized—this was a challenge. Try it, Mr. Richardson was saying. It was hard. Many, many crumpled sheets of paper filled up the wastebasket in David's room. He borrowed Borden's Thesaurus and looked up synonyms. Slowly it began to appear, and he turned it in, finally, just before the end of the winter marking period.

The Boy and the Purple Purse

> He marches down the sunlit winter street
> He's on his way to Porter's "Kiss Me Kate"
> He puffs his smoke, he smiles a smile so sweet
> He laughs and flicks his ashes in the grate
>
> Then looks up just in time to see
> A woman with a dangling purple purse
> One eye is blind, she mumbles to her knee
> She's walking toward him like a funeral hearse
>
> Legs marbled, pasty white start out
> Below a garish checkered coat
> She stares Cassandra like, then shouts
> "What are you so goddamn happy about?"

Then whomps him with the swinging purple purse
And mumbles on still looking at her thighs.
He pauses, stunned. He had not known such creatures
Walked beyond his shining bright blue eyes.

It was still not right, he knew. Some of the rhymes were kind of weak, but he was excited about parts of it. He'd changed it from "South Pacific" to "Kiss Me Kate" for the rhyme; it didn't make any difference what the show was, and he changed his eyes from brown to blue because blue was a better symbol for innocence, like the sky. "Cassandra" he had remembered from *The Iliad*, and he knew it was good to have a Classical allusion. He was proud of the poem, because it was true, because he had been scared by the woman. He hadn't really known there were people like that. It was cold, and she was sick, and he was full of the joy of getting theater tickets, and he had no thought for such people. That's what Father Perkins meant by letting Jesus into Christmas. He meant getting involved with the needy, the poor, and here he was thinking only about himself. The woman was a call—what was it? She was a sign. That was it, she was a sign, and he hadn't really noticed it until he wrote the poem. Now he needed to do something about it.

Of course, he didn't. School went on, the daily round of tests and papers and hockey practice, and the snow turning to rain, and the beginnings, the hints of spring again. The Sunday before spring vacation was warm, and David and Wally Hinson and Billy DuPont went for a walk in the woods after lunch. That was when Wally pulled out the cigarettes. David could feel his heartbeat rise. "Don't, Wally," he said. "It's not safe. We'll get caught."

"Come on, D.J.," said Wally, "you want one as much as I do. Don't be such a fucking chicken." He laughed when he said it. That was the thing about Wally that David loved. Even when he was mad at the system, he was mad in a crazy, funny, easy-going way. He just did what he wanted and laughed at the rules. So the three of them smoked a cigarette somewhere in the woods halfway up Mt. Algo under the protection of an outcropping of rocks. He loved it. He loved blowing the warm smoke out into the cold air, watching the

Anthony S. Abbott

wind carry it, watching the grey ash turn red as he drew the smoke in. There was something exciting about this stolen moment. No one talked. They just each smoked a cigarette, put the pack away, and walked back down the mountain. No one saw them. At least that was what David thought until he got called into the Headmaster's office on Monday morning.

He had never been in the Headmaster's office, but he had walked by and looked in on his way to the mail room in the basement. It was simple, bare, unpretentious, nothing like the office of Mr. Armbrister at Lowell. The walls were cement block, painted white, a few books rested unevenly on three shelves, a desk cluttered with papers sat in the middle of the room, and there were a couple of chairs. "Simplicity of life," David thought. He was not scared, the way he had been at Lowell, but he was angry at himself.

"Sit down, lad," Father Perkins said, cigarette in hand.

David sat.

"So you like these, do you?"

"Yes, sir," David said.

"And you were smoking on the mountain yesterday afternoon."

"Yes, sir."

"That's too bad," the Headmaster said.

"Yes, sir."

There was a long silence and a look from Father Perkins which hurt David more than any blow the Headmaster might have given him, a look he would remember long afterwards.

"Hinson I would have expected it of, but not you. You know, we can't have that—we can't have people like you breaking the rules. It sends the wrong message. It tells others that you don't care, and I don't believe that's true."

"No, sir. It's not true. I do care."

"You're not busy enough. You need more to do. You have the second best academic average in the school, but you have no extra-curriculars. Have you ever read George Bernard Shaw?"

"No, sir."

"You should. He's our greatest living playwright. Read *Saint Joan* or even better, read *Major Barbara.* You'll like those. It was Shaw who said that it was useless to try and be happy. He was only happy when he was so busy doing what he called the work of the Life Force that he didn't have time to worry about whether he was happy or not. We Christians call the Life Force God. We call it doing the will of God. 'In His will is our Peace.' I think you are one of those people who will never be happy unless you're really engaged. You're not happy now—so you let Hinson or DuPont tempt you. You like to write, don't you?"

"Yes, sir."

"Then, go write for the Wicker *Sentinel.* That will keep you busy on Sunday afternoons. Change your sport. Find one that engages you like soccer. You don't really like hockey, do you?"

"No, sir."

"Then why not try wrestling? You look like a wrestler. Get involved in theater. You were in plays at Lowell. Why not try out for plays here? Get involved. Find out where your passion is."

"Yes, sir."

"For now, I'm giving you indefinite hours, including three vacation days. You can stay here and work over the weekend, and then resume when vacation has ended."

"Yes, sir, and thank you, sir."

"For what, lad?"

"For what you told me."

"You knew that already. Give yourself credit. Don't ever undervalue yourself, David."

"No, sir."

He got up and walked out of the room. How was he to explain to Elizabeth and Phil why he would be three days late for vacation? What could he say to them? He couldn't face the idea of telling them that he had been caught smoking. And so he went back to his room and wrote them a note. "I've decided to stay at school until Monday. Some of my friends and I are going to help Mr. Lee build his new house on the hill above the playing fields. I'll be down on the usual train Monday." He sealed the letter and mailed it quickly. It was wrong, he knew, but that was the best he could do for now.

It turned out that he was not entirely wrong. Mr. Lee took the six of them—David, Wally, and Billy and three other boys they didn't know—and he worked them hard, all Friday afternoon after the school had let out, all day Saturday and all Sunday afternoon. They were allowed to go to church on Sunday morning. Even with school in recess, there were still Sunday services in St. Matthew's Chapel. David prayed for strength before he took the bread and the wine, he prayed to change, he prayed for God to make him bolder, more honest. He always prayed for these things, but this time it seemed more important.

The air outside was brisk, but at least it was not raining. They worked at the school on Friday afternoon, raking the leaves from under the bushes and stuffing them in canvas bags. "Getting ready for spring," Mr. Lee said, smiling, puffing on his pipe, as he moved them from the dining hall to the administration building. "Work builds character, boys," he said, and he meant it. No one else could say it and mean it the way he did, and the boys knew it. They had seen the house going up on the mountain, and on Saturday and Sunday they would see it more closely, because Mr. Lee was allowed to use the boys to help him with his own work during vacation time. They hiked up his driveway at nine o'clock in the morning, and were greeted at the door by Mrs. Lee, who immediately invited them in for hot cocoa. David looked up at the giant beams across the ceiling, and tried to imagine how Mr. Lee had gotten them up. Each of them was sixteen feet long, Mr. Lee said, and every board in the house had been cut from timber on the land, hickory and pine and elm. Today the boys were going to work on fence posts. The posts had been cut, but the post holes had to be dug and the poles placed, and the barbed wire strung. Mr. Lee was going to have sheep in his pastures, and he didn't want them wandering down to the river to drown, nor did he want dogs attacking the sheep. Sheep had no sense, nor did they have any protection. That's why the Bible always talked about God as a shepherd. Humans are like sheep in the larger scheme of things, Mr. Lee said.

So they had to get the post holes dug, and the boys were here to do it. He gave them heavy work gloves, and sent them out in two groups of three. The time went fast, and there was little talking. Even Wally Hinson was strangely quiet, and when they walked back to their dorms on Sunday afternoon with the sun beginning to set behind Mt. Algo, all he could say was "Shit, that's the hardest I've ever worked in my life." David kept thinking about Mr. Lee and the pioneers and how Mr. Lee wanted to live the way people had lived before machinery. He wanted to build a house the way men had built houses for thousands of years. "I know every board in this house," he had told them. "In the living room there is one hickory board, and only I," he laughed, "know which one it is."

On the train going down on Monday, Wally Hinson said, "Anyone want a cigarette?" Billy DuPont laughed. David shuddered. He couldn't understand how Wally Hinson had the guts to keep his cigarettes. One more mistake and he was out for good.

At Elizabeth's he sensed right away that something was wrong. The kids were in the back when he let himself in the door with his key. Elizabeth was sitting in the kitchen smoking. She didn't get up.

"Would you like a cigarette, David?" she asked.

"No, thank you," he said, turning red.

"Do you smoke?"

"No," he said.

"Then what is this?"

She handed him a letter written on official Wicker School stationery, signed by Father Perkins, explaining why David had been detained.

"Did you really think we didn't know? Did you think the school wouldn't inform Molly Ariel or us? Come on, David, have some sense."

"I didn't think."

"No, you didn't think. Now, I'm going to tell you something. I don't particularly like you smoking. It's a filthy habit, but I do it, and I can't be one to judge. And I won't try and stop you if you really want to. But, please, David, don't do it behind my back. If you want to smoke, for God's sake don't hide it from me. Now, do you want a cigarette?"

"Yes," he said, smiling feebly.

She got up and hugged him fiercely. "Take your coat off and sit down, then. I'm your sister. You don't have to hide things from me. I love you."

"I know," he said.

"When you were very little," she said, "you were full of light and life, and you laughed all the time. Do you remember how we played tricks on Mommy and Bernie?"

"Like when we made up our own language?"

"And how you pretended you knew how to read?"

"*Ferdinand the Bull*," David said, and they laughed together, and chanted in unison, "He just loved to sit and smell the flowers."

"Now it's hard to get two words out of you."

"I'll be better," he said. "I really will." He reached into the pack of Pall Malls, took one out, and lit it with his sister's match. For a few minutes they smoked in silence.

"This is really strange, don't you think? I just can't believe I'm sitting here smoking with you. I'm supposed to be punishing you or something."

"The look on Father Perkins' face was the worst punishment," David said.

Then he told her about the weekend and Mr. Lee's house, and about what Father Perkins had told him. He talked until Alex came bumping around the corner.

"Unca Dave!" he shouted.

And then Maggie's curly brown hair appeared and her big smile, and he crushed his cigarette in the ashtray and picked them up and went off to the back to play.

CHAPTER TEN

It was June, and David was glad that summer was here. It had not always been that way. Many times he had dreaded the end of the school year and the start of summer vacation, wondering what each summer might bring and how he would deal with it. But he felt good this year. He knew he would have two weeks at Elizabeth and Phil's before he left for Lambertville, and he knew that he would have a summer job once he arrived there. Aunt Louise had written him: "David, I have found you a position as a soda jerk at the Purple Onion Grill in New Hope. It is run by Peter Karriker who lives nearby. You will work from seven in the evening until one in the morning. I will drive you to work, and Peter will bring you home. It's not very glamorous, I know, but it is a good income, and Peter is a reliable young man, who raises cocker spaniels in his spare time." David loved the letter. It was clearly the cocker spaniels that made Peter Karriker respectable. Next to art, Aunt Louise loved dogs best.

Financially the spring had been lucrative for David. He had begun typing papers for other students, and toward the end of the year, when term papers were due, he had more business than he could handle. He used all his spare time on weekends for typing, except for Sunday afternoon when he went up to the Wicker *Sentinel* room and worked for the newspaper. He was glad that

Anthony S. Abbott

Father Perkins had suggested it to him. At first, because he was just a fourth former, they gave him unimportant assignments like covering the chess club or the debating society, but as the spring wore on and the sixth formers turned over their responsibilities to the fifth form, David's role grew. Jim Moffet was named as the new editor, and immediately he took David under his wing. "You're a good writer, Dave," he said, "and I'd like to use you next year as assistant head of the news department. You'll work directly under me, and I'll show you the ropes."

The last three issues of the year were put out by the new board, and David's name appeared prominently. Billy DuPont was working in the sports department, and David's new friend, Dennis Vogler, was working in editorials and features. Dennis had arrived at the school after spring break, having transferred from a day school on Long Island after his mother died. He was the tallest boy in the school, and, almost immediately, the most popular, because he played a mean piano. At night, after supper, people would gather around him while he played Dixieland and progressive jazz and popular songs from the movies and Broadway. He never used music. Students who knew the words sang along or rapped the beat with their hands against their chairs. He and David and Ralph Wisdom went to the Wednesday night debates together, and watched the techniques of the graduating seniors. David was fascinated with Dennis Vogler, with his ease, with his talent, with his kindness, and one day in the mailroom he just blurted out:

"Dennis, would you room with me next year?"

Dennis looked down at him with his big brown eyes and then took those huge arms and wrapped them around David. "I'd love it, Dave, but the Headmaster has asked me to room with Ralph Wisdom. Ralph's going to live on campus next year instead of commuting from home. You know I'd do it otherwise."

There was no competing with Ralph Wisdom. David knew that, so he and Borden stayed together and asked for a room over the dining hall as close to Dennis and Ralph as they could get.

And now it was June, and they were on the train to New York, he and Wally Hinson and Billy Dupont and Dennis Vogler, all smoking like chimneys and making plans. Dennis wanted them to go to Jimmy Ryan's on 52nd Street. It was the best Dixieland in New York. You were supposed to be eighteen, but during the week they let anybody in who looked close. Sixteen was close enough, and besides Dennis knew the piano player. Billy and David were going to Yankee Stadium and watch the Yankees play the Red Sox, and one day they would all go to Jones Beach.

David had money, that was the difference this summer. He had saved a lot by typing papers, he didn't have to pay his way to California, and he had the money from selling pennants. The idea was Wally Hinson's. He had a catalogue where you could send away for pennants real cheap.

David now had a job at the Stat Store, where they sold pads of paper and notebooks and pens and pencils, Wicker School stationery, and rulers and compasses and graph paper—everything you needed at school. They also sold stamps. There was a scale where you could weigh packages and letters and figure out how much you needed. And that's how the boys paid for the pennants—with stamps.

The first time David stole stamps was in late April. It was a slow day, and no one was watching when he took ten six-cent stamps out of the book and only put a quarter in the money tray. He never stole them outright. He just didn't pay the full amount, and this went on for weeks. Each time he took a few more and paid a little less. No one had suggested he do it. He just did it, and he didn't really feel guilty about it, because no one ever said anything. The store manager never kept records. No one said that there wasn't enough money in the drawer, because as far as David could see, they just sold stuff and took in the money. There were no receipts. Still, by the end of the year, David was glad it was over. He promised himself he would not do it again in the fall. He didn't like doing it, and he prayed to God to help him stop, but God didn't seem very interested. God had bigger things to worry about, like the Russians and the Red Chinese and the H-Bomb, and whether or not to punish Ingrid Bergman for having a baby with Roberto Rosselini.

God was tricky. You could go for days, for weeks, without really thinking about God. You could go to chapel every day and say the prayers, mumble the words in the book, think about dinner. You could even go to the Sunday Eucharist and take the wafer on your tongue and drink the wine and then go out into the sunshine or the rain and get on with the rest of the day without really thinking about God. And then at the most surprising moment something would grab you, and there God was in the midst of everything.

There God was— in the rhythm and beauty of the crew as they rowed by on the river in perfect harmony, in the click of the oars and the single splash of each stroke. God was there in the voices of the glee club, the harmonies that could come from nowhere else but heaven. And most of all, David thought, God was there in the letters he got from Tracy Warren. They were his most precious possessions, and so afraid was he that someone would find them, he carefully read each one over and over and then destroyed it, tearing it into tiny pieces and mixing the pieces with other scraps of paper in the trash. He never went to his mailbox at the usual times, when everyone was in the mail room screaming and yelling and lining up for packages at the window. He'd go during morning classes when only the honors students could be out of study hall. He'd go on his way back to the room from English or math. He'd tuck the letter in his notebook and read it in the privacy of his room. Knowing Tracy Warren was there was kind of like knowing God was there. She just loved him, and he didn't have to do anything to earn it, it seemed. It was like grace, her words flowing so easily he could hear her voice in them, hear her speaking to him as she wrote. She told him simple things, like what she was doing, or what she ate for dinner, she told him about driving lessons, and how she would meet him at the train when he came in June.

He had not been able to see her during spring vacation. They only had ten days and David had spent four of them at school working off his hours, and the rest of the week he stayed close to home, playing with the children, going to an occasional movie, but nothing much. "You were working off your guilt," she said in a letter to him after he returned to school. "You can't fool your heart," she said. "You had to do that to make things right. You had betrayed your sister by lying to her, and you needed to let her know you were sorry by staying at home. You boys don't ever speak your hearts, do you? But you act it out in some way. I know."

Her wisdom stunned him. Somehow he was not worthy of it, he felt, and he wrote her back and thanked her the best he could. He signed his letters, "Love," but he did not say, "I love you." That was different. He wrote her about the pennants and the stamps, which was terribly hard for him, because he knew that once you wrote something down, it was true. It was proof that it had happened, and there could be no denying it, but he could not keep it from her. He was beginning to truly understand the nature of their friendship. "I have to tell you," he said, "because lying to you is like lying to God. You would know, wouldn't you? We would be together, and you would say, 'There is something you want to tell me, isn't there?'"

"Yes," she wrote back. "I would know. I'm sad for you, David, because you don't need to do this. Money is not that important. You said you wanted money so you could take me to the movies or dinner. We don't need movies or dinner. We don't need anything except each other. You're too good for this kind of petty theft. That's what it's called, isn't it? 'Petty' means small. You're not small. Don't ever be small." Then, she surprised him. "SHIT" she wrote in capital letters, and underlined it. "That's what my dad says when he gets mad. He says I can't say it, but I can say it to you. God, I love you, David. That's all, Tracy."

She loved him, she not only loved him but said "I love you" in the letter. David wondered why. He wanted to talk to her about it, to ask her the next time he saw her, wanted her to tell him. Then maybe he would feel more comfortable, more secure. Now he just worried that her love might vanish as quickly as it had appeared. She liked secrets. Perhaps she had other secrets that she wasn't sharing with him. There was the dark thing she had said the night they pricked their thumbs. "I'm bad," she had said, and the scar under her eye had whitened. It was not good for him to think this way, he knew, but he could not make his fears go away.

Anthony S. Abbott

The money burned in his pocket for a while, but he kept it, and he and Billy DuPont went to Yankee Stadium and cheered for the Yankee Clipper. The sight of Number 5 trotting to center field brought tears to his eyes. Talk of Joe's retirement was everywhere. His batting average had slipped almost to .300, and reporters asked him how he felt about his brother Dominick having a higher average. But he was still Joe DiMaggio, and without him the Yankees would not be the same. He was still the one they counted on to win the big games. Now it was only June, and Joe was at his best in September when the pennant race was feverish, but he always gave his best, and David could never watch him without a lump in his throat and a pounding of his heart.

After the game, they took the subway back to Grand Central and met Dennis Vogler and Wally Hinson at the Information Booth. It was always the Information Booth or the clock at the Biltmore. Tonight they were going to Jimmy Ryan's on 52nd Street to listen to Dixieland. There were six players—trumpet, trombone, clarinet, bass, drums, and piano—Dennis explained, and each player took turns improvising off the number's main tune. Dennis had played some of his favorite records to them at school, so David understood what he was talking about, but he had never seen and heard Dixieland live. He couldn't believe how different it was to actually be there. The audience stomped and yelled, and stood and screamed for "Saints" until finally, after eleven, the band took up the challenge and played the universal favorite, "When the Saints Go Marching In." The fever was catching. They got in a line and danced around the room and shouted their joy 'till they were hoarse. Then they stomped out into the street and walked back to Grand Central where the other boys caught the last trains back to the suburbs, and David went down the stairs to the subway.

He was not afraid, coming home on the subway late at night. Elizabeth trusted him, and he had his own key to let himself in if the family had gone to bed. David felt cleansed by the day's events, purged of whatever tension lingered after the school year. He loved the ball game and the music and the easy camaraderie of the other guys, but what he didn't realize until he got home was that he had forgotten his key, left it in the pocket of a different pair of trousers. It was well past midnight, and David didn't want to wake his sister or Phil. There was only one hope—the front window. He climbed the stairs and then slid over the railing and stretched until he could reach the window. It was unlocked. He raised it up, and then bent over and squeezed through into the dark living room. Then he closed the window, and looked back into the street. No policemen, no one watching him that he could see, and so he undressed and quietly went to bed.

In the morning Elizabeth received a call from a neighbor, wanting to know if she had been robbed in the night. Her husband had seen someone crawling in her window, and was going to call the police.

"You're lucky you weren't shot," Phil said at breakfast.

"Don't do it again," Elizabeth said.

"Bad David," said Alex.

"Bad," said Maggie and laughed.

And Phil went to work, and the rest of them went to the beach, to Orchard Beach, up at the northeastern tip of the Bronx. It was a long subway ride and a bus ride, and a job to open and close Maggie's stroller, but with two of them they managed. They settled their blanket on the beach, and David led the kids down by the water. They were going to build the biggest sand castle that ever was, just like the ones David and Elizabeth had built when they were little. David loved making turrets and tunnels and various paths for the water to get in when the tide came up. When they were hot, they picked the kids up and carried them into the water for a dip, and then went up to the cafeteria for hot dogs and Cokes.

"I wish Mommy were here," said Elizabeth, out of the blue. "I miss her. She would have loved little Maggie. My God, she looks just like her." Then she started to cry and wiped her eyes on her napkin and blew her nose. "It's silly to think of her now, I know. But she loved the water, and watching the waves come in made me think of her. I know she could be awful, just awful, but still there's such a hole when your mother is gone, such a hole."

David didn't know what to say. He and Elizabeth hadn't really talked about their mother since her death. David had simply avoided the subject, and he knew this wasn't the time to talk. Still he understood what Elizabeth meant. He missed her, too. There were some things he might have said to her had she lived a little longer. Maybe he would have learned more about her. As it was, her life simply got smaller and smaller in his mind. If he didn't think about her, pretty soon she would go away altogether, and David knew that wasn't right. He wouldn't find out anything if he didn't ask, but he was not much of an asker. He would have to talk to Tracy Warren about it.

And he did. She met him at the station in the family car in a red top and cut off blue jeans and sneakers with a bandana around her head. He loved the little chip on her front tooth. It made her look cuter when she smiled. Tracy was going to have it capped, but David preferred it with the chip. It seemed to suit her. He got in the car beside her and just couldn't stop smiling.

"Where do you want to go, good sir?" she asked.

"To Compo Beach in Westport," he said. "It's where my mother used to take my sister and me when we were little. I want to see if going there makes me remember better."

"That's neat," she said, and they drove home and changed, fixed a picnic lunch, and got back in the car. Tracy looked the same, except she had her bathing suit on underneath. It was a two piece suit, and she had tied her red top under her breasts, leaving a brown stomach exposed.

"How'd you get brown so fast?" David asked.

"I work at the club as a life guard. I'll be there 'till August when we take our family trip out west."

"Will you see Ellie?"

"I hope so. Now light us a cigarette and tell me about your mom."

"I didn't know you smoked."

"I didn't until now, but my parents said it was up to me. There was no point in telling me not to, because that would just make me want to more. So I just started with a bunch of other girls at school. It just seemed natural. They're in my bag."

It seemed strange reaching into Tracy's bag. It seemed personal in an intrusive way.

"Don't be shy, silly," she said. "Nothing in there will bite you. The worst thing you could find is a Tampax."

David blushed, and found the cigarettes. He pulled one out, put it in his mouth, and lit it with the Zippo lighter. Then he passed it to her. She drew on it, and passed it back, holding the wheel with her left hand. Their fingers lingered in the exchange.

"Your mom," she said. "Do you think she was ever happy?"

"I don't know. Maybe when she was young, when she and my father were first married. When she played the piano and sang, and all the men stood around her."

"Then what happened?"

"I don't know."

"You don't know," she laughed. "Then, make it up. Imagine what might have happened."

"She kept saying to me, 'When I was a boy.'"

"When I was a boy," Tracy echoed.

"It scared me."

"She liked to tease you."

"Yes, I think that's true. I remember her driving the car, the green Plymouth, a cigarette in her left hand, her right hand on the wheel. And she would say, 'When I was a little boy, I did such and such,' and I would say, 'You can't be a boy,' and she would say, 'Yes, I was, before I was a little girl.'"

"And now," Tracy said, "It all makes sense. She was a tomboy, she climbed trees and played like a boy, and then they made her be a little girl. My parents didn't do that to me. They just let me be. You know what I mean?"

They continued like this at the beach, between swims. She asled him questions, and he answered. They lay side by side on the blanket, covered with lotion and sand. They smoked one cigarette at a time between them, passing it slowly back and forth. They touched each other's faces, as each placed the cigarette in the other's mouth. He could feel himself growing, and he put a towel over himself to hide it. Tracy laughed.

"Come on," she said. "Let's go swim," and she grabbed his hand and pulled him up. They ran to the water, pushing against the incoming force of the waves, and swam out to where they could stand up to their necks. She put her arms around him, and they held each other there in the water, and rubbed against each other until he finished. Then they went back to the blanket and talked.

"I think your mother had a lot of love in her," Tracy said, "but she never found the right man. Your father was so—I'm trying to find the word—remote, that's it. He thought he was too good for college, too good for work. He kept his distance waiting for something to be given to him. So she left him, and then met Bernie, who was kind of fun, but he went his own way, too, and left her sitting there with two kids, not coming home. No wonder she drank. I would never marry anyone except someone who loved me terribly. I mean he wouldn't have to hang around all the time, but I would just know that he loved me the most and that he was always there, no matter what. You know what I mean?"

"I do," he said, and they talked some more and then walked to the showers and stood together as the cold water washed the sand and the oil and the salt from them. They toweled dry and slipped their clothes back on over their wet bathing suits. Then they drove home.

"I'm not allowed to drive alone after dark until I'm eighteen," Tracy said. "My parents are good about rules. They don't make any silly ones, but the ones they do make they're very serious about. I like that."

The Warrens were glad to see David. It was different from the winter. They sat outside on the terrace, and Mr. Warren cooked steaks on the grill, and they drank gin and tonics. David and Tracy were each allowed a very small one. "It's better to drink at home and learn how to do it properly rather than going off on the sly. Drinking can be very civilized in moderation," Mr. Warren said, and they clinked their glasses.

"You're welcome here any time, David," Mrs. Warren said.

"Right," said Butch, and after dinner they shot baskets until it got really dark.

Later, David and Tracy sat on a blanket in the grass and looked at the stars. When David tried to kiss her, Tracy turned away.

"No," she said. "We need to talk about the stealing."

It was the first time he had heard the word.

"You can't lie to yourself, David," she said. "That's the worst kind of lie. You should write to the Headmaster and tell him what you did."

"It's all over, Tracy," David said. He was frightened by her words. No one else spoke to him the way she did. "I can't do that. I'll never do it again, I promise you. It's all over, and I know it was wrong, but I can't go through two things in the same year. I can't."

She was silent for a while, and then turned to him. "I know you can't. I know you better than you know yourself. But, still you should." She reached out and took his hands. "You have this secret side of yourself, the side that keeps everything inside. You think that if it's inside, it didn't really happen. You and I, we can be secret, but nothing else. You have to be true to yourself and true to me, OK?"

"OK," he said.

"You're going to your aunt's for the summer. You'll meet girls at this restaurant where you're working. I'll meet boys at the club. We have to date. That's part of the deal. We have to date other people to find out what they're like, then we can tell each other about it before school starts. You can come back here before school starts, OK?"

"OK," he said.

"You're so funny," she said. "You're so scared of life. You want it so badly, but you're so scared at the same time. That's why you need me."

"Yes," he said, "I need you," and he began to cry, and she saw his tears.

"Jesus, David," she said. "I love you. It's all right, I love you," and she began to kiss him, and they lay on the blanket in the dark and held each other.

At his aunt's everything was dogs and paintings, the way he had remembered it, except now there were four dogs, the two cocker spaniels and two Afghan hounds, a kind of dog David had never seen before. It was hard for David to describe them. They were large dogs with long, smooth, golden hair, both bitches, as Aunt Louise said. They had long, pointed noses and quizzical eyes. Aunt Louise parted the hair on top of their heads in the middle, and combed each side down, giving the dogs an almost human look. They lounged on the furniture in the living room. If one was on the couch, the other took the yellow stuffed chair near the kitchen door. Aunt Louise loved to watch them run. She had a large back yard, which she had fenced in so the dogs could never run loose onto the road. The grace of their movement was what she loved most, and she painted it.

David could see in the house a mixture of Aunt Louise's and Uncle Swen's paintings. Louise's were mostly animals, many of them studies of the Afghans in different positions. The curve of their tails fascinated her, as did the way their heads and their front paws hung down from where they lay on the couch or the chairs.

Swen's painting were filled with swirling water and rocks, and fish and birds, birds that looked like dive bombers, swooping down toward the sea's surface. And there were more religious paintings to accompany those David had seen at the gallery in New York. One was called "Entry into Jerusalem" and another "Carrying the Dead Christ." He would send them to New York for his next show, opening in the fall. Sometimes there would be visitors, coming to look at the paintings, and David was allowed to sit in the studio and watch as Swen and Louise showed different paintings to them. Swen had been painting since the early part of the century, and David could see how his style had become more and more abstract. Some of the visitors liked the new paintings, but many were entranced by the oils and watercolors he had done in New Mexico, when he lived in Santa Fe. He had lived in Santa Fe for over twenty years, and it was when he left Santa Fe and came to Minneapolis that Aunt Louise had first met him and studied with him. He considered the Santa Fe paintings old fashioned now, Aunt Louise said, but a sale was a sale, and the New Mexico paintings sold well, especially the landscapes and the ones of the Indians in their religious rituals.

David started work in the Purple Onion on the Tuesday after he arrived. The weekend was the busiest time, and Peter Karriker wanted to break David in on the slower days. He liked working at the counter, where his main job was to make sodas and milkshakes. He had to learn how much ice cream to mix with seltzer water, and how much syrup to put in a soda, and how to make the milkshakes blend smoothly without spilling all over the counter. If business was light he was allowed to talk, but he was not supposed to go out from behind the counter unless he was carrying a soda or a milkshake to someone.

The restaurant was on the main road from New Hope to Doylestown about a half mile from the Delaware River. It was the only place that stayed open late, and when the movies and the summer theater got out, there was a rush of business. The crowd fascinated David. There seemed to be lots of college kids working at the theater for the summer who came for cokes and hamburgers, and often, a little earlier, groups of teenagers out for a drive.

Among the teenagers were two girls that David came to know, Jill Landers and Margie Sorenson. They were from Philips Mill, a tiny town just up the road to the north, where Jill's mother weaved wall hangings that Margie's mother sold at her craft shop in New Hope. There were craft shops everywhere in New Hope, up and down the main street and on the small streets going up the hill— there were craft shops and artists' galleries and a toy store and a bookshop that specialized in children's books, and a small grocery store where Aunt Louise always shopped rather than going to the big A&P over in Lambertville. New Hope was an artist's colony, like Provincetown at the tip of Cape Cod, where Uncle Swen had worked when he was young making woodcuts and designing sets for the Provincetown Players, where Eugene O'Neill had gotten his start. Aunt Louise had showed David a picture of Uncle Swen in one of O'Neill's plays. "When they needed a Swede," she laughed, "they always asked him."

Jill was a tall girl, soft and pale and big-breasted. She always wore blue jeans. Margie, her sidekick, was dazzling. That's the way it always is, David thought. It was like Tracy and Ellie. The beautiful girl always had a not-so-beautiful friend at her side. Margie was a strawberry blonde, short, slim, and brown-skinned. She looked like she had spent the summer in the sun. She usually wore Bermuda shorts and a sleeveless top with two buttons undone. She and Jill would come into the restaurant and sit at the counter and talk to David when business was slow. He was fascinated by them. They were juniors at New Hope High, and Margie's boyfriend was Johnny Packer, a senior, and the star running back for the football team. He sometimes came with them and sat on the stool with his hand on Margie's thigh.

During the day the girls worked in the scene shop at the summer theater, and at night they cruised around in Jill's car, an old Ford her family had given to her for her seventeenth birthday. She would take it to college. Once in a while they would drive David home after work to help Peter out, Margie and John making out in the back seat, while David sat up front with Jill, trying to keep his mind off what was going on. Aunt Louise knew Mrs. Landers, and so she didn't mind the girls bringing David home. "Jill Landers is a lovely girl," Aunt Louise said, "but I don't know the Sorenson girl. What is she like?"

"She's very cute, Aunt Louise," David said, and that was that until the Sunday of the picnic.

David was sitting on the side porch when the girls came squealing into the gravel driveway. Jill hopped out and ran to the front door and rang the bell. Aunt Louise answered it.

"Hello, Mrs. Swenson," said Jill in her sweetest manner. "We came to take David over to Washington Crossing Park for a picnic. We'll drop him at work afterwards. Is that OK?"

Aunt Louise was delighted. She thought it would be "lovely," and off David went, dashing down the front steps after kissing his aunt on the cheek. He was glad to get away. It had been a long week, and David had gotten himself into trouble with Uncle Swen twice. The first time was when he was bouncing the tennis ball against the studio wall. Usually, during the afternoons, he read. Ralph Wisdom had told him the Russian novelists were the best of all. He should read *War and Peace* by Tolstoy. It was a huge novel, nine hundred pages, and he was working his way through it, remembering as he read how Debbie Rossiter had played the 1812 Overture by Tchaikovsky, celebrating the Russian victory over Napoleon. He could hear the bells ringing and the burst of joy in the Russian national anthem, and he could see the figure of Debbie Rossiter bending over the record player at Lowell School, revealing a hint of her beautiful breasts. It was hard to read and think of Debbie Rossiter at the same time. So he got up from the porch and walked over to the studio with his tennis ball. If he stood ten yards from the south wall, he could bounce the ball against the studio wall and then catch it. If he threw it really hard, the ball would sail over his head, and he would have to race back to make the catch like DiMaggio in center field. Or he could deliberately throw it short and race in. He could even invent games. He'd done it before but never when Uncle Swen was inside painting. That was his mistake. It didn't last long.

"David," said Aunt Louise from the studio door, "Please don't throw the ball against the wall while Swen is painting. It is extremely distracting." Then she went back inside.

David resumed his reading, but he had lost the heart for it. In his room, he turned on the small radio next to his bed, and found the Yankee game. He couldn't always get it. Lambertville was closer to Philadelphia than New York, and sometimes he could only get the Philadelphia stations, but today the Yankee game came in. He lay on his bed with his eyes closed. The Yankees were in Chicago, at Comisky Park, and he could hear the roar of the fans for the home team. The Yankees needed his support. As each batter came to the plate, David closed his eyes and tried to imagine how he looked. He could see the gray road uniforms, the numbers on the back, the dark blue Yankee hats with the letters NY intertwined. He could hear the crack of the bat as each one hit the ball, and he could see the flight of the ball as Mel Allen described it. Inning by inning the game went on, and David become more and more immersed in the world of sounds and voices coming from the radio. He forgot the time completely.

Suddenly the door to his room opened. It was Uncle Swen calling him to dinner.

"I'm sorry, Uncle Swen," David said. "I didn't hear you."

"Of course not," said Uncle Swen. "You never hear. You lock yourself in there and listen to the radio for hours. How do you expect to hear?"

And so David was glad to get away on that Sunday afternoon. Only when he got to the car, something was strange. Johnny Packer was sitting in the front seat next to Jill, and he waved David into the back. David tried to figure it out. John was supposedly Margie's boy friend. Why was he sitting up front with Jill?

Margie smiled at him, then eased over toward him and kissed him on the cheek. "You're cute," she whispered. "It's such a waste to have you secluded way out here." She slid back to the other side, lit a cigarette, and handed it to David. "Relax, kiddo," she said. "It's OK, I don't eat up virgins." He took a puff, and handed her the cigarette back. He was afraid to look at her.

They squealed out of the driveway and spun up the gravel road to the top of the next hill, then down toward Washington Crossing State Park, where they crossed the river and wound their way up the hill on the other side. They spread their blanket on the grass and stretched out in the sun. The girls had brought picnic baskets, and John had brought beer. Margie popped open a Ballantine and handed it to David.

"I don't drink," he said quietly.

"Oh, come on. No one cares. Your auntie isn't here."

So he started, a little at first, and then more, and soon the four of them had finished the six pack. "Gimme the keys," said John. "I'll get some more in town. They all know me."

"I'll drive the car," said Jill. "You get the beer," and they were gone.

"He's a real bastard," said Margie. "We're breaking up. Jill can have him if she wants, but I'm sick of him."

David didn't know what to say. The beer had made him a little light-headed, and he felt more like lying down and closing his eyes than like talking. But he wanted to know what was going on. He thought immediately of Tracy. What would Tracy want him to do? Experience life, he thought. Well, this was certainly an experience.

"What does he do?" David asked.

"He does what he damn well pleases. He takes me for granted. Everybody takes me for granted. I know what they think of me. 'Makeout Margie.' That's what they call me. You think I don't know? John just thinks because he's Mr. Popularity, Mr. Hot Stuff, he can make me do whatever he wants."

She was crying now. "So I said, 'Go to hell, Johnny Packer,' and he laughed and walked away, and then this morning he and Jill pulled up to my house and said they wanted to go for a picnic and did I want to go, and I said OK and then we came to get you."

"But why me?"

"You're amazing. You don't even know you're cute. You just sit there with that sweet face looking so goddamn innocent. Jesus, maybe you are."

And then she leaned over and kissed him, not the way Tracy had kissed him, but hard as if in kissing she was trying to work some pain out of her system.. She pushed him back, and he lay on his back on the green plaid blanket in the shade at Washington Crossing State Park, while Margie Sorenson kissed him and cried.

They left him at work at six, and David didn't say anything to Peter Karriker or any of the others about his afternoon. He tried to think while he worked. He could make sodas and milkshakes and scoop ice cream and talk to the customers now, all at the same time. He liked his job, with his blue button-down shirt and the white apron tied around his waist, and the little white hat to keep his hairs from falling in the drinks. But he couldn't be the friendly soda-jerk tonight. He kept thinking.

He knew Margie was just trying to make Johnny jealous, but what about Jill? Wasn't she Margie's friend? Why would she go out with Johnny? David was way over his head. He liked being kissed by Margie Sorenson, and he could feel the sexual excitement of her body on his, but it seemed wrong to him somehow, like she was just using him and he was letting her. Tracy wouldn't approve of that. Yes, David thought, he would have to break it off, not see her again, at least not be alone with her.

But he never had the chance to tell her that. In the morning, Aunt Louise broke it off for him. She had come back to the kitchen from the studio while David was having his breakfast in the kitchen. She was stern.

"Pete Karriker rang me this morning, David."

"Yes?"

"He told me that you arrived at work yesterday with beer on your breath."

"That's true, Aunt Louise."

"You know that it is against the law to drink beer until you are eighteen."

"Yes, Aunt Louise."

"And you did it anyway."

"Yes."

"Why?

"Because everyone else was doing it, and I didn't want to be different. I don't know. It helped me to relax."

"But you know about your mother and your grandmother. It's not just the law, David, it's your family. I think it's better for you not to drink at all."

David started to speak, but Louise didn't stop.

"Peter says that if it happens again, he will have to let you go."

"I understand that, Aunt Louise. It won't happen again."

"And I think it best that you not see those girls, especially the Sorenson girl."

"Yes, Aunt Louise."

"Now, get dressed, and put on something nice. We're going to drive to Philadelphia and visit your Aunt Estelle."

David took a deep breath and sighed, really sighed.

"It's not so bad as all that," said Aunt Louise, laughing. "We can't have you bouncing balls against the wall, and we can't have you driving off with these wild young women, so we'll just go see Aunt Estelle. You haven't been to visit her all summer."

She was right. He hadn't been to see Aunt Estelle all summer. Louise had moved her to a nursing home outside Philadelphia, "a beautiful, comfortable place with excellent help," Aunt Louise said. But Aunt Estelle had not adjusted well. She wouldn't talk to the other residents, and sometimes she just stayed in her room and cried. It was hard to persuade her to get dressed. David knew that Louise had gone over to see her at least once a week, but she had not taken David, because it would be "too unsettling," she said. But today she was taking him in hopes of cheering Estelle up.

"You'll see quite a change," she said to David as they pulled out of the driveway. "She's very angry at me for moving her, and she will not forgive me. But there was no other choice. She simply could not care for herself any more. She's not like your grandmother, her sister, who was always a lady, always gracious about everything. Estelle is a woman of strong opinions, very stubborn if she's crossed."

Louise was a good driver, slow but not too slow, careful but not too careful. It was nice to be in the car with her away from the paintings and the dogs and the demands of the telephone. While she drove, she talked about her life before she met Swen, about their marriage and how important letters were. They had gotten to know each other through letters, during their periods of long separation and after they were married and he had moved to Lambertville alone. While she was caring for her mother in Minneapolis, he wrote her almost every day.

"You must read those letters one day when you're older. They're full of wisdom about art, about life in general. I realized when I married him that my most important job was to make life comfortable for him so that he could paint. He likes a regular life, his bowl of oatmeal at eight o'clock, lunch at twelve, dinner at six, a game in the evening. He's not used to children. He doesn't like visitors very much, unless they're artists. I know it's been hard for you, but his needs must come first."

She patted him on the leg and smiled. He smiled back—he could not help liking Aunt Louise, really admiring her. She had studied

French at the University, she had traveled to France to study at the Sorbonne, she had married the man she loved, she did what she wanted, and she had the guts to be herself. She didn't care what people thought. If one of the dogs had a tick, she just took it off with her fingers and threw it in the fireplace, or burned it up with a match. If one of the Afghans sat in her chair at the dinner table, she'd just get another one. She wore what she liked, she ate what she liked, and she did what she liked. Well, David couldn't fault that. He just realized her home was not his home. He couldn't live there, cut off from friends his age. He'd have to find another place for next summer. That was certain. Still, he did admire her.

Aunt Estelle was worse than ever. She was in her room, in bed, and wouldn't get up or get dressed. She sat in bed, staring ahead of her, her hair combed by the nurses, but looking thin and hanging down straight on either side. She looked like someone in a Dickens novel, David thought.

"Here's David to see you, Estelle," said Aunt Louise cheerfully.

David edged toward the bed, and smiled tentatively. "Hello, Aunt Estelle," he said, "How are you?"

"I know where I am," she said. "Have you come to take me home young man?" but she showed no look of recognition.

"You know David, Estelle, Allan's son. You loved to see him in New York."

"I know you," Estelle retorted, "and I know where I am."

"Would you like to get dressed and go to luncheon with us, Estelle?" Louise responded, determined to be cheerful, but it was no use.

"Why don't you go outside and wait, David," Louise said, turning to him. "I will be with you in a few moments."

It was cool for August, and ceiling fans kept the air moving in the residents' rooms and in the dining room. The nursing home was shaded with oaks, and the staff was both courteous and well-trained. Louise was right, she had not lied to David about Aunt Estelle's care. She had done the best thing, but Estelle could not live outside of her beloved New York City. She could not live if she could not walk down the streets, hailing her yellow cabs and asking the driver to take her to the Plaza.

David thought about all of this as he waited for Louise in the reception area. People came and went, old people using walkers and canes, others being pushed in wheelchairs. Sons and daughters and grandchildren, he guessed, came to visit and eat with them in the dining hall. David was glad that Estelle did not want to eat. He did not think he would have any appetite here in this place. It was clean and orderly, lovely and quiet, but it depressed him, and he hoped that Louise would suggest they eat their luncheon elsewhere.

CHAPTER ELEVEN

School, blessed school. They had smoked their way north on the New York, New Haven, and Hartford Railroad and tossed their packs of cigarettes into the waiting baskets of the sixth formers—David and Billy DuPont and Wally Hinson and Kosmo, the crazy Pole. Then they dumped their bags in the waiting truck, strolled down the main street of Wicker, and turned to cross the bridge to the school. It was a beautiful September day, with a hint of autumn in the air. Leaves mostly green still, but a touch of yellow and orange on Mt. Algo. Straight ahead Numeral Rock looked down at them with its blue 51 on a yellow background.

"We're next," said Wally Hinson. It was one of the great rituals at Wicker School, the painting of the rock by the rising sixth formers during the final month of school, part of that turnover of power, where the fifth formers got to act like sixth formers for three weeks before the older boys graduated, a kind of practice run.

"I wonder who our Senior Prefect will be," said David.

"Jesus, Lear," said Wally Hinson. "You gotta be a complete idiot not to know that. That's the only sure thing there is."

"You mean Ralph Wisdom?" said David innocently.

"You're goddamn right," said Wally Hinson.

Of course, David knew. But he liked to ask, just to hear other people say it, just to be sure that it couldn't possibly be anyone else. It was Ralph Wisdom's class, and they were Ralph Wisdom's people. They would do anything for him.

"Why do you think JAP had him move into the dorms?" said Wally Hinson. "He wants him around. He wants to train him. You just watch."

They turned and walked up the hill, past the tennis courts and the North Dorm, where they had suffered as third formers, past the Auditorium to the Dining Hall. They were all on the second floor of the dining hall together—David and Borden Smith, Wally Hinson and Ted Barber next door, and Ralph Wisdom and Dennis Vogler two doors down. Everything was buzzing. School, blessed school, David thought. "Thank God the summer is over."

He plunged into his work with new gusto. He joined the debating society and got a bit part in *Hamlet*, which the new English teacher, Reginald Barnes, was directing. He thought it was amazing that Wicker School would do *Hamlet*. How could a bunch of seventeen year-olds do *Hamlet*? At first he didn't believe it was possible, but day by day, as rehearsals went on, he was more and more convinced that it could work. He didn't have to rehearse every night, only once a week or so, because his part was so small, and so each time he went back, he could see the changes, the way the characters had begun to speak the lines so that they made sense.

Reginald Barnes was good, and so was Jerry Klein, the sixth former who played Hamlet. He wasn't just good, he was terrific. He was angry and disillusioned, sick to death of the corruption in Denmark. It fit exactly the poem David had written about the movie. He spat his lines out with venom, and hated the stupid, bumbling Polonius. David reviewed the play for the paper and called it the best piece of work that had been done since he'd been at school. Everyone agreed. The students stood and shouted as each of the cast members came forward for their bows, and the two faculty wives who played Gertrude and Ophelia got the biggest cheers of all.

But happy as he was, David couldn't solve the problem of English. The fifth form English teacher was the feared B. Nicholas Benson, known to the students as B.N. or Bad News. Nobody could get an A from him, not even Ralph Wisdom. In the first marking period the fifth form averages plummeted. David led the class but was way below his usual average, and the redoubtable Antonio Black had slipped temporarily even lower. Ralph Wisdom didn't care; he had other things on his mind like the Korean War and his hero, General of the Army Douglas MacArthur. Wally Hinson loved it. "Boy, has Bad News got your butts!" was his favorite phrase.

David was puzzled. He couldn't figure out what he was doing wrong. So he wrote to Tracy. He missed her terribly. He had hoped to meet her in New York and take her out when he got back from Lambertville, but when he called her house there was no answer. He brooded. Here he was in New York with money in his pocket from the summer and no one to spend it on. He had moved back to New York at the end of August for a week at Elizabeth and Phil's before school started, and he had counted on her. Where could she be? Out West on a family trip again? In Europe? Her school didn't start until a week after David's, and maybe they were still traveling. He had told her not to write him in Lambertville, because he felt funny about getting letters there. He just wasn't ready to get Tracy mixed up with Aunt Louise and Uncle Swen. He wanted to keep her secret.

So he wrote her from school and got a letter back immediately. He tucked it into his notebook and walked back to his room before opening it. Borden would be in the library working in Mr. Parkinson's office.

"Dearest David, I'm so sorry I missed your call. I was at my grandmother's funeral in Wisconsin, and we stayed there for several days. I helped my mom and my aunt start going through their mom's stuff. It was awful and it was beautiful both. You know what I mean? I cried and cried. I loved my grandmother so much. When she came and stayed with us at Thanksgiving or Easter or Christmas, she slept in my room, and I moved in with Butch. But I would go into my room to dress, and we would talk. She treated me like a grown up, like I was a special friend. I can't believe she's gone. I dream about her. Do you dream about your mother? Of course you do. You've told me about those dreams.

"I have so much to tell you. I hated not being able to write you all summer. That was stupid.

"Let's do something at Thanksgiving, maybe on the Saturday after I can come to New York and we can go out, and then you can come home with me on the train and spend Saturday night and catch the train to school from Stamford. I'll drive you there, OK?

"What to do about English! Talk to Father Perkins. You admire him. He'll know. In my French class we are reading Pascal. Have you ever heard of him? He said, 'La coeur a ses raisons que la raison ne connait point.' Can you translate that? Sure you can. Think about it. I love you, David J. Lear, remember that."

He held the letter like the Holy Grail, like the cup itself. She could make him laugh and make him cry. She knew him. "The heart has its reasons that the reason doesn't know at all." He had studied the French word "point" which was the strongest negative, much stronger than "pas." "Point" meant "not at all." Tracy was right. The heart did have its reasons, and David was afraid to trust the heart. He knew that. But what did that have to do with English and with asking Father Perkins? He couldn't figure that out. He put the letter away in his third bureau drawer under his sweaters. It was safe there. Borden would never touch any of his things.

The next day during his free period he knocked on Father Perkins' door.

"Come in, lad," the Headmaster said. "To what do I owe the honor of this visit?"

"Well, sir," said David. "I need some advice."

"Advice on what subject?"

"English."

"Well, that's hardly my field. I should think you would consult Mr. Benson on that subject."

"Mr. Benson is the problem, sir. I can't seem to write an essay for him that gets higher than a B. I feel like all my essays are stupid. It's not as if I get lots of red marks for spelling or grammar. I just get B's and he doesn't find my essays very. . ."

"Very what?"

"Well, very interesting."

"Do you know Pascal?"

David couldn't believe it.

"No, sir, I mean, yes sir. I mean I know one phrase by Pascal."

"And what would that be?"

"La coeur a ses raisons que la raison ne connait point."

"Very good, and do you know what that means?"

"Sort of."

"Let's do better than sort of."

"Yes, sir."

"It means that there are two different kinds of knowledge, the knowledge of the heart and the knowledge of the brain, the reason. The heart's knowledge is deeper, wiser, more mysterious, more emotional. You won't get A's from Bad News Benson until you learn to write with the heart, with that deeper knowledge. You have to take risks, be original, talk about how the book, the novel speaks to the heart. Don't just recite what you think English teachers want to hear. You can do that."

"Yes, sir."

"God lives in the deep places. If you can find where God dwells within you, you can do everything else. Do you know what the word 'inspiration' comes from?"

"From the Latin word 'spiritus?'"

"That's right. Think of the Trinity. God the Father, Son, and Holy Spirit. Inspiration—when the spirit is in you—when you find where the spirit is. We all find it in different places. You have the capacity for some great achievement. Pray for the presence of the spirit, pray for God's breath—without God's breath we are only animals."

He paused and lit his customary cigarette, then smiled. You didn't see a smile from Father Perkins very often, but when you did, it changed everything. "You didn't expect that, did you?" he said, and then laughed. "Well, I didn't either, that's the joy of it."

They were reading *The Scarlet Letter* in English, and it was Bad News Benson's second favorite book, second to *Moby Dick*, which they would read after Thanksgiving. At least that's what all the sixth formers said. As David read the book chapter by chapter, the words of Pascal kept coming back. "The heart has its reasons."

That was it. Hester and Dimmesdale had followed their hearts, and were punished by the Puritans for it. They were drawn together by some powerful force. Why was it so wrong what they did? David couldn't figure it out. He asked in class.

"Well, Mr. Lear," said B.N. Benson. "What do you think?" He turned toward David, pipe in hand, smiling, his eyes lit up with a fierce passion. "That's a good question, a damned good question. Now, go after it."

Later, he would look back on this moment as a turning point in his education. He had always been afraid of being wrong. He answered questions when he knew the answer, and most of the time he knew the answer. But to this question, there was no answer, no right answer. He had to say what he felt. He had to speak from the heart.

"I don't think they were wrong," he said. "They loved each other. She took the scarlet letter off and they loved each other. She never had any love from Chillingworth. She needed love, and so did Dimmesdale."

"But he wasn't married to her," said Antonio Black. "The Puritans viewed their act as a sin—A for Adultery."

"But Hawthorne didn't like the Puritans," said Ralph Wisdom.

"True," David said. "The Puritans were cold, they were mean."

"Just the same," said Antonio Black, "they were right."

"Wait," said David. "I just thought of something. What about Pearl? She's the one who tells her mother to put the letter back on."

"So?" said Billy DuPont.

"Sew letters on your chest," said crazy Kosmo, and everyone laughed.

"Back to the issue, gentlemen," said B.D. Benson, and off they went some more, going back and forth.

"I know," said David. He was very excited now. "'Thou wast not bold, thou was not true.' That's what Pearl says to her father, the minister. She knows. She wants him to come out in the open. It's not what they did that was wrong. It was keeping it secret, trying to act respectable."

Anthony S. Abbott

"She is one really weird kid," said Kosmo.

"But she's right," said David. "That's it. She is like the voice of God, the voice of conscience."

"Well, Mr. Lear," said Mr. Benson, "you might have to write your essay on that," and the bell rang, releasing them into the hall. David took a deep breath. He'd never had so much fun in class, and the time had gone by as if there were no time at all. That was it. It had nothing to do with grades, or answers, but the excitement of discovery, the give and take of debate.

For days he scribbled in his journal. He wanted to write a poem about Pearl, not only an essay, but a poem to go with it. He went back through the pages of the book where she appeared. The baby Pearl made him think of Maggie, with her dark curls. He could see her stamping her little foot and insisting on her way, her sturdy little legs, her perfect lips, her pout, and her smile when she got her way. He tried to relate Pearl to his own life. Who was his Pearl, he wondered, and then he knew.

It was Tracy Warren, Tracy who would never let him do anything but his best. She had told him to be true to himself, she had told him to see Father Perkins. Pearl wouldn't leave the forest with her mother until Hester put the letter back on. The letter was about truth. He hammered out the poem:

DEVIL OR ANGEL
Imp child, you love to stomp
your foot, you love to romp
through the halls of high people
and make those dark-hatted, regal
folk call you devil child.
But you abide no lies.

You take the minister's hand
and ask him if he'll stand
on the scaffold with you on Election Day.
But instead, hand on heart, he stays
in the dark, afraid to part

with his holy reputation. His heart
is with you, he says, but you
shake your head and say, "Thou
wast not bold, thou wast not true."
He cannot prove his love for you
Except to stand and hold your hand
Before the entire land.
Then you can love him, then he can pray
Up high in the brilliant light of day.

He had wrestled with what kind of poem he would write, rhymed or unrhymed, but he settled on rhyme because Mr. Richardson had said it was good verbal exercise, a way of working out your vocabulary by trying to find good matches for words. The poem seemed kind of lame to him, though, because the matches were so ordinary—"hand" and "land." or "pray" and "day." The surprising rhymes were more fun, like "part" and "heart." He wanted to make it better, but he just didn't have any more time. The essay was due, and the poem had to accompany it, and every time he made changes, he would have to type it over, so he just ran up to Mr. Benson's office, turned it in, packed his bag and ran down the path to catch the others on the way to the station.

Elizabeth was waiting for him at Grand Central.

"What a surprise," David said, putting down his bag and hugging her.

"Phil let me out," she said with a nervous laugh. "Let's go have dinner. He said I had to be back by nine."

They walked back to Donatello's on Third Ave., the same place they had gone for dinner when David had taken the train down from Lowell for his mother's funeral. It had not changed at all. David liked that—the same dark booths, the candles on the table in Chianti bottles, the wax dripping down the sides.

"Well," Elizabeth said, "I'm afraid I've got bad news for you."

David didn't want to hear it, whatever it was.

"Aunt Estelle died about two weeks ago."

"Aunt Estelle? But why didn't you. . .I mean why…?"

"Didn't we tell you?"

"Yes, why didn't you tell me? I would have come down for the funeral."

"There wasn't any funeral."

"No funeral? But why?"

"Because Aunt Louise thinks funerals are morbid. She doesn't believe in God, anyway. She just thinks that's all superstitious nonsense. 'When you're dead, you're dead,' she said."

"I didn't know that."

"Well, there's a lot you don't know, and it's probably just as well. So we just decided it was better not to bother you, not to make you miss school."

"They all just die and disappear, don't they?" David suddenly said. "I mean I don't know what happened to Mommy, what happened to Grandma. Do you?"

"Actually, I don't. Your grandfather made arrangements, that's all I know. I didn't want to know any more."

"Is there a grave somewhere to go visit?"

"David, I don't know, OK? Let's just leave it."

"All right. Then what about Aunt Estelle?"

"Well, I do know where she is. She's scattered."

"Scattered?"

"Her ashes. Louise had her cremated, and then brought the ashes to New York. We scattered them in Central Park, across from the Plaza. You know how much she loved the Plaza. Well, Louise just thought she'd like to be scattered nearby."

"But how did you do it?"

"Real early in the morning. It was cold and rainy and no one was around, so we just walked through the grass and scattered her bit by bit. We ended up over near the Carousel, that you loved so much."

"Jesus," said David.

"She just died of discouragement. Poor Louise blamed herself, but there was nothing else she could do. I think Estelle just stopped eating, stopped caring."

"She'd already started that when Louise took me to see her last summer. I should have known."

"There's nothing we can do now," said Elizabeth, and then she started to laugh. "You know, it's pretty funny, thinking about Estelle scattered over Central Park, people stepping on her and not knowing. As Louise said, 'It's an original idea, and I like original ideas.'"

"How's Phil?" David asked, "And how are the kids?"

"The kids are fine," Elizabeth answered. "They can't wait to see you."

"And Phil?"

"I don't know." She reached out her hand to touch his across the table. "Don't say anything to anybody, especially not Louise or Molly Ariel. I think Phil's having an affair."

"Having an affair?"

"He's just out all the time. He never takes me anywhere. I'm always at home with the kids, all day and all night. He says it's work. I know he plays a lot of dates, and I know he has to meet with musicians and rehearse the pieces he's arranged. A lot of that goes on at night. I know that. It's just that I'm so lonely."

David didn't know what to say. He had been careful to stay out of all this, away from the complications of adult lives. The more you knew, the worse it was. That's what he thought. If you didn't know, then you didn't have to think about it, but once you knew, then you felt like you had to do something.

"There's nothing you can do, David," Elizabeth said. "It's good to have you here. It makes me happy, and it makes the kids happy. Maybe he's not having an affair. I don't know. But he sure doesn't have any love for me these days."

David ate while she talked and picked at her food.

"Tomorrow's Thanksgiving," he said.

"I know, but there sure isn't one hell of a lot to be thankful for this year."

"It'll be better," he said.

"That's what Mommy used to say, and look what happened to her."

But things were better in the morning. Alex and Maggie came running down the hall and jumped on David, and he made his monster face, and started clumping down the hall like Frankenstein. They screamed with joy and ran back to their room, David following slowly arms stiffly out from his sides. But in their room he relented when he saw they were really scared. He lifted Maggie up and hugged her and said in his own voice, "Look at you, how big you are!"

"I big," she said.

"I big too," said Alex, copying her baby talk.

"You're HUGE, Alex," said David. "You're almost big enough to play for the Yankees."

"I hit the ball far. Over the fence. Home run," said Alex and ran around the room like he was rounding the bases. His pajamas were white with black stripes and a Number 5 on the back.

"Joe DiMaggio," said David.

"Go Joe!" said Alex, and David picked him up and hugged him.

After breakfast he took them up the hill to the playground behind the elementary school, where Alex would go in another year. He pushed them on the swings, and watched them go down the slides, while big kids rattled basketballs into rusty baskets with chain nets. Everything in the playground looked old or tired or beat up. "I think we'll move," Elizabeth had said to David at dinner. "I don't want the kids to go to school here. Maybe Phil can find work in L.A. The music business is good out there. It would be much better for us."

David hadn't said anything in response. He'd just nodded his head in understanding, but it scared him. Somehow it wouldn't be right for them to move, especially so far away. How would he get to California? Even if he could get there, how could he afford it? He couldn't ask Molly to pay his way. She'd already done enough for him. No, David didn't want to think about their moving.

It was a good Thanksgiving. The oven worked, the turkey was brown, the kids didn't break any dishes, and Phil was in a good mood for once. When David offered to baby sit, he smiled and said he'd like to take his wife out for a date. Elizabeth smiled, and they went back to the bedroom to change, while David started on the dishes. He told them goodbye and locked the door when they went out. The kids didn't care. Life with "Unca Dave" could be pretty good, and when Elizabeth and Phil came in at eleven the kids hadn't been asleep for more than an hour, but they didn't have to know that. David and the kids had read stories and built castles with blocks, and knocked them down. They had created machines and robots with the new erector set Alex had been given by Aunt Louise, who felt that toys should be educational. It was too old for him, but with David doing most of the work, he could build whatever he wanted.

When he woke on Friday morning, David felt a sense of contentment. Maybe things weren't as bad with Elizabeth and Phil as she had suggested Wednesday night. Phil was up and dressed in his best suit, off to work downtown, and he kissed Elizabeth goodbye at the door with a big smile and picked the kids up and hugged each one. Maybe they were all right, maybe they wouldn't have to move to California, at least not yet. There was, for the moment, a kind of fragile peace. That was it, David thought. He liked the phrase. He would have to write a poem with that title.

At Grand Central Station he checked his bag in a locker and stood at Gate 26 waiting for the New Haven local. He thought of his mother, and the time when he was eleven he had come in on the train from Lowell School for his weekend. He thought of how terrified he had been when she wasn't there, how slowly it had penetrated his consciousness that he was on his own. He wondered what he would have done if Elizabeth had not answered the phone. Alone in New York at eleven, what could a person do? There was a place called Travelers Aid. He could have gone there, but then what would they have done? Called the school, kept him somewhere overnight and put him on the train back to school in the morning? He tried to imagine.

Then, suddenly, a voice he recognized, "Hey, Butter Rum."

He turned. "Oh my God," he said, "Terry Roche."

Anthony S. Abbott

There was Terry, blonder and handsomer than ever, with his big, goofy grin, standing six feet away. They moved slowly, almost unbelievingly toward each other, then stood and hugged and hugged, rocking back and forth.

"Jesus," said Terry, "I thought I'd never see you again."

"Me, too," said David.

"I'm sorry I didn't write," said Terry.

"Me, too," said David, and they both laughed. For a moment they stood there in silence, just looking at each other, neither knowing quite what to say.

"Where you going?" David asked.

"To New Haven, to my cousin's for the weekend, then back to school."

"When are you leaving?"

"As soon as the local gets in. They just turn the seats around and it goes back."

"Back by Port Chester, and the Life Saver factory," said David.

"Yeah, I know. I think of it every time I go by there."

"What about Griff?"

"I don't know."

"You don't know? I thought, if anyone would know, you would."

"Griff is strange."

"But why?" David started, but he really didn't know how to continue. He looked at Terry, then looked away, toward the waiting room where he had searched for his mother that time.

There was an odd silence, which Terry broke.

"It's all right, Butter Rum. It's just. . ."

"Just what?" David asked.

"Just. . .I don't know." And then, "You doing any plays?"

"No," said David.

"Me neither."

Then from the track a familiar figure. It was Tracy Warren striding toward them with her long polo coat open, her black skirt down to her leather boots, her breasts moving slightly under her white sweater, red scarf hanging loosely around her neck.

"God," said Terry, "I know her."

"You know Tracy Warren?"

"She was at Deerfield this fall with a senior. I don't really know her, I just saw her."

Terry stuck out his hand. "Hi, Tracy Warren," he said. "I'm Terry."

"Terry," she said softly. "Oh my God, not that Terry?"

"Yes," he said, "that Terry."

"The one who stood up when David got the prize," she murmured.

"That's me," he smiled.

David didn't know what to say. Here were his two favorite people in the world standing there talking to each other, and they had met at Deerfield.

"Terry, why don't you. . ." David started.

"No, Dave, I gotta go. Nice to meet you, Tracy." Terry paused, picked up his bag, and turned toward the gate, then back. "You still got that bag with M.H. on it?"

"Oh, yes," said David.

"See you around, Butter Rum."

"Till the next time, Cherry," said David, and then he turned to Tracy Warren.

"He said you were at Deerfield this fall."

"I was."

"But you didn't tell me."

"You didn't ask. Maybe you did some things I don't know about. It doesn't matter. We're together now. That's all that matters."

"It just seems so weird you're being at Deerfield and meeting Terry and not knowing who he was."

"I know. But let's not think about it tonight. Tonight is for us." She opened her arms to him. "Give me a hug," she said, "and let's just have a good time, OK?"

"OK," he said, and they walked slowly up the stairs to Vanderbilt Avenue and out into the evening.

Later they stood in front of the skating rink at Rockefeller Center. They had gone to dinner at the Automat, David's favorite restaurant in New York. It wasn't something he did very often, and it certainly wasn't very romantic, at least on the surface, but he was mesmerized by the idea, by the nickels you placed in the slots for each dish. He liked not having to give his order to a waiter, but just walking from window to window and looking at the dish inside, then slipping the requisite number of nickels in the slot, turning the handle, and hearing the click when the door opened. He liked the little pots of macaroni and cheese or spaghetti, and so did Tracy—or at least she seemed to. They raced around the room, their pockets full of nickels picking what they liked, then carried their trays up to the balcony where it was easier to talk.

"So tell me about seeing Terry," she said, throwing her coat on the back of her chair and the scarf on top of it. "I only heard the end of it."

"He just appeared," said David, "like Hamlet's ghost, but smiling as if we'd seen each other yesterday. I was so glad to see him, and then. . ."

"And then?" she asked.

"And then, it was like we could never be friends again. . . As if our friendship was in a glass bowl and it couldn't exist outside of it."

"Maybe he's right. . .the magic would be gone."

"But still. . ."

"Don't you see, David, that's why we're so special. We don't belong to your school or my school, we don't belong to anybody or anyplace. We just are. . .outside of time and space. . .we create ourselves. That's what's so beautiful . . .anywhere, any time, all we need is just us."

"But you went to Deerfield."

"David, David, David, David, David," she murmured. "You don't understand. That doesn't count. It means nothing. Girls go to boys schools for dances, for weekends. It has nothing to do with us. Didn't you meet any girls this summer?"

David reddened. He hadn't told her about Jill and Margie. "Sort of," he said.

"Come on, brother of mine," she laughed. "Out with it."

And so he told her, haltingly at first and then laughing at himself for his own ineptness.

"But you missed your chance, didn't you?" she asked.

"I guess so."

"You guess so. You drink two beers and then let Auntie Louise tell you off, and you don't see the girl again. That's more than 'I guess so.'"

"But Tracy."

"No buts, brother of mine. We have to live every day."

David looked at her, her face across the table from him. And he saw the scar.

"You want to know about this?" she asked.

"Yes."

She took his left hand and placed his index finger on the thin line. He could feel the small edge of the scar as he traced its length across her cheek bone.

"It was a knife," she said. "He could have cut my eye. He missed."

"But how?"

"I told you that I used to go to Greenwich high school. I ran with a pretty rough crowd. I liked it, David. I hated the prissy little kids. The rough ones had more life, more energy. I don't know. A guy was taunting me, and I said something, and he swiped me with the knife. It scared him. I think he meant to miss. My family moved me to Country Day, where I would be safe. No more street kids. I have you instead."

"Let's go to the Music Hall," he said suddenly. "I want to take you to see the Christmas show at the Music Hall. We can sit upstairs in the balcony, way up, and hold hands, and watch the Rockettes and listen to the organ. I've never taken anyone there. No one will know. Just us."

"That's better," she said. "That's more like it." And she kissed him, right there in the balcony of the automat in front of all those people.

They walked up Fifth Avenue and across 50th Street to the Radio City Music Hall and sat in the balcony for the stage show and the movie. David put his arm around her shoulders, and she took his hand with hers and placed it on her breast and held it there for what seemed a long time. Then she took his hand and kissed it, and he let it rest easily on her shoulder. He completely lost track of the picture.

When the show was over they walked to the skating rink. It was closed for the night, and the few others who were passing by just looked and walked on, but Tracy wanted to stay. "Come on," she said, "let's go out on the ice. Let's pretend we're skating."

"But we can't," said David. "They'll kick us off."

"Who?" she said. "Do you see anybody there? Come on, be brave." And she lifted one long leg and then the other over the wooden barrier, and began to slide on the ice. David followed her and caught her, and they spun crazily and fell, then got up and slid, step by step to the other side.

"Look up," she said, and he looked up and saw the snow begin to fall.

They stood and looked at the snow, and stuck out their tongues and let the snow fall into their eyes and onto their tongues, and they held each other there for a long time, before they climbed back over the wall and walked to Grand Central in time for the last train to Greenwich.

When they got home, the house seemed asleep. It was one-thirty in the morning, and only the small light by the front hall table was on with a note next to it. "Welcome kids," it said. "Turn off the light so we'll know you're home."

They went down to the playroom and sat on the couch in front of the fireplace. Tracy put a log on, and smoke began to curl around it from the remnants of the evening's fire.

"Your parents are so trusting," David said. "I can't get over it, how they let you do whatever you want."

"Not with everyone," she said. "Because it was you, they let me stay out late tonight. They trust you, too. They're probably awake upstairs. My dad always stays awake until he hears the car come in the drive. Then he knows I'm OK and he can go to sleep."

"And I don't even know how to drive."

"You will, when you need to."

"Thank you," he said suddenly, "thank you for being you."

"Sweetheart," she said and turned to him, and they began to kiss, more passionately than they ever had before. She opened her mouth, and whispered to him. Their tongues touched and their hands touched places through their clothes they had not touched before, and at the end when they finished she placed her hand over his mouth so his cry would not wake her parents.

The next day they slept late and had Saturday brunch and told the family about Music Hall and the skating rink and the snow.

"It snowed when I came last Christmas," David said. "I guess I'm good luck, if you like snow. Driving from the station to the house, you could hardly see the sides of the road. It was like we were the only ones in the world." He looked at Tracy.

"We were," she said.

In the afternoon he played chess with Butch, while Tracy watched and gave suggestions.

"I used to be really good when I was little," David said. He told them about the camp and then about playing chess with Mr. Hackett at Lowell. "His nickname was Rabbit," David said, "and some of the kids called him the Sick Rabbit."

"Why?" asked Butch.

"Because he—I didn't really understand this at all when I knew him—but Terry told me our sixth form year it was because he—because he liked boys."

"Liked boys? What does that mean?" asked Butch.

Tracy laughed. "I hope he didn't like you too much, David."

"No, I didn't know about it at all. He never did anything to me."

"Maybe he never did anything to anybody. Maybe the boys just made that up," said Tracy.

"Made up what?" Butch asked. "I still don't understand."

"That's OK, you will some day," said Tracy.

CHAPTER TWELVE

David returned for the winter term with renewed energy. The first day back Mr. Benson returned their essays on *The Scarlet Letter*, and David got his first A. "Brilliant job, David," the comment said. "This is the kind of work I had expected from you. I like the way you combine textual analysis with personal insights. Some splendid writing." His essay, like his poem, had been based on the character of Pearl as the living embodiment of the Scarlet Letter, Pearl as Dimmesdale's conscience. David had tried for the first time to wrestle with something he didn't really know the answer to, and as a result he had written a more original essay. He had explored answers rather than sticking with the safe path. Father Perkins had been right.

The next day he went down to the gym and tried out for the wrestling team. It was something he had thought about for some time. He really hated hockey, and there was no reason for him to suffer outdoors in the cold and get blisters on his Achilles tendons from the skates when he could be doing a sport that he might be better suited for. Mr. Benson was one of the wrestling coaches, and David had approached him after class about trying out.

"We'll be glad to have you, lad," his teacher had said. "But you better be prepared to be more tired than you ever have in your life. There's nothing more strenuous than three minutes of wrestling."

David found that out quickly enough. They started out practicing holds, the younger and newer wrestlers being paired with the more experienced ones, who taught them sit-throughs and half nelsons and leg drops and then made them practice these holds over and over until they were almost rote. David loved the practices, and he learned quickly to take advantage of his strong arms and shoulders. He could drop to the mat like a cat, grab an opponent's legs, and wrestle him to the ground. He could turn an opponent over, driving him with his shoulder onto his back, flipping him with his half nelson. What he couldn't do was last very long. He had played soccer for three years, but soccer was nothing like this. In practice matches, he would be exhausted by the third period and he would feel his opponents doing things to him that he knew perfectly well how to stop. It was as if he wasn't there, as if someone else were in his body, and he had lost control of it.

"You better do some running to build up your wind and strengthen your legs." Mr. Benson told him. "You tend to wrestle with your arms and shoulders. You need to drive with your legs, push with your whole body. You can't do it with your upper body alone."

He and Wally Hinson's roommate, Ted Barber, started running together. He liked Ted, but hadn't really gotten to know him. Ted had transferred to Wicker from Salisbury, where he lived most of the year, but he also had a house in Florida, where his family went after Christmas. Ted wrestled in the 177-pound class, and rowed on the JV. crew in the spring. He was strong and smart, and unlike Wally Hinson, he was a hard worker. They talked while they ran, and it made the time pass. One Sunday in February, his mother drove over to Wicker and took David and Wally Hinson back to their house in Salisbury for Sunday dinner. It was fun being away from school, if only for a few hours, and for a while David let himself relax. He and Ted and Wally decided they would go to Princeton and room together.

"Fat chance you have of getting into Princeton," said Ted to Wally.

"Hell, I'm a legacy. My dad went to Princeton."

"Yeah, but your grades really stink."

"I can do better any time I want," said Wally Hinson, "and D.J. here can help me if I need it, can't you, old buddy?"

David laughed. "You'll have to make the honor roll if you want to study in your room. The only way I can help you is if we're both in the dorm together."

"Well, I'm not going to make the fucking honor roll until we finish reading *Moby-Dick*. That's the stupidest book I've ever read. It goes on forever. Jesus, who cares about all the different kinds of whales anyway?"

David loved *Moby-Dick*, and he loved the way Mr. Benson taught it. The weather was cold, and the steam radiators chugged and hissed and clanged, and Bad News Benson would pace fiercely up and down at the front of the room. He was Captain Ahab himself, hunting his implacable enemy, the White Whale, who had maliciously bitten off his leg. Ahab paced the quarterdeck on his ivory leg. Bad News Benson paced and puffed on his pipe, and sometimes he brought his dog to class, his brown boxer, Max, and the dog would lie by the radiator and fart, and the room would fill with the smell of the dog's farts, but no one would laugh, at least not until they got out of the room at the end of class. They would stagger down the hall laughing and gasping for breath. It was awful, still there was this aura of excitement as the book approached its climax, Benson taking them forward step by step, getting them to argue about who was right, Ahab or Starbuck, the first mate.

"The whale is just a dumb brute. That's what Starbuck says. Ahab sees the whale as a kind of angry God," said Mr. Benson.

"Ahab is full of it," said Wally Hinson.

"Full of what, Mr. Hinson?" asked Benson, puffing on his pipe.

"Bull, full of bull, sir," said Wally Hinson.

"The hunt for Moby-Dick gives his life meaning," said David.

"Go on," said Mr. Benson.

"If he didn't have the whale, he'd have nothing to live for. It's not just any whale. He doesn't care about making money. He cares about figuring out the meaning of the universe."

"Meaning of the universe," said Dennis Vogler. "That's a big one."

"The Whiteness of the Whale," said Antonio Black cryptically.

"What about it?" asked Mr. Benson.

"It shows us that Melville meant the whale to be a symbol."

"Right," said David, "and we see that again in 'The Quarterdeck.'"

"Strike through the mask," said Ralph Wisdom, who then proceeded to quote from memory the whole passage that ended with those words.

David remembered that winter later as one of his favorite times at Wicker. It was as if, for the first time, he was really there, almost all the time. The rhythm of his days was pure. Class in the morning, wrestling in the afternoon, homework or debate or writing for the newspaper at night. His only problem was finding a topic for his final English essay.

He was trying to figure out why he was so sympathetic to Ahab, despite the fact that Ahab was so clearly wrong--he was a murderer-- his crazy desire for vengeance caused the death of his entire crew, but that surely wasn't Melville's point. David remembered the passage Ralph Wisdom had memorized: "Hark ye, yet again, the little lower layer. . .all visible objects are but pasteboard masks." The words stayed with him. The whale was a symbol to Ahab, a symbol of God's injustice. Ahab was like Job, protesting against the cruelty of things, the pain of things.

But they were different. That was it—he would write about Ahab and Job, how they were alike and how different. He found a book in the library called *Melville's Use of the Bible* by Nathalia Wright, and he began reading it. At first he was excited. He learned that Ahab was named for Ahab, the seventh king of Israel, and Ishmael for the son of Abraham and Hagar who was banished with his mother to the wilderness because Sarah did not want him competing with her son, Isaac. Some of these things they had talked about in class, but it was not until David saw them in the book that he realized their importance. Melville had read the Bible, he had named his characters for Biblical characters because he expected his readers to pick up the echoes. But David didn't really know the Bible that well, and neither did anyone else in the class, and so they missed the meanings. The more he read and the more notes he took, the more complicated everything got. His original idea got lost in the pile of parallels.

Still he loved what he had discovered, and he loved wrestling with ideas, and the fact that he didn't have an answer to his original question didn't discourage him.

He was approaching his seventeenth birthday, one more birthday that no one would remember except for Molly Ariel, who always remembered everything. She would send him a check for $100, signed "Affectionately, Molly." Like David, she never said, "Love." It was interesting. Elizabeth would remember later, and send a card, and Aunt Louise would laugh and say that birthdays were unimportant. But she would write him all the family news, and even if she didn't think birthdays important, David knew that she thought he was important. She would tell him about Uncle Swen's new show in New York and send him clippings from the *Times*. She would tell him what his father was doing, and why she was worried about Elizabeth and Phil living in the Bronx.

With Aunt Louise there, David felt less obligated to worry about his family. It was as if she had things under control. He could simply be at school, and when his birthday came, he would just be silent and let it pass. It was better that way.

More important was Lent. Easter was early this year, and at Wicker classes were delayed by an hour on Ash Wednesday so that everyone could go to St. Matthew's Chapel for a special service. On Ash Wednesday, Father Perkins said, we wore ashes on our foreheads to remind us of our mortality. "Ashes to ashes and dust to dust." Why "ashes," and why "dust" David asked himself, and Father Perkins answered in his sermon.

"Our text for this morning," said the Headmaster, "is Genesis 2:7: 'The Lord God formed a human being from the dust of the ground and breathed into his nostrils the breath of life, so that he became a living creature.' What an extraordinary text this is, gentlemen—this one verse."

The Headmaster paused for a long time, and stood still, so still that it was if he had stopped breathing. David could not see him as well as he had during his first two years. Each year you moved back, until you became a sixth former and were allowed to sit in wonderful carved wooden seats along the side. As a fifth former, close to the rear, he could not see the Headmaster's expressions in the same way that he had, and he missed that closer view. Still, he was frightened by the silence, the stillness.

"Did you hear the silence, my young friends?" the Headmaster finally said. "That was the silence of death. Now, take a deep breath. Go ahead, a really deep breath. Then let it out, slowly. Hear the air, the wind, go out, and then back in again. The Hebrew word for wind is 'Ruah,' and it is the same word as the word for breath. 'Ruah' is wind, and it is also the breath of God, without which we have no existence. It is that simple. Without 'Ruah' we are as dust, as ashes. If you stop breathing, you are dead. If God is not in you, if the breath of the living God is not in you, then you are as death itself, like stone, like ashes, like dust."

Except for the flickering of the candles, the chapel was dark, and at the end of the service, as each student came forward to receive the ashes, David felt the darkness. He knelt at the rail and looked forward. There was Father Perkins and his sidekick, Father Andrew North, Daddy Drew, as the students called him. There, under the flickering red light that signaled the presence of the Eucharist, sat the man they called Pater immobile in his wheelchair, his head slumped down, the saliva dripping from his bottom lip. A student with a handkerchief wiped it. The darkness was palpable. David liked that word. It meant, *able to be touched*. He knelt at the rail, bowed his head and closed his eyes.

Father Perkins approached him, and made the sign of the cross on David's head with the ashes.

"The breath of God be in you, David Johnson," he said.

David was stunned. He could not be mistaken. Over and over afterwards he wondered if he had dreamed it, but it was real. Father Perkins had said that to him, but by the time David opened his

Anthony S. Abbott

eyes, the Headmaster had moved on to someone else, and he could not be sure.

That night he went down to Ralph Wisdom and Dennis Vogler's room, and he went in and closed the door behind him. "I need to talk to you both," he said, "about something really strange."

Ralph was writing at his desk, and Dennis was stretched out on his bed, reading. David sat on Ralph's bed and told them what had happened.

"He does that sometimes," said Ralph Wisdom, "at early morning communion. He will see someone who he thinks is particularly needy, and he will hold the cup to the boy's lips and say, 'The blood of God, James Francis, or whatever the boy's name is.'"

"So it wasn't just something I imagined."

"Oh, no," said Dennis Vogler. "He did it to me last spring near the end of the year. I'd gotten a letter from home saying my sister was in the hospital with pneumonia, and I was really down and thought communion might help, and he came up to me and put his hand on my head, and said, 'The love of God, Dennis Benjamin.' I almost started crying right there."

"And your sister?" asked David.

"She got better."

"For JAP," said Ralph Wisdom, "God is not just an idea, He's a real presence."

"But why me? Why today?"

"Because he knows you are needy."

"But how does he know?"

"He just knows," they said together, and both of them laughed.

David was needy. What he needed was to figure out Tracy Warren. It was driving him crazy. He really didn't know her. First there was the Deerfield thing, and then her story about the scar. He was sure there was more, but he wasn't sure how much he wanted to know. It was like the Yankees, he thought. If you didn't know the score of the game, it was always possible that they had won. He'd rather not know than know they had lost. He had tried to find out something over Christmas vacation.

They were in the playroom, downstairs, in front of the fire, lying back on the couch, smoking. Their hands touched easily with a quiet familiarity.

"My mom says I jump into conversations at level four," she said suddenly.

"What is level four? I never heard of it," David said.

"You haven't heard of it because you don't read psychology books." Tracy laughed, and kissed him on the cheek. "Listen to me a minute.

"She says that there are five levels of conversation. One is like 'nice day'—polite weather talk. Two is information—current events and stuff like that. Three is talk about friends and family. Four is deep—it's about what you're really feeling and thinking. Five is life changing."

"You're life changing for me," he said.

"I know," she smiled, "but I like hearing you say it." She took a puff and smiled and then went on. "Shit, where was I?"

"My mom says there are five levels," David echoed.

"Ok—level four. I know. You need me because I'm the only one that you can really talk to and feel safe, but I'm not always going to be there. You can jump in at level four with someone else. You have to get your radar out and test that person. If it's right you'll know. Don't think too much about it. If you do, you'll just find reasons not to do it."

David felt brave. "OK, level four," he said. "Tell me about you. Do you date other guys?"

"What do you mean, other guys?"

"Besides me."

"But you're not a date, you're my blood brother."

"OK. Do you date guys?"

"Yes."

"Do you kiss them? Do you let them touch you?"

"Yes, sometimes, if I feel like it."

"Do you enjoy it?"

"Most of the time."

"And do you ever feel guilty, like you're cheating?"

"Wait a minute, wait just a minute. What is this? I'm not married to you. What do you mean cheating? Don't be so possessive, David. You don't own me. I like kissing. If I'm with a boy, and he's a good kisser and I like him, then we kiss. It doesn't change how I feel about you. Don't you see?"

But David didn't see, and he really wanted to talk to someone about Tracy.

So he picked Ralph Wisdom and Dennis Vogler because his radar said it was right. He started going down to Ralph and Dennis's room in the evenings after study hall, or after debate, and the three of them, and sometimes Ted Barber, would sit on the beds or the floor and just, as they said, "have bull sessions."

But the thing never happened. As close as he felt to Ralph and Dennis in some ways, he could never bring himself to talk about Tracy to them. He thought about Griff and Terry and his friendship with them at Lowell School, how they had been inseparable, how their club had sustained him during his years there. He would have told them. But this was entirely different. It began falling together for him. It was not an issue of friendship, but an issue of the class. At Lowell, he had never had a sense of his class as a group, but at Wicker the class was everything, because of the exciting and terrible responsibility of the sixth form in running the school. Everything in the school depended on the quality of the sixth form. What Ralph and Dennis were interested in talking about was not girls, it was the class. The Tracy question would have to wait.

David's class was preparing itself for that moment when they would assume leadership, and they wanted to be the best sixth form in the school's history. Friendship was subordinate to the class. The class was everything, and Ralph Wisdom was the leader of the class. He was shaping it for the changeover that would take place in the spring. The breath of God was in him and in Dennis Vogler and in David, and they would use it to turn Wicker from Kansas into Oz. That was it. They would transform the school.

They talked about it in Ralph and Dennis's room at night, and they talked about it in class meetings in the Headmaster's study. They talked about the relationship between the sixth form and the rest of the school and how the sixth formers continued to abuse their privileges. They couldn't do anything official about it until the transfer of power, but they could think about what they wanted to do.

Wicker had improved vastly since David's early days, when the sixth formers roamed the halls like barbarians on the streets of Rome in the waning days of the empire. Father Perkins had put an end to the rampant abuses of those times. There was no more running the gauntlet, being flicked by the sharp edges of towels, no more turning of second and third formers' rooms inside out in search of contraband, no more swats with split baseball bats. But there were subtle abuses, which not even Father Perkins could control if there was no real leadership at the top. The senior prefect was the key, and then the other prefects who would, in turn, take their example from him.

Ralph Wisdom had a vision of what Wicker School could be if the sixth formers took their duties seriously, and during those winter and spring nights he and Dennis and David and any others that happened into Ralph and Dennis's room tossed his ideas back and forth.

"It's all about respect," said Wally Hinson one night. No one took Wally Hinson seriously, not even Wally himself. The idea of respecting Wally was sort of a joke, but Ralph turned it into something else.

"You have to earn respect," he said. "You don't get respect just because you wear a badge of office."

"You mean like Douglas MacArthur?" said Dennis Vogler slyly.

Everyone in the room laughed, because they knew that Douglas MacArthur was Ralph Wisdom's hero. Ralph knew everything about MacArthur's career from his graduation at West Point first in his class to his appointment as Commander-in-Chief of the UN forces in Korea.

"MacArthur's in deep shit," said Ted Barber.

"Indeed," said Ralph Wisdom, who could imitate MacArthur's voice and his walk, his long easy strides. MacArthur had just been relieved of his duties by President Harry S. Truman, and he was on his way home. He had openly criticized the President and the Chiefs of Staff, and that could not be tolerated. So America's most beloved leader had been ignominiously sacked.

"There can only be one President," said Ralph Wisdom. "Even MacArthur must bow to that, and he didn't. It was sad, but necessary. Still, that does not in any way reduce MacArthur's magnificence as a general."

"We all know he can walk on water," said Ted Barber.

"He did, when he came back to the Philippines," said David.

Three nights later, on April 19, 1951, General MacArthur was to speak to a joint session of Congress, and on that evening Ralph Wisdom was nowhere to be seen.

"He's gone home to watch the speech on television. You can be sure of that," said Dennis Vogler. "He'll be back by lights out."

And he was. The word passed quickly down the hall that he had returned, and his friends, mostly in their pajamas, filled his room.

"It was," said Ralph Wisdom somberly, "one of the great speeches in the history of the United States." He put up his hand for silence, and then he began:

"The earth has turned over many times since I took the oath on the plains at West Point, and the hopes and dreams have long since vanished, but I still remember the refrain of one of the most popular barracks ballads of that day, which proclaimed, most proudly, that old soldiers never die; they just fade away.

"And like the old soldier of that ballad, I now close my military career and just fade away, an old soldier who tried to do his duty as God gave him the light to see that duty. Good-bye."

There was a quaver in Ralph Wisdom's voice, as he spoke the final words, but was it his quaver, or MacArthur's? It didn't matter. The imitation of the General was so grand, so perfect, so immediate that the entire room was spellbound into silence. For a moment no one spoke, and then someone, maybe Wally Hinson, began to clap, and then others, and pretty soon everyone in the room was standing up and clapping.

One of the sixth-form prefects stuck his head in the room and asked what was going on?

"It's OK, Jack," said Kosmo, the Pole. "We're just fading away."

Sometime around the first of May, rumor began to circulate around the school that MacArthur himself would be stopping on his way somewhere. The students were to assemble in the North Dorm parking lot at 9 p.m. for the General's appearance. It would be brief. Sure enough, on the given night, just before the appointed hour, a series of cars drove across the bridge from town and turned into the school. In the third car, an open convertible, stood the General, in uniform, his famous sunglasses on, his pipe in hand, his free hand waving in his own special manner. He spoke briefly, the voice unmistakable, and then the cars turned and drove away, disappearing into the night from which they had come.

It was astounding. David and Wally Hinson and Billy DuPont and Ted Barber cheered furiously as the motorcade drove away. They looked around for Ralph Wisdom, but he was nowhere to be seen. Of course, he was nowhere to be seen. He had fooled them all.

And so the legend grew, and when the day came in mid-May for the graduating sixth form to turn over its power to the incoming class, the coronation of Ralph Wisdom was no more than a formality. The prefects, one by one, descended the stairs from the stage and walked out into the auditorium in search of their successors. Each came up behind the appointed person and tapped him on the shoulder. Hugh Packard, the new captain of the soccer team, was tapped, as was Ted Barber, who would stroke the crew his senior year. David was tapped by the Editor of the *Wicker Sentinel* as his successor, and Dennis Vogler was tapped as the Sacristan, the sixth former who was in charge of St. Matthew's Chapel.

When Ralph Wisdom was finally tapped, as the climax of the evening, the student body rose as one, and cheered. The new prefects took their seats on the stage, and the turnover was complete.

David was thrilled to be the new Editor of the *Sentinel*. He had worked hard during the year, writing articles, revising other students' work, and writing headlines every Sunday afternoon in the news room in the attic of the library. He had walked down to J.K. Richardson's house for tea when the Editors took the paper down to him for his final perusal, and he had been trained in every aspect of the paper's operation, except for advertisements, which he really knew nothing about. He picked his staff with care. Dennis Vogler would be his assistant editor in charge of the front page, Antonio Black would write the editorials, Billy DuPont would be the Sports Editor, and Borden Smith the photography editor. David divided the news room into sections, and each section worked on a page. David went from section to section, giving suggestions, and helping the page editors with particular problems.

On the Sunday they were working on their last issue of the spring, Kosmo came up to him. "D.J.," he said. "Let's go for a walk. I need to talk to you."

David didn't know Kosmo very well, but he liked him. He was the funniest guy in the class. He had a gift for satire and parody. He could imitate all the masters, and even the Headmaster. He lived in Doylestown, Pennsylvania, which was about ten miles from New Hope, where David had worked when he spent the summer with Aunt Louise. Kosmo had come into the restaurant a couple of times with friends. Once he had invited David over to spend the day with his family, but David hadn't been able to go.

They walked around the triangle.

"I want to work for you," Kosmo said. "You need something to juice the paper up. No offense, but it's kind of boring."

"So?"

"So, I write a weekly humor column, no name, no by-line, and no one knows who writes it."

"People will guess."

"No they won't. Hell, no one thinks I can do anything like that. I won't even be on the news staff. You save me the space."

"Suppose I don't like it."

"You will. I promise you. Here it is, the first one."

David opened it. It was called "The Silver Sphere."

"Why 'The Silver Sphere'?"

"I don't know. It just came to me."

"Suppose JKR doesn't like it?"

"He will. There's enough crap in the paper for the alumni. This is for the students."

David took the column from Kosmo. As he read it, he laughed out loud. "Not bad for a dumb Polack," David said.

"You ain't seen nothin' yet," said Kosmo.

They shook hands.

Kosmo beamed. "You passed the test. Now get back to the peons, and send my regards to JKR. I never could understand all his goddamn comma rules, but he's a good guy."

And so "The Silver Sphere" made its debut, and Kosmo was right. Nobody suspected it was him. There were all kinds of guesses. Some of them thought it was Bad News Benson writing in the style of a student. Some thought it was Wally Hinson because he had that kind of humor, and there wasn't much they could do about finding out, because it was the end of the term and exams were starting. The hunt for the Sphere's identity would have to wait for fall.

The day after the paper came out, Kosmo came into David's room during their morning free period. Borden, as usual, was in the library.

"Listen, D.J.," said Kosmo. "I got a great idea."

David laughed. "I don't know if I can stand another one."

"I'm serious," he said. "How about if you come spend the summer with me at my house. My dad's got pull, and he can get you and me and my brothers jobs with the State Highway. We earn money, you have some place to stay, and my family won't kick me out of here."

"Kick you out of here?"

"My dad says I can't come back unless I develop more disciplined habits. Those were his words—'more disciplined habits.'"

"So where do I come in?"

"Christ, D.J., you're famous. The goddam paper goes home to all the parents. You're in it for something every week. I might well start calling you C.C."

"C.C.?"

Anthony S. Abbott

"Columbia Cup. Come on, don't act like an asshole. You got the cup locked up. Hell, the only person who could beat you out is Father Wisdom, and prefects aren't eligible. My dad thinks you'll be a good influence on me—teach me disciplined fucking habits."

He laughed. "Well, what do you say?"

"I like it," said David. "I like it very much."

"Good fucking deal," said Kosmo, and walked out. Then he opened the door again. "My mom and dad will make the arrangements."

"Wait a minute," said David. "What arrangements?"

"You know, all that adult crap, where so-and-so calls so-and-so and then Mrs. Such-and-Such writes to Dr. Whatsisname, and they all agree. My mom and dad know your aunt and uncle. He's famous. They've already talked about it."

"If I spend the summer with you, everyone will figure out you're the Sphere."

"No, they won't, not unless you tell 'em."

CHAPTER THIRTEEN

"It's all about the shared secret," said Tracy Warren.

"The shared secret? Where do you get these phrases?" David asked.

They were lying in the sun at the beach. It was their last day together before David left for Lambertville and then Doylestown for the summer. David loved the sun, he had always loved the sun—the sun and the beach and the water—even from the time he was little. His dark skin tanned easily, and after three or four days he looked as if he had spent a summer at the beach.

"You like Kosmo because you have a shared secret. That's like level five stuff. You and me. We have a shared secret."

"We certainly do."

"If you trust somebody with a secret it ups the ante."

"Right."

"Then the friendship has more value. If you have the power to break the pact, then you can hurt someone. If you can hurt someone, then the trust really means something."

"I don't have a shared secret with Ralph."

"Yes you do. You have that thing about the Headmaster saying, 'Breath of God, David Johnson.' That was wonderful. You went in and told him about the Headmaster saying that."

"I would rather have told you."

"Of course, but I wasn't there."

David pushed himself up and turned toward her. She was lying with her eyes closed, her small breasts almost flat as she lay on her back, her straps down, a touch of white showing between the top of her bathing suit and the tan of her neck and shoulders. David bent over and kissed her there on that white, and her arms reached up and held him.

He took her sun glasses off and looked in her eyes. "I'm afraid I'm going to lose you," he said.

She sat up, pulling up her straps, and put her glasses back on. "We've been through this before," she said. "I'm tired of this, David. I don't want to have this conversation again."

"But we won't see each other all summer."

"We didn't see each other last summer."

"That was different."

"How was it different?"

"You're older now, you're more. . .more beautiful."

"So you're jealous?"

"No."

"Then what do you call this?"

"Insecurity."

"But you know the rules. . .we ARE. Don't you know that? We ARE. Nothing else IS in the same way. It's not a game. It's not something to be tested. It just IS. Do you believe that?"

Suddenly, as he faced her there on the beach, he felt cold. He was looking over her shoulder toward the water, and there was a woman who seemed to be his mother walking toward them. She wore sunglasses, like Tracy's, but her hair was curly and brown, and her skin was pale. She wore a white beach robe over her bathing suit, and she carried something in her right hand. "Help me, Maggie Hope," he said to himself. He closed his eyes and opened them again. The woman was gone.

"Hey, Mister, where are you?" Tracy's voice brought him back.

"I don't know," he said. "I'm scared."

"Of what?"

"I just saw my mother walking down the beach toward us."

"Maggie Hope?"

"She was there, and then she was gone. I think she wanted to tell me something."

"About me?"

"Maybe, about you."

"What?"

"To warn me."

"What?"

"Not to love you too much."

"And. . .?"

"And what?"

"And if you do. . ."

"I don't know."

"I do."

"So tell me."

"You want me all to yourself. You think that's love, but it isn't."

"Why not?"

"Oh come on, David. You know."

"I don't."

"It's just ownership. You can't own me."

"I don't want to own you."

"Then let me go. Don't you see, you can't have me unless you let me go. You don't understand that. David, David, David, David, David."

And suddenly he just felt like laughing. "Tracy, Tracy, Tracy, Tracy, Tracy," he said, and then again, laughing, "Tracy, Tracy, Tracy, Tracy, Tracy."

And then she laughed. "Do you know e.e. cummings?"

"Tell me about e.e. cummings," he said.

"He doesn't use capital letters," she said.

"So?"

"He's original. He does everything his own way. We studied a poem of his called 'somewhere I have never traveled.' It was about you and me. I memorized it so I could say it to you. I was saving it for tonight, but I think you need to hear it right now."

And she spoke it to him, line by line, halting a little at places she had almost forgotten, but the halting only made it more beautiful, he thought, as he watched her lips make each word, each sound. At the end he could feel the tears in his eyes under the dark glasses, and he tried to speak, but she put her finger on his mouth and said, "Not yet."

And when it was time, he said, "Say the second stanza again. I want to learn it."

And so she said it, teaching it to him line by line:

"your slightest look easily will unclose me
though I have closed myself as fingers,
you open always petal by petal myself as Spring opens
(touching skillfully, mysteriously)her first rose."

"But that's me," he said. "You are the Spring opening me. I'm the one who's closed. As fingers."

He clenched his fists, and then opened his fingers slowly. "That's what you do to me," he said.

"The voice of your eyes is deeper than all roses," she said. "Stanza five."

"I'll learn the whole thing," he said, and they came together and held each other very close, out there on the blanket on the beach in June in Greenwich, Connecticut, in front of all those people, and David didn't care about the people seeing them or what Tracy did when they weren't together. He just wanted her, right there on the beach, and all he knew was that if he had to let her go in order to have her then he would try.

She had copied the poem for him, and when they got back to the house, they took showers and dressed and came downstairs to have cocktails and dinner with her family, and she gave him the copy of the poem to put in his suitcase and take to New Jersey with him. Her father cooked steaks on the patio, and they sat with Butch and her parents at the table outside in the dusk and ate dinner and talked about baseball and colleges and grades and President Truman and the war in Korea.

"Did you know they booed President Truman in Washington when he threw out the first ball of the baseball season?" said Butch.

"I didn't know that," said David.

"Because they loved MacArthur, and they were really mad when MacArthur was called home," said Mr. Warren.

And David told them the story of MacArthur's visit to Wicker School and how Ralph Wisdom had tricked everyone into believing he was really MacArthur.

They talked about their summers and about the ranch in Wyoming where Tracy would be going as a riding teacher and swimming instructor. Butch would go with her, and the family would come out for two weeks in August.

"That sounds a lot better than the Pennsylvania State Highway Department," David said, and everyone laughed.

Later that night David lay in his bed thinking. He was happy. He loved the rhythm of the family—father, mother, sister, brother. Demon or angel, Tracy was his twin, his other self. They were joined and they would stay joined. Whatever she asked for he would give. Whatever darkness she carried, he would accept. That was it. They were halves of the same person, and he could only find himself by loving her. He was satisfied. But during the night the dream came again. He was on the beach with Tracy. They were laughing, and then the sky darkened and the woman appearing to be Maggie Hope came walking out of the water toward them. "No," she said mournfully, and again, "No" until he woke to his own cries.

It wasn't so bad working for the Pennsylvania State Highway Department. He liked living with the Kosmalskis, or the Spheres, as David thought of them. There was an order, a symmetry, to their lives. Kosmo had an older brother and a younger brother, and each morning promptly at seven the three brothers and David were awakened. They ate breakfast in almost absolute silence in the family dining room, and at eight o'clock Mrs. Sphere gave each of the boys their lunch boxes, and then John, the older brother, drove them in his battered blue Ford to their jobs. David and Kosmo worked in the sign shop, and their main job was to drive all over the county with their teams replacing the signs that had been battered and beaten by weather and drunk drivers. They also put down lines on new roads. On rainy days they stayed indoors in the shop and did whatever the boss told them, usually as little as possible.

The most fun was riding in the truck. The boss drove, and his sidekick, Eddie, sat up front. David and Kosmo rode in the back with Elmer and Frankie. It was a whole new experience for David, meeting what Kosmo called "the great unwashed." Elmer and Frankie must have been in their forties, and they had worked for the State Highway all their adult lives. Elmer was bald and a little soft around the middle, kind of high-voiced. Every day he wore the same outfit to work—khaki pants, a blue denim work shirt, and his big brown boots.

He loved to travel. Every summer he got in the car and drove somewhere all by himself during his vacation. He hated flying. "They aint gettin' me in one o' those things," he told the boys. "Hell, when one of them goes down, it's all over. In a car you got a chance." He brought postcards to work, postcards of The Everglades and The Great Smoky Mountains, of Lake Tahoe and Yosemite, Mount Rushmore and Niagara Falls. "I'm gonna hit every state before I die," he said. "I got twelve to go."

Frankie was a little guy with a club foot, and a big black shoe with a built-up heel. He was afraid of nothing. When they painted lines on the road, Frankie was the one who sat in the little seat at the rear of the truck right down on the road. He was the one who put the little stands with their red flags on the road so drivers wouldn't mess up the fresh paint. The rest of them made a chain and handed the stands down and then back up to the pile. Frankie's favorite words were swear words. He was Italian. Everything was "fuckin' goddamn sonofabitch" this and that, but with Frankie it never sounded obscene. It was just the way he talked. He was usually hung over on Monday morning, and there was a bar in town, Kosmo said, where they could usually find Frankie on Friday and Saturday nights, but the boys never went there. Kosmo didn't like mixing up his social life with his work life.

Vladimir Kosmalski, or Sphere Senior, as David liked to think of him, was an autocrat. "A goddamn fascist," Kosmo said, but David liked him. He gave lectures at the dinner table about diligence and the value of hard work, lectures that seemed particularly pointed toward "those specially gifted young men who don't apply themselves." On hot nights he would come to dinner without his jacket, but he never appeared at the table without a tie. It was always a long sleeved shirt, starched, with a dark tie and suspenders. Between lectures he talked about current affairs and business and economic systems. He reminded David of his grandfather Everett. A little less hair, perhaps, but the same values. At one meal he told the boys, "I voted for Dewey in 1948, and I'll vote Republican in 1952 for anybody that runs. The Democrats, they just give everything away."

"Who will the Republicans nominate for President next year?" David asked.

"Senator Taft," said Mr. Kosmalski.

"What about Ike?" asked David.

"He's not interested."

"Who cares?" said Kosmo. "They're all the same. Just politicians. Change the faces, change the names, they're all the same."

"Not so," said Mr. Kosmalski.

"Not so," mimicked Kosmo in his best Sphere Senior accent.

"Go to your room," said the father, and the son stomped up the stairs and closed the door. Kosmo just couldn't help himself. The humorist in him was too strong. But dinners didn't always end so violently. Often they spilled out onto the porch with Mr. Kosmalski explaining to John, who was a freshman at Princeton, the fine points of international banking, and Kosmo taking David off in the car for driving lessons.

Kosmo was a good driving teacher, and even though David had no access to a car, he wanted to learn to drive. He had to learn to drive. Everybody over sixteen had a driver's license. Kosmo made sure that he would be a good one. He drilled him in fundamentals. "Who's behind you?" he would say, suddenly, or "How much gas have you got?" He made him check his gauges, use the rear-view mirror, and know exactly how fast he was going. "Always parallel park by coming alongside the car in front of the space you want to back into. Never try to park by going forward. You'll never get your tail in. You've got to go in reverse. Put your right arm on the back of the seat, your left hand on the wheel, and look backwards through the rear window."

David learned to let the clutch out slowly and not apply too much gas. They practiced at first in the big parking lot down at the State Highway Department, which was empty at night after the workers went home. Most learners either stalled out or jerked the car forward in a huge lunge. If you did either one on your test, you were through. Kosmo was patient and funny, but serious.

"Sometimes you piss me off, C.C.," he said one night on the way home. "I just wish you weren't so fucking perfect. You're the goddamn son my mother wanted." Then he laughed. "Still, it's easier with you here. My dad's not so testy. Having another person around takes some of the pressure off."

Over the Fourth of July weekend they went to Atlantic City for three days, and rented a house three blocks from the beach on Indiana Avenue. It was a family tradition. Kosmo's girl friend was Lydia Morris. She and her friend Melinda were staying with their families around the corner on Baltic.

"Do the street names sound familiar?" Kosmo asked David.

"What do you mean?" David answered.

"The street names, stupid. Boardwalk, Park Place, Baltic, Kentucky, Indiana."

"Oh my God, Monopoly."

"The guy who invented Monopoly used the streets in Atlantic City."

"I never thought of that before."

"You've never been to Atlantic City before."

Friday night it rained and the four of them, David, Kosmo, Lydia and Melinda played Monopoly on the screen porch. David couldn't get over it. He wanted to walk up and down the Boardwalk. He wanted to find every street that was in Monopoly and figure out if the price in the game was based on how ritzy it was in real life.

"Baltic's pretty cheap in real life," said Lydia.

"You can say that again," said Melinda. She was short with dark skin and black hair pulled tight against her head in a pony tail.

She wore a boy's shirt tied around her waist and cut off blue jeans. Her toenails were painted. David could tell by the way she held her mouth that she was tough. Her body was hard, her eyes had that "don't mess with me" look. David was spoiled. Next to Tracy, every other girl was—not boring—but an effort, that was it, an effort. You had to start at level one and level two and go through all the regular conversation about school and families and then grope toward something to talk about that really interested the girl. Tracy said it was important for David to get to know other girls, to figure out how girls worked. "Tell whoever it is you're a poet," Tracy had said. "That always gets their attention."

But sitting on the screen porch in the rain playing Monopoly was not a place where you suddenly said, "I'm a poet." Besides, he wasn't a poet. He didn't have the right to call himself that. Robert Frost and e.e. cummings were poets. He was just a kid who wrote poems. The day after he left Tracy's he had gone to the bookstore at Rockefeller Center and bought a copy of e.e. cummings' poems, and he had taken the book with him to Lambertville and then to Doylestown.

In Lambertville, at Aunt Louise's, he could read the book and work on his own poems. He had a room to himself there, and no one bothered him. It was so interesting what you wanted at different times. The summer before he had craved company, but now for these three days before he went to Kosmo's he was glad to be alone. He read the poems and tried to figure out what cummings was doing. He read "somewhere I have never traveled" over and over, and every time he came to the last line, "nobody, not even the rain, has such small hands" he thought of Tracy and how she had read the poem to him on the beach.

He played with poems in his notebook, he tried to write a letter to Tracy, and everything he said seemed stupid to him. That was the trouble with poets, real poets. They said things so well you couldn't approach what they said. But he had to try. He liked the way cummings used words, the old-fashioned words, in a fresh way, the way he turned things upside down and inside out without being pretentious. David practiced writing his name in small letters, "davidjohnsonlear" all run together. He practiced phrases, lines—

learleapslilybylilly
over thefarstars
to(Christ)whereyourhands
myhandstouchthescar
where yourwoundwas

He thought he would write a poem for Tracy, but then Christ got into it somehow and wouldn't go away. That was all right. He thought of writing to Dennis Vogler. You just didn't talk about Christ to anyone. It was too hard, too scary, but with Dennis you could, like the morning David had awakened really early and gone to communion before breakfast, something he never did, and Daddy Drew was the priest that day, and Dennis was the acolyte, holding and presenting the bread and wine, and there had been only four or five of them in the chapel, kneeling there in the stalls up in the choir where the prefects sat, and afterwards he and Dennis had walked to breakfast together, and Dennis had looked down and put his arm around David and smiled, and said, "I really felt the presence of Christ this morning, didn't you?"

And David said, "Yes, I really did, in my bones."

"I like that, in your bones, I like that," said Dennis Vogler.

"If Jesus had touched you," David said, "you would never be the same."

"That's right. We just guess at it, don't we?"

And they talked like that until they came to the dining hall and went their separate ways. But you didn't talk like that very much. It was scary, and most people would just think you were weird.

So here was David now with hard-faced Melinda Menkhaus trying to figure out how to make conversation.

"Hey, Dave," she said with her Philadelphia accent, "you wanna trade Tennessee for Kentucky and Reading Railroad?"

"But that will give you a monopoly. In fact, more people land on that monopoly than any other."

"How do you know that?" said Kosmo.

"Because of jail," said David. "Every time you get out of jail you land on either St. James or Tennessee."

"So, I'll give you Kentucky and two railroads."

"And $500."

"Done," she said, and smiled, and thirty minutes later she had a hotel and was, in Kosmo's words, "beating the shit out of the rest of us."

After the game, they walked the girls back to Baltic. Their house was dark except for a lamp in the front hall. The girls were supposed to lock the door after they came in.

Kosmo whispered to David, "I'm gonna sit on the porch with Lydia for a while. You know."

"I know. So, what do I do?"

"Whatever you want, just don't use the porch."

Melinda yawned and said she was going to bed. David walked back to Indiana.

Saturday was beautiful. After lunch they got the girls and walked down to the pier. They wore their bathing suits with tee shirts and sandals. Some of the places wouldn't let you in with bare feet. They played skee ball and ate foot-long hotdogs at Nathan's, and then sat on their blankets on the beach and swam and bodysurfed in the waves.

That night they came back after dinner and sat on the beach in the dark looking at the stars and listening to the music coming from the Pier. After a while Kosmo and Lydia disappeared, and David was left alone with Melinda.

For a while they smoked and talked and watched the remaining rockets that soared out over the ocean from the pier. Then there was a huge crescendo, rockets everywhere and the band playing "God Bless America," and then it was quiet up and down the beach except for the scattered applause.

"Have a swig," Melinda said, and pulled a tiny flask from her purse.

"Where'd you get that?" David asked.

"Just a little gift from Lydia. She's got one too."

He took a swig, and felt it burn his throat on the way down. "What is it?" he asked.

"I don't know, but it makes me feel good," she said. So they drank and talked, and then drank and smoked and talked, and

David felt a pleasant dizziness in his head and a hardness in his groin. He thought about it. He was turned on. He wanted to kiss her, to rub against her, to feel her hard little body against his. It had nothing to do with love, with friendship. It was just sex, pure sex. He put out his cigarette, and turned to her, putting his arms around her. He searched for her lips with his, but she was gone somehow. She had turned away and stood up.

"Listen," she said, "why don't you walk me back to the house? Hell, Lydia and Kosmo, you can never tell when they'll be coming back."

David was glad for the dark. If it had been light, she would have seen the redness in his cheeks. He was burning with shame. He felt so stupid, so clumsy. And besides, he shouldn't have tried it in the first place. If it wasn't natural and easy and born of the heart, then it was no good. He knew that. Tracy had taught him that, but still he had to learn it for himself. They walked up the stairs to the Boardwalk and down to Indiana. When they got to the girls' house, Melinda said goodnight and disappeared through the screen door.

On Sunday they drove home. Mr. Kosmalski had to be back at work on Monday morning, and the boys would be back at the State Highway Department. The weekend was over. That night, in bed, Kosmo talked to David:

"I'm sorry about last night," he said.

"Sorry about what?"

"About you and Melinda."

"Did she say something to you this morning?"

"No, she told Lydia and Lydia told me."

"What?"

"She said she could never love a guy with legs like that."

"You're kidding."

"No, that's what she said. I'm sorry. Melinda's into bodies, into what people look like. You just didn't turn her on, that's all."

David hadn't really thought much about his legs in a while. His arms and shoulders and chest were powerful from wrestling, and his thigh muscles had developed in the last year, but from knee to toe there were these almost fleshless calves, ankles so thin he could put his fingers all the way around them, and tiny feet that still caused him to run almost entirely on the toes and the balls of his feet. He had learned in soccer to wrap his feet and ankles carefully with tape, and the shin guards he always wore compensated for the hurt and the thinness. But on the beach, he had no protection. In shorts he had no protection. In the water he was fine. No one could see his legs there.

And Tracy, God bless her, didn't care. She thought David was a miracle. She knew about his shortened Achilles tendons and the operations and the doctors. She knew how hard it had been on David during his childhood, and she just loved him for who he was. But Melinda. . .he knew he shouldn't care, he knew Melinda wasn't important, but still her words had hurt, and he found himself glad for the blue jeans he wore to work where no one could see how funny his legs looked.

In mid-August David made his way back to Elizabeth's via Aunt Louise's. Louise had come to pick him up in Doylestown the day before the Kosmalskis packed up for their annual vacation. The two Afghans were in the back side, each with a head out a window, letting the air blow through their long blond hair. David put his bags in the way back, shoving them between frames and pieces of canvas and bags of dog food.

"Well," said Aunt Louise as they started off, "how was your summer?"

"Fine," said David. "The family was very nice to me, and the job was. . ." He paused. "The job was my favorite job of all time."

"Of all time," Aunt Louise echoed. "How many years does that include?"

"Well, my camp job and my job at the restaurant last summer."

"And why was it so wonderful?"

"Because I got to know a whole different class of people."

He told her about Frankie and Elmer, and how everyone had made fun of him because he couldn't hit a nail straight. "But not in a mean way," he went on. "If they were putting up a sign, they'd ask me if it was straight, and if I said yes, then they knew it wasn't.

And they would laugh in a friendly way that made me feel like they really liked me."

"Not 'feel like,'" said Aunt Louise. "'feel that.'"

David laughed. Aunt Louise was a purist. She always got her grammar right. David knew his grammar, but he liked using slang. He liked talking more informally than he wrote. Aunt Louise would correct him if he said 'me" instead of "I," but David felt pretentious saying "I" when he said something like "It's me." But Aunt Louise kept him sharp, kept him on his toes.

He stayed at the house for three days, and while he was there he helped her and Uncle Swen clean up the studio and build new racks to hold the paintings. In September they were going to drive to the Southwest and then to Mexico to paint, and they wanted to leave everything in order. The dogs would go to the kennel, and the house and studio would be closed up for two months.

"We'll be visiting your father in Arizona," she said at dinner the last night. They were eating at Colligan's Stockton Inn, a few miles up the river, the inn that inspired Irving Berlin to write the song, "There's a small hotel/with a wishing well." David had dropped a quarter in the well and wished that he could see Tracy before he went back to school.

"Why is my father in Arizona?" David asked. "I thought they had moved to California, to Carmel."

"Diane and the children moved to California, but your father moved to Scottsdale, just north of Phoenix. He and Diane have separated. It's very sad about your father, David. He's very gifted, He was always more gifted than I."

David noticed the "I." Uncle Swen puffed on his pipe, and looked out over the river.

She went on. "He never wanted to work for things. If they came easily to him, he did them. If not, he just gave up and did something else. Diane told him that unless he stopped drinking, she wouldn't stay with him. So, he just decided to move to Scottsdale. He's invested in some land there. Swen and I will stop and look at it on the way back from Mexico. It seems that people are moving to Arizona for the climate. People from New York and Pittsburgh and Chicago are retiring and moving to Scottsdale. The land will be developed."

"But what about his drinking?" said David. "Will that get him into trouble?"

"Of course it will," said Aunt Louise, "but we can hope that the trouble is just enough to make him stop and not enough to put him out of business. If Diane's leaving him didn't make him stop, I can't imagine what will."

"Like my mother," said David suddenly. It had surprised him the way the words just came out. He hadn't planned on saying that.

"Yes," said Aunt Louise, "like your mother."

"I was thinking," David said, "that I never really knew my mother."

"It's probably just as well," said Aunt Louise. "She was a very unhappy woman."

"But you should know your own parents," David said. "At the Kosmalskis' at dinner, Mr. Kosmalski would ask questions. We had required dinner conversation."

"So that's what this is all about," said Uncle Swen. "I have never seen you this conversational except about baseball."

"Baseball didn't cut it with Mr. Kosmalski," David laughed. "We discussed current events and family histories and values. Kosmo hated it, so I had to talk enough for both of us. Mr. Kosmalski quizzed us about everything at school, and Kosmo was afraid I'd say something about the Silver Sphere, but I didn't."

"The Silver Sphere?" asked Aunt Louise.

"It's a humor column in the paper. The name of the author is a secret."

"I see," said Aunt Louise, "and only you, as the editor, know the identity of the author."

"Right," said David, and then he told them about how much he enjoyed being editor of the paper and how Ralph Wisdom had fooled them all into believing he was Douglas MacArthur.

"I wish your father were here," said Aunt Louise. "He would have enjoyed this night and your sparkling conversation. He said you were very quiet at the Ranch, very diffident, I think he said."

"And what does diffident mean?" asked David.

"It means reserved or timid," said Uncle Swen. "It comes from the Latin 'dis" and 'fidere' which means to distrust."

"That's really interesting," said David. "You're diffident if you distrust someone."

"Or yourself," said Uncle Swen. "It can come from lack of self-confidence. I know, I've been that way myself. By the way, David, I have something to tell you. While you've been in Doylestown, I've become a baseball fan."

"A Yankee fan?"

"No, A Dodger fan. Duke Snider and Roy Campanella and Don Newcombe. I listen to the games on the radio at night. The Dodgers just appeal to me. I needed something to relax with, and they're just the thing."

"Dem Bums," David laughed.

"Dem Bums," Uncle Swen echoed. "They're looking mighty good."

They talked back and forth over coffee and ice cream, and by the time they were ready to leave, the sun had disappeared behind the hills and the sky had turned the darkest of blue. David could see lights on the Pennsylvania shore, and he thought how much fun it would be to glide down the river in a canoe with Tracy Warren. On the way out he dropped another quarter in the wishing well.

He rode home in the back seat of the station wagon, and wiped the gold hairs of the Afghans from his pants before hanging them up in the closet in the yellow room. He hadn't really learned anything about his mother or father, but he had felt closer to Aunt Louise and Uncle Swen than ever before. It came to him how much they were family too, and how much easier it was when you weren't so diffident.

The next day in New York, he and Elizabeth smoked and drank coffee in the kitchen after the kids had gone to bed. He told her about his evening, and she hugged him and told him she was proud. "We were worried about you," she said. "You seemed kind of depressed in June."

"No, just diffident," he said, and went off to the movies.

The next day he took Alex to the Yankee game. Alex was five now, and growing like a cornstalk in July. He had his blue Yankee cap with the white NY, a white Tee shirt with a blue NY, blue jeans, sneakers, and his glove. They sauntered down Morris Avenue in the bright sunshine and turned onto 161st St. Maggie had screamed with anger when they left. "No fair," she had said with her pouty lips, and the big tears coming from her eyes.

"Next summer, Maggie," said David. "You have to be four."

"No next summer," said Maggie. "I go now."

"Just boys," said Alex.

"No just boys," said Maggie, but they went anyway.

They sat out in the right field stands to catch home runs. It wasn't a big game, and the crowd was smaller than David remembered from before. It was easier to get around, and if a home run came, they had room to run after it. David didn't know if DiMaggio would be playing. He'd had a bad year, a humiliating year for him. His average had sunk into the .270's for the first time in his life, and his injuries made him a question mark from day to day. At the end of the season he would retire, and a young kid named Mickey Mantle from Joplin, Missouri, would take his place. No one could take Joe's place, of course. There was only one DiMaggio. But Mickey was a phenomenon. He was just twenty years old, and he was a switch hitter. He was not as consistent as Joe, but he could hit the ball farther. Some of his home runs soared out of the ball park like shells from a cannon. And he was fast, too. He could run out infield hits and cover great distances in the outfield, but he also struck out a lot, missing curve balls and change ups by a foot with his huge, powerful swing. Joe was supposed to teach him.

"Go, Mickey," said Alex, when the young slugger came up to bat in the first inning. DiMaggio wasn't playing today, and Mickey had taken his place in center field, his clean-up slot in the batting order. David was mesmerized by the size of Mickey's shoulders and his forearms. Even his practice swings had seemed huge. He swung at the first pitch and missed, and David could hear the crowd's long "ooooh"; then he took two balls, and on the fourth pitch he lofted a fly ball high toward them in right field. The Chicago right fielder camped on the warning track and waited, and waited, and waited. The ball seemed as if it would never come down. When it finally settled in the outfielder's glove, there was another sigh from the crowd. Suppose he had connected perfectly instead of getting under it? Where might it have gone? David thought into the future, years and years of Mickey and Yogi. DiMag would be gone, but they would still be the Yankees.

That night at supper, Alex told Elizabeth and Phil about the game. "Mickey, he hit the ball so high, so high. . .what, Uncle Dave?"

"So high it disappeared in the sky."

"Right, in the sky. Later, he hit the ball to the monuments."

"To the monuments," David echoed.

"And he run all the way to third base."

"Ran," said David.

"No run. He comes home. That's a run."

"Right," said David.

"And what was the name of the other team?" asked Phil.

"Sox," said Alex.

"What sox?" asked Phil.

"Right," said Alex. "White Sox. Not Red Sox. Red Sox really bad."

"Really bad," said David and hugged him.

CHAPTER FOURTEEN

And now the rock was theirs, now their own class numerals were on the rock, white on a royal blue background, as they trudged over the bridge to begin the fall term of their senior year—David, and Wally Hinson full of the latest tales of his sexual prowess, and Billy DuPont, who could talk of nothing but the National League race between the Giants and the Dodgers, and Dennis Vogler singing "When The Saints Come Marching In" with the voice of Louis Armstrong. They were happy to be home, all of them, home in what they had come to call "The Happy Valley." It had started as a joke that Antonio Black had made when they were reading "Rasselas" by Samuel Johnson fourth form year, and then it stuck. The school, like the Happy Valley of Samuel Johnson, was isolated from the world. Once you crossed the bridge, the world out there was gone until Thanksgiving or Christmas. No television, no radios, only the *New York Times* in the library, which no one read except for Borden Smith, who lived there and kindly let David know if there was something going on in the world that they needed to find out about.

David thought of the spring before, in Bad News Benson's class, when Ralph Wisdom stood up and recited from memory, word for word, Robert Frost's poem, "The Death of the Hired Man." David

Anthony S. Abbott

could still hear the words themselves, the moment in the poem where Mary and Warren talk about the hired man coming home:

"Home is the place where, when you have to go there,
They have to take you in."
                    "I should have called it
Something you somehow haven't to deserve."

David remembered how long they had talked in class, trying to figure out what the lines meant, the first lines Warren's definition of home, and the second ones, Mary's.

"They have to take you in, because you're a family member," somebody had said.

"But it's more than that, isn't it?" Dennis Vogler replied. "It's a religious thing."

"What's so religious about it?" Wally Hinson had asked.

"It's grace," said David.

"Ah," said Bad News Benson, "and how is it grace, Mr. Lear?"

"Because God takes us in whether we deserve it or not. We don't have to earn our home with God."

"And it's about dignity," said Ralph Wisdom, who knew all about dignity. "Silas comes home to Mary and Warren because it's the only place he can die with dignity."

"The only place he still feels valuable," said David.

"Gentlemen," said Bad News Benson, "you are all right, all magnificently right. Now let us pray that you will remember these lines when you are called upon to act accordingly."

And so it was that Bad News Benson, who had never been known to give such lavish praise, conferred upon all of them a kind of grace, and the Happy Valley had become home for them, never more so than on that fall day when they walked across the bridge to begin their sixth form year. They came with the new boys, the second and third formers, a week before the rest of the school. They came to teach the new boys how Wicker could be home for them. They came to prepare themselves to be, in Ralph Wisdom's words, "the best sixth form ever."

That preparation had begun in the spring during the official changeover from the old sixth form to the new. It had begun with dozens of meetings in Ralph Wisdom's room, meetings of different class leaders with the new prefects to discuss what they could do to run the school more efficiently and gain the respect of the underclassmen, and what they came up with in these meetings was a set of "new traditions" that would set off the sixth form from the rest of the school.

Wally Hinson liked to play the Devil's Advocate. "How can you have a 'new tradition?'" he asked. "A tradition is something that goes on for a long time."

"Well, it has to start somewhere," said Hugh Packard. "If it works, then it will continue."

"And it will only work if we earn it," said David.

"These traditions," said Ralph Wisdom, "are signs of the status of the sixth form. They will be not only privileges, but status symbols that all the underclassmen will look forward to achieving when they become sixth formers."

Ralph Wisdom would announce the changes on the day of the changeover, the day he formally assumed the role of Head Prefect, two weeks before graduation. David would prepare an article for the Wicker *Sentinel*. The night before the ceremony, Ralph read his speech to those gathered in his room: "A fundamental principle of the Wicker School—as founded by Pater—is that the sixth form is responsible for a large part of the running of the school. Obviously, then, the sixth form must have the respect of the entire student body. . . . Therefore, we have instituted certain 'new traditions' which are designed collectively to distinguish markedly the senior class from the rest of the student body and to serve as daily reminders of the responsibility and the position of the sixth form. . ."

Under the new rules, only sixth formers, along with faculty and guests, could enter the rear door of the chapel, only sixth formers could serve as table heads in the dining room, and only sixth formers were permitted to wear blazers with the school insignia. The privilege of smoking in the Headmaster's study after underclass lights out was preserved, and the privilege of going to the mail room at any time of day was also reserved for sixth formers.

Anthony S. Abbott

But none of it seemed real until the fall, until the old sixth formers were gone. During that first week, when they realized it was their school, the new sixth formers began to feel the magic and the mystery of their responsibility. David loved it. He was never happier. He liked being part of this new community, this new band of brothers—the sixth form of Wicker School, Ralph Wisdom's cohorts. The key was that every member of the form must serve, must do something, even the guys with names like Veg and Sack Artist and Satchel Ass. They had to rise to the moment, they had to find something in them that made them part of this unit. "The whole is greater than the sum of its parts," Ralph Wisdom said, "if each participant is doing his part. We can't criticize one another in front of the underclassmen. We can't pretend to love the system and then disrupt it by abusing our power. We must believe in ourselves and our mission."

David was a believer. He and Wally Hinson and Hugh Packard were the leaders of the soccer team, and even though the team was not very good, that didn't matter. It was just a joy to play, and a joy to debate on Wednesday evenings, and to study English with Reginald Barnes, who treated them as adults and simply expected them to think for themselves. He was no Bad News Benson. He didn't have the fire to stimulate the class with his own wild energy, but he was wise and thoughtful and made the study of literature a kind of search for truth. They never got bogged down in silly details. They dug for meaning and searched for the truth under the truth in Shakespeare and Milton and, of course, in the dreaded *Beowulf.*

Beowulf provoked the Sphere into writing his most popular column, his very own version of the ancient epic. Called "Beowulf's Last Stand," or "Beowulf and the Draggin' Dragon," the Sphere's masterpiece permanently changed Wicker vocabulary. It was no longer possible to refer to the Monster Grendel as anything but the "draggin' dragon," and "mede," as the Sphere spelled it, soon became the favorite beverage of all Wicker students, many of whom were to go to Charlie's bar in New York at Thanksgiving and ask the perplexed bartenders for it.

"I'm sorry, we don't carry that. What is it?"

"A kind of beer."

"We have Schlitz, Ballantine, and Schaeffer, but no. . .whatever you said."

"Mede."

"That must be a foreign beer."

"Oh yes, very foreign, very old."

And then gales of laughter.

Second and third formers had been made to memorize lines from the Sphere's epic as punishments for being late to meals or to assembly. Reciting "Beowulf and the draggin' Dragon" replaced running the triangle for a while:

Midst the roaring shouts of knights and princes
Entered the mighty Beowuf draggin' his new slain dragon
That was daid as daid could be.

To the long oaken table his eye wandered and there he spied old Hrothgar's queen.
Boldly then he done strut right up to slumberin' Wealtheow,
And watched her as she snored away.
"Wake, Queenie!" he shouted to her ear.
As she slowly arose from her slumber deep
He hurled the monster at her feet.
The fair damsel lept back in fright and he said,
"Look, Queenie, here am mah latest draggin', all for you.
Back to him she screams with pride,
"Dat aint no draggin' dragon; dat am Grendel!"

That was the point at which the young memorizers stopped, to the applause of the whole table. Everybody in school knew the last line, "Dat aint no draggin' dragon; dat am Grendel!" Even Bad News Benson, himself a match for Beowulf, quoted it in class, and Father Perkins congratulated the Sphere obliquely with some clever references to circles and orbits. David thought it was time for Kosmo to reveal himself.

"It's the perfect time," he said to Kosmo in the privacy of his room. "Your fame is at its height. In the next issue you can come forth."

"Not 'till after Christmas," Kosmo said. "We've got other fish to fry right now."

"What's that?" David asked.

"The Sixth Form Dance."

"What about it?"

"You, Mr. Columbia Cup, don't have a date, do you?"

"Well, no I don't."

"And you're not going to ask Melinda Menkhaus."

"Hell, no."

"Or that whatsername from Phillips Mill."

"You mean Margie Sorenson?"

"Right, you're not asking her."

"Nope. I'm just going to be celibate."

"That's not permissible," said the Sphere and walked out.

The next night they all attacked him, Wally Hinson and Billy DuPont and Ted Barber, who knew more about girls than anyone in the class.

"You ever done it, D.J.?" Wally asked, rumpling his hair.

"You want me to get you a date?" asked Ted Barber, smiling.

"A little Spanish pussy?" Wally leered.

"I don't need a date," David said. "Besides, Ralph Wisdom doesn't have a date. I'll hang out with him."

"Ralph Wisdom doesn't need a date," said Ted Barber. "He's our Father. He's a Catholic priest. They're all celibate. Hell, he may never have a date."

"If he does, it won't be with a girl," said Wally Hinson.

"What's that supposed to mean?" asked David curtly. He didn't like this kind of talk.

"Come on, D.J.," said Wally, "Don't be so damned serious. I was just kidding."

"Don't," said David. "Just don't kid around about Ralph. He's special."

"Well, he's not God," said Ted Barber.

"Well, pretty damn close to it," said David.

"Jesus Christ, D.J.," said Billy DuPont. "Even I have a date."

They grabbed him and held him down on the bed. Wally sat on his legs, Ted and Billy each had an arm. "Swear you'll get a date," said Wally Hinson, "or we'll fix you good afterwards."

David didn't struggle. He wasn't even mad. It wasn't their fault that they didn't know about Tracy. "OK," he said, "I'll swear. Now get off me."

He and Tracy had talked about this very moment several times. The last was the night before school started. They were lying on beach towels in her back yard, looking up at the sky. Her parents had gone to bed, and Butch was spending the night with a friend. Tracy's radio was playing music softly. It was dark enough to see the stars. Their hands were touching.

"Will you come to the Sixth Form Dance at Wicker?" he asked.

"No," she said.

"Why not?"

"You know, David. We've had this conversation before. Why do you keep asking?"

"Because, you might have changed your mind."

"I haven't. You know what would happen. Just think of it, David. All those rules, all those boys with their dirty minds thinking of nothing but what they're going to get."

"I'm proud of you. I want them to meet you. I'm tired of secrets. Everybody thinks I'm queer or something. I never talk about girls. As far as they know, I've never had a date, except for Melinda Menkhaus and that was hardly a success. Come on, Tracy."

"No," she said. "I'm not coming to Wicker just to prove your manhood. We're secret. We have to stay secret, or it will all be ruined.."

"But why?"

"David, David, David, David, David."

"Not that again. Not the five Davids."

She started again, and he clamped his hand over her mouth. She jumped up, laughing now, dancing in her bare feet, her shirt half-unbuttoned, whispering the words again and again, David chasing her, laughing too, then catching her, tumbling her to the ground, then kissing her, her mouth opening to his, her laughter gone, his

Anthony S. Abbott

hand inside her shirt feeling the hardness of her nipple, his body moving against hers.

"Wow," she said afterwards. "What was that?"

"It was like we were. . ." David started.

"Out of our bodies," she said.

"Our bodies just. . ."

"That's the problem. We have to be careful."

The music played, a song they had heard before. . . "For all we know, we may never meet again."

"What's the worst thing that could happen to you?" she asked.

"Losing you," he said, without hesitation. "And you?"

"Losing Butch or one of my parents, I guess."

"Not me."

"No, not you."

Then something happened. He started to cry, and he said, "Oh God, Tracy, I love you, I love you so much."

And she took him and held him, held his head against her breasts. "Thank you," she said, "I've been waiting for a long time for that."

"I know. I didn't think I could. Then it was like a string snapping, and I could say it, a broken string that had been so tight before."

"Say that again."

"What?"

"You know, the string snapping. Did you make that up?"

"No. It was something we read in class. I like it, though."

They were lying side by side on the blanket, their hands touching.

"Listen," she said.

"What?"

"Don't count on me too much, David."

"Why not?"

"Because I might hurt you."

"Why?"

"Because of who I am. You can love me. Just don't idealize me. There's a part of me you don't know."

"So tell me about it."

"No," she said. "Not tonight. Let's not spoil tonight. Tonight's too good."

And that, for the time being was the end of it. He had told Tracy he loved her, and was willing to let the dark thing go. He was happy to keep her secret. But now he'd promised under oath to get a date, and not knowing what else to do, he followed a hunch and went to Ralph Wisdom's room.

"Ah, Brother Lear," said Ralph with a smile. "Sit down, sit down." He patted the bed next to his desk.

David started to explain his problem, and Ralph listened with that combination of quizzical curiosity and seriousness that was his trademark. All that was missing was the pipe, which he could only smoke in the Headmaster's study or, of course, at home on weekends. Ralph had gone home on the Saturday of the first football game of the year and come back with a goat wearing a Wicker banner, and had pronounced the goat to be the class mascot.

Wicker had no mascot, a fact which had bothered Wally Hinson more than anyone else. "What are we?" he exclaimed. "The fucking Wicker Nothings? We're not Lions or Tigers or even a color like Dartmouth. At least they're the Big Green." But Wally was not pleased with the goat. There was something about the Wicker Goats that seemed even worse than nothing. But you couldn't fault Ralph Wisdom for trying, and he just took the goat home and kept it in a pen in the back yard for future uses. Ralph was always thinking and always laughing at himself. He had learned early on not to take himself too seriously. That was one of the things that David liked most about him.

"I have a girl friend," David said. "Her name is Tracy Warren. She can't come to Dance Weekend, and I don't want to ask anyone else."

"No blind date with someone's sister?" Ralph asked.

David laughed. "Ralph," he said. "Tracy doesn't want me to mention her to anyone her. She wants to be secret."

"Indeed."

"So this conversation is just between us, OK?"

"OK."

There was a moment of silence. "Well, Brother David," said Ralph, "I have an idea."

"What?"

"You can come to my house Saturday night. I'll check you out after classes on Saturday morning, and we'll come back Sunday in time for the Eucharist. "

David was amazed. He'd never been invited to Ralph Wisdom's except with a group of other boys. "I'd love that," he said.

Ralph put his hand on David's knee. "Good," he said. "We'll make it a special evening."

The next day something happened that made Ralph Wisdom's proposal unnecessary. David received a letter from his Aunt Louise. It was postmarked "Austin, Texas."

"Dear David, I have very sad news for you. Your Uncle Swen has died. I thought that I would have a longer time with him, but it was not to be. As you know, we had left Lambertville and worked our way south and west to Mexico, where Swen and I painted watercolors in the Mexican desert. The work he did there was splendid, simply splendid. A week ago, Saturday, we packed up and returned to Texas, to visit friends Swen had known when he taught at the University.

"He suffered a heart attack in Henderson and died in the hospital within hours. I have had his body cremated and will spread his ashes on his beloved Pacific Ocean on my next trip to the coast. Your father has flown to Austin to be with me and to help me drive home. He will stay with me in Lambertville for a few weeks. There will be a memorial tribute to Swen in New York at the Passedoit Gallery on Saturday, November 10, at 3:00 pm. It would mean a great deal to me and to your father if the school would permit you to attend this event. I feel the loss of Swen deeply. He had just reached, in his new work, another level in his artistic growth, and I blame myself for pushing him too hard on this trip."

David had never been close to his uncle until that evening at the end of the summer when Swen had suddenly declared his fondness for the Brooklyn Dodgers, and so he could not really feel the loss himself, but he felt sad for his Aunt Louise. At the same time he felt an enormous relief. November 10 was the day of the Fall Dance, and he had found a perfect excuse, one that even Wally Hinson could not quarrel about. Father Perkins would approve his request, he was sure, and David no longer had to worry about the demon of dance weekend.

Or so he thought. The Thursday night before the weekend Wally Hinson and Billy DuPont burst into his room.

"You're not getting away with this, D.J.," said Wally Hinson.

"You're gonna pay big time," said Billy.

"It's not like I made my uncle die," said David.

"Yeah, well, it's too damned convenient," said Wally.

"We're gonna fix you, when you least expect it," said Billy.

And they were gone, to evening study hall. It was just bluster, David was sure, and then he was not so sure.

On Saturday morning, David left early to catch the train. He felt strange walking by himself over the bridge, then turning left down the Main Street to the station. His feet crunched the year's last leaves. At the drug store he stopped to buy a pack of Chesterfields, then shoved it in the pocket of his overcoat. He had brought a change of clothes, his shaving kit, and a copy of *King Lear*, which they would begin reading on Monday in Reginald Barnes' class. And he had brought his journal. He had been trying for weeks to write a poem for Tracy's birthday, which came just before Thanksgiving. She would be eighteen. He had tried and tried to find the words he needed for her, and he found himself coming back to the moment when she had asked him what he feared most. "Losing you," he had said. And he had meant not only her death, which was unthinkable to him, terrifying to him, but the loss of her love, the possibility that she might stop caring for him.

"I do not know," he wrote in his journal as the train began to move south, "about kissing, the placement of the hands or the lips, or whether the tongue goes this way or that."

And then the lines began to come, in the rhythm of the train's movement, the image of the moon as they had watched it from the chairs on her terrace:

"I remember only that on certain nights
when the full moon hung low on the horizon
there was the beginning
of something more than you and me
something more than self
and if I lost that forever
It would be losing God
or whatever God is."

His hand trembled in the excitement of the words, the sudden realization that his passion for Tracy was somehow connected to his passion for God. He wasn't sure if it made any sense, and then he remembered the poems of John Donne they had read in October in Reginald Barnes' class, he remembered "Reggie" almost blushing as he read the ending of one of Donne's Holy Sonnets. What was it? The one where the poet asks God to ravish him. That was it. "nor ever chaste except you ravish me." Donne asks God to overwhelm him. There is a parallel between human passion and divine passion. The poet can't be free unless God takes him prisoner. David could remember Reginald Barnes, soft, white Reginald Barnes, reddening with passion when he talked about this poem. "He can't save himself. Only God can save him by taking over his body, by literally 'raping' him," Reginald Barnes had said. "That's what original sin means," he went on. "It means nothing we can do can overcome that dark place unless God takes it over, and by taking it over, makes it whole." What a great topic for his long paper, David thought, as the train rattled toward New York. "Human love and Divine Love in Donne's *Holy Sonnets*." He wrote on in his journal, notes about his paper, notes about Tracy, notes about God all mixed up together.

He walked up the familiar ramp at Grand Central into the huge concourse, up the stairs to Vanderbilt Avenue, then to Madison and up to 57th. As he reached the gallery, he could see others walking in and many more inside. He had not expected so many. Inside, Uncle Swen's paintings and water colors were everywhere. There were two rooms, one as he came in the door and a second room off to the left full of folding chairs, where people were gradually seating themselves. Across the room he saw Aunt Louise in the front row and Elizabeth next to her and then next to Elizabeth a man he didn't recognize at first. It wasn't Phil. And then he knew. It was his father. Elizabeth and his father were talking, so engaged with one another they had not seen David yet, and Louise was receiving condolences from a tall blond woman in a black jacket and a long, flowered skirt.

For a few moments, David watched from his vantage point at the entrance to the room. He was not yet ready to go in. He felt awkward, knowing that he was never good at these moments. With each one of these people he could be at ease, be himself, but somehow seeing them all together made him distinctly uncomfortable, as if he were somehow on display. He preferred watching. His father wore light brown trousers, a gray-brown jacket and a blue shirt, open at the neck, with an ascot. His hair was silver, beautifully combed. He looked older, thinner, but clearly more distinguished, more elegant than David had remembered him. He had changed. David could see that in his gestures, in his eyes. Elizabeth adored him. David had never seen her look at anyone quite like that. Having him back, if even for a short time, was a gift for her.

David moved forward, walked around the rows of chairs, and approached them from the front.

"Hi everyone," he said, and they looked up at once, the three of them, and rose from their seats. He kissed Aunt Louise on the cheek, hugged Elizabeth, and shook hands with his father.

"You've turned into a fine young man," his father said.

"Thank you," David answered. He wasn't quite sure what he should say back.

Aunt Louise patted the seat next to her, and David sat down. "They're getting ready to start," she said. "See that man next to the podium. That's Howard Devree, the art critic for *The New York Times*. He's the Master of Ceremonies. He's always been one of Swen's greatest supporters."

Howard Devree spoke first, talking about Swen's courage and individuality, his development as a painter, and how his work had changed after he married Louise Lear. She had studied with him in Minneapolis, they had corresponded when he went off to Texas, and those letters gave him encouragement during a time when no one seemed interested in his work. He returned to Minneapolis, where they married, and then they moved to New Jersey, where he did his finest work. Her love and support had kept him going when no one believed in him, and now people were beginning to recognize that he was a major artist, one of America's most important.

David looked at Louise with pride. He understood. She had really given her life to him, she had made him comfortable, cooked his meals, worked side by side with him, and kept him free from bother. Now, he wondered what she would do.

Others got up and spoke about Swen's work. Gerald Peters from Santa Fe talked about his unique achievement there during the 1920's and 1930's. Someone else talked about his pioneering woodcuts, etchings, and lithographs in Provincetown during the First World War and his set designs for the Provincetown Players, the group that had discovered Eugene O'Neill. Swen had been everywhere, David realized. He was not just that crotchety uncle who complained about his noise and his bouncing a ball against the studio wall. He was a major American artist.

At the end Louise got up to speak about their time together in Lambertville. "When we came east," she said, "we searched for a place where we could have a studio and a few acres for privacy. We found a ninety-acre farm with a burned out barn and a house sadly in need of repairs. But the farm offered such glowing possibilities that we capitulated.

"It proved to be all that we hoped for. A wonderful studio, space and good light, and a place where Swen could paint with perfect freedom. He loved nature and wanted to portray it as he felt and saw it—not realistically, but with deep feeling and emotion. From sketches and memories, canvases came alive with pictures of the sea, rocky coasts, mountains, fish, birds and flowers." She raised her right arm and gestured to the room where they sat and the room beyond it. "Please, when we have finished, take some time to look at these paintings, which are his gift to us. I only wish that he had been given more time."

She turned toward her seat, a small, dignified woman who spoke the truth as she knew it, and as she sat, the assembled guests rose to applaud her and thank her for what she had given them.

Later the family walked to dinner, two couples walking arm in arm, David and Aunt Louise leading, Elizabeth and her father following. "There is much to be done," Aunt Louise said while they ate. "We must catalogue all the paintings, write to museums, arrange shows, solicit articles. We need a book-length study of his work. Nothing happens in the world of art without effort. We must all work hard to be sure that Swen is not forgotten."

"I'll stay for a few weeks," his father said, "and do what I can to help. We'll put the paintings in racks, fix up the studio, make it habitable for scholars or visitors."

"I can help, too," said David suddenly. "I can come out for Thanksgiving vacation."

"That's wonderful," his father said. "Maybe we can get to know one another. I'm afraid our last time together was not very successful. But I'm a different person now. I almost died last year, when Diane and the children left me. I just drank more to kill the pain and ended up practically killing myself. A friend of mine in Phoenix took me to A.A. I've been sober for six months. I know that's not very long, but it's a start. At every meeting, if I wish to talk, I must stand up and say, 'My name is Allan Lear, and I am an alcoholic.' I didn't understand, until I joined A.A., that alcoholism was a disease. Some people can't drink at all. That's what A.A. wants people to understand. Your mother was an alcoholic, Diane is probably one, and I certainly am. Whenever I feel as if I might slip, then I find a meeting. There are A.A. chapters everywhere. They're like churches. You can go to them and feel as if you belong, and you do."

David watched and listened, as his father talked about real estate in Arizona and land deals and "big bucks" to be made. He wanted to talk to him, to ask him questions, but this was not the time, here in the restaurant with Elizabeth glowing and Aunt Louise fascinated. He had his audience, and he loved it, but David was not his audience tonight. He would have to wait until they were alone. He remembered his conversation with Uncle Swen. He did not want to be diffident, but he could not find a way to get in.

CHAPTER FIFTEEN

On the train back to school he began to read *King Lear,* which they were going to begin discussing in class on Monday. He hated to be unprepared, hated not to be able to take part in discussion. He was no good at what Wally Hinson and his friends called "bull shitting" or "bull" in general. To Wally and his crowd, "bull" was good. It was a sign of mental quickness, the ability to sound as if you knew more than you really did. "Bull artists" were clever, they were good liars, good conversationalists. If Ralph Wisdom weren't so wise and so eloquent, he might have been dismissed as a bull artist. Ted Barber was a borderline bull artist, smart, clever, handsome and muscular, full of stories of his family's Mexican jack-of-all-trades who had taught him everything there was to know about becoming a man.

There was a thin line between bull and philosophy. To Wally Hinson religion was "just a lot of bull" that couldn't be proved. So was philosophy. How did you know the difference between "bullshit" and "truth"? That was what David wanted to know. If he didn't feel passionately about something, he couldn't just make up something about it. He had to believe it was true. He had to believe that underneath all the bull and all the hot air and fancy talk there was something real, something he could claim as truth. That's what he was trying to learn from Father Perkins—whether or not Christianity was part of that truth, maybe was that truth.

That's what he liked about the first act of *King Lear* and hated at the same time. It was a strange story. The aging king wants to give up ruling and pass his power on to his children. He has three daughters—two evil daughters named Goneril and Regan—and a beautiful, true daughter named Cordelia. She is his favorite. He divides his kingdom into three parts with the intention of giving the largest part to Cordelia, because he loves her best, but before doing that he asks each daughter to tell him how much she loves him. Goneril—David could hear Wally Hinson in class already— "Sounds like gonorrhea to me," he would say, and everyone would laugh—Goneril and Regan make beautiful speeches, but Cordelia cannot say anything. She says she loves him according to her bond—according to her duty. And the king goes crazy and throws her out of the country with nothing. Then he banishes his best servant, Kent, for telling him he's made a mistake. The king has lost his mind.

This was a play about telling the truth. That's what David thought. He was anxious for class to begin. By the time the train got to Wicker, he'd written some notes in his journal. "People who speak the truth get screwed. The ones who suck up to the king get rewarded. If you're slick you win. That's the way it seems. But why does the king do this stupid test in the first place? He already knows Cordelia loves him. He already loves her best. Why this stupid test?"

For three weeks, six days a week, they hammered away at *King Lear* in class. They argued, they fought, Reginald Barnes jousted with them. Everything about the play was controversial. It wasn't like studying *Moby-Dick* with Bad News Benson, which had been David's favorite time in class until now. It wasn't really better, just different in an exciting way. Bad News Benson *was* Ahab; he was so powerful, so dynamic that he carried the class. Reginald Barnes gave the class a new identity by letting it have its freedom. That was it. What David learned was that there were no right answers, that with Shakespeare, at least, every production of the play was different, and the characters themselves became different depending on who played them. David loved Cordelia. He wrote his essay on her character and why she cannot lie just to make her father feel good. Wally Hinson and Ted Barber hated her. They said she was proud and selfish and cold. They couldn't understand why, if she loved her father best, she couldn't say a few special words. Antonio Black agreed. "If she's so wise, she must know what will happen to her father when he's stuck with Goneril and Regan."

"She just can't. Her mouth won't say the words," David said. He understood her. He was more like Cordelia than anyone else in the play, he thought.

They all had to memorize passages and perform them to the class, not just recite them but perform them, and then they had to talk to the class about their passage. Wally Hinson stole the show when he did the soliloquy of Edmund, the bastard son of the Earl of Gloucester, who ends his speech with the stirring line, "Now gods stand up for bastards!" The class rose and cheered for the vigorous villain, who ends up with both the wicked sisters in love with him. He was Wally Hinson's favorite character, of course.

David did Lear's short soliloquy in the third act, when Lear, out in the storm, alone, realizes for the first time what it must be like to be poor:

"Poor naked wretches, whereso'er you are,
That bide the pelting of this pitiless storm,
How shall your houseless heads and unfed sides,
Your loop'd and windowed raggedness defend you
From seasons such as these? O I have ta'en
Too little care of this! Take physic, pomp,
Expose thyself to feel what wretches feel,
That thou mayst shake the superflux to them,
And show the heavens more just."

He could see the scene in his mind's eye, the old king looking like his father, standing there in the rain before the hovel, telling the disguised Kent and the fool to go in because he wants to "pray." He's never prayed before, never needed to pray—never realized what the real job of being a king was. He didn't even know how to dress and undress. Someone was always helping him, someone was always saying, "Yes, your Majesty." His suffering has made him see the world's suffering. That was it. We can't understand what we don't see.

David talked to the class. "We're like King Lear," he said. "We've never been really poor or hungry or homeless. When I went to New York, two weeks ago, for my uncle's memorial service, I came out of Grand Central Station and started walking uptown, toward 57th. It was cold, and there on Vanderbilt Avenue just across from the station was a man kind of hunched up, sitting on the sidewalk, with a blanket over him and a ski cap on his head, a black ski cap, I think. And he had a bowl or a dish in front of him with money in it, and a sign that said, PLEAS HELP. No E on the 'please,' I thought. And I walked by and thought of Father Perkins and the parable of the Good Samaritan and came back and put a quarter on his plate. It clinked, and I looked in his eyes and wondered what it would be like to be that hungry or that cold. So when we read *King Lear* and we got to that scene out on the heath when King Lear thinks about the fool being cold and how awful it is to be poor, I knew I had to memorize that passage. Thank you."

Ralph Wisdom leaned over and touched him on the arm as he sat down. "I hadn't thought about the name before," he whispered with a half wink.

"What name?" David whispered back, and then it came to him. "Oh, my God," he said. "I really didn't think about it, either."

At Thanksgiving he took the train to Grand Central, subway to Times Square and then to 34th Street, and the Pennsylvania Railroad to Trenton. When the train to Trenton left Penn Station he pulled out the letter and read it again. It was from Terry at Deerfield, and it had arrived at school just the day before, just in time to totally disrupt his life. "Dear Butter Rum," it read, "I hate to be the one to tell you this, but someone needs to warn you about Tracy Warren. She's bad news, Dave. My advice would be to break it off with her. She's nothing but trouble. I say this in friendship, old buddy. Yours, Terry."

He had lain awake for hours going over the letter. What did it mean? How was Tracy bad news? David knew that she had gone to Deerfield for a weekend, but what had she done. Part of him wanted to do nothing, to say nothing. Part of him wanted to take the letter and tear in a million little pieces and simply go on as if it had never come. He knew what Tracy's reaction would be: "It has nothing to do with us," she would say. "We're secret," she would say. She would do that level five stuff with him and make him forget the letter, which was of course what he wanted to do. He was going to her house on Saturday for their "last night before vacation" ritual. And he couldn't spend a night with her and just ignore the letter. She'd see through it. "What's the matter?" she would ask. She would know he was hiding something. And so that other part of him knew that he had to confront her with it, show it to her, let her say what she would. Still, it terrified him, because it might mean losing her. He would show her the letter, and she would tell him to go home. That was what he feared most.

His father met him in Lambertville in Aunt Louise's station wagon. He wrapped his arms around David and hugged him. "It's good to see you, son," he said. "I want us to learn to know each other."

"Me, too," said David.

"Elizabeth and the kids are already there," he said. "I drove up to New York and picked them up this morning. Let's go across the street and get some coffee. We can tell Louise the train was late. They're all busy making paper turkeys and pilgrims. They won't miss us."

David could envisage the scene, the children spread out on the living room floor, a little nervous about those big dogs, paper, scissors, glue, paint everywhere. Louise didn't believe in buying things. She didn't really believe in holidays, but if she was going to have to celebrate them, then everything would be done by hand.

David and his father sat in the coffee shop at the Lambertville House where Swen had lived when he first came east, before he and Louise were married.

"I drink a lot of coffee now," his father said when they were served. He measured in two spoonfuls of sugar and stirred.

"I know," said David. "I loved what you said about A.A. at Swen's funeral. I was really listening. I feel like I never knew you before."

"You were awfully quiet. I was wondering if you still held it against me, the summer you came out to the ranch."

"Oh, no," said David. "I was just listening because Elizabeth and Aunt Louise, you know… "

"I do know. Women are great talkers. That's why I wanted this time with you before… "

"I know," said David, and they both laughed. "And how are the dogs?" Then they laughed again.

"Jesus," said his father, "they're everywhere. I have to keep my door closed to keep them out of my room."

They talked for a long time, and something happened to David. He forgot himself. He forgot to be careful and plan what he would say, he forgot to treat his father as a grown up. Before he knew it he was talking about Tracy Warren and Ralph Wisdom and the odd meeting with Terry Roche at Grand Central. His father listened and talked back, like a friend, an older, wiser friend, but a friend, not a parent. David liked him, he liked him very much. But he didn't tell him about the letter. He was not ready to do that.

When they arrived at the house, it was dark, and the two children came bursting out the front door and down the stone steps to the driveway. David got out and lifted them up, Maggie in one arm and Alex in the other.

"You bad, Uncle Dave," said Maggie.

"You take too long to get here," said Alex.

David looked at his father and laughed and carried the kids into the house. There was something special here that David couldn't quite put his finger on, a brightness inside that kept the dark away, a brightness among the children and the autumn leaves and small pumpkins on the dining room table and the figures of the Puritans the children had made that afternoon by folding and cutting out magazines. David walked into the kitchen to greet Aunt Louise and

Elizabeth, who were cooking dinner, and for a moment the house seemed like home

At least until later that evening. The kids had been put to bed in the little yellow room next to the kitchen where David had slept two summers before. Elizabeth would sleep in the guest bedroom next to it, and David and his father would sleep in the studio in the room his father was fixing up for Aunt Louise. The adults were sitting in the living room talking when suddenly Elizabeth, who was sitting on the couch next to one of the Afghans, burst into tears.

"What is it, sweetheart?" her father asked. He stood up and walked toward her, shooing the Afghan off the couch so that he could sit down next to her.

Louise looked puzzled and embarrassed. She was a no-nonsense woman, and there was little place for tears in her world. David understood that and admired her. He was very much the same, except when he was with Tracy.

Elizabeth started talking. It was about Phil. She didn't know what to do. He had been talking about moving the family to Cincinnati or Cleveland or even Los Angeles. He had been studying a new music theory called the Schillinger method. There were already too many Schillinger teachers in New York, and if he wanted work, he would have to go elsewhere.

"I don't know if I have the strength to start all over again," she said, and began to cry softly.

"It's not really that, is it?" Allan asked. He took her hand.

"Well, no," said Elizabeth tentatively. "It is and it isn't. It's just that I. . ."

"That you don't love him anymore," said Allan, "or he doesn't love you."

"He's so cold. I don't know what to do. I don't have any friends. I can't go out. I want to go out by myself, but he won't let me. It's like he thinks I'm going to have an affair. How can I have an affair? I don't even know anyone."

"He's jealous and insecure," said Allan. "At least he doesn't drink, at least he doesn't hit you. That's what I see in A.A."

"He just watches me all the time."

"Maybe moving would be good."

"I'm just so tired. I don't have any energy. I really need to get away from him. This is the first time I've been out of the apartment in months, except to go to the grocery store or the playground."

"And the children?" asked Aunt Louise. "How are they?"

"I don't know. OK, I guess, though Alex is getting a little Bronx accent."

She laughed, and David laughed. He tried to imagine Alex with a Bronx accent, and little Maggie as a tough teenager, popping her gum.

"I'd like to go back to California," Elizabeth said, "but not with him. I just don't think I can live with him anymore, and I don't think I could support the children on my own. I asked him about a divorce once, and he just glared at me and said 'Never in a million years.' I'm useful to him. I'm the children's mother, I'm a convenience."

"You have to think of the children first," said Louise.

"I do, Louise," said Elizabeth. "I do, all the time. That's the problem. I don't sleep at night. I wake up tired. It's just a rat race."

"We'll work through it together," said Allan.

"Perhaps you will, but I will excuse myself and go to bed," said Louise, and walked up the stairs to her room.

David was way over his head. It was as if he was there and not there. He could be everyone and no one at the same time. When each person spoke, he listened and understood that person's point of view. If someone had asked him what he thought, he would not have known what to say. It seemed so complicated. It seemed as if whatever Elizabeth might do was wrong. Leaving was wrong, staying was wrong, moving was wrong. They could talk about it all night, and it wouldn't get them anywhere. His father was so kind, so understanding, but he really couldn't offer any solution. He would go back to Phoenix and try to make money buying and selling land, Elizabeth and the children would go back to New York, Louise would write letters to museums and galleries and try to get Swen's work shown in exhibits. And David would go to Tracy Warren's and find out what the hell had been going on.

Tracy Warren met him at the station, but she didn't get out of the car. That's the first thing David noticed. She sat in the car smoking. He put his bags in the back and slid into the seat beside her. He reached to kiss her, to turn her head toward his, but she just sat there, looking straight ahead. She had been crying.

"What is it?" he asked.

"Don't be so goddamn nice, David. Just get it out. You know. You got the fucking letter."

He had never heard her speak like this before.

"Yes," he said. "I got the letter."

"I knew. I knew that's what he would do. He threatened to do it, and I begged him not to, but he did anyway. Your friend is a real bastard."

"But what happened, Tracy? What happened?"

"Listen, David. Do me a favor. My parents don't know, OK? Butch doesn't know. It's dinner time. We're going home, we're going to act normal during dinner. Then I'll tell you—after they go to bed? OK? OK, sweetheart?"

David had never seen her this agitated, this insecure. It was as if she were fifteen again. "OK," he said. "Now, please give me a hug."

And she turned and buried her face in his shoulder and cried. "They're all such bastards," she said. "Oh, David, I'm so glad I didn't come to your dance weekend."

Dinner took forever. It was as if they were eating and drinking in slow motion. The conversation was strictly level two. David and Butch and Mr. Warren talked about the Princeton football team and how great Dick Kazmaier was, and Mrs. Warren asked David about his family. He told them about his uncle's death and the memorial service they'd had at the gallery. "I know that gallery," Mrs. Warren said. "You know, Tracy, the one that had all the bird paintings." But Tracy would not play the game.

"Don't you guys stay up too late tonight, David," Mrs. Warren said. "I don't think your buddy is feeling up to par."

At ten o'clock Tracy abruptly sent Butch to his room. "Get out of here, Tiger," she said. "Your big brother and I need to have private talk."

"Come on, Tracy, you're not my boss."

"Butch, I mean it."

David looked at Butch and tried to signal with his eyes that it would be wise to obey her.

For a moment he stood his ground, his brown eyes confronting her green. Then he turned and stomped up the stairs.

"Your friend, Terry," she started.

"Wait, Tracy," David began, "I think we'll both need a cigarette for this."

He pulled the pack from his shirt pocket, and shook one out to her. He watched her as he lit it, watched her as she sat on the couch and looked past him to the outdoors. He sat next to her, but not too close.

"Your friend, Terry," she began again. "I begged him not to write you, not to tell you."

"About what, Tracy? Start at the beginning."

"I went back to Deerfield, David. I had a date with Paul Montgomery. He's a senior. I've known him since I was ten. He's from here."

"But you wouldn't come to Wicker with me."

"And it's a damn good thing I didn't. At least I didn't get you in trouble. Here I was in this godforsaken town in the middle of nowhere. Everywhere you turn, you're looking in the woods. It's like a time warp. I was staying in this faculty house across the street from the school, down one of those little side roads, and at the end of the road there was nothing but woods. You know all the rules. You have to be in your house by eleven, and I couldn't stand it, so I told Paul I'd meet him at one at the end of the street. My room was on the first floor. I'd just climb out the window."

"But he was supposed to be in his dorm by midnight."

"Of course he was. But he was a sixth former and he could get away without causing too much trouble. It was me that caused the trouble. I met him at the end of the road and went into the woods. I loved it, David. That's the problem with me. There we were in the middle of the night sitting in the woods smoking, and one thing led to another, and we started messing around, and then there were flashlights and the next thing we knew we were surrounded. God, I felt like we were being arrested or something, and they dragged me back to the house where I was staying and sent me home on the first train Sunday morning. Paul got suspended."

And Terry?"

"Terry is Paul's best friend. He hates me for getting Paul suspended. I begged him not to tell you."

"But we're supposed to be honest."

"We are. I would have told you myself. I just didn't like someone else telling you."

She reached toward him, but he felt suddenly cold. She put her hands on either side of his face and drew him towards her. She kissed him, but he did not respond. She drew back. "What is this, David?" she asked. "You've never been like this before."

"You've never been like this before," he echoed.

"You don't see, do you?"

"See what?"

"I need you now more than ever. I need your love. I need your support."

"But Tracy, you don't come to Wicker and you go off to Deerfield and get into trouble, and I'm supposed to support you? I'm so. . .I'm so. . ."

"Well say it, then. So. . .what?"

"I'm upset. I feel betrayed."

"You're not, David. Don't you see? We're forever. I was just having fun with Paul. It didn't mean anything."

"How could it not mean anything?"

David got up and walked across the room. He felt himself on the edge of tears. He didn't want to cry in front of Tracy, not tonight, not this way.

"I need your support," she said.

He turned and looked back. "I don't think I can do it," he said.

Between Thanksgiving and Christmas they finished *King Lear*. The end of the fourth act was terrifying—the mad king meeting the blind Earl of Gloucester on the beach at Dover. Gloucester blind because his eyes have been put out by the Duke of Cornwall. "It's the grossest thing I ever heard of," said Wally Hinson with some delight. He had memorized the Duke's line, "Out vile jelly, where is thy luster now?" and he enjoyed saying it, as he pretended to push out someone's eyes with his thumb. But the final act was even worse, as Lear carries in the dead Cordelia, who has been hanged by the order of the villainous Edmund. The stage is scattered with bodies, and only Edgar and the Duke of Albany are alive to speak the ending.

Reginald Barnes told the class that an alternate ending had been written in the 17th century and that the play was performed with that ending for a hundred years. "People couldn't stand the injustice of Cordelia's death and Lear's," he said. "The great Samuel Johnson was appalled by the ending of the play."

The class argued about it.

"Hamlet dies, Othello dies, Macbeth dies," said Antonio Black. "What's wrong with Lear dying? It's a tragedy, isn't it?"

Antonio Black was showing off because no one else in the class had read *Othello*, not even David. But Reginald Barnes was quick to respond. "That's a good question," he said. "But there's a difference between Lear and the others. All the others have killed someone. There is a kind of poetic justice about their deaths, even if we sympathize with them. Lear hasn't done anything except make an error of judgment."

"But he can't go on living without Cordelia," said David suddenly. "He dies of a broken heart. If she had lived, they could have been happy together. It's her death we hate, not his."

David had been thinking about Tracy Warren since he got back to school. She had not gotten up on Sunday morning, and Mrs. Warren had taken him to the station. "I think she's come down with something," Mrs. Warren said. "I hope you don't get it." David almost laughed at the irony. Indeed, she had come down with something, and David didn't know what to do about it. The more he thought in class about Lear and Cordelia, the more it made him think about himself and Tracy. Somehow he had failed Tracy, just as Lear failed Cordelia. That was it. What was it he had said to Tracy? "I don't think I can?" Tracy had done something wrong, and she needed him to love her despite that. But he had failed her, and now it was as if she was dead. She might as well be. In his room, during evening study hall, with Borden in the library, David wrote to Tracy:

> You asked for love and I gave you
> Only a stone. You asked for love
> And I turned away, turned my face
> From day to icy night. I thought
> You were Pearl, but now I know
> You are Hester and I, I am Arthur
> Dimmesdale. Can we start again
> In the glare of common places,
> Can we walk together in the spaces
> I have left behind? Let the Puritans
> Howl. I will not be one of them.
> Forgive me.

"Well, Maggie Hope," he said to himself, "be with me now." He folded the paper carefully and stuffed it into an envelope, sealed it quickly, and then addressed and stamped it. He carried it to the mailroom, now filled with milling students getting out of study hall. He slammed it in the mail slot.

"So, who's the letter to?" asked Wally Hinson, coming toward him with a big smile.

"To my girl friend, Tracy Warren," said David. He had never said it before, never spoken her name to anyone at Wicker except Ralph Wisdom, whom he could trust to keep his secret. But now Wally Hinson knew, and if Wally Hinson knew, the whole world would know soon.

Reginald Barnes invited him for tea the next afternoon. He had a small apartment in the basement of the North Dorm, where David had lived his third form year. There were books everywhere: on shelves supported by concrete blocks, on tables, in piles on the floor—books and papers, old spiral notebooks, and blue examination booklets. David sat in an overstuffed chair whose springs seemed almost ready to break through its thin fabric.

"It reminds me of my room in Cambridge," said Reginald Barnes, smiling and stirring sugar into his tea.

"How do you know where anything is?" asked David, who was nothing if not organized. He and Borden kept the neatest room in the school. It was kind of joke as to which one was more compulsive.

"My own personal filing system. Instinct, I guess. You reach and hope," said the English teacher. There was a momentary silence. Then he continued, "You know, David, we've all been wondering what you will do after college."

"After college is a long way, sir," said David.

"Indeed it is, but if you were intending, for example, to be a doctor, wouldn't it be best to be sure and get the right courses in preparation?"

"Yes, sir."

"And the same would be true, would it not, if you were hoping to become an English teacher?"

"I don't know, sir."

"Mr. Benson and Mr. Richardson and I have been talking about your work, and we are very proud, very proud indeed, of what you have accomplished here. Perhaps you will major in English in college and eventually go on to graduate school. You have the potential to be a fine teacher-scholar."

"Thank you, sir," David said, and then he thought of something. "Mr. Barnes," he said, "I think I just realized why I like English best. I don't think I could really major in anything else. All the other subjects here seem—not easy—that's not the word—they seem mechanical. You read the book, take tests, and answer the questions. If you answer them right, then you get good grades. It's a matter of hard work, but afterwards there's nothing left. In English, there are no right answers. English is my lowest grade but my best subject because I spend more time on it than anything else, trying to figure out what the books mean. English is more exciting than anything else."

"I'm glad you feel that way," the master replied, and then went on. "While I have you here, take this script home with you for the holidays. It's Ben Jonson's play, *The Alchemist*. We're going to do it this winter, and I'd like you to play the part of Face. You can start working on the lines—there are a lot of them."

"But aren't you having tryouts?" David asked.

"Some," said Mr. Barnes, "but in your case, I've already decided. I'd like the chance to work with you. Have a good Christmas, David. I'll see you next year."

David stood and shook hands with Reginald Barnes. Then he walked out into the December night, stunned at all this. He felt honored.

CHAPTER SIXTEEN

Thee St. Regis was as beautiful as ever. Every time David walked through the revolving door it was like entering a magical world belonging only to Molly Ariel. No one else knew he stayed there, and no one else would do it justice. His meetings with Molly usually took place during Christmas vacation, when she came to Washington and New York to see Jack's children and her other Eastern friends. Usually they had lunch, and she took him shopping for things he would not have thought of buying himself – things like rubbers or galoshes or pajamas or new luggage. He'd dragged his old trunk and the M.H. bag around for so long that they seemed as much as a part of his limp or his cowlick, which he was forever wetting down.

David knew he didn't walk like anyone else, and for the most part it didn't bother him. He had been hurt terribly by Melinda Menkhaus, but Tracy had helped him get over that, and as long as he had Tracy he didn't have to worry about his thin legs. He was proud of his legs and his bleeding Achilles tendons he'd wrapped so lovingly before every game. His proudest moment at Wicker had been during the week before Christmas break at the soccer banquet in the Headmaster's study. David and Hugh Packard had played on Wicker's first soccer team four years ago, and Wally Hinson had joined them the next year. And now they were graduating, leaving their beloved team to another generation of feet. The school had instituted a new award, the Whitfield Trophy, given for team spirit and aggressive play. It was named for James Whitfield, the wonderful English coach who had helped them so much as fourth formers.

"It is my pleasure," Coach Jumping John had said, "to award the initial Winfield trophy to David J. Lear and Wallace B. Hinson." David and Wally had risen together and taken the trophy between them, each holding a handle as they posed for pictures. It was a new thing for David, getting an athletic trophy. He was used to academic prizes, he'd been getting them all his life. He'd won the Latin Prize as a fifth former at Wicker because he was completing sixth form Latin a year early. They just didn't have any more Latin for him. But this was different because he'd paid for this with his body and his blood. Once in a game he'd been hit in the balls with a savage line drive as he tried to cut off an opposing halfback. For a moment he couldn't breathe. He lay on the field, crumpled, curled up in pain. "No cup," Jumping John had whispered afterwards, when he was better.

"I can't run with one of those cups," David had said. "It just scrapes the hell out of me." The coach had not answered.

Walking back to the room after the banquet, Wally Hinson held forth. "I love this goddamn school, and I love you guys, but Jesus, they've got to change the way they give letters."

What Wally Hinson was talking about was the tradition of major and minor sports. Major sports like football and basketball and baseball and crews got big letters, big blue W's. Minor sports got little letters with even smaller letters to indicate their sport, like sWt for Wicker Ski Team, or tWt for Wicker Tennis Team. They called soccer Association Football, so the soccer players got aWf, which all the students called Wicker Air Force, or even worse, Women's Air Force. So they never wore their letters. They just stuck them away in their bottom drawers to keep for posterity.

"This aWf stuff really eats shit," said Wally Hinson with a big grin. He was mad, but he was also happy.

David arrived at the St. Regis on the second night of Christmas vacation for dinner with Molly Ariel, full of the joy of his soccer trophy, full of the joy of his tea with Reginald Barnes, his part in *The Alchemist*. He looked in the mirror next to the elevators and liked what he saw.

Molly brought him back to earth. They sat in the dining room with candles on the tables. She was smoking and drinking a martini. David was smoking and drinking wine, being as sophisticated as he possibly could.

"I'm very proud of you, chum," she said. "I couldn't have asked any more from you than you've given."

"Thank you," David said modestly.

"But I think," she said with a change in her voice, "that you need to begin taking responsibility for your own life from now on. You'll be eighteen in the spring. That's a big birthday."

She smiled and reached toward him, put her hand on his for a moment. "Now don't give me your big, sad, scared look. It's not so bad as all that."

She had caught him by surprise and he hadn't the time to stop his face from registering the shock of this news.

"Your tuition is paid until the end of the year, and your allowance will continue until June. After graduation, you're an adult, a grown up. With your grades, you'll probably get a full scholarship to Princeton, and the only difference will be that you'll have to earn a little money for clothes and things."

He smiled weakly and tried to say something, but nothing came out.

"I think a job at college is a good thing, David. The university has jobs for scholarship students, like waiting on tables in the commons or working in administrative offices. It'll keep you busy and introduce you to a different group of students than you'd otherwise meet. It's not really that different from Wicker, is it? At Wicker, everyone works. It's part of their philosophy, part of the reason I wanted you to go there instead of Deerfield or Groton."

"I know," he said, "and I'm glad. I'm really glad I went to Wicker. It was a good choice." He had his breath back now and his presence of mind. "Thank you for everything, Molly," he said. "I can't begin to imagine what might have happened to me without you. Even if, even if. . ."

He paused and started again. "Even if you aren't paying for my education, will you still be there, you know, to help me? I can talk to you. I need your guidance."

"Of course, chum," she said. "I'm not throwing you to the wolves. I'm just making it a little harder for you, giving you a challenge."

"Like when I took the bus to California," he laughed.

"That's not very good grammar for an English major," she said, "but, yes, like that."

They ate their dinner and talked about Elizabeth and Phil and Aunt Louise and soccer and wrestling and the theater. Molly was going to see *The King and I* the next night. David knew the songs, because the record had come out, and the sixth formers could play records in the Headmaster's study at night and on Sunday afternoons. He loved the story of the woman who tries to teach the King of Siam how to be a human being. He could "whistle a happy tune," if he was alone. That had become David's theme song. "No one will suspect I'm afraid" the verse went on, and he understood how important it was to keep whistling.

Molly kissed him goodbye in the lobby and told him she would come to his graduation in June. It was nine o'clock, and he wasn't ready to go home, so he walked over to Times Square and looked at the marquees of the theatres. *Guys and Dolls, Call Me Madame, The King and I, The Rose Tattoo* by Tennessee Williams. *Mr. Roberts* with Henry Fonda had just closed, and David was sorry he had missed it. There had been a lot of talk at Wicker about the young lieutenant who throws the Captain's palm tree overboard at the end of the play and the heroic Mr. Roberts. David walked down Broadway, past the Paramount, to 42nd Street and turned right. Between Broadway and Eighth Avenue were a group of theatres with cheap admissions, theatres that featured double or triple features with old movies. One of them had erotic movies. Wally Hinson had talked about going to these movies, "dirty flicks" he called them, but David didn't know if he'd really done it. Maybe he'd done it on a dare with a group of friends.

David stopped in front of the theater and looked at the advertisements, the suggestive pictures. He turned toward the box office, took out his wallet, then stopped, pulled away, and walked back across town to Sixth Avenue. He couldn't do it. It was too scary. He'd heard talk at school of people going to sex movies and being picked up by strange men, who would come over and sit next to anyone by themselves and make advances. No, he would not risk that. He would take the D train home to the Bronx.

The next day after breakfast he told Elizabeth about Molly's decision. She was not at all surprised. In fact, she thought it was good for him, too.

"I think I need to start earning money right now," David said. "Maybe I can find a job. Don't stores put on extra workers for the Christmas holidays? Maybe I could go back to that grocery store and do deliveries. I don't know where to start."

"Slow down, sweetie," Elizabeth said, laughing. "It's not as if you're going to go broke. You've got six months before your allowance stops."

"But I want something in the bank to fall back on. You know."

"What do I know? I never have anything to fall back on. You know that. I just get by from day to day. That's what we do. And once you're eighteen, I don't get money from Social Security any more."

David felt guilty. Now he really had to get a job. He had to help Elizabeth AND save money.

"Maybe I can go out to Lambertville," he said. "And work at that restaurant."

"Well, maybe you can," she suddenly yelled, and then burst into tears and went into her room.

"What's the matter with Mommy?" Alex asked.

"Matter Mommy!" Maggie wailed plaintively.

"Mommy's just tired," said David, and he took the kids back to their room to play. Eventually Elizabeth came out and apologized to him. Things weren't any better with Phil. He just seemed to avoid everything by going to work all the time, and her nerves were bad. She told him to do whatever he had to do. She understood.

"I just love it when you're here," she said. "It's nice to have another adult in the house, someone to talk to, someone to help with the kids. It means a lot."

"I know," he said.

He decided to stay until after Christmas. Then he would go to Princeton and talk to the Admissions and Financial Aid Director, and Aunt Louise could pick him up there, and he would help her with the cataloguing of Uncle Swen's paintings for a few days before he headed back to school. Maybe she would pay him something.

He got his old job back at the grocery store. They always needed someone to carry groceries to the elderly and the shut-ins, and there weren't many people who were willing to do it. David didn't mind. He was much stronger now than he had been before. Wrestling had built his body up, and his arms and shoulders were powerful. He'd been elected captain of the second wrestling team, but if he could beat the person in his weight class on the varsity, he would move up. He thought about that. The problem was you never knew who would wrestle at what weight. David usually wrestled at 130, but sometimes at 137. The coaches tried to figure out the best combinations for the team, and often a bigger, stronger wrestler could sweat down to a lower weight, if he was willing to go through that arduous process, so David wasn't really sure who he would have to beat. All he knew, as he walked up the long hill to the Concourse with his boxes of groceries, was that he loved wrestling and was ready for the season to begin.

Most of his deliveries were in the big apartment houses on the Concourse, but sometimes he had to go down the hill on the other side to Phyllis Shapiro's on Jerome Avenue where the IRT subway rattled overhead on its elevated tracks on the way to the north Bronx. He could tell that people were getting ready for Christmas. It was his job not only to carry the groceries to the people, but he also took their orders on the phone and packed their boxes. A lot of the little old ladies lived alone, David knew, but they were ordering enough food for a month. There would be people coming for Christmas or after Christmas, sons and daughters, grandchildren, nieces, nephews. There would be great feasts, family members sitting around the table and telling stories, children opening presents, aunts and uncles falling asleep in the overstuffed chairs in the living room after dinner, after turkey and wine and mince pie or apple pie with ice cream. Before Christmas the old ladies would stock their larders in case it snowed, in case they had a blizzard and the stores were closed and they were trapped in their apartments. Sometimes they called and asked David to go down to the hardware store and buy them flashlights and batteries. By the time Christmas day came David had been to some apartments two or three times. On December 24 three of the ladies asked him to come by and pick up "a little Christmas thank-you" if he was in the neighborhood.

He had trouble with the heat in their apartments. He'd come in from the outside, where it must have been in the twenties, and they all kept their heat on high. It was boiling. He'd take off everything and still start sweating and then have to put it all on again to go back out, and the sweat would turn cold. He couldn't figure out how they stood it.

"When you get old," Mrs. Baumgartner told him, "your circulation stops. Your blood don't run good. You're just cold all the time, so you gotta have it hot. Enjoy your life now. Enjoy every minute of it." She handed him a card in an envelope. "Merry Christmas. Find a girl. Take her to the movies or something. Don't wait, kiddo. Old age stinks."

He thought about Tracy. He hadn't heard from her since he mailed the letter at school the day before vacation, but he had given her Elizabeth's address and phone number, and said that he would like to come, as usual, for the Saturday night before he had to go back to school. "I know I was wrong not to support you, Tracy, and I ask your forgiveness," he had written. "I can't imagine life without you." His image of her kept him sane as he trudged up and down the steep hills in the cold. He didn't care what she had done. He would keep the faith. The words of the Lowell School hymn kept coming to him—"Fight the good fight with all your might"— he sang to himself as he walked down the Concourse. He would

Anthony S. Abbott

fight to keep Tracy. That was it. He would not wait for her to call. He would take the fight to her and ask her to take him back.

On the day before Christmas Phyllis Shapiro, his Jerome Avenue friend, asked him for tea. She sat him at her kitchen table and put his "little envelope" next to his place. Her brother Nathan and his kids were coming for dinner and presents that night. She would go to his house in Queens on Christmas day. "I hate Christmas," she told David. She wasn't as old at the others, and she was almost pretty in a rough, hard kind of way, black hair turning gray, a kind of New York street savvy about her. "I grew up here," she said. "It was nicer then. It's changing. You tell your sister, kid, to get out of here. I been working at the bank on 167th St. for ten years. You can tell—blacks, Puerto Ricans moving in, Jewish families moving out. It's like the rats deserting the sinking ship. I can tell by the customers in my line." She was standing next to him as he drank his tea. Then she bent over and kissed him on the cheek. "I'd like to get you in bed," she said.

David blushed.

"Don't worry, kid, I'm just giving you a compliment. You're a nice lookin' kid. We don't see many like you around here."

He got up and put his coat and hat and gloves back on and slipped the card in his pocket. "Thanks, Mrs. Shapiro," he said and edged toward the door.

"Merry Christmas, kid," she said.

At five he was back at Elizabeth's and kissing her goodbye as she headed out the door for her Christmas ritual. She would meet Phil downtown for dinner and they would finish their shopping, picking up bargains at the stores, sales on everything. They would come home around ten with shopping bags full, and the children would be in bed. At least they hoped the children would be in bed. David wasn't much of a disciplinarian. Elizabeth had left their dinner on the stove, and after dinner, David was good at baths and stories and play time. But getting them to sleep was another matter altogether. There was always one more potty trip or one more drink of water or something in the room that scared them.

But on Christmas Eve, despite their excitement, there was always the bribe: "Santa can't come unless you're asleep." So David read them "The Night Before Christmas," and they put out cookies and milk for Santa, and he led them to their room.

"Uncle Dave," said Alex, as David tucked him into bed. "In the story Santa comes down the chimney."

"Right," said David.

"But we don't have a chimney."

"We don't have a chimley," echoed Maggie.

"Nope," said David. "No chimley." He loved Maggie, and he especially loved her baby talk. He didn't want her to say words right. If she said "pasketti" for spaghetti, he thought it was wonderful. Elizabeth told him it was not good to encourage her to talk baby talk. She needed to grow up. "Not yet," David thought.

"So how does Santa get in?" asked Alex.

"Through the window," said David, remembering his own trip through the window when he had forgotten his key.

"Where do the reindeer land?"

"On the street," said David.

"But the cars," said Alex.

"Cars," said Maggie. "Cars go on street."

"No cars in the middle of the night. Everyone is asleep," said David.

"Santa eat cookie," said Maggie.

"Santa eat cookie," echoed David.

"Santa fat," said Maggie.

"That's right, Maggie Hope," said David. "Santa is fat because he has so many cookies to eat."

"Santa couldn't go to all the houses," said Alex, who was by now thinking much more complex thoughts.

"He has to send his helpers," said David.

The conversation went on, but finally they tired and David made his way down the hall to the living room. It was 8:45. With luck, they'd be asleep when Elizabeth and Phil came in.

Then the thought of Jesus came to him—it was not invited, nothing conscious he could put his finger on. It was there. He could see himself walking to the manger. He was in his blue jeans and his hat and jacket, and his old gloves, his scarf thrown around his neck. He was out in a field, walking in his galoshes, his galoshes unbuckled, walking through the field toward the manger. Jesus was out there somewhere. Everyone was walking. He could see old Mrs. Baumgartner and Phyllis Shapiro, and fat old Santa Claus—everyone walking, and somewhere out there was the manger, and they would all come to that place and kneel, and there would be a moment of terrible and beautiful silence and the world would be different somehow.

Father Perkins had reminded them again, as they left for the holidays, not to leave Jesus out of Christmas. David missed school. It was strange how Jesus was there in St. Matthew's Chapel, there in the bread and wine and in the voice of Father Perkins who spoke with such assurance, his deep voice echoing off the stone walls. "We bring our daily acts to Jesus, and He takes them and makes them new. He sanctifies them. That means 'to make holy.' Jesus makes holy that which cannot be holy without Him. Our best is never good enough without His sanctifying grace."

David would have liked to go downtown to church, but he didn't know what church to go to. How strange to love St. Matthew"s Chapel at Wicker School and never go to church anywhere else. No one in his family seemed to believe in God, not Phil or Elizabeth or his mother or Aunt Louise. He wondered why. He felt the need to find a church. Maybe he could go with Tracy Warren and her family. Maybe they would go on the Sunday morning after New Years. He missed her terribly, missed her smile and her touch and her green eyes, he missed her questions and the softness of her low and musical voice. He would call her on Christmas Day.

CHAPTER SEVENTEEN

The winter term was glorious for the sixth form at Wicker School. Though David didn't believe God had anything to do with athletics, God seemed to have blessed the Wicker basketball team in general and their Captain Robbie Tillman in particular. They charged through the season winning game after game, and then, just when it seemed they had the championship, they were unexpectedly routed by the Gunnery School, 71-50, to fall into second place. But on Valentine's Day they came back to defeat Gunnery, 58-55, and retake the lead.

When the final buzzer sounded, the entire school poured from the stands onto the court and carried their heroes off on their shoulders. All the home games had been attended by boisterous crowds, but none like this one. They had all stood from beginning to end, each form together, trying to out cheer every other form for every basket and gasping when things went badly. David had never seen such spirit—such absolute devotion to a team. At first David was a little tentative, standing next to Wally Hinson, worried that Wally would utter some incredible curse and get kicked out of the gym, but by the end David screamed with all the rest until his voice was shredded.

As the players finally climbed down from the shoulders of their fans and started toward the locker room, someone began a chant,

"We want Robbie," and then others picked it up, and soon they were all yelling, "We want Robbie!" until he came back through the door and into the gym, his arms raised in victory, his eyes filled with tears.

This is what Ralph Wisdom had meant when he talked about the leadership of the sixth form, how every member of the form had a role to play. Robbie Tillman had played his with passion and dignity and humility. It was beautiful. Now it was David's turn in *The Alchemist*, which was to be performed twice, once for the student body and once for the parents. They had rehearsed all winter, it seemed, sometimes late into the night. One night Father Perkins came in and sent the cast to bed. The next night Reginald Barnes let them go on time.

It was a huge struggle, and David wondered if they had overreached themselves. The play was terribly long, and full of opportunities to make mistakes. The play had to go fast—this play about three con artists who take over a house while the master is away and disguise themselves in order to take advantage of a whole series of gullible fools. It was a great idea, but if it bogged down, if the three tricksters themselves were not totally believable, then the whole play fell apart. There were no women cast in the play. Reginald Barnes had decided to follow the Elizabethan practice of casting boys in the female parts, and this, of course, made the play funnier. David was the chief trickster, Jeremy, the servant of the house's absent master, who disguises himself as Captain Face and brings the poor gullible fools to Subtle, the Alchemist, who promises to turn all their lead to gold.

Rehearsals were slow, people kept forgetting their lines, and sometimes their entrances. David kept getting angry and losing his patience. "Shit, D.J.," said Wally Hinson one night after rehearsal (Wally was Abel Drugger, the pharmacist). "You gotta stop treating us all like we're professionals or something. We're just kids trying to have a good time, you know? Slow down."

Reginald Barnes asked David to stay one night after rehearsal. "Are you having fun, David?" he asked.

"Well, sort of," David said.

"It's got to be more than sort of. If you're not having fun, no one else will have fun. You've got to enjoy being Face. What you're doing is trying to direct the play and take responsibility for everyone. I've seen you up there, whispering people's lines to them. Every time someone makes a mistake, you look angry. Face isn't angry. Face is having the time of his life. Let me be the director. Your job is to have fun."

They talked about the character of Face and how he was different from David, and as they talked, David thought of Debbie Rossiter. He hadn't thought of her in years—Debbie Rossiter his music teacher at Lowell School, whom he had fallen in love with as a student there, Debbie Rossiter who directed him as Frederick in *The Pirates of Penzance,* Debbie Rossiter who had told him the same thing that Reginald Barnes was telling him. He needed to relax, to have fun, to enjoy being Frederick.

It was funny, David thought, that he had stopped singing when he got to Wicker. He had not even tried out for the Glee Club much as he loved music. And he had not tried out for any plays. Now he wondered why. Was it lack of confidence, fear that his voice in changing had simply disappeared? Fear that he would not be any good. He just didn't like doing things that he was not good at.

"I've lost you, David," said Reginald Barnes. "Where were you?"

David told him about Debbie Rossiter and Frederick.

"Maybe if I was as beautiful as Debbie Rossiter, you would relax," he said. "Let's go to my place and have a smoke before you go to bed."

"That's a deal, sir," said David. He was feeling better already.

In the night he dreamed of Tracy Warren. He had been dreaming of her a lot since Christmas. It was as if she had replaced Maggie Hope as his central dream figure. Their time together after Christmas had been extraordinary, and David had returned to school in a state of high excitement.

He had called her on Christmas day from Elizabeth's, and she had cried into the phone. "Your poem is so beautiful," she said between sniffles. "It was my favorite Christmas present. You don't know how much I needed that."

"I do," said David, and then ". . .can I come before school?"

"Yes, yes, yes," she said, and David's heart lifted, but nothing prepared him for what happened when he got there.

They had been sitting together in the playroom. Butch had gone to bed, and Tracy's parents, if not asleep, were in their room watching television. They had bought a second television set and often watched it in bed before they went to sleep. David could hear it as he walked by their room to Butch's, where he always slept in the bed closest to the door.

Tracy Warren sat on the couch facing him with her legs folded under her. He loved the way she could sit on her legs. He couldn't do that—he couldn't begin to do that.

"We always talk about you," she suddenly said. "Sometimes you forget that other people have suffered too."

He started to protest, but she put her hand over his mouth. "Just hush, David, and let me talk. I'm not mad at you. I'm not criticizing, I just want my turn. I just need to let you know that I've suffered too."

She leaned over and kissed him lightly on the lips, then drew on her cigarette.

"When I was four, my older sister died. She was my favorite person in the world. I idolized her."

With the word "died" the air in the room changed. It became charged with something that David could not describe.

"Her name was Caroline, Caroline Baker Warren. She was named for my mother's mother. She knew things, David. She just knew things. She was seven and in the first grade. She could read, and sometimes she would read to me. I would climb onto her bed, and she would pat her hand on the blanket next to her and say, 'Come over here, sweetie.' It was something she heard our mother say, I guess.

"One day, after school, we were playing dolls, and we had the little blanket for the dolls spread out on the floor, and we had the tea cups and the plates and knives and forks out—the table was set for the dolls, and her eyes just rolled back into her head, and she fell over onto the blanket, and the little metal teacups rolled across the floor."

She started to cry. "I still see them, those little teacups rolling."

David put his arms around her and held her. "She taught me things, you know, what to wear, how to play, what words were."

"Do your parents talk about her?" David asked.

"No," she said.

"Never?"

"Never."

"And you?"

"Not until now. You're the first."

"It's our secret."

"Yes," she said, "and here's another one. She came to me in a dream two nights ago. I couldn't wait for you to get here, I wanted to tell you so bad. She was grown, she was the age she would have been if she'd lived. Like twenty-one. She had long dark hair, and blue eyes, very blue eyes. She walked into my bedroom from the hall as if she'd lived here all these years, and I sat up in bed, and she touched me with her hand, her right hand, right here." She took David's right hand and placed it on her left shoulder. "Then I reached out to touch her, and she said, 'No,' and then she said, 'All is well, all manner of things are well,' and then she just disappeared, and I woke up, sitting on the edge of the bed."

"I feel like I've heard those words."

"Yes, exactly," Tracy said. "Me, too. We've been reading T. S. Eliot, and he uses them in one of his poems, but he got them from somewhere else, from a famous woman saint, Julian of Norwich." She was breathless with excitement. "Don't you see, David? Caroline has continued to grow in heaven. She must have heard Julian's words, too."

"What did she die of?" David asked.

"Encephalitis," Tracy said.

"What's that?"

"It's a virus that attacks the brain cells."

"Did you see her, you know, after. . ."

"No. I don't know what happened. I can't remember any more. I went to my aunt's and stayed there until my mother came. She said Caroline was at peace, that she had gone to be with God."

"Do you believe in heaven, Tracy?" David asked.

"Of course," she smiled. "I just told you. Caroline learned those words in heaven."

David told her about Christmas and Jesus and how nobody in his family believed.

"You do," she said.

"Sometimes," he said. "But there's so much it's hard to believe, like the way everyone in the church talks about seeing people in heaven. I can't imagine what that would be like. I think of my mother and my grandmother. What would they look like in heaven?"

"I don't know. You'd just know, that's all. You'd see them and you'd know. I would know Caroline anywhere."

"Of course, you would, but she was beautiful when she died. I'm thinking about old people and people killed in wars. Think of all the millions and millions of people who have died. Where do they go?"

"Our imaginations just aren't strong enough. That's the problem," Tracy said. "We just read 'Song of Myself' by Walt Whitman. He said, 'To die is different from what any one supposed, and luckier.' Isn't that wonderful? It made me think of Caroline, like she's still growing somewhere, just becoming more and more beautiful. Your mother will, too."

"I don't know, Tracy. You're really the poet, not me. You can imagine those things."

"One day, you will, David, I know you will," she said, and then they held each other close, and David could feel his need, and he began to kiss her.

"Not yet, sweetheart," she said. "There's one more thing we have to do." And she got up and pulled him with her. They walked upstairs and put their coats on, their hats and mittens, and walked out to the car.

"Where are we going?" David asked.

"You'll see," she said, and she drove them down the road to St. Thomas's Episcopal Church. Behind the church was an old cemetery, weirdly lit by the one bluish streetlight. David could read the names, old names, Connecticut names—Hooker and Carver, Wainwright, Carpenter, and Dickson. Then he saw Warren, and the small stone in the ground with Caroline's name.

They knelt next to her marker, and Tracy took from her jacket pocket a small glass bowl with a candle in it. She lit the candle. She had planned this—of course, she had planned it, David realized, this ritual. She unzipped her jacket and held in her hands the small gold cross that had hung down between her breasts. "Unclasp the cross," she whispered, and David took off his gloves and undid the tiny clasp with his fingers. She placed the cross next to the candle, and then drew from her other pocket a small trowel, which she used to dig in the hard earth in front of her. Then she handed the trowel to David, who dug also. Then she took the cross and placed it in the hole, and together they covered it with the loose dirt. Then they stood and packed the fragments of earth down hard with their boots. There were no words between them, only Tracy's movements and David's following hers almost instinctively. Tracy reached down and picked up the candle and blew it out.

"It will snow tomorrow," she said as they turned to leave. "It always snows when you are here." Then they kissed in the strange silence of the night and walked back to the car, their arms around each other.

And now he was back at school and dreaming of her. He had come back from Reginald Barnes' room a little dizzy from his cigarette, and he had undressed and slipped into bed quickly. Borden was asleep. He curled up, fell asleep and dreamed of Tracy Warren. They were on a beach—or she was on a beach, and he was on a cliff above the beach looking down at her. She was beautiful, her hair longer, her eyes alight with joy, and she was holding her arms open to him. He had to jump. "It's OK," she kept saying. "Nothing will happen to you. Just jump." But he couldn't. He was there, on the edge of the cliff, his feet tiny like bird's feet, and he leaned and reached toward her, but he could not jump. He woke in a sweat.

In the morning he still remembered his dream, which was unusual, but he didn't have time to write it down. He had to get an English paper finished. It had been due the week before, but Reginald Barnes had given the cast members extra time. David could use the morning job period and the first class period to finish it. That would give him two hours. He was trying to write something about T. S. Eliot's "The Waste Land," which they had been reading for the past two weeks. It was hard, and they only did a few pages a day in class. David asked Mr. Barnes about the lines from Julian of Norwich, and Mr. Barnes told him they were in a later and even harder poem called "The Four Quartets."

They had read "The Love Song of J. Alfred Prufrock" in January, and it had been a big success. It was as if everyone in the room understood Prufrock and his fears. They whispered to each other lines from the poems. "I have measured out my life with coffee spoons," Antonio Black would whisper as he passed David in the hall, or Ralph Wisdom would point his finger and hiss, "In short, I was afraid." They all knew Prufrock with his nice clothes and his fear of women, they understood how terribly he wanted to change his life and how hard it was for him. They were sad for his failure, and they all hoped to do better, but they weren't sure they could. "I am not Prince Hamlet, nor was meant to be," Wally Hinson would proclaim, and he meant it.

Then, on the first Sunday of Lent, Father Perkins stood in the pulpit in St. Matthew's Chapel and spoke a new set of lines from T. S. Eliot. David could hear the lines reverberating in the Headmaster's deep voice, reverberating to the back of chapel. "This was a decent, Godless people, their only monument the asphalt road, and a thousand lost golf balls."

That was the postwar generation, the Headmaster said, in their gray flannel suits, anonymous, faceless, going to work every day—pouring from commuter trains into Grand Central Terminal and going home at night to the latest gadgets—new dishwashers, color television sets, station wagons with fake wood on the sides. Then the Headmaster had quoted from "The Waste Land." He read:

"A crowd flowed over London Bridge, so many, I had not thought death had undone so many."

He talked about the crowds of faceless men and women who poured over London Bridge, who poured in and out of Grand Central, men and women who had ceased to believe, who had lost the ways of their parents and the parents of those parents, men and women who had no real spiritual center. He called on the students to use Lent as a time of repentance, a time of turning away from "the butt ends of their days and ways," as Eliot had said in Prufrock. And on the next Sunday students had brought to church clothing for the needy, clothing from their own closets, not old clothes, but new clothes. As a kind of symbol of caring, they had brought sweaters and jackets and shoes and shirts, and they had walked forward and placed these clothes in baskets at the foot of the altar. And the Headmaster had blessed their giving.

All this David tried to work into his essay for English, and as he wrote, he remembered the dream of the night before, and suddenly the dream itself made sense. He was Prufrock in the dream, he was one of those men who walked over London Bridge. He was "decent and godless." He knew that. Only he didn't know quite how to change. "*The Waste Land,*" David wrote at the end of his paper, "ends with the protagonist sitting on the shore fishing. He is trying to make a change. He has seen the wrongness of his ways, but he has not yet found a solution. Neither have we, who read the poem, but like the protagonist, we can make a start."

And they did. Rehearsals got better and better. Everyone learned their lines, and the sheer joy of the play radiated through the cast, and when the play was finally put on the weekend before the term ended, the school roared its approval. It was part of the magic—first the basketball team and then the play. Ralph Wisdom's dream, to make this the best sixth form in school history, everyone doing his part, all the fingers and toes and even the follicles of hair, every organ, every muscle in the body playing a part.

At Sunday morning breakfast after the second performance of the play, Father Perkins asked David to meet him in his study. David couldn't imagine what it might be. Something for the Wicker

Sentinel perhaps. He tried to think of something he had done wrong, some rule he had broken. The only other time Father Perkins had called him in was when he had smoked with Wally Hinson. He certainly hadn't risked that again. He had stayed up after lights out working on papers, but everyone did that, and Father Perkins certainly wouldn't bother himself about such a small thing. And then, suddenly, he remembered the stamps, he remembered stealing the stamps. Maybe someone had found out about it and told the Headmaster.

Father Perkins asked David to sit down and offered him a cigarette.

"Are you sure it's all right, sir?" David asked, surprised.

"Of course, lad. You deserve it. Splendid performance last night. I don't know how you find the energy. You boys don't seem to require sleep."

"Except during early morning classes," David said.

There was a pause, and the Headmaster continued. "David, how would you like to be the English Exchange Student for next year? I have decided to nominate you, and the faculty has enthusiastically supported my choice."

He was flabbergasted. Of course, he knew about the exchange system, how a Wicker boy would go to an English "public" school, which meant private, of course, and an English student would come to Wicker. He had just never thought of himself as the one who would go. Then he thought of Tracy.

"I can't, sir," he said suddenly. He hadn't really thought before speaking. The words just came out.

"What do you mean, you can't?"

"I haven't any money," he said quickly. He couldn't tell the Headmaster it was because of Tracy.

"David, this is a great honor. It is a full scholarship. Everything is paid for by the English Speaking Union—tuition, room and board, travel allowance."

"Mrs. Ariel. . ." David started.

"I have talked to Mrs. Ariel. She told me of her decision not to pay for your college education. That need not be a factor. In fact, that is precisely why Wicker School would like you to have this scholarship, because you would not have been able to go to Europe on your own. Many students can afford a trip to Europe. You can't, and we'd like to send you. Mrs. Ariel will continue your clothing allowance for another year. You will have an interview next month in Wallingford along with the candidates from the other Connecticut schools. I am confident you will be selected by the committee and that you will make an outstanding representative of this school and of this country."

"It's scary, thinking of going that far away, all of a sudden."

"Of course it is, lad. But that's what growing up means—taking those kinds of risks. You, above all, should know that."

"Father Perkins," David began, "there is something I need to tell you."

Now it was the Headmaster's turn to be surprised. "What is it, lad?"

"During fourth-form year, when I was working at the stationery store, I stole stamps."

"More than once?"

"Yes, sir."

"Tell me about it, lad."

And David did, pouring out the whole story, not emotionally but calmly almost, glad to be relieved of the secret.

"Well, lad, that is why the church has confession."

"Yes, sir, I think I understand that now."

"Good. Now run along."

"And the scholarship to England?"

"That changes nothing, David. It only makes me more certain we have made the right choice."

"But the penalty for stealing. . ."

"That was two years ago, lad. You were a different person then. If anything further is needed, I will inform you."

"Yes, sir," David said.

"And David."

"Yes, sir."

"Everything we do we pay for ultimately. When the payment for this action comes, you will recognize it."

"Yes, sir."

"Good lad," the Headmaster said, and they stood and shook hands.

"Of course you'll go," Tracy said vehemently. "There's no question about it. I'd kill to have that chance."

It was almost spring. They were shooting baskets in the driveway, Tracy as tall as David, not as strong, but quick and graceful in her moves. They talked between shots, bouncing the orange ball, leaning against each other in an easy way.

"Maybe you could come visit me," he said.

"Not bloody likely," she said in an English accent.

"A year's a long time."

"It's nothing, David. Don't you know that?" She bounced the ball three times and put up a perfect jumper from fifteen feet. He missed.

"You're an H," she said. "What you need to do is take art history. Do you have any idea what's over there?"

"We don't have art history at Wicker," he said.

"But you know what's there," she said. She dribbled toward him, stopped, turned and hooked with her left arm over his head. Swish. He missed again. "You're an H-O," she said. She was laughing now, her teeth shining, her eyes sparkling with mischief, Tracy Warren, in her Radcliffe sweatshirt.

"Don't make it so hard," she said. "You can be my eyes and ears, OK? You can go to all these places and see these incredible things and write about them. Keep a journal."

"I know," he said. He drove to the basket and laid it up with a sweet backward spin. She followed him and did the same.

"What do you know?" she asked, and threw him the ball.

"I'll write you letters. My letters to you will be my journal. If I think I'm talking to you, then I'll pay closer attention."

"What do you mean 'think'?"

"I mean 'know.'"

He stood still and put up a one-hander. It bounced off the rim. She took it and dribbled up to him and held the ball. She kissed him on the lips and then spun away, stopped, and swished another jumper from the side. He missed.

"You're a H-O-R." she laughed.

"I can't be an H-O-R."

"Go see the Sistine Chapel," she said, "and go to Madrid to the Prado and see the Goyas and the El Grecos. Go to Paris. . ."

"And see the Mona Lisa," he said.

"And Notre Dame," she said.

"And the Eiffel Tower," he said.

"And best of all Saint Chappelle," she said.

"What's that?"

"It's all glass, all stained glass. They showed us slides in class, David. It's pure beauty, absolutely pure beauty."

"We'll go there together some day," he said.

"Yes," she said. "OK, but next year you'll be there alone. Write me about it."

He could feel the tears almost start. She did that to him, even out here in the driveway in her sweatshirt, shooting baskets.

"You're my good angel," he said.

"It's really the other way around," she said, and shot another basket.

"What do you mean?" David was holding the ball. He wanted to think for a minute.

"You know. I'm the dark one. I'm Hester. You said so. And it's true, David. When I'm with you, I think I have a chance."

"A chance for what?"

She knocked the ball out of his hands. "Shit," she said. "Don't act so dumb. You know perfectly well. Then she made him an S and an E, and they went inside.

That night they looked at her art books, at pictures of Michelangelo's statues. The David was in Florence, the Moses in Rome, the slaves in Paris at the Louvre.

"Where are you going this summer, Tracy?" he asked.

Anthony S. Abbott

"To Wyoming, to work on a Dude ranch. I'll get to ride a lot. I'll work as a waitress in the dining hall and take the kids out riding some. The head of the ranch is a friend of Dad's. Butch and the family'll come out for a month."

"That's nice," David said.

"You're jealous, aren't you? I can tell by your voice."

"I guess."

"Well, don't be. You're going to Europe. Goddamit. Just don't forget that. In Paris you can see all the impressionists—Degas and Renoir and Monet. You can see the Water Lilies."

She paged through the art book until she came to Monet. "Look," she said. "Look at that. You'll see that next year in Paris."

But he wasn't happy. He knew he was supposed to be happy, and he tried to look happy for her. She knew what was wrong. "Sweet Jesus, David," she said. "We have our whole life. This trip is a gift. Everything you learn you'll bring back to me, and I'll bring Wyoming and Cambridge back to you."

"I know," he said, but he didn't really mean it. He didn't have her faith in the future. He only knew there was this space that had to be filled and that without the touch of her body, without her arms around him and her lips against his, their tongues intertwining, her beautiful small breasts against his chest, that without all this, he could not imagine being happy.

"I don't like you like this," she said. "I'm going to bed."

"Don't," he said. "Please don't."

"Why not?"

"Because. . .I want to. . .you know."

"I *don't* know," she said, and she walked out of the playroom and up the stairs. He could hear the door close in her bedroom.

CHAPTER EIGHTEEN

In the spring they slowed down, all of them, even Ralph Wisdom, even David. There was about this spring something different from any other time in David's life. The spring of his sixth form year at Lowell had been different. The reality that they were leaving had sneaked up on them suddenly, and it was really not until the last night that David and Griff and Terry had looked back on their time together. But here at Wicker, the looking back had begun the first day after spring vacation and continued until the day they left.

They talked about colleges and where everyone was going and why. David and Wally Hinson and Ted Barber were going to Princeton. Ted and Wally would room together as freshmen, and David would join them a year later when he got back from England. Antonio Black would go to Harvard, of course, and Dennis Vogler to Yale, where he had lots of musical friends. Ralph Wisdom chose Amherst and Hugh Packard Williams. He would play soccer there and ice hockey. Billy DuPont and the Sphere would go to Penn. Mr. Sphere, being a Philadelphia banker, had pull there, and besides, the Sphere said, it was a great party school. You either went to an Ivy League school or a little Ivy or very occasionally to a Southern school like University of Virginia or Duke, but no further south than that. Nobody went to the Midwest.

Anthony S. Abbott

They all talked of the freedom of college. No more rules. No more chapel, no more getting up at 6:45 and staggering to breakfast, trying to tie ties with one hand and button shirts with the other. Their world would change. Women would become suddenly available. It all seemed so glorious, and yet there was an undertone of sadness, a knowledge that they would never have anything like this again, a world where fifty or sixty guys could somehow create a real community by working and living and studying together. College would be totally different.

They had built something special together at Wicker, and as they staggered back from Florida or California or Alabama or wherever they had gone to seek the sun during their last spring vacation, they came back with a unity and a nostalgia that even the Sphere could not be cynical about. They talked long into the night, and the Headmaster would come to the study at eleven o'clock to kick out the last stragglers and send them to bed. And when the next class climbed Skiff Mountain to paint its own numerals on the rock, David and his friends looked the other way. Things were starting over. Father Wisdom would step down, David would pass on the *Sentinel*, the Sphere would be retired.

"Let no one presume," he wrote in his farewell column, "to imitate the Sphere. He is unique in his circular and rounded brilliance. He will return to the skies whence he came, his brilliance absorbed by the sun, his memory honored in the stars. Go thy ways, fools, and do not presume to follow. *Dixi.*"

"I know where you got that *dixi*," David said that afternoon in the newsroom. "It's from Dostoyevsky, 'The Grand Inquisitor.'"

"Yeah, but who else besides you and Antonio Black would know that. The peons don't know that." He laughed. "Listen, C.C., I'm feeling a little sentimental today. I know I'm a shit sometimes and a pain in the ass."

"But a funny pain in the ass," said David.

"That, too," said the Sphere, "but for today I'd just like to tell you something nice. I'm really glad I had the chance to get to know you, and I'm really glad you got to go to England. Now get the hell out of here and let me finish this column. I'll bring it down to JKR's in half an hour."

When the final column was printed, the Sphere revealed himself in all his glory as a credit to Poland and to all those whose names ended with "ski." Maybe everyone had known before, but no one had ever actually come up to David and asked, "Is it Kosmo?" That would have been difficult, because David, who was not very good about lying, would have blushed or stammered. But they didn't, and maybe it was because they liked the secret and wanted the mystery to continue to the end.

After the changeover, they hung out in Ralph Wisdom's room and talked about the future. They talked about professions and what they wanted to be. They had been given vocational tests earlier in the spring, and all David learned was that he shouldn't be a farmer. Well, he'd known that already. All the other professions came out nearly even. They talked about what was the best profession, the most important. Father Perkins had talked to them about vocations. The word "vocation" came from the Latin word "to call." A vocation was a calling, in which we could serve God through our work. Luther, he said, believed in "the priesthood of all believers." It wasn't only priests and ministers who could serve God. Anyone could serve God, even the executioner, Luther had said, if he did his job reverently and with devotion.

But they didn't really believe that. Some callings were better—you could be a doctor, a minister, a teacher, a lawyer. Those were all professions in which you could help people. Ralph Wisdom would be a priest, perhaps. They hadn't called him Father Wisdom for nothing. David would teach English. Maybe he would come back to Wicker and teach, or even go back to Lowell. He could imagine himself as a young teacher coming back and standing in front of the classroom telling stories about what it had been like in the old days. Dennis Vogler would go to Yale Law School and live in New York and play the piano after hours in a bar. The others would come see him. Wally Hinson said they were all a bunch of stupid idealists. He was going to make money and have a good time. Ted Barber would try and keep Wally Hinson from destroying himself.

They talked about women and marriage and the difference between "nice girls" and "good girls." They talked about how to do it and who had done it and who would never do it. They talked about their high school girl friends, their friends from Miss Porter's or Emma Willard's or Ethel Walker's and whether they would keep dating them in college.

"So, D.J.," Wally Hinson said one evening, "tell us about Tracy Warren."

"Who the hell is Tracy Warren?" asked Ted Barber.

A shout went up. "Tracy Warren! Tracy Warren! Tracy Warren!"

"O.K., O.K.," said David. "I'll tell you." And he did, the best he could without giving too much away.

"So that's why you've been getting on the train in Stanford," said Dennis Vogler. "I suspected something was up."

"So, are you getting any good stuff, D.J.?" Wally Hinson asked. "Those Greenwich Country Day girls are supposed to be pretty hot."

David didn't answer. He didn't need to.

"I can't believe you never ran into one of us in New York," Billy DuPont said.

David was happy. Somehow he had kept her safe from them all this time, and now it didn't matter. They couldn't hurt her. And for the first time in his life he was the center of a conversation about girls. He just smiled and took the good-natured ribbing of his friends. No one was really mean. They were just having a good time.

He had come back to school after vacation depressed about his last night with Tracy She wouldn't even take him to the train on Sunday. She asked her mother to do it for the second time in a row. Then, about a week later, David got a cryptic letter from her. It contained a copy of John Donne's poem, "A Valediction Forbidding Mourning." "Let me know what you think of this," she said. "Love, T."

He went to the library and found a book about Donne's poetry. They had read some of Donne's "Holy Sonnets" in class earlier in the year, but not this poem. He studied it. It was hard: According to the notes in the book, Donne wrote the poem to his wife before leaving on a trip to France. A "Valediction" was, the notes said, "a farewell." That scared David. Was the poem Tracy's farewell to him? He read it:

> Dull sublunary lovers' love
> (Whose soul is sense) cannot admit
> Absence, because it doth remove
> Those things which elemented it.
>
> But we, by a love so much refined
> That ourselves know not what it is,
> Inter-assured of the mind,
> Care less eyes, lips, and hands to miss.
>
> Our two souls, therefore, which are one,
> Though I must go, endure not yet
> A breach, but an expansion,
> Like gold to airy thinness beat.
>
> If they be two, they are two so
> As stiff twin compasses are two:
> Thy soul, the fixed foot, makes no show
> To move, but doth, if th' other do.
>
> And though it in the center sit,
> Yet when the other far doth roam,
> It leans and harkens after it,
> And grows erect as that comes home.
>
> Such wilt thou be to me, who must
> Like th' other foot, obliquely run;
> Thy firmness makes my circle just,
> And makes me end where I begun.

He didn't know quite what to make of the poem. He thought of taking it to Reginald Barnes, but then he thought he ought to be able to work it out by himself. Besides, if he did it on his own, he might even be able to use his analysis as an essay. He struggled with it. He read it again and again. He looked up words. And then it began to fall into place.

The poem contrasted two kinds of loves—those who love with their bodies and those who love with their souls. Donne's lovers are like a drawing compass, attached by their souls. When they part, their bodies get further and further away from each other, but they are still attached by their souls. They don't have to have their bodies together to keep loving each other. He took out his math compass and held one foot in the center and let the other one move toward the side of the paper. The inside foot, the one that stayed at home, kept leaning farther and farther away from the center, but never separated from the other foot. That was it. He was going away, but they would still be together in their souls. It wasn't a poem about her leaving him, but about her NOT leaving him. It was about his travels. He was the I of the poem, not she.

He realized how stupid he had been that last night at her house, how wrong he had been not to trust her. It was all right to go, she was saying, and he didn't have to be afraid.

He wrote to her, explaining all this with great excitement. She wrote back. "Not bad for a beginner. Next time see if you can figure it out without a poem. God knows, though, eyes and lips and hands are pretty nice things. I love you very much, T."

He carried the letter with him like a talisman for days. When he had moments alone, he read it again and again until he had memorized it. Then he tore it into tiny pieces and threw it in the trash barrel in the mail room.

April became May, and the leaves came out, and the crews practiced silently except for the click of their oars. Sometimes, on the way back from baseball practice, David stopped by the wall of the North Dorm to watch them. They were very good, and if they won the big regatta in Worcester, they would go to England to row in the Royal Henley Regatta. David was the manager of the baseball team, and each day he would go down to the gym thirty minutes early to get the equipment out and prepare the field for practice. After practice he would pick up all the equipment and take it back to the gym and clean up the locker room after showers. On game days he wore a uniform like the rest of the team and coached third base. None of the players treated him any differently from anyone else. He was part of the team; he had a role to play, and at the end of the season, he won his varsity letter. Now he had letters in soccer, wrestling, and baseball.

On the morning of June 2, the class rose early, and in their graduation uniforms—white pants and shoes and shirts, blue blazers and ties—they marched into St. Matthew's Chapel for their final communion. It was fitting that no guests—no parents or sisters or nieces and nephews—be allowed in the chapel for this occasion. This was their last time together as a class, Father Perkins at the altar, the prefects, the sacristan, and the editor of the newspaper back in their familiar positions in the stalls, the rest of the class in the front rows. David held the moment in his heart and froze time. He could see, forever, the hands folded together at the altar rail to receive the communion wafers, the cups in the hands of Father Perkins and Daddy Drew in their spring robes.

"The peace which passeth all understanding" was the subject of the Headmaster's meditation. "You have been a great class," he said to them, "one of the truly great classes in Wicker history, because you have taken your responsibilities seriously and have become models for the rest of the school to follow. But greatness has a price. Jesus never said we wouldn't suffer. Jesus never said that there would be an end to injustice. Jesus never said that man could bring the kingdom of God into being by hard work. That is naïve idealism. He only said that if we gave ourselves to Him and to his kingdom, we would have peace, not peace as the world knows it, but *his* peace, a different kind of peace, a knowledge that we are in God's hands and his protection no matter what befalls us. Peace does not mean happiness. Happiness is just another kind of death, a contentment with things as they are. Jesus knew that.

"You, my young friends, have been given very special gifts, and as you leave this place, it will be your destiny, your calling, to use those gifts to bring forward Christ's kingdom. Some may laugh at you for it, some may persecute you, some may say you are foolish not to strive for the good things of this earth. But only striving for Christ's kingdom will bring you his peace, his special kind of peace."

"*Dixi*," the Sphere whispered to David as they walked out into the sun and marched to the chairs arranged in rows in front of the dining hall. There they were in this bright June world, the mothers and fathers and sisters and brothers and aunts and uncles and friends who had come from all over the world to celebrate this moment. The boys could hardly see as they marched from the darkness of the chapel into that June light, and as they took their seats in the front rows to the applause of the guests, David could see his family sitting there. Molly Ariel had come all the way from California, Aunt Louise from New Jersey, and Elizabeth from New York.

There were speeches and expressions of thanks and many awards and a huge standing ovation for Ralph Wisdom. And then, at exactly 11:35 a.m., as the last award of the morning, the Columbia Cup for "that student who has shown the most comprehensive grasp of his life and work at Wicker" was presented to Dennis Benjamin Vogler.

David was stunned. "Well, Maggie Hope," he said under his breath, "we sure screwed it up this time," and then almost at the same moment he knew what had happened, and he composed the face he would need to get through the rest of the day. He walked down to where Dennis was receiving congratulations, and worked his way through the crowd of boys.

Dennis saw him, and moved toward him with his big arms. He wrapped David in his warmth, and whispered in his ear, "You should have gotten it. I didn't deserve it."

"Yes, you did," said David. "There's something you don't know. I'll tell you after, in New York, when we're alone. I'm glad you won it, Dennis. It was the right choice," and he hugged the bigger boy back as hard as he could.

CHAPTER NINETEEN

"Look," David said, "there's actually sawdust on the floor."

"And red-checkered table cloths," Elizabeth added.

"And Chianti bottles with candles in them," David went on.

They were sitting in a booth at an Italian restaurant on 8th Street in Greenwich Village gawking like tourists.

"You shouldn't do this," David said. "What if Phil finds out?"

"He won't. He thinks you're taking me, and that makes sense to him as a man."

"Well, I should be taking you."

"No, David. You've given me all the money from Mommy's Social Security, you've babysat for us, you've been a wonderful uncle and brother. You're going to need every penny you have to get through this year. Now, we won't talk about it any more, OK?"

"OK."

"Besides, we may not be here when you get back. Phil is looking for jobs in other cities, and I'm not going to. . . " She stopped, and David could tell she was on the verge of tears. He waited, while she gathered herself.

"I'm not going to break up this family, even if. . ."

"Even if you don't love him any more," David said quietly.

"That's right," she said firmly. "I can't raise Alex and Maggie by myself, and he's going to damn well support us until the kids are grown up. So maybe we won't be here."

"I love New York," he said suddenly.

"Of course you do. You spend two or three weeks a year here and you go out with your friends and see plays and movies." She reached out and put her hand over his. "I loved it too when I was single and living in the Village and going to plays and concerts in the evening. But it's no good for raising a family. Can you imagine what Alex and Maggie would be like in five years? They'd be hoods."

They laughed together, and she pulled out her package of cigarettes and offered him one. He pulled two from the pack and lit them both, then handed one to her.

"Do you mind if I have a glass of wine?" he asked her. He was eighteen and it was perfectly legal in New York.

"Why not?" she said. "I can't stand the stuff, but if you like it, a little won't hurt you. I don't think you're the alcoholic type."

"What's the alcoholic type?" he asked.

"You know, someone that can't stop, that has no self-control."

"I know," he said. "I have some friends at Wicker like that. They scare me."

"Mommy was like that," she said. "She'd have a little drink, and then a little more, and the next thing she'd be hiding the stuff, sneaking off to her secret places for a quick swig. I think Sugie was the same way."

"Do you miss them?" David asked.

She shook her head. "I don't know. I don't know which is worse, not having them around or having them around they way they were."

"I was the lucky one, wasn't I, getting sent off to school?"

"I guess you could say that."

"I mean you were the one who had to deal with everything. If she got sick or. . ."

"Drunk," she said.

"If that happened, you had to take care of her, didn't you?"

"Most of the time."

"I'm sorry. I keep thinking that it isn't fair how I got to go to school and have Molly pay for it and now I get to go to England, and you just end up sitting up in the Bronx with two little kids and a. . ." He stopped.

"I'll have mine one day," she said. "I'm only twenty-seven. I'm glad you're having yours. You deserve it. I want you to just love the hell out of every minute of it. We're all happy for you, Toots."

The sound of the word made him dizzy for a moment, hot, then cold.

"God," he said, "I haven't heard that in years. That's what Mom used to call me."

They ate slowly, relishing every bite. David had heard about English food, about how awful it was. He wouldn't have a piece of beef like this for a year, Elizabeth told him. English beef would be dry and brown. They ate and talked and walked up Sixth Avenue holding hands in the September dusk. They rode the D train home.

In the morning David kissed the kids goodbye and said he would send them postcards from his boat, the Queen Elizabeth.

"Is it a big boat, Uncle Dave?" Alex asked.

"Very big."

"As big as this house?"

"Bigger. Much bigger."

"How big?"

"As big as this street," David said, and Alex laughed, and Maggie laughed with him.

"See you later, alligator," he said.

"In a while, crocodile," they said, and he turned and walked out the door.

He hauled his three bags up the hill, the M.H. bag in one hand, a duffel bag slung across his back, and his new suitcase, given to him by Molly Ariel, in his other hand. He should have taken a cab, he knew, but he couldn't bring himself to spend the money, and so he made his way slowly past Grant, Sheridan, and Sherman, those tough Union generals, to the Grand Concourse. He was sweating by the time he made it to the top of the hill, and he stopped.

He knew it was stupid, this penny pinching habit of his, but he couldn't control it. It was in his blood as much as his competitiveness, his desire to be the best. He would just have to live with it, so he bumped his way through the turnstiles and waited for the D train to take him to Rockefeller Center. There he would change to the crosstown bus, which would take him to the pier. He checked his pockets: passport, tickets, wallet, traveler's checks, cash. Molly Ariel had gone over everything with him the day before. He was glad she had come.

They had lunched at the St. Regis and gone out shopping in the afternoon for a new suitcase, for shirts and ties, and shoes. She would not see him for a year, and she wanted to give him a good send-off, she said. After dessert, they smoked cigarettes and drank coffee, and he had felt very grown up. "Well, chum," she said. "I'm very proud of you, and I'm not going to tell you what to do and what not to do in Europe. You'll do what you have to do. Just remember that you are responsible for your actions. The world out there isn't like Wicker School. And if something goes wrong, then you just have to take the consequences. We all do, chum."

"I understand," he had said, but he wasn't sure just how much he understood. Her words could have meant all kinds of things. He had lain in bed at Elizabeth's thinking about her words. It was about sex, he thought. She was saying that he might want to have sex, but that if he did, then he was responsible. If he got a girl pregnant, it was his responsibility. That was it. Or, if he got some disease, he had to "take the consequences."

He knew something about that. The Wicker crew had gone to the Henley Regatta in July, and Ted Barber had come back from England with all kinds of stories. They had all met in New York for a night of Dixieland before college started—David and Ted and Wally Hinson and Dennis Vogler. They had gone down to Luchow's on Fourteenth St. for dinner and then to the village. Ted Barber was full of stories about prostitutes on the streets of London and how you could get the clap if you weren't careful. You always had to use a rubber, he said, in the most casual and knowing way. The whole thing scared David, not the idea of sex itself, but the idea of sex with a perfect stranger, sex as a kind of business proposition. "When you go to Paris," Ted Barber had said, "look up my friend Robert LaBouchere. He'll show you a good time, and fix you up with a girl you know is safe."

They had all got a little drunk over dinner and even drunker at the Village Barn, and when the band played "When The Saints Go Marching In," everyone screamed and jumped up and down and spilled their drinks and told David he damn well better get laid while was in Europe. That was his obligation. If he didn't, he wasn't a man. David had laughed with them, but still the idea scared him. He would have to be responsible. After all, Molly Ariel had made him promise.

In the Tourist Class Lounge of the Queen Elizabeth David waited. He had arrived early at the ship and checked in, and the porters had brought his luggage to his room, deep in the bowels of the ship, a tiny room with no portholes that he would be sharing with another exchange student. He had claimed his bed and put his stuff away and walked up to the Lounge, where he now sat and waited for Tracy Warren.

They had arranged this during his last visit to her in Greenwich. He wanted an image of her to keep with him during his year, and they had both loved the idea of having their last meeting on the ship. She could stay for a couple of hours, before they sent the visitors off, and then he could wave to her as the boat backed out of its berth into the Hudson River. He could hold that image of her during the months they would be apart, he could keep that sense of her presence with him during the crossing and long afterwards, and he would give her, in return for her coming, the poem he had been working on. He said the words to himself:

FOR TRACY
You are not like the moon
 the moon is too cool
 up there in the hard sky.

Nor are you like the sun
teasing with its rays
burning us by surprise

You are like the eye
of a storm, calm
at the center while everything

around you rages and rages
and the winds sweep by
in a terrible swirl.

You teach me to love myself
in a way I never knew
to love myself as I love you.

The poem was in the pocket of his blue blazer, and he would take it from his pocket and give it to her when they said good-bye. She would read it later, at home, in the privacy of her room and then write to him, or she would read it when she got to Radcliffe on Friday. He imagined her sitting in her dorm room unfolding the poem, reading it, and then folding it again and secreting it away, somewhere safe, in her bureau drawer perhaps, beneath her underwear.

He knew her love of secrets and his own. She would be careful with his letters. He knew that. But it also scared him. She had other secrets that he knew nothing about. He was sure of it. The boy at Deerfield was just one example. There were others. He sometimes imagined her with a whole secret life that would blossom like a dark flower when he left, a life that had taken root and would continue to grow the whole time he was away.

Over the summer he had thought about ending it, about using the trip to Europe, the year away as a conclusion. It seemed, to his mind, like the best thing. He composed letter after letter to her, telling her he had decided this, but he never mailed them. There was a part of him that could sit back and look at her and say, "She is bad for you. She is using you," but in his heart he never believed that. All he knew was that without her his life would be smaller—simpler, of course, and easier and less fraught with danger and surprise—but surely smaller. The adventure would have to end itself another way. He would not end it.

When she appeared in the doorway, she was smiling and holding a bouquet of flowers, and David forgot his fears. She wore a yellow blouse, open at the neck, and a dark grey skirt. Her face and arms were tan from the summer sun. Her hair was bleached enough to look almost blonde, and it hung down easily over her shoulders. They came together and kissed, and she held the flowers behind his back.

"You look beautiful," he said.

"So do you," she said, and they walked down the stairs, the many stairs to his room, where she put the flowers on the little table next to his bed. He closed the door. There was still no one else there, but they might have only a few minutes before the other boy arrived, and so they were careful. They did not want to be caught half-undressed, their bodies sweating on the small bed. They kissed. They kissed for a long time and held each other. Then Tracy got up.

"Come on," she said. "Let's go to the bar and have a drink and talk," and they worked their way back up to the main deck and higher still to the bar, where they ordered scotches and took them to a table by the window, where they could see the city shining in the afternoon sun. There was the RCA Building on 50th Street and the Chrysler Building on 42nd and the Empire State on 34th. Farther downtown the tall buildings of the financial district shot up.

"I feel like it's my city," David said, and then told her about Elizabeth and Phil and how they might move away.

"You can come to my house," she said smiling. "We'll just adopt you."

"I know," he said. It was their little joke, their continued refrain, but it wasn't quite real.

"I won't have any address," he said. "People always ask me where I live, and I say in New York with my sister. I like that. So, when they move, I won't have any address at all. It's weird. You know, when you fill out all those forms for college, you have to put your home address. So what do I put?"

"You'll figure it out when you need to. For now, just let it be," she said, and then she paused and went on. "Listen, David, I want to ask you something important."

"OK."

"Promise me you'll write me the truth. That you'll write me real letters about what you really feel. You can send travelogues to your sister and your godmother, but not to me."

"I'll try," he said.

"Trying isn't good enough. Your problem is that you edit everything. You're afraid of having bad feelings. You don't like to criticize anyone or talk about things that upset you. I know you. You can say anything to me. You know that, don't you?"

"I know that."

"So promise me."

"I promise you."

"Good," she said. "Now let's go see this amazing ship. I've never been on anything like this. It's like a huge hotel, like a movie set. I had no idea it was this big, and this is only tourist class."

And she took his hand, and they walked all over the ship, up and down the narrow hallways and out onto the deck, where they came to a chain with a sign on it that said, 'FIRST CLASS ONLY." Tracy ducked under the chain and said, "Come on, don't be afraid," and she reached her hand and brought him through.

At the end, when the horn blew and the announcement came that all visitors must leave, she told him where she would be standing, and asked him to go out on deck and wave to her. Then he handed her his poem, which she put in her purse, and she handed him a letter, which he put in his pocket. She kissed him one last time, turned her back and walked down the gangplank, and he watched until she appeared in the waving crowd. As the boat backed out, he could see the swirl of her hair and the gold blouse and the silver bracelet on her bare arm. Then she was gone.

Their last time together except for the farewell on the boat itself had been the week before. David had spent the summer in Lambertville working at the restaurant and helping Aunt Louise. It was different there with Uncle Swen gone. Everything was more relaxed. David slept in the same yellow room next to the kitchen, and when he woke up, he would have breakfast and then go over to the studio and help Aunt Louise with the cataloguing of the paintings.

Every painting had to be marked on the back with its title, its date of composition, and its number. Then each painting had to be photographed, and placed in chronological order. Then these paintings would be listed in the book along with the ones already in museums and private collections. In this way, Aunt Louise would know where every Swenson painting was, and if a show were organized, she could find the paintings quickly and organize them. She would move paintings back and forth between the house and the studio, trying different ones in different places. She invited art professors and curators to see the paintings, she wrote long letters to museums, asking them to buy paintings. She was amazing. It made David understand that artists didn't succeed just because they were good painters, but because they had someone like Aunt Louise to promote them.

David liked working at the restaurant. He was quicker, more efficient, more comfortable than he had been two years before. He was happier, more at ease with himself. He didn't spill milkshakes or break glasses or confuse regular and cherry coke. If Aunt Louise wasn't going out at night, she'd let him drive her car to work and drive himself home in the early morning. It was one of his favorite things, the drive home at two a.m., when the moon shone over the hills as he came up from Lambertville out into the high plain near Aunt Louise's. Sometimes he would just stop at the turnoff from the highway to her gravel lane and turn the engine off. He would look at the moon turning the hills to silver and feel the stillness, and talk in his mind to Tracy.

When Tracy returned from Wyoming, he left Lambertville and went to her house for a last weekend.

On Friday they cooked out in the back yard. Tracy wore a red halter top and blue jean shorts. She was barefoot, and her toenails were painted. She and Butch and David tossed a baseball back and forth for a while and talked about their summers. It always amazed David what a beautiful athlete she was, how she could be so pretty and so feminine and so wise and yet throw like a boy. She could really hum it in, and when his hand stung she just laughed. Butch was taller, and he was getting muscles. Mr. and Mrs. Warren were sitting on the verandah drinking gin and tonics, and the smoke was coming up from the charcoal, the sun was setting and casting its gold reflection on the house.

"Look, Mom. Look, Dad!" Tracy suddenly said, and cast down her glove and ran to the verandah, pulling them each up by an arm. She brought them out, and the four of them stood, mesmerized by the glow of the evening light. "This could be my family," David thought. "We could all be happy here." And then he thought, "I won't see her for a year. A lot can happen in a year."

They ate hamburgers and corn on the cob fresh from the farm, and drank beer and red wine, and smoked cigarettes and talked about college and England and the war in Korea, which seemed to go on forever. They talked about Eisenhower and Stevenson and the elections and the threat of nuclear war. David enjoyed the talk. He was better at it now, since he had been debating at Wicker. He had learned much from Ralph Wisdom.

They talked about school, and how Tracy had won the Art History award and David had won the English Prize at Wicker. He told them about the Columbia Cup. When he started he didn't know that he was going to tell the story, but it just came out. Maybe it was the wine, but whatever it was, the words took control. "I heard the name, Dennis Benjamin Vogler, and I froze, and then all of a sudden I remembered Father Perkins' words. He said I would know and I did know. Isn't that amazing?"

Tracy got up from her seat and hugged him, right there at the picnic table.

"I'm so proud of you, David," she said, and Mrs. Warren dabbed her eyes with her napkin. It was a new experience for David, this telling of the sad truth, and he had not understood until now that losing is not always bad.

On Saturday David and Tracy took the train to New York for the day. They held hands as they walked up the ramp into Grand Central and then across 43rd to Fifth Avenue. Tracy was taking him somewhere, but she didn't tell him where until they got in line at the Museum of Modern Art on 51st Street. David had heard of it, of course, and he had walked past it many times, but never gone in.

She bought two tickets and then led him up to the second floor. There was a painting she wanted to show him, she said, and when they turned into a large gallery just across from the stairs, he was immediately seized by it, even though he didn't know what it was.

They sat on a bench in front of it, and she told him about it. "It's called *Guernica*," she said, "and it was painted in 1937 by Pablo Picasso. We studied it this spring in my art class, and our teacher brought the whole class here just to see it. You would have loved it, David, standing here with the class while my teacher talked. The Germans had bombed the city of Guernica during the Spanish Civil War. They killed so many people, David, so many people. All these innocent people, slaughtered, for no reason. All these. . ."

She stopped, and turned her face to his shoulder. She was crying.

"Look at it," she said almost in a whisper.

David could see it, the woman on the left side of the painting, mouth open, screaming, holding her dead child. The woman on the right being consumed by flames, the horse in the middle, neighing in terror. The man in the middle lying on the ground, a broken sword in his hand. The bull on the top looking on without feeling.

"Those people hadn't done anything," Tracy said. "They were Basques. Maybe Franco hated Basques. He just let the Germans kill them all. I love this painting. It shows you how much you can say without words. I might major in art history in college. Maybe I'll be an art teacher."

She was almost breathless with excitement. She took his hand and led him into the next room. On the south wall was another painting of Picasso's, *Les Demoiselles d'Avignon*.

They stood there, hand in hand, looking at the painting. She didn't say anything, but David knew that she could if she had wanted to. She was testing him, letting him look at the painting and come up with something.

"The other one was all black and white and grey. This one is much brighter."

"Yes," she said. "Go on."

She was playing teacher.

"There are five women," he said. "They're naked, but not sexy, not appealing. They're scary."

Tracy smiled. She liked that.

"The one on the top right has a kind of mask on," David said.

"That's right. We learned that in our class. Picasso was studying African art, African masks."

"Why Avignon?" David asked.

"It was a street in Barcelona where there were lots of whorehouses."

"Of course," said David. "I see it. They're showing off their bodies. They're selling themselves. But you don't want to buy."

"No," she said. "You don't want to buy."

"Because they're dangerous."

"Right," she said. "So remember that when you go to Spain."

He laughed. "Who says I'm going to Spain?"

"I do."

"Why?"

"Because you have to see the Prado."

"Ok, I have to see the Prado."

"You have to see Goya. He was the greatest Spanish painter before Picasso."

"Was that in your class, too?"

"Yes."

"And you were in love with the teacher?"

"Yes," she said, and then suddenly, "No, I was not. You just tricked me into saying that."

She was even more beautiful when she got flustered. Her color heightened, and she tried to say something and gave up. They were both high, high on the power of the art and the power of one another. They walked from room to room, from painting to painting, hardly knowing where they were. They wanted to touch the paintings, smell them, put their ears close and listen to them. Twice blue uniformed guards motioned them further away.

Finally, they just had to leave to keep from being thrown out. They wandered over to Broadway and then to Eighth Avenue, and on 48th between Eighth and Ninth found a little café, where you went down three steps into a quiet room. They sat across from each other at a small table with a burgundy table cloth and a white candle in a glass stand. They drank red wine, and took turns blowing on the candle and watching the way the air took a second or two to reach the flame. If you blew too hard, it would go out, David thought, but it never did.

"Sweet Jesus, Trace," David said.

"Sweet Jesus, what?" she answered.

"I feel like there's no time, like we're not in time any more. We're in eternity."

"Eternity?"

"When I'm with you, then time doesn't exist. We could be together forever and there would be no time."

"And so?"

"And so. . .I don't know."

"Yes, you do."

"I don't."

"You do. You're just afraid that if you say it, it won't come true."

"I love you."

"I love you, too. But not that."

"What, then?"

"You know."

"No, I don't."

"Go back. . .to eternity."

"Oh," he said. "I see."

"Yes," she said.

"I want us," he said, "to be together forever, for eternity."

"Yes," she said. "Now that that's settled, let's eat."

After dinner they went to see *The African Queen* with Humphrey Bogart and Katherine Hepburn, and all the way home on the train David called Tracy "Rosie," and she called him "Charlie."

On Sunday the family went to church together, and all through the service David could feel her next to him, in the hymns, in the prayers, in the taking of the bread and wine. And then at lunch, on the verandah, David found a large box at his place. "For your trip, from the Warrens," the card said.

"I can't believe this," David said, as he opened the box and saw the small, compact Olivetti typewriter snug in its case. His hands began to tremble. "There's nothing, there's absolutely nothing I needed more."

He got up and hugged Mrs. Warren and shook hands with Mr. Warren and Butch, and when he got back to Tracy, he couldn't look at her.

"For your poems," Mrs. Warren said.

"For your term papers," Mr. Warren said.

"For your letters," Tracy said.

As the ship continued to back out, David brought his mind back to the present. He looked down at the crowd, but there was no sign of her yellow shirt. A moment before she had been there; now she was gone. "It's not fair, Trace," he said to her. Then he remembered the letter and pulled it from his pocket. "For David, to be opened at sea" it said. "Well," he thought, "we're moving. That ought to count," and he walked back to the bar where they had just sat and ordered another scotch. He took it to the same table and watched his city once more. He was afraid to open the letter, and for a long time he sat and looked out the window at the passing buildings. Then he opened it slowly:

"Dear David," it started out. That wasn't good. Not "Dearest David" or "My precious David" or something like that. Just "Dear David."

"Our friendship has been the most special thing in my life during these past three years. Maybe I should say that it has saved my life.

I had hoped, believe me, my special friend, that our relationship could be the beacon for me, the light that would allow me to come through the darkness of this time. I know, the word 'darkness' seems strange. I can see the look of surprise, even of unbelief on your face. I can see your lovely, sweet eyes turn away from the word. My parents have always known, and they have supported my friendship with you more than anything I have ever done in my life, because they hoped you might 'cure' me.

"But it hasn't worked, and I feel the fairest thing I can do for you is to set you free, to tell you to go forth in this wonderful, wonderful adventure and meet other people, fall in love, find out how glorious life can be. I will only hold you back. Please write me, please send me your journals. I will treasure them, and if I am not here, my mother and father will save them for me. Don't worry—they won't open them. But don't send them to Cambridge. It's too risky there. You may not hear from me for a long time, but don't worry. I will never stop loving you, and we will never stop being friends. But for now, at least, we must be free of each other.

" Love always, from your dark sister, Tracy."

CHAPTER TWENTY

September 20

Dear Tracy,
Tomorrow the ship will dock at Southampton and I guess it will turn around and go back to New York with this letter. Tracy, I'm so confused. I read your letter as soon as the boat left dock, and I almost tore it into a million little pieces right then and there. I don't know what you intended, but what I really wanted to do was get off the damn ship and come after you and shake you. I was so angry.

I was sitting in the bar, where we had our last drink together, and I got up and walked around and around the deck trying to figure out what you meant. Then, I thought, "Oh my God, I have a roommate. I've got to get myself together." So I calmed down and went downstairs to the horrible little room and just opened the door and walked in. Christ Almighty, Tracy, my roommate was Terry Roche. There he was big as life, standing there unpacking his stuff, putting his shirts in the little drawers built into the bed.

My hand is trembling as I write this. You knew, didn't you, and you didn't want to be there when he came on board. Is that it?

Terry and I are friends again. I'm glad. I never had a friend at Wicker like Terry, a real best friend. I had lots of people I liked and admired, Tracy, but no Terry. You know that. He just walked over and gave me a big hug and said, 'Dave, I'm really, really sorry about my letter, but I was really mad. She got my best friend kicked out of Deerfield. He couldn't graduate with the class. He'll have to come back and finish next year. I couldn't forgive her for that, but I'm sorry I hurt you.'

That's what he said to me, and now we're friends again. We spent the whole trip over together with the other guys just having a good time. I showed him your letter finally, and he said you were doing me a favor, that I was better off without you, and then we agreed not to talk about you anymore. It was too hard. We would be friends, and we would go to Paris for Christmas with Brad Christian from Choate and Little Billy Wheeler from Lawrenceville, and in Little Billy Wheeler's unforgettable words, 'We shall get laid.'

So now I am writing you this letter to tell you good-bye, to tell you I understand that it's better if we break it off. But I can't, Tracy. I just can't. I love you so much, I don't care what you've done. I don't like being so angry. I don't like being so wild. It scares me. What is all this stuff about 'cures' and your 'dark' self? It doesn't make any sense to me. Tell me something, please, something that makes sense. OK? I don't like all this weird stuff. Help me, Tracy. Just write me at school and tell me what is really going on.

Your blood brother and best friend,

David

October 1

Dearest Tracy,
How far away I feel. It's like I live on another planet. It's like playing Monopoly and working your way all the way around the board to Boardwalk and then being sent back to Baltic Avenue and having to start all over again. Rules, rules, rules. There are so many. Worse than Wicker. We have uniforms. Can you imagine? Of course you can. We wear, from the bottom up, black shoes and socks or gray socks, gray trousers, not pants. In England "pants"

means "underpants." No belts. Gray trousers with "braces," not "suspenders." A white shirt with a detachable collar. That's right. No button downs here. There is a front stud and a rear stud, and the collar is held on this way. Very hard to do. The first morning everyone helped me get dressed. It was crazy. Black tie with a tie clip or a sweater, and a black jacket. And here is the worst. Your trouser pockets are sewn shut. You can't put your hands in your pockets. As my friends at Wicker used to say, "No pocket pool!" Only prefects or "pollies" as they are called here can have their pockets unsewn.

It's a hierarchical (I like that word) society here. The lowest of the low are called "fags"—they are kind of like slaves. Really! The pollies can have the fags do anything they want like polishing their shoes, going to the Buttery (that's like a soda shop) to get food, buying newspapers, cleaning up their messes. It's weird. I'm so independent I wouldn't dream of having a fag do something for me. Anyway, there are houses here. Everybody is assigned to a house—thirty or forty students to a house, and the houses compete in everything, in sports, academics, extracurriculars. There are pollies in every house, and there is a head of each house. All the house heads and some others are also school pollies. They wear boater hats to distinguish themselves, and they run everything, kind of like the sixth formers at Wicker.

We don't have rooms here. There's no real privacy. There are dorms. They call them "dormies." Isn't that cute? The dorms are upstairs on the third floor and on the second floor. Then there are studies. Everyone has a study, a tiny little room just big enough for a desk. Everyone decorates their studies with pictures and banners and curtains. The studies are on the first and second floors. On the first floor is the dining room, and in the basement our lockers and the shower rooms and bathrooms. In the morning you get up and race down the stairs to get dressed. It's cold in the dorms, but warm in the basement. The dining room doubles as a study hall for the younger boys in the evening, and the pollies have to supervise study hall.

I love my typewriter. Everyone does. They've never seen a typewriter that small and compact. Please thank your parents again for me. It's hard to get much private time to do things like write you. Just when I settle in, there comes a knock on my study door, and someone wants to talk. It's as if I'm a celebrity. Well I guess I am. I'm the only American in the school, and so I'm the expert on all things American. I don't know what the rules are about talking, but I sure do a lot of it. American movies, American sports, American schools, American politics, American girls (well, I'm not going to tell them about you. If I did, they wouldn't believe me)….The other day I was talking about Senator McCarthy and how awful he was, and one of them said he thought McCarthy had been a great general in the war. They got McCarthy and MacArthur mixed up.

You notice I haven't said anything about you. Well, I trust you. That's what I want to say right now. You know me better than anyone in the world, and you're the only person I've ever been completely honest with. Even if you're not my girl friend, you're still my muse. Right? I love you very much, and I wonder what you're doing. I think of you all the time!

Your blood brother, David

Sunday, October 10

My dearest Tracy—
Still no word from you. I hate it. You could be dead for all I know. I know you were saying goodbye in your letter to me, but you can't just turn your back on me and walk away, not after all we've been to each other. Just let me know you're OK. Please? I was thinking about my last letter to you and how ordinary it was. I remember how you told me that I wanted everyone to like me and that's why I didn't take risks. There are things I want to say to you, but I don't because I'm afraid to take risks. I know that.

I want to tell you how beautiful your breasts are, I want to tell you how I loved you with my whole soul and my whole body when we took communion next to each other at St. Andrew's on that last Sunday, how kneeling next to you with the sun breaking through the stained glass windows was the most beautiful moment of my

Anthony S. Abbott

life. It was like we were being lifted up and carried somewhere. There, I did it!

Still, I want you to have a record of my year. Maybe I will write poems about it or a novel when I come back, and I thought that my letters to you could be my journal, and so a lot of this will be stuff that I could send to my sister or my aunt. It's not all just for you. For you I'll enclose a separate page, one you can burn. Burn this one!

Your friend and blood brother always, David.

Monday, November 1

Oh Tracy, Tracy, Tracy—what a time I have had. It's so strange. Everything takes so long. It's at least a three-week turnaround for a letter from here to get to the U.S. and then a response to come back, and no one wants to telephone. It's too expensive. Anyway, the day after I wrote you last I got a telegram from Elizabeth saying, "Buying car. Please send money. Need help." I had no idea what to do. I knew they were going to move, but I hoped maybe they'd stay another year, at least until I got back. Why else would they buy a car except to drive to wherever they were going to live? Anyway, I called the English Speaking Union, the organization that sponsors my scholarship—they're wonderful, and the Secretary there said she could wire the money to my sister in New York, and I could pay her back when I came to London in December, so I sent $200. It wasn't much, but for me it was a lot.

Then day before yesterday I got a letter from my aunt about the whole thing. Here it is: "Dear David, Well, your sister and her little family are on the way to California. They left this morning, and I have grave doubts about their future. They arrived yesterday afternoon from New York in their Chevrolet, looking like the family in Steinbeck's *The Grapes of Wrath*. Philip was driving the car, and your sister in the front seat next to him, with the children in the back reading comic books as the car pulled into the driveway. The trunk was entirely full, and the roof of the car was covered with boxes and suitcases tied down.

"'What will happen if it rains?' I asked. They didn't know.

"I fixed them some supper, and we put the children to bed in the little yellow room you like so much. Then I sat down and talked to them both about their move. They had no money, and I could not see how they were going to get to California without starving to death. They were going to look for a house when they arrived, and Philip had a number of prospects for work in Hollywood, writing music for the movies. But they had nothing to live on until his first paycheck. So, this morning, I drove down to Lambertville, with them following, stopped at the bank, and took out $500 in cash, which I handed to Elizabeth. And then, of course, she started crying, and that made little Maggie start to cry also. It was a dreadful scene. She clung to me, and I told her that I would look out for them until they were settled, and then she calmed down and got back into the car, and they went off across the bridge into Pennsylvania.

"They left some things for you here, which I have put in the studio for you, some books and records they thought you might like at Princeton."

Thank God for Aunt Louise. She is amazing. She always seems to do what needs to be done. She took care of her mother and Aunt Estelle and her husband and now Elizabeth. I think she will end up taking care of my father, too. He's in Arizona now, but he'll be back. I can just feel it.

Anyway, I tried to imagine what their trip was like. They must be there by now, don't you think, somewhere in L.A. looking for a house? I think of Alex and little Maggie and how grown up they'll be when I see them again. I'm trying to imagine when that will be. Probably a year from Christmas. I'll have to go out to California for Christmas, won't I?

So I sit here, six thousand miles away, waiting for news. I've felt really strange these last two days, thinking about them being gone and landing in New York with them not there. If I didn't have you, I would feel really lost. We were reading Shakespeare the other day, and my English teacher, Mr. Griffin, just started reciting one of Shakespeare's sonnets from memory, and it made me think of you. As he read it, I could feel the hairs on my arms rising:

Let me not to the marriage of true minds
Admit impediment; love is not love
Which alters when it alteration finds
Or bends with the remover to remove.
O no, it is an ever fixed mark,
That looks on tempests and is never shaken;
It is the star to every wand'ring bark
Whose worth's unknown, although his height be taken. . .

I just love that, Tracy. It's what you were trying to tell me before, isn't it? Elizabeth's leaving, your going to college, my being over here—those are alterations, but they don't change us and our love. Still, I wish I were in Cambridge with you, walking the foggy streets at night and thinking of T. S. Eliot. Oh Tracy, I don't know. I just reread what I wrote and it seems so positive, so strong. You are "my ever fixed mark"—but I'm not yours, and the whole love thing is just my illusion. Is that it? I get so angry at you. Just tell me SOMETHING, ANYTHING. Maybe if I cut my wrist and spread the blood on the paper, you'd pay attention. What do I have to do to break your silence? Sweet Jesus, Tracy, help me!

Your David

Sunday, November 20

It's almost Thanksgiving, and the school is letting me go to Birmingham to spend Thanksgiving with a family that is very active in the English-Speaking Union. I get to miss two days of classes and for the first time since September put my hands in my pockets. I can wear my own clothes when I leave the school!

Thanksgiving makes me think of Elizabeth and Alex and Maggie. I always had Thanksgiving with them except when I stayed at school. One year, I don't remember it very well, I had two Thanksgiving dinners, one with Elizabeth on 115th Street and one with my mother. I can't figure out why they had separate Thanksgivings, unless Elizabeth just wasn't talking to her then. My mother had moved into a little hotel on Broadway, about five blocks from Elizabeth, and I remember walking down there and not telling her that I had already eaten. She took me to a restaurant. I remember spilling gravy on my tie and her dippng her napkin in her water glass and leaning over the table to wipe it off. Then she kissed me on the cheek and said, "I love you, Toots." I had almost forgotten that.

The big news here is that I have been made a house polly. I was promoted a couple of weeks ago, and it has really changed my life in the house. It's a tricky thing, this system. Once you're a polly, you have to administer the system. You have to enforce the rules, so my friendship with the sixth formers who aren't pollies has really gone down the drain. There's a guy named Churchill (like the Prime Minister) who's pretty funny, pretty wild, and he keeps pushing at me to let him get away with stuff because we were friends before I was promoted. Now I just have to stay away from him and hang out with the other pollies. He calls me a hypocrite, says I'm a real bastard. Makes me think of my first roommate at Wicker, Jackie Callaghan. Did I ever tell you about him?

We're going to Paris for Christmas! I'm making the arrangements. Terry and Brad and Little Billy Wheeler and I are renting hotel rooms for a week in Paris, and then we'll split up. O my God, I forgot to tell you—I found my grandfather, or I should say my aunt Louise sent me my grandfather's address, which she got from Elizabeth. He's living in Monte Carlo, and I'm going there to see him after Christmas. I can't remember the last time I saw him. It seems like he just vanished after my mother and my grandmother died, but Aunt Louise says he's been living in Europe all this time and that he has a French mistress named Madame Lucas, who lives in Antibes on the Riviera. Isn't that amazing.

I think I'll go to Rome after Monte Carlo. Isn't that the right thing to do? Tell me about the art I should see in Paris and Rome. You're my art person. I want to see stuff that you're studying, so we can talk about the same art. Then, someday we can come here together and see all this. Remember how you told me once that we should lie down on the floor of the Sistine Chapel and hold hands and look up at the ceiling together? Come on, Trace, give up this crazy silence and get on a plane to Paris after Christmas, and we'll go to Rome together.

I miss you so much. Each day I look in the mail for a letter from you. The other night I dreamed of you. You were kissing a man under a streetlight, and I was upstairs in a building, like a dorm or something, looking out the window, and crying, "No, don't!" And Maurice Taylor, who sleeps next to me, shook me until I woke up. "You were having a nightmare," he said. "You kept yelling, 'No. Don't.'"

Think of me when the snow falls.
Your loving brother, David

Paris, December 29

Tracy, Tracy, Tracy—I have to put all this down before I forget it. It's all so crazy, so full, so funny and sad and mixed up. You are the only one I can tell it to. We've been in Paris for a week, and we're leaving tomorrow, the four of us—Terry and Brad and me and Little Billy Wheeler, of course.

We met in London, at Victoria Station, and took the boat train from New Haven to Dieppe. It was wild. When we got off the boat in Dieppe, suddenly everyone was speaking French, and the porters were saying things no one could understand, and one took our luggage off to the train, and we thought we would never see it again. Well, I had more French than anyone else, so I took off after him, and found that all he was doing was taking the bags to our compartment. So, when we got there, I had no idea how much to tip him, and gave him a hundred franc note and asked for "la monnaie," which means "the change." But he just said, "Merci, monsieur" and walked off. I was really mad, you know me and money, and started after him, when Terry caught me by the shoulder and said, "A hundred francs is only worth a quarter." It was such a relief. We all laughed and settled into our seats for Paris.

"The first thing I'm gonna do in Paris," said Little Billy Wheeler, "is get laid."

"Me too," said Brad.

"What about you, Butter Rum?" Terry asked.

"Who's Butter Rum?" Little Billy said.

"I am," I answered. "That was my nickname at Lowell. Didn't Terry tell you guys we went to Lowell together? We had a club—The Lifesavers—and I was Butter Rum. . ."

"And I was Cherry," said Terry.

"Cherry Terry," said Little Billy Wheeler.

"And Griff was Orange," Terry and I said together.

Brad and Billy didn't know what to make of that.

We arrived at Gare Saint Lazare, and walked to our hotel, which was only four blocks away, not far from American Express and the Opera. Very central. We got two rooms and went out for dinner. It was great. I could read enough French to order for everybody, and we got three bottles of cheap wine (Wine is absolutely essential in Paris. Nobody in their right mind would order milk), and decided to explore a little. We broke up into two groups—Terry and I went down to the Place de la Concorde and then up the Champs Elysee. It was glorious, just glorious. I've never seen a city glow like Paris at night, the outdoor cafes open even in the winter with large awnings and glass sides protecting the tables from the weather. We sat and drank absinthe, which is supposed to be cool. It has a licorice taste and leaves your tongue green.

When we got back to the hotel, Brad was there, but not Little Billy.

Billy had gotten laid. At least that's what Brad said. They had gone to look for the Moulin Rouge up on Rue Pigalle, and that's when they started encountering prostitutes. Think of this as Brad telling the story to us, Tracy. These prostitutes came out from doorways, wearing feathered hats and long skirts with slits up the middle. They would stick out a black stocking and say,

"Voulez-vous faire le jig-jig?"

And we kept saying, "No thanks." But finally Billy said, "This is what I came for, and I might as well get it done," and he just said, "Oui, oui, mademoiselle," to one of them, who looked a little younger than the others, and off he went. "See you back at the hotel," he said, and he just disappeared in the doorway, and I kept walking.

"They're all over the place up there," Brad said.

The next afternoon Brad and Billy took Terry and me up there, Tracy. We walked along the Rue Pigalle, and it was pretty quiet. It was December 24, Christmas Eve. And we saw this incredible church in the distance, called Sacre Coeur, up on a hill called Montmartre. I'd heard of Montmartre, how artists lived up there, but the church I didn't know about. It was absolutely beautiful, white, shining in the sun, and we walked up into the church and around it, and I felt like I was being lifted up. I just wanted to stay there, but it was getting dark, and they were getting ready to close, so we walked down the hill, back down to Pigalle, and that's when the prostitutes came out. All the way home, every corner we turned, there were more. "Hey boys," they'd say in English, "want ficky-ficky." Or "voulez-vous faire le jig-jig?" I was walking a little ahead of the others, you know, and each time I turned around, someone was gone, first Brad and then little Billy Wheeler, who had spotted the girl he'd laid the night before and was so excited he could hardly stand it.

"Hey, Beelee," she called. "You come back with me?"

"You said it, Baby," Billy answered, and he was gone.

For awhile Terry stayed with me, and then he suddenly said, "Oh shit, I just have to try it. Are you OK on your own, Butter Rum?"

I nodded yes, and he headed for a doorway where two girls were standing. Now it was just me, and I kept hearing church bells. It was Christmas Eve, and the voice of Father Perkins was ringing in one ear and Molly Ariel's advice in the other ear, and you were there in my heart, Tracy, and I would have just called you on the telephone, except I didn't know how to make a long distance phone call, and so I just went back to the room and wrote this poem:

PARIS, CHRISTMAS EVE
Four young men
boys still in the brain
ramble Paris streets
in the December rain.

They are all virgins
first time away from home
fresh arrivals on the evening train
what they want is too well known.

Two by two they march up hill
"Pigalle," one yells, another "Moulin Rouge"
They've seen the pictures of the can-can girls
Stockings black, their skirts aswirl.

But most of all they look for whores
With feathered hats behind half-open doors.
They wonder where their rapid steps will lead
and then they hear the booted women plead:

"Want ficky-ficky, boys?" "Want faire
le jig-jig? Come closer, boys,"
They beckon with enticing smiles
—the boys respond, they haven't traveled all these miles

for nothing. Tonight they will get laid
though Christmas bells are played and played
and the white church of the Sacred Heart
glows like a beacon set apart

for on this the night the Savior lay
in a manger, and Mary prayed
in thanks to God for this her son
who'd bring salvation to every one.

Anthony S. Abbott

The one boy left of all the four
runs on and on and up the wide stone steps
he sees the church, the candles bright
the rain will turn to snow this Christmas night.

I know it's not finished, Tracy, but I wanted you to have it as a Christmas present. It's really about you, about how I can't imagine just going to some prostitute and paying money. It's not a moral thing. I don't think I'm a Puritan. It's just that you've spoiled me. I dream of the way your hair shone in the sun on the day you left me. Don't you see, Trace? Don't you see?

One more amazing story, and then I'll get this in the mail. The next day was Christmas. Everyone slept late, and there was a strange kind of quiet in the hotel. We went out to a restaurant for Christmas dinner, the one we'd liked so much the first night, and then we came back to the room to share presents, presents we'd got from our families and from each other. It was funny how no one wanted to talk about the night before. Not even Little Billy Wheeler. It was like everyone knew something was wrong, or they were thinking about their families and just missing home.

About six o'clock Terry and I decided to walk over to the left bank, where the intellectuals hang out, and stopped for coffee in a café on the Boulevard St. Germain. There weren't many people there—maybe twenty or so, and a young man across the room from us stood up and started to sing. It was like we were in a movie. He sang in Italian, in a rich, baritone voice. He sang so beautifully he brought tears to everyone's eyes. And when he finished, everybody stood up and cheered and clapped.

"Magnifique," I said, and went over to shake his hand. He was blond with a big head of tight curls, a barrel chest and thick thighs. He looked like an opera singer.

"Thanks," he said in perfect English, and asked if he could join us. We were thrilled. His name was Robert Touchton, and he was an opera singer, or at least training to be one. We bought him a drink, and he sang again. I liked him a lot, not just as a singer, but as a person. He was warm and funny and he knew Paris inside and out.

The next night I went back by myself, and there he was, still singing, picking up a few tips from the fans. I guess the owners of the café liked him. He came over and sat with me, and we started sharing stories, and the next thing I knew, he had invited me to come back to his apartment for a nightcap. I had a new friend.

He had a tiny apartment, just two rooms and a kitchenette, full of paintings and odd drawings and music books galore. He gave me some cognac, and we drank and looked at photographs of cathedrals and stained glass windows, and it all seemed so perfectly what I had imagined, when he bent over and kissed me on the lips.

I was scared to death, Tracy. I didn't know what to do. I stood up and went to get my coat.

"Please don't leave," he said. "I won't do that again. I just needed to find out if you were interested. I won't do anything you don't want to do."

"OK," I said, and I took my coat off, and sat in a chair by the little table he used for his meals and kept my distance from him.

"Do I disgust you?" he asked. "Do you find me morally offensive?"

"No," I said. And that was true. I suddenly realized that it was true.

"Then what troubles you? I promised I wouldn't do anything you didn't want to do. I couldn't force you to do anything, even if I wanted to. I've got a big voice, but I'm soft. You're hard. I can see your shoulder muscles under your jacket."

"I like you," I said quickly. I don't know where that came from, Tracy, but I'm glad I said it. It's like you don't know what you think until you say it or write it. "I like you," I said again, "and I want you as a friend, but not that kind of friend. I'm not condemning you. I don't think you're wrong or bad, if that's what you want and that's what the other person wants. It's just wrong to. . .impose it on someone else that doesn't want it."

"And you don't think less of me for it?"

"No, truly. I just don't want it for myself. I'm really attracted to. . .girls."

Robert laughed. "Damn," he said, "you're something else. I like that very much, David. I've never met anyone like you. Everyone either is like me, or they hate me." And then he stood up, and came over and stuck out his hand, and I got up and we shook hands on it, and then we hugged, not in a sexy way, but kind of the way you'd hug your dad," and the next day he took Brad and me and Terry all over Paris, and I'll tell you about that in another letter, because I've got to get this off. We swore we would stay friends, and I told him I'd come back to Paris in April, on my spring vacation, and we would go to Chartres together.

Tracy, I'm absolutely exhausted, and I can't wait to get on the train and just sleep all day. Brad and Terry and I are headed to Monaco to see my grandfather, and then they're going skiing and I'm going to Rome to see all the stuff you've told me about. And, oh yeah, Little Billy Wheeler is going back to London to spend New Year's with his parents. Getting laid in London seems very unlikely.

I love you more than life, David.

CHAPTER TWENTY-ONE

Rome, January 12

My dearest Tracy— I fly back to London tomorrow and then take the train to school on Saturday. When I get there, I will find a letter from you waiting for me. I know that. I just feel that with my bones. You wouldn't let Christmas and New Year's go by without a letter. I count on it, Tracy.

What a time it's been. There's so much to tell you I hardly know where to start. I found my grandfather, and he's just the same, except even more so. He doesn't look any older than I remember. He's so elegant. Brad and Terry and I got into Monaco on the train, and found a wonderful little hotel just a block or so from the station, cheap, but a nice big room with three beds, 300 francs apiece. We'd been up all night on the train and looked terrible, so we took showers and changed into our coats and ties and marched ourselves like good Boy Scouts down to the main square by the sea to meet my grandfather.

"Now remember," I told them, "he won't let us drink, so don't order wine or you'll get a ferocious sermon. That's one of the last things my sister Elizabeth told me before we left in September. 'If you see your grandfather,' she said, 'for heaven's sake don't have anything alcoholic. He's afraid you'll become an alcoholic just like your mother and your grandmother.'"

"Well, that doesn't mean we can't," said Brad.

"Shut up, Brad," said Terry. "We can get through one lunch!"

"One lunch," I laughed. "I've got three days."

And so there we were, at the Hermitage Hotel across from the Grand Casino, Brad and Terry and I having this incredible lunch, white table cloth, silver, linen napkins with E. Everett Sampson himself, who seems to have found his money again. We talked about Democrats and Republicans and how lucky we were that Eisenhower won the election. We talked about alcohol and its evils (he would be furious if he found out how much we'd been drinking in Paris). Lets see—oh yes—the devastating effects of smoking cigarettes, and the importance of education. Well, at least we scored well on the last one, with Brad and me going to Princeton and Terry to Harvard. My grandfather said that education had replaced family as the most important key to success. He sat, white hair beautifully combed, eyes dancing with pleasure, in his gray suit, dark blue tie, and black shoes and socks. Perfectly dressed, for lunch in his hotel room.

After lunch he took us to the Casino and let us play the thirty-franc machines in the outer room. We weren't allowed in the big room, the famous private casino, because we were under twenty-one.

The next day Brad and Terry took the train to Milan and then up to Innsbruck to ski, so I had my grandfather all to myself. He drove me up the mountain on this winding road called the Grand Corniche, all the way to the top and then to Nice, with these astounding views of the blue Mediterranean, and we had lunch in a hotel above Nice with his mistress, Madame Lucas. Her name is Lucas because she was married to a British naval officer named Lucas who was killed in the war. I don't know where my grandfather met her, but he had a room at her Villa, which he considered home, and said he was just in Monte Carlo for a change of scenery.

She is a funny little woman, who speaks perfect English with a French accent and laughs at everything my grandfather says, but is just as opinionated about things as he is. They are a riot together. He hates her driving, which he says is too "French." I think that means very aggressive with lots of gestures and horn blowing, but when he criticizes her he always does it with a big laugh. He seems younger now than he was when I last saw him. Maybe my mother's and grandmother's dying kind of freed him up. Do you know what I mean? Maybe Madame Lucas was there before, and he couldn't get to her, and now he's got what he always wanted. I don't know. It's funny to think how little we know about other people's lives.

He talked a lot about the old days in New York—about my grandmother and her family—the Johnsons—for whom I was named, about Uncle Joe Johnson, who was Police Commissioner in New York, and other aunts and uncles and cousins and what a great bridge player my grandmother was and how funny she was and how sad it was to watch her deteriorate at the end. We said good-bye that night, and I promised I would come see him again in April, and the next morning I was on my way to Rome.

And here's my confession, Tracy. I met a girl in Rome, not right away, but toward the end. Her name is Peggy Urbano, and she's studying art at the University of Madrid. Here's how I met her. I was in the Sistine Chapel, looking at the ceiling, and it was pretty empty. Maybe it was the time of year or the weather—it was raining and cold—but whatever the reason, there was plenty of space, and I just lay down on the floor and imagined that we were together there.

I tried to find the panel where God is touching Adam, giving him life, and I heard this voice next to me, "Mind if I join you?" and suddenly this girl with red hair in a blue jacket was lying on the floor next to me, and we both were laughing and looking up, and she started showing me different stuff she had studied. Finally the guard made us get up, and we stood there looking at each other. "You look just like. . ." I started to say. And she laughed and said, "Little Orphan Annie. I'm trying to outgrow that."

So we introduced ourselves, and then she took me off to see the Raphaels in the Stanze, and we ended up having lunch in a little café down the street and then walking back to the Spanish Steps to American Express, where she was meeting her roommate. One thing led to another, and the three of us ended up having dinner together. They talked about how much they loved Madrid and how much freedom they had compared to the U.S., where they went to a Catholic college. And I said I hadn't talked to a girl since September, and they couldn't believe how strict my school was.

The next morning Peggy and I went to see the apartment where John Keats died and we read his love letters to Fanny Brawne, and then we went to see Michelangelo's Moses at some church I can't remember the name of. It was just unbelievable, Tracy. I've never seen anything like it. God touching Adam was good, but it was tiny, it was so far away, and the paint was kind of faded, but the statue of Moses glowed. It was like it was alive, and the skin shone. You felt as if Moses could get up and walk. His eyes were on fire. We were just standing there looking at the Moses, the two of us, and I suddenly realized I had my arm around her, and she had her arm around me, and then we just turned and kissed each other.

And I thought, I can't do this—I love Tracy—but you were right. Being there at that moment had nothing to do with you— no, that's not true. It had everything to do with you. "Live your life, experience everything, and bring it back to me," you said, and somehow that's what I was doing, just letting the moment happen. So after the Moses, Peggy and I walked back to my hotel, hand in hand, and we went up to my room for a while and lay there on my bed with all our clothes on and just kissed and kissed, and then we straightened ourselves out and I took her out for coffee, and we talked. Nothing more really happened except that she invited me to come visit her in Madrid in April. April is filling up, isn't it?

I am sitting here rereading what I just wrote. It's so strange. Why do I feel guilty telling you about Peggy? Why did I think of you when I kissed her? Why don't I just crumple up this whole letter and say to hell with it? I don't owe you anything. Right? You said good-bye, and as far as you're concerned what I do or don't do with a girl is meaningless. Or is it?

That's the thing. I still feel attached to you, and you are still my blood sister. Right? You want to know everything I do, and you want what I tell you to be true, to be honest. That's what I've done. Now, please, for God's sake, just give me some response!

Your still faithful blood brother, David

February 1

Oh my God! It all makes sense now. When I saw your letter sitting there in the big pile on the hall table, my heart started beating so fast and so hard I thought I was going to faint. I grabbed your letter and headed upstairs to the privacy of my study. I was afraid to open it. I'm such a coward, Tracy. It's like I'd rather have no news than bad news. So I waited, I waited until night when there was less likely to be a knock on the door. And then I read it. Tracy, Tracy, Tracy, what can I say? I understand everything. You knew when we were together for the last time in September, but you didn't know for sure. It was too soon.

I wish I could be with you. I feel like you could use me as a true friend and brother, during this time. I think of you out there in Wisconsin at your aunt's house getting bigger and bigger. Six months now. I'm glad you decided to have the baby. I almost wish it was mine. Isn't that a strange thing to say? You say that you will give the baby up for adoption and go back to school in the fall. I try to imagine that—I try to imagine this beautiful little Tracy being raised by someone else and not knowing you, or you not knowing her. That's the thing, isn't it, Tracy? Maybe your parents would take care of the baby until you finish school, and you and I could get married and raise the baby. How about that for a wild idea? Keep writing me. Please. I don't care what you did. I don't care that you don't know who the father is. I just love you. Burn this!

I have been made a school prefect, not just a house polly but a school polly. That's huge. Now I can have my pockets unsewed, and when I go out I wear a white boater hat with a blue, white, and black ribbon around it. I have all kinds of privileges, like going to town during free periods and studying in the house in my study instead of the library during free class periods.

There are also lots of responsibilities. I have to lead a morning exercise group every day. They call it "breathers," which is a funny name, isn't it, and I have to be in charge of either the new or the old library during study hours once or twice a week. All the pollies take turns doing these things. I must say I'm not very good at discipline. I'm such a softy. I hate to give demerits, and unless you're strict the kids take advantage of you. Most of the time they're nice to me because I'm an American, but there are a few tough customers.

The worst thing about being a prefect, house or school, is having to give whippings. I thought Wicker was bad, but it's nothing compared to here. It reminds me of the headmaster at Lowell School, Mr. Armbrister, but I think it's even worse than him, because here the paddling is done by the students.

At our house we do the whippings in the changing room. It's a long narrow room with lockers on both sides. At the end of the room are steps going up to the shower. The victim has to take down his trousers (and his pants) and kneel on the cold stone steps. Then the four house prefects line up at the opposite end of the room with large switches and run at top speed the length of the room before laying huge smacks on the boy's bottom or on his thighs. The other day, Tracy, we had to beat a boy named Kiddiminster. (What a name!) It was horrible. Taylor, the head house prefect, called us together in the changing room, and Wardlaw, the newest house prefect, brought the kid in. The minute he saw us and saw the switch in Taylor's hand, he started bawling, and he struggled to get away. Underwood had him under one arm, and Taylor grabbed the other arm. I was standing there feeling very uncomfortable.

The boy goes wild. He starts screaming and swearing and telling us that everyone hates him and that all his dorm mates have set him up to take the punishment for their offense. So Taylor and Wardlaw drag him over to the stairs and pull down his pants, and he's there on his knees sniveling, with snot coming from his nose. Taylor goes back to the doorway with his switch and comes running down and smacks him on the bottom. Wardlaw lets him go, and he doubles up in pain and says Taylor hit him in the ribs, which would be impossible. Then Taylor and Wardlaw held him while I hit him, and Taylor and I held him while Wardlaw hit him, and finally he just collapsed in a pool of tears and urine, and Taylor stood him up, and we pulled up his pants and his trousers, and put him back together and sent him to bed.

Afterwards I went up to my study, but I couldn't work. I couldn't concentrate. I kept seeing him lying there. And what good did beating him do? Did it make him a better person, did it deal with what makes him so difficult all the time? Once you beat someone, how can you talk to them? I feel like I want to do something for him, something to help him, but now I'm part of the enemy, part of what he hates and will always hate about this school.

Tracy, Tracy, Tracy, I miss you so much tonight. I just don't feel myself right now. I feel so far away from who I am, and who I am is always part of you. I wish we could be close, I wish we could lie down and touch each other from head to toe. I wish I could kiss your beautiful breasts and touch your nipples with my tongue, and listen to the baby's heart beat. Then the ice would begin to melt, the coldness would begin to go. I can't write any more right now. I love you, David.

February 20

Valentine's Day has come and gone and nothing from you. I thought surely my letter would reach you in Wisconsin and that you would have time to write back. I keep worrying about you, thinking about something going wrong with the baby. The problem is that we're so much closer than anyone knows. Everything special about our friendship is secret. Your parents wouldn't think to write me if something was wrong, and Butch certainly wouldn't. Does Butch know about the baby? Do your parents know you told me? Could I call them in Greenwich? Can you give me your number in Wisconsin? I keep seeing you sitting in your bedroom in a farm house in Wisconsin with the snow coming down outside and no one to talk to. What do you do all day?

I've been thinking about my last letter and all that stuff about Peggy Urbano. What I realize now is how lonely I was in Rome, how much I needed a real friend, and how Peggy was a kind of gift, a kind of angel—an answer to my need just then. I don't know whether I'll go to Madrid in April or not, Tracy, but I do know that I need love and that even though no one could ever replace you, it's just too painful to go without. Does that make sense?

Winter is nasty here. It has snowed a couple of times, but mostly it's cold rain or drizzle. A lot of gray. Elizabeth sent me a picture of the family in their new house in southern California, the four of them standing in their sunny back yard with palm trees and fruit trees in the background. She loves it there and says she can't wait for next Christmas when I can join them. They live in a place called Van Nuys in the valley north of Hollywood. Wouldn't it be great to be there now! Elizabeth sent me a book for Christmas called *The Catcher in the Rye*, by J. D. Salinger. It just came out last year, she says, and she was sure I would love it. She was right.

Tracy, you've got to read it. I want to talk to you about it. Holden is so much like me. He's sixteen in the book and has been kicked out of prep school and goes to New York and stays at a hotel instead of going to his parents' apartment. The elevator operator sets him up with a prostitute, but when the prostitute comes to his room, he just can't have sex with her. He talks to her instead, and she thinks he's weird. But I understand him. There's this incredible section later on where he goes to his sister Phoebe's school, and someone has written "Fuck you" on the wall. He erases it, and then when he leaves the school, he goes out a different way, and sees that someone has scratched the same words on the wall with a knife. "It wouldn't come off. It's hopeless, anyway. If you had a million years to do it in, you couldn't rub out even *half* the 'Fuck you' signs in the world. It's impossible."

I love that. That's what Holden wants to spend his life doing—being a "catcher in the rye," catching all the little kids that would run off the cliff if he wasn't there. He wants to erase all the "Fuck you" signs. He wants to save people. I love him. He's so mixed up and depressed, but in his heart he's really good. His problem is that he's too good. What do you think, Tracy? Have you read it yet? I can't wait to hear from you.

Your loving brother, David

March 10

Tracy,
I don't know what to say or where to begin or even if I should begin. I've thought about this a long time. Your letter came, or I should say, your note. What does it mean? "Thou wast not bold, thou wast not true!" I know they're Pearl's lines from *The Scarlet Letter.* You don't have to tell me that. But what are they referring to that I've done? Is it kissing Peggy Urbano in Rome? Is that it? I don't think it is, because we had already agreed about that. So it must be something else.

My mind is working. Then, all of a sudden I get it. I get it. It's about whipping that boy—I wasn't bold, I wasn't true to myself. I should have stood up and said I was against it. I should have done something to help Kiddiminster instead of just making it worse by participating. Of course, you know me too well. I'm a guest over here; they've made me a prefect; prefects conduct whippings, so I participate. I adapt. I'm good at that. In fact, very good at it. They love me here; I'm doing really well in my studies, I'm participating in debate, and I'm in the Shakespeare play, which is just coming up. We're doing *As You Like It,* and I am Charles, the wrestler. How do you like that? Wrestlers are supposed to talk funny, and everyone thought it would be a great joke to make the wrestler American. The neat thing is, Tracy, that Mr. Hall, who runs the gym, has taken me and the guy who's playing Orlando, and he's teaching us judo. We practice wrestling almost every day, and we've got this huge fall worked out where he flips me and I do a somersault and land on my neck, and then get carried out unconscious. It's great, because it looks so real. I really land on my arm, and slap the mat very hard to break the fall.

Why do I tell you all this? Just to let you know who I am, dear friend. You're right, I wasn't bold or true, but I do really like it here, and I will do my best to make it up to Kiddiminster by trying to help him. Still, all I get from you after two months is a stupid note chiding me for not being brave. OK, I deserve that. But what is going on with you and the baby?

Meanwhile, my beloved Tracy, I have something to tell you, something for all time. I want to say it now, because I feel strong enough to say it. I want to become a writer. I want to go to Princeton and major in English and learn how to become a writer. I don't know what's going on with you, but somehow becoming a writer and loving you are tied together in my mind, in my heart. I want to keep sending you these letters, because I want to use these letters to practice my writing and I want you to read them. You are my audience, the person for whom I write. Please don't destroy my letters. Save them somewhere, and when I come back, if you don't want to keep seeing me, at least give me the chance to meet you once and talk, and if I can't convince you to keep loving me, then you can give me the letters back, and I'll go my way.

Shit, Tracy, all that sounds so brave, but I don't feel brave at all. I feel very shaky. Just write me and tell me what the hell is going on. I can't stand your silence.

Your needy blood brother, David

Paris, April 10

Christmas in Paris, Easter in Paris. What a change, Tracy. I think at Christmas I had lost my focus on the "Christ" in Christmas, and looking back on it, I realize that I did not set foot in a church during that week. But this past week has been my cathedral week, and I feel dazzled, renewed, restored. Brad and Terry and I found a hotel called the George V, not far from the Place de l'Etoile. It's an expensive part of town, but the hotel is on a little side street and not well known, so it's pretty reasonable.

I called my friend Robert, the opera singer, and the next day he took me to Sainte Chapelle, the church you told me I had to see. I didn't know what to expect, and he said he wanted to surprise me, to see my face when I went in there. So, I met him at Shakespeare and Company, the famous English bookstore, and we walked to the chapel, and on the way he told me that it had been built by Louis IX, Saint Louis—that's how it got its name—to house the holy relics he had gotten from Turkey—the crown of thorns and a piece of the true cross and something else I can't remember. Probably a nail. Apparently, when the chapel was built and the relics arrived, St. Louis walked barefoot with them for several miles in order to place them in their new home.

When we went in, I was disappointed at first. The chapel was beautiful, but dark, and Robert said, "Wait!" Then we walked up a narrow staircase to the "upstairs" which only the king and his family could enter from their private doorway in the palace. The upstairs was pure light—pure light, Tracy, just as you said, as if there were no walls at all, just glass everywhere and the dazzling reflections of red and blue and gold on the floor. I stood there in utter unbelief and just let the light bathe over me, and of course I thought of you and how the only thing that could make the experience more beautiful would be if you were here with me.

"You're crying," Robert said, and I was.

"It's my favorite place in Paris," he said. "I come here when I'm sad or feel lonely."

He handed me a piece of paper. "Keep it," he said. "I have memorized these words. They're from a fourteenth-century poet named Jean de Jandun."

Here are the words, Tracy: ". . .on entering one would think oneself transported to heaven and one might with reason imagine oneself taken into one of the most beautiful rooms of paradise."

So the two of us just stood there in awe and felt like we had been transported to paradise.

The next day we took the train to Chartres, which is the most perfect of the medieval cathedrals. It was Good Friday, and Robert wanted me to see the cathedral on good Friday, because all the lights were off inside, he said, to help us remember the crucifixion of Christ. Chartres is a small town about an hour's train ride from Paris, and when you come in, you can see the cathedral towering over the village. The whole town seems to exist for the cathedral. It was a beautiful day, and inside the cathedral we could imagine what it must have been like for the people in the middle ages who had no light except the light that shone in through the windows.

Before this week, Tracy, I don't think I ever cared about stained glass. It was pretty, of course, but I never paid much attention to it. Chartres is even more stunning than Sainte-Chapelle. Robert says it's because it has the most perfect stained-glass windows in all of Europe. He's been here several times, he says, and taken the tours with the English guide. The whole story of creation from Adam and Eve to the Last Judgment is told in these windows. It's incredible. The people were mostly illiterate. They couldn't read the Bible, and the priests didn't want them to, anyway. So they could "read" the windows, which told the stories in pictures.

We worked our way down toward the transept, starting at the West and moving toward the East. I never know whether to capitalize these words. Do you? The altar is always in the East, where the sun rises, the sun which is a symbol for the "son" who rises. The West is death, the East is Resurrection, and at the transept, the center of the cross, you can stand and look to the North and South, and here are two absolutely magnificent rose windows. We went and sat down on a bench and looked for a long time at the South window. Everything was dark, black almost inside, and the windows seemed to be floating, floating in eternity, as if they needed no support. There was an old man in a wheelchair. . .but let me give you the poem I wrote:

CHARTRES CATHEDRAL, GOOD FRIDAY
I sit with my friend before the South Rose Window
on Good Friday, lights off, candles snuffed,

nothing but the shifting April sun behind the glass
and the walls so black they seem to have vanished

In the midst, color and glass float blue and white
in the circled light, the silence deep as love.
I think of you kneeling at your own altar somewhere
to the West where the sun still shifts upward.

I sit with my friend, watching the afternoon light
and the old man in the wheel chair next to us
old man paralyzed in leg and arm staring
with his one good eye at the center of the Rose

Christ eternal, angels, elders, beasts
chant songs of praise. He dreams of the Last
Judgment when limbs will be made whole
souls and bodies mixed in new-made harmony.

Suddenly the sun gives way and darkness
slides through the colored glass. A woman
comes to guide the man outside, and my friend
and I follow down the nave, out under

the window of Jesse's stem into the cobblestone
street. "Tres belle," I murmur to the old man's ear,
the only French I have. He gurgles some strange
laughter. "Oui," he says, "Ah oui, tres belle."

I don't think it's quite finished, Tracy, but I like it. I like the old
man and my struggle to find words for him in French for what I
felt. Anyway, after that Robert and I walked back to the station
and took the train to Paris. We didn't talk much. I had bought a
guide book, and kept going through it, looking at the pictures of the
windows and marveling how the craftsmen told each story, each
parable, each event in Christ's life, in these beautiful, tiny pieces
of glass. And the people, cold in their thatched huts or whatever

Anthony S. Abbott

miserable places they had to live in, came to the cathedral and saw the windows and were comforted.

Tracy, I just reread what I wrote, and there's really nothing personal, nothing about you and me, my feelings. It's sad. I don't know what to say. I doubt myself. She'll just think it's stupid, I say. It's amazing how affected I am by small things. Visiting Chartres and Sainte Chapelle made me feel like God was really there. Then the God in me goes away, and I wonder if He really does exist. Same with you. Sometimes, I wonder if you are really there, if everything we had together just adds up to nothing. Shit, Tracy. If you can say it, I can say it. Let me know what happens with the baby. I think about her all the time, Tracy. It's as if I were her father, and not whoever it is....What does that mean?

Your devoted and loyal brother, David

CHAPTER TWENTY-TWO

Madrid, April 17

Oh Tracy, Tracy, Tracy—I hope you read this. Even if you didn't know me, it would be scary. I'm sitting at the desk in my hotel room in Madrid, writing as fast as I can. I want to get all this down while it's still fresh in my mind. I'm still trembling, and I will not sleep tonight. So here goes.

I had written Peggy Urbano that I was coming to Madrid and given her my arrival time and hoped she would be able to meet me. It was a night train from Paris that worked its way south and then west over the Pyrenees as the sun came up. Suddenly we were in Spain and the train stopped and bunches of soldiers with rifles came aboard and worked their way through the cars checking our luggage and our passports. This was Franco's Spain, the country of the man who had Guernica bombed. This was a military dictatorship, not pleasure-loving France.

Anyway, we got to Madrid around nine in the morning, and when I walked out the gate, there was Peggy Urbano looking absolutely fantastic. She was different. It was as if she had stopped being an American and had become Spanish. Her hair was different, and she wore a long flowered skirt and a scoop-necked blouse, and she wore make-up. She looked like a woman, not a girl. When I had seen her at Christmas, she looked like an American college girl still—you know what I mean—knee socks and loafers and one of those plaid skirts with a pin in it, and a wool sweater.

I was just knocked out. She hugged me, and we got a cab, and we drove to this beautiful hotel near the university, and she took me in and talked to the desk clerk in Spanish and got me a room with bath, a modern, gorgeous room with bath, for 65 pesetas, that's a dollar and a half. And she said she had to go to class and she would call me after lunch, and we would go to dinner together and she would show me the night life.

So here I was in Madrid, and I took off my clothes, which I'd been in all night and got under my covers and went to sleep, thinking about Peggy and what might happen next. When I woke up it was three o'clock, and I took a shower and got dressed and wrote in my journal and waited for her to call. Finally at five o'clock she called:

"David," she said, "I have bad news for you."

"What is it, Peggy?"

"I've been quarantined."

"What do you mean?"

"The university has put me in the infirmary, and I'm not allowed to leave for five days. I have the mumps."

"You're kidding."

"This morning, at the station, I felt funny, and had a swelling in my neck. Didn't you notice it?"

"No." (Obviously I had not noticed it; I was too busy being overwhelmed.)

"I'm sick about this, David. I was really looking forward to your coming."

"I don't know what to do," I said. "I don't know anyone in Madrid except you, and I don't speak Spanish."

"Just ask the concierge at the hotel. He'll tell you where to go and what to see. You'll be fine. Go to the Prado tomorrow, and I'll call you at five o'clock, and you can tell me about it. OK?"

"Five days?" I asked.

"Five days," she said.

Well that was my whole time in Madrid. Blown all to hell by the mumps.

What a development. Now what was I to do? I went to the lobby and asked for the concierge, and he gave me a bunch of stuff, and I realized that the restaurants didn't even open for dinner until nine o'clock, and most people ate at ten. Great. Six o'clock was the middle of the afternoon in Madrid. Everybody slept from one to four! To make a long story short, I just had dinner in the hotel and was on my way up to my room in the elevator, when the elevator boy said, "You wanna girl? I get you nice girl. Send to room."

"No thanks," I answered.

"You virgin? You want someone teach you? I get you nice girl."

"No," I said again.

"OK. You change mind. Ask for Felix."

"Thanks, Felix," I said and got out at my floor.

Holy shit, Tracy. This is a regular way of life over here. I felt like Holden Caulfield in New York.

Tuesday morning I went to the Prado. I got an English guidebook, and started working my way through the rooms. I remembered what you told me—Velasquez, El Greco and Goya. They were the big three, and Picasso, of course, but the best Picasso's were in New York.

Did you know that each of these artists has a room of his own with his name over the door? Huge rooms. I started with Velasquez, and was standing in front of a picture called "Las Meninas" ("The Maids of Honor")—my guide book said it was his masterpiece. I was standing, looking at it, when I heard a voice in an English accent:

"Notice that the king and queen are visible only in the mirror on the back wall."

I turned around, and there behind me was an elegant-looking man in his thirties, I guess. He had sandy brown hair and a small beard. He wore gray trousers and a brown tweed jacket with a suede vest. He had little round glasses with silver rims.

"Archibald Henderson," he said, extending his hand. "I teach art history at the University of Manchester. I'm here on sabbatical, working on a book. You can call me Archie."

"David Lear," I said. "I'm an exchange student at Rutland College."

"Fine school," he said. "Are you here for long?"

"Just a few days," I said.

"Let me take you around," he said. "Spanish painters are my specialty."

I was astounded. What an opportunity, to see the Spanish paintings with an art history professor, and a delightful one at that.

"Think of the irony," he laughed. "Velasquez makes himself the central character in the painting. He tricks the king and queen who are sitting in the viewer's space being painted, so what we get is not the king and queen, but a completely different painting, so that Velasquez is really in our space with the king and queen looking at the children and the dwarves and the dog."

I loved listening to him. We walked from painting to painting and room to room and went upstairs to the cafeteria for lunch. Before I knew it, I found myself telling him the story of Peggy Urbano and the mumps. A perfect stranger.

He laughed again. "You really think she has the mumps? It sounds quite like a dodge to me. She's got a boy friend here."

"But why would she invite me, if she didn't want to see me?"

"Perhaps she didn't have the boy friend then."

I didn't want to believe him, and I was glad when we went back to see the Goyas and the El Greco's. Goya just blew me away, Tracy, just blew me away. There's a big painting called "The Third of May, 1808"—I think it's one you told me about—where a French firing squad is murdering a group of Spanish men, and the expression on the men's faces is absolutely astonishing. The soldiers have no faces. They are just shooting machines, and the light in the painting is on the victims, on the man in the white shirt and the yellow pants with his hands up. The soldiers are dark, dark, dark. Just killing machines.

Then Archie said we had to go up to the second floor to see Goya's "black" paintings. They were too dark to be exhibited in the main room, and he was right. They were terrifying, and the most terrifying of all was one of Saturn eating his own son. Archie said that Goya suffered terribly during his last years from nightmares of human cruelty and savagery and painted these pictures to relieve his agony.

The museum was closing, and I stuck out my hand to thank him. He took my hand and held it for a long time.

"Why don't we have dinner together?" he asked. "I know a wonderful little restaurant where they serve great paella Valencia."

I told him I would love to join him, and we agreed to meet at the restaurant at ten o'clock, the fashionable hour for dinner in Spain. It was delightful. We ate and drank Spanish wine, which he knew all about, and we talked. I told him my life story, and he seemed so interested and sympathetic that I just kept talking. Then he invited me back to his apartment for a nightcap. He had worked out an exchange with a Spanish friend, who had taken his apartment in Manchester for the year. It was a perfect arrangement.

So, off we went to his apartment, and took off our jackets and ties and had some cognac and looked at art books, and then had some more cognac and the next thing I knew he wanted to show me something in his bedroom, some wonderful painting on the wall, I think, and I went in and sat on his bed to look at the painting, and I was having trouble focusing on the painting. I guess I had drunk too much cognac. Suddenly, his arms were around me, and he was trying to kiss me. He wasn't really big, Tracy, but he was bigger than I was, and I could feel him pushing me down on the bed, his body on top of me, his body moving on top of me like I would move on top of you. I struggled. I turned and twisted, and finally was able to throw him off. He stood in the doorway of the bedroom looking down at me.

He laughed. He was a great laugher. "You're awfully naïve, aren't you?" he said.

I gave him the same speech I gave Robert. He wasn't amused. "That sounds lovely, dear boy," he said, "but you have no business leading me on this way. You are so charming, so confessional. My goodness, you don't think I was just being nice to you?"

"I better go," I said.

"Maybe I won't let you," he said, and laughed again. And then he pulled from his pocket a black-handled knife, which he held in the palm of his hand. Click, and the blade opened and he was standing in front of me, holding the knife to my chest.

"Unbutton your shirt," he said.

Tracy, I've never been so scared in my life. So I did what he said. I unbuttoned my shirt and took it off.

"Stand up," he said.

I did not move.

He flicked the knife against my chest, and I saw a tiny bubble of blood on my skin. "Now stand up," he said again, and I stood up.

He told me to unbuckle my belt and drop my trousers and then my underpants, and he told me to turn around and put my hands on the bed, but I wouldn't, and then he cut me again. I turned around and did what he said, and began to sob, not just to cry but to sob, and I felt him against me, and I started to pray, and I prayed and I sobbed. And then, I heard his voice.

"Oh go on," he said. "I can't stand this baby behavior. You're not worth my time. I don't want your silly company anymore. You're just a stupid boy. But, Master David, let me tell you something. You had better be very careful. The next man you meet may not be as civilized as I am. You could be badly hurt. Didn't your mother ever tell you not to talk to strangers?" He turned and walked out into the living room.

When I came out, he was holding my coat and tie.

"It's all right," he said. "Don't be frightened. There's a taxi stand on the corner. Turn right." He handed me my things, and looked into my eyes.

"Too bad," he said. "We might have had a wonderful time."

I took a cab back to the hotel and went up to my room and stood in the shower for a long, long time, just washing myself, trying to wash myself clean. Then I held the white towel against the cuts on my chest until the bleeding stopped. I couldn't sleep.

Jesus, Tracy. I kept thinking about myself and how stupid I was not to recognize what Archibald was doing. He was so much slicker than Robert. Then I thought about you, and the irony of the whole thing. Here I had come to Madrid to go to bed with Peggy Urbano, just to let you know I could live without you, and this is how I end up, nearly getting raped by another homosexual. What is it with me? I love to travel. I love to meet new people and make friends. Now every man I meet I'm going to worry about.

All this happened tonight, Tracy. In the morning I will call my grandfather and ask him if I can come to Nice right away. I can't stay here.

Well, Tracy, I'm finishing this up in the airport here in Madrid, waiting for my flight to Nice. I'm tired of traveling right now. I'm tired of the salesmen who peddle Parker 51's outside of every museum. I'm tired of the pimps who peddle their prostitutes and the strangers who prey on boys. I think I'm ready to go home, Tracy, but where is home? If I got on a plane and flew to New York, that wouldn't be home any more. So I'll go back to school, to my study there, which is my home in England, where the walls are covered with postcards from my trips and newspaper clippings my Aunt Louise has sent me. And in my study I will read a letter from you about the baby.

I have never loved you more or needed you more, David

May 10

Thank God for school. I still love it, even here. It's like putting myself on again, the grey trousers and the black coat and the white boater hat and walking down the main street (they call it High Street here) and saying hello to everyone—good old Maurice Taylor and my new best friend, George Henderson, who I will see next year, because he's going to be Rutland's exchange student. George is the one I stay with in London.

When I got back from Madrid, I had a few days in London before school started, and it was wonderful to be with George and speak English again. One night we went to his father's club, and we sat in the smoking room, and there were these old, fat men in black suits sitting in every overstuffed chair, and they were all reading newspapers. When George and I sat down on the couch, it made a noise like a fart. It hissed. And then it hissed again if you got up, and we got laughing so hard at these stupid old men and the farting couch, we were asked to leave. His father was mad at us, but not really mad. He thinks the club is pretty pompous, but he asked us not to go back there.

The weirdest thing happened, Tracy. The school has been sending reports about my work to Molly Ariel in California, and two days ago I got a letter from her with my fall and winter term reports. She thought I ought to see them, now that I was almost on my own. It was so strange to see what they were writing about me. The one that really bothered me at first was the report from my English teacher, Mr. Griffin. I really like him. I think I've told you that. He's a superb teacher, and when I get a good grade from him, it gives me huge pleasure. He gave me a really nice report for the fall, but then in the winter report he said, "His work has continued to be well above average. I believe his next task must be to try and make his written work less impersonal, to convey some of his conversational self into his essays, so that they seem less obviously donnish."

It really upset me to read that, Tracy. I don't think of myself as "donnish," and certainly my letters to you convey my "conversational self." Then I went back and read a couple of my essays, and damned if he wasn't right. I have two styles, one in my essays and one for you. I guess I thought being more formal was what the English liked.

Oh God, I almost forgot to tell you about the end of my vacation. I flew from Madrid to Nice, and my grandfather met me and took me to Antibes where I stayed for three days and slept and read in a folding chair on the beach just across the road. It was a pathetic beach, full of little pebbles, no sand. But the sun was warm. I was so tired, Tracy, I could hardly keep my eyes open, and I told Mme. Lucas and my grandfather about Peggy Urbano and the mumps. Nothing about Archibald, of course. He laughed and she gave me a knowing smile, as if to say, "Well, women are like that." I don't know. I still don't know. My grandfather said he was proud of me, and he looked forward to seeing me at Princeton. He had to come back to New York at least once every five years in order to keep from losing his citizenship. He would write me when he was coming back.

I took the sleeper, second class, from Nice to Paris, and spent the next night in the same hotel I had stayed in before. I called Robert, and we went out for dinner. I told him about Peggy Urbano and Archibald Henderson. It made him sad.

"Don't turn cynical," he said. "What I like best about you is your idealism. You'll get what you want one day. Just don't give up on it. If you do, then you'll never find yourself."

That's so important, Tracy, what Robert said. I really love him, not the way I love you, of course, but like the brother I never had. Robert seems kinder and wiser than almost anyone else I've met, except maybe Ralph Wisdom. It's as though being a homosexual has made him more sensitive, more understanding. I guess that's what disappointed me so much about Archibald Henderson. He was so mean once he found out he couldn't use me. But not Robert.

Here's the best part. Robert took me to the station in the morning, and gave me a present—a book called "The Diary of Anne Frank." Have you heard of it? It had just been published in America the year before, and his mother had sent him a copy. He wanted me to have it, and he wanted me to go by the house in Amsterdam and pay my respects to her memory. I didn't understand what he meant, but I do now. Oh Tracy, what an extraordinary book. I read it on the train all the way to Amsterdam, and then I went to the Travelers Information desk in the station and found a hotel near Anne Frank's House. Everyone knew where it was. As soon as I got to the hotel, I just put down my bags and finished the book.

Here is this girl, Tracy, who is only thirteen in 1940 when her family has to hide from the Germans in a very small apartment they call "The Secret Annex." They hide there for two years, until someone betrays them, and the Germans catch them and send them off to concentration camps. All during this time she kept her diary, and when her father found it after the war (he was the only one who survived), he had it published, and it was just translated into English.

She shames us, Tracy. My letters to you are nothing compared to what she writes, and she was only thirteen and fourteen. I'm just amazed. Listen to this: "I am becoming still more independent of my parents, young as I am, I face life with more courage than Mummy; my feeling for justice is immovable, and truer than hers. I know what I want, I have a goal, an opinion, I have a religion and love. Let me be myself and then I am satisfied. I know that I'm a woman, a woman with inward strength and plenty of courage.

"If God lets me live, I shall attain more than Mummy ever has done, I shall not remain insignificant, I shall work in the world and for mankind."

All that, Tracy and she's only fifteen. Of course, she makes me think of you. I can't tell you how hard it is not to have your letters anymore. It's not just the love I miss, though that is everything. It's your knowledge, your wisdom, the things you share with me, it's what you're reading and thinking. I understand your decision to let me go, "at least for now," as you say, but I feel like a part of my body is missing. I'm a man with an amputated leg, limping along on crutches, but still feeling the missing limb. (Maybe there's a poem in that. Maybe it's too pitiful.)

Sweet Jesus, Tracy, the baby! I got so involved telling you about myself that I just ignored the most important thing. It must be time. The baby must have come by now. Are you all right? Is the baby all right? Will you be going home? I have so many questions. I may just have to call your mom and dad. I can't stand not knowing anything.

Your loving and faithful brother, David

May 30

Oh my beloved Tracy I'm so stupid, I'm so naïve, and so ignorant. Of course, it all makes sense. When I saw your letter on the table in the hall and snatched it up to take it to my study, someone saw me, and the next thing I knew there were all these knocks on my study door and voices hooting in the hall. "David has a love note!" So I tucked it into Milton's *Paradise Lost* (they'd never think of looking there!) and opened the door and just stood there smiling. "Well, why don't we go down and change and play some cricket!" I said, and off I went down the stairs to the changing room. I figured they'd forget about it by evening and they did.

Tracy, you weren't being punished. God doesn't work like that. I just can't believe that. You are the most loving person I know. Your mistakes are mistakes of the heart. God didn't take your baby from you as a punishment. It just happened. I'm so glad you got to hold her and know her for a few days. Maybe that was worse, I don't know. I can't imagine being a girl and giving birth and then losing my baby. I think of baby Caroline's little grave next to her namesake, her aunt, in the cemetery where we buried the cross. Will you take me back there when I come home? You say you don't think you will ever be able to love again. You feel ugly with a big scar down your stomach. You feel empty and drained. But you will get better, Tracy, I know. I want to help you heal. Please let me, Tracy. I think I know more about love now than I did, and I know that I love you and will always love you. David

Edinburgh, July 4

My dearest Tracy, this will be my last letter, or at least the last letter I mail from Europe. I had an experience just before school ended that I want to tell you about. It's very important, so please read this. All the school prefects, the pollies, take turns reading the lessons in chapel, and my turn came up in late June, just before our exams. The lesson was Romans 8:18-25. I had to practice it in the huge chapel several times, the last time with the Headmaster.

He helped me tremendously. He had me read the lesson once, and I kind of stumbled over some of the words. Then he told me to sit down and he thanked me for being such a credit to the school, and he said he wished all the exchange students would contribute as much as I had. So then I read the lesson beautifully, and he sent me back to the house just beaming.

I got back to my study, and I opened the Bible to read the lesson to myself one more time, and suddenly two lines just danced off the page: "Now hope that is seen is not hope. For who hopes for what he sees? But if we hope for what we do not see, we wait for it with patience."

And I thought of you, of course, and how, until you, I had not loved and didn't really know what love was, and how you were the first person I could say the word "love" to. I know what love is now because of you, and I won't ever be fooled by something that looks like love but really isn't. But I never understood hope before. "But if we hope for what we do not see, we wait for it with patience." What I do not see right now is you and me together. I don't see, and I never realized until I practiced that lesson what hope really was. If we are meant to be together, we will be together, and I will wait for it with patience. I don't have to see us together, but I have to hope. After all, I am Maggie Hope's son.

So if it is to be, dear Tracy, meet me at the boat. I arrive at noon on Friday, August 2 at Pier Ninety on the Queen Mary. I will be looking for your yellow shirt and your red bandana. Maybe you won't be there. Maybe you'll be in Montana or Wyoming or someplace else. But I will hope and try to hope with patience. All my love, David.

CHAPTER TWENTY-THREE

He was on his way home. He kept saying that. Then he would say, "No, I am on my way back to the United States, where I will learn where home is or what home is or whether it is something I will have to live without."

He and Terry were sharing a room on the Queen Mary, and David was glad the others weren't there. They had decided to stay in England for an extra week. David loved Brad and Little Billy Wheeler, but he was tired of the drinking and the card playing and the conversations about girls. He needed some time to himself, and Terry understood it, because Terry knew him so well. And for Terry, making new friends on the ship was easy. He just picked out the prettiest girl he could find, walked up to her, introduced himself, smiled, and off they went as if they had known each other all their lives. That was Terry. He had not told Terry about Tracy's baby, and he was sure that he would never tell anyone without asking Tracy first. That was a private thing, the most private thing of all. That was a true secret between them, and would remain a secret as far as David was concerned.

"Do you still love her?" Terry had asked.

"Yes," David answered truthfully.

Anthony S. Abbott

Terry shrugged his shoulders and smiled. "I don't know, Butter Rum," he said. "It doesn't make sense to me, but it's your call. I'm staying out of it, OK?"

"OK," said David, and that was the end of their Tracy conversation.

The first couple of days on the ship David got up around nine and went to breakfast, leaving Terry snoring away. Then he would take his tea (he was a tea drinker now) to the paneled library, where he sat at a small table by the window and wrote letters, which would be mailed from New York when the ship docked.

He wrote to Elizabeth, telling her about his final month at school and his trip to Edinburgh. He sent Alex a postcard of the Queen Mary and Maggie one of the Queen herself. He knew they would fight if he sent only one. He wrote to Molly Ariel, a long, carefully composed letter thanking her for what she had done for him and especially for her support during this "extra" year. He had decided, he told her, to use his Aunt Louise's address in Lambertville as his "home" address, since it was so close to Princeton, and he asked Molly if she would forward any mail that she had received over the summer.

All this business about letters bothered him. Mail from Princeton probably went to Molly Ariel, since she had been listed as his legal guardian, but mail from his friends like Wally Hinson and Ted Barber had probably gone to the Bronx and disappeared somewhere, marked "return to sender, addressee unknown." But he had plenty of time to contact them before they headed down to Princeton. He would go to the campus himself before school opened and find out about his status, his room, and everything else he needed to know.

He had passed his A-level examinations with distinction, and he would show his certificates to the Dean at Princeton to make sure he received credit for his freshman year. He carried them home with great pride. It was one thing to be the best English student at Wicker School, but it was another to do it in a foreign country where he was competing with "specialists." The French he had not been worried about, but in English he had felt all year that there was something missing, some step he hadn't taken.

Maybe it was what Mr. Griffin had pointed out in the school report which Molly Ariel had sent him, but he thought it was something more than that—a feeling that there was something in the literary texts he just missed, a secret code or something that he could not unlock. His essays always just missed. Lots of Alpha minuses and Beta plusses. He was always very good, but never the best.

He wrote to Father Perkins, thanking the Headmaster for selecting him as the exchange student from Wicker. "You made it possible for me to experience a world I never dreamed of seeing, a world so different from my own that I can't find the words to describe it, and yet, Father Perkins, I hope it will be my business some day to find those words. I want to go back to England, back to the Continent, and see these places again when I have finished college, particularly the places associated with writers. I saw Shakespeare's tomb at Holy Trinity Church in Stratford, and Thomas Gray's country churchyard and Donne's sepulcher in the basement of St. Paul's in London. It was you who taught me the lines from Donne, "Seek not for whom the bell tolls, it tolls for thee," and it was you who read us "Death be not proud" in your Lenten sermon on death my third-form year. I thought of Donne, preaching his sermons in St. Paul's and wouldn't have known about him if it hadn't been for you and Mr. Barnes. Thank you for everything."

The crossing was lovely, so different from the turbulent, stormy passage on the Elizabeth in September. There were no storms on the North Atlantic now, and he dozed in the deckchairs in the sun, accepting gratefully the cookies and the cups of tea brought round by the stewards. He dozed and dreamed and scribbled poems.

The one he most wanted to write was the one about Vermeer. It had haunted him since the end of his Easter vacation in Amsterdam when he stumbled into two paintings of Vermeer in the Rijksmuseum in Amsterdam. Vermeer had caught him by surprise, completely by surprise. He was not a painter David had learned about from Tracy Warren or from any of his teachers. He was just walking down one of the halls in the museum, when he saw these two paintings side by side and gasped. One was called "The Milkmaid" and the other was "A Woman in Blue Reading a Letter."

Anthony S. Abbott

He reached out to touch "The Milkmaid," it was so three dimensional. "No touch," said the guard in English. "I'm sorry," David said. "Pardonnez-moi." He had forgotten where he was, the painting was so real, the bread with its seeds so tangible David could feel the crumbs, the broken pieces falling to the floor, the milk pouring from the pitcher, the woman's face pock-marked, nail holes in the wall. "Here," he would say to the milkmaid, "you dropped this," and he would lean over and pick up the piece of bread, and hand it to her, and she would put her pitcher down and wipe her big hands on her blue apron, and thank him.

But the other—the woman in blue—was the one that had made him gasp, and he could not look at it long without tears. The woman reading the letter was Tracy, she was clearly Tracy, and not only was she reading a letter, she was reading his letter, David's letter. There was a map on the wall, and the girl was standing next to the map reading a letter from far away. She was thinking deeply, she was engrossed so deeply in the words of the letter that if someone had knocked on her door, she would not have heard. She *was* Tracy, Tracy in seventeenth-century clothes, to be sure, but that didn't matter. The eyes were Tracy's, the quiet concentration in the eyes, the soft, slightly parted lips, the hands, the way she held the letter carefully with both hands. And she was pregnant, she was clearly carrying a baby.

David would walk away and look at something else, and then come back to her again, and it was still the same. He went to the shop and bought postcards of both paintings and pasted them in his book. At first he thought he would send them to Tracy, but he couldn't bear to part with them. And that was when he got the idea of the poem, the poem he would write her for his homecoming, the poem that he would write whether she was there or not. If she was not there, he would mail it to her.

And now, as the Queen Mary neared New York, he still had not finished it. He couldn't get it right. The poem he would have written in April he could no longer write, and the poem he needed to write now he could not find words for.

It had been almost a year since he had seen her last, a year since their trip to New York, their "Rosie and Charlie" trip, a year since they had come home and called upstairs to her parents that they were back and heard her mother say, "Goodnight, sweetheart." David remembered that so vividly, how her mother stayed awake just to be sure they were safe, and how Tracy said with such sureness, "She'll go right to sleep now. She won't come down," and how they had gone upstairs to change into shorts and Tee shirts and come down and taken their blanket out to the backyard and had spread it out and lay on their backs smoking and watching the stars, and how they had sat up and Tracy had taken her shirt off and showed him her breasts, bare, for the first time, and how he had touched them first with his fingers and then with his mouth, how he had buried his head there for a long time and felt that this was home.

She must have known about the baby, even then, and she had brought her letter and the flowers to the boat to say good-bye to him, to let him know that she could no longer see him because of the baby, and he had not known the letter meant that. She had hung the letter A on her own breast and told him to stay away from her. Terry had told him to stay away from her. She was bad.

But David knew better now. He knew that she was different, different from what she had seemed to be and different from what anyone else thought. He could hear the boys at school calling her "slut." That's the way Terry felt. The word had got around from school to school. "That Tracy Warren is just a slut." Even the sound of the word made David sick. He hated it, because it was such a lie. He could see Tracy, alone in her room, pale and beaten from losing the child. He could see her kneeling at the grave of the two Carolines, the stones cutting into her knees. She had lost weight, and the scar from the Caesarean section must burn. He couldn't write a poem about that.

Now it was the morning of his third day at sea, Sunday morning, and the ropes dividing the classes would be taken down for church services. David had decided to attend the Anglican communion service in the first-class lounge, and he was excited about seeing that part of the ship. He took his seat in the third row of chairs and picked up the familiar prayer book, which he had become used to during his year in England. Then the piano

Anthony S. Abbott

started to play the opening hymn and the priests processed down the center aisle. David turned his head. There in the procession was Father Perkins, the Headmaster to whom he had just written. He was mesmerized.

As the procession reached the front of the room, David opened his program, and found his name. The meditation was to be given by the Rev. James Alexander Perkins, Rector and Headmaster of Wicker School.

The lesson was from the fourteenth chapter of the Gospel of John. Jesus has been explaining his mission to the disciples, and as usual they have difficulty understanding him. Jesus says, "I am the way, and the truth, and the life; no one comes to the Father, but by me. If you had known me, you would have known my father also; henceforth you know him and have seen him."

Then Philip says, "Lord, show us the Father, and we shall be satisfied," and Jesus answers him, "Have I been with you so long, and yet you do not know me, Philip. He who has seen me has seen the Father. . .Do you not believe that I am in the Father and the Father in me?"

David loved listening to the Headmaster read. The deep sonorous voice, the piercing eyes, the strong and pointed pauses. He seemed to be speaking directly to David. "What an extraordinary passage of scripture this is," he said quietly, "and what a comforting one, and yet so many miss the comfort. Surely the disciples did. 'Show us the Father,' Philip says, and isn't that just like us? 'Show us the Father,' and we will know what God is like, we think, and Jesus says that we don't need to see the Father, that He is the way, the truth and the life, and that He and the Father are one; they are the same. How do we know what God is like? We know because of the Incarnation. How do we know that God loves us, that God cares about us infinitely? We know because we have seen that love in Jesus, His love for the poor, the outcast, the troubled.

"God takes joy in His creation of us, and we are to take joy in our lives. We are here to love, to be joyful, not to be eaten up with guilt and remorse. 'Don't be afraid' is what Jesus says over and over. Don't be afraid of God, don't be afraid of God's judgment, but live your life to the fullest in love, and love one another as God has loved you. That is what Jesus says."

The words made their way into an empty space in David's heart. He understood. He had spent so much of his life trying to please people, trying to excel, to win prizes, to be the best. That wasn't what it was really all about. It was really about loving, about trying to see people as they saw themselves. That was it. It was about young Kiddiminster, the boy they had whipped at school, the boy David could have done something for if he had really loved in the way that Jesus told us to; it was about the boy that they had called Satchel Ass at Wicker, the least popular boy in his class; it was about Ian Stuart, the little Scottish boy David had made fun of at Lowell in order to be popular with Griff and Terry. It was about the people who stood on street corners in Paris and Madrid and London begging for coins, because they had nothing. It wasn't so hard, opening the heart to these people, and if he opened his heart to them, then he would know God in a new way, in the way that Jesus had meant him to know God. That's what Father Perkins was saying.

And when David came forward and knelt down to receive the wafer, Father Perkins stood before him and spoke the words that David had heard once before, "The body of Christ which is given for you, David." At the end of the service, David remained in his seat until the Headmaster came back to greet him.

He stood and shook Father Perkins' extended hand.

"You look like you've just seen a ghost, lad," the Headmaster said.

"I couldn't believe it was you, sir," David said. "It was, it was…"

"Don't try and say it, David. I know what you mean. I was in Canterbury for a week, for the Lambeth Conference. They have it every three years. Church business.

Now, come have lunch with me."

"But I'm in tourist class."

"You're my guest," the Headmaster said. "You can stay as a guest."

And so they sat for a long time, the two of them, near the window in the first class dining room, white linen and flowers on the table, the sun beaming in. They drank wine and talked about Uppingham and Wicker and the sixth form that had followed David's.

"You've had a grand year, lad," said the Headmaster, "just what I had hoped for. What will you do at Princeton?"

"Major in English, learn to become a teacher," David said.

"Fine, lad. Maybe you'll come back to Wicker and teach. We'd be proud to have you."

"Thank you, sir," David said.

For a while they ate in silence. The Headmaster's white collar shone brightly against the black of his shirt. David wondered why ministers wore their collars turned around, but he didn't think he would ask.

"You know, David," said the Headmaster, wiping his mouth with his linen napkin, "college is very different from prep school. There's no center, no sense of God as the central meaning of our lives. It's all open, and you may find it much more difficult at Princeton to keep focused. Even choosing classes is difficult. There are dozens of departments that didn't even exist at Wicker. Take some religion courses. You might even decide to go to seminary one day. Had you thought of that?"

"Not really, sir," said David. And then, before he had time to take it back, he said, "Can I ask you something, sir?"

"Certainly, lad."

"I actually have thought about it. I love thinking about God, and I feel very close to God sometimes. Like this morning, during your meditation, or when I was in Sainte Chapelle and Chartres over Easter break."

A flood of words came out from somewhere. He told the Headmaster about the stained glass windows and the color and the old man in the wheelchair, and then he told him about the boys on Christmas Eve and the poem he had written.

"But I have always felt funny around religious people. They seem so pious and holy and I just don't feel comfortable around them. I seem to like my religion in art and in stories and poems, but not in church. Do you know what I mean?"

"We're all called differently, lad. Wearing these silly collars is only one way to serve God. You'll find your ministry in your own way. That's good. Do you know the work of Alan Paton?"

"No, sir."

"Here," he said, and reached into his brief case. "I always carry an extra copy of this novel with me. Read it, David. It's one of the most powerful Christian books I've ever read, and one of the most simple and beautifully written. There's nothing pious or churchy about it."

"*Cry, the Beloved Country,*" David said, pronouncing each word of the book's title out loud.

"Yes," said the Headmaster. "It's a book about faith and love and the overcoming of hatred in South Africa. Read it, and read it again. Then, buy one and give it to someone else. It's exactly what you were talking about."

"Thank you, sir, I will," said David, and he held the book as if it were a talisman.

All afternoon David read the book, turning each page as if it were holy scripture. Maybe it was. Maybe God's word was not only in the Bible but in novels and poems. He read with a peculiar intensity, this story of sorrow and pain and the courage to overcome prejudice. He felt the terrible agony of the black people of South Africa. He had not known really about apartheid, and he had not really thought very much about black people in America. He knew in his heart that segregation was wrong, but he hadn't done anything about it. He had simply ignored it. At Princeton he would have to learn more about these things.

On he read into the night. Terry thought he had lost his mind.

"Here we are on the Queen Mary," Terry said. "Enough is enough. You can read later."

"It's not just a book," David said. "It's an emotional experience. I'm in it so deep, I can't come out until it's over. Do you know what I mean?"

"If it was anyone else, I'd say 'no,' but with you it makes sense, I guess. Come join me and Gwendolyn later, if you're done," said Terry.

By midnight David had finished the book, and he walked up on the promenade deck to look at the stars and think.

"Goddammit," he whispered fiercely to the night sky. He was angry at himself, angry at the stupid cruelty of human beings, and he was angry at Tracy. He could do nothing important without thinking of her. Maybe she had read it during her short time at Radcliffe or in her lonely room out there in Wisconsin while the baby grew. He ached to talk to her about it.

He went to the little bar up on the boat deck and bought a scotch and soda. He took it out to one of the tables on the deck behind, which was protected from the wind. He drank, and he copied into his journal his favorite lines from the novel:

"That men should walk upright in the land where they were born, and be free to use the fruits of the earth, what was there evil in it? Yet men were afraid, with a fear that was deep, deep in the heart, a fear so deep that they hid their kindness or brought it out with fierceness and anger, and hid it behind fierce and frowning eyes. They were afraid because they were so few. And such fear could not be cast out, but by love."

He went back to the bar, bought another scotch and soda, and carried it back to the table. He began writing in his journal.

"My dearest Tracy, everything I write is for you whether you want it or not. Maybe I should learn to do things just for myself, but that seems silly. What is one person alone? If I did not have you, I would want someone else, and I cannot imagine anyone else I would want. That's my problem. All day today and tonight, as the Queen Mary churned toward New York, I read *Cry, The Beloved Country* by Alan Paton. It is the most beautiful book I have ever read, Tracy, and if you are there at the dock, when we arrive, I will give it to you and give you this journal to read. If you are not there, I will send you the book and tear out these pages and send them also.

"I keep trying to figure everything out. That's my problem, isn't it? Some things you can't figure out. My father, when he stopped drinking, memorized this prayer: 'Lord give me the strength to change the things that I can change, the serenity to accept the things which I cannot change, and the wisdom to know the difference.' Or something like that. I can't remember the words exactly. I love it. I think it's true, but with you my problem is that I don't know the difference. Can I change things with you by changing myself, by being different, or do I have to accept things as they are? I don't know. Your silence frightens me.

"And so I must live in hope and not in fear. I understand that completely, but to do it is so much harder than I imagined. I have it all in my head, Tracy, right now, with two scotches in me. Maybe I shouldn't be drinking, with my mother's problem and my father's. Here I am sitting on the deck drinking scotches, but only two, and I feel a wonderful sense of freedom to say what I want to say and not be afraid, so I'll say it.

The worst tragedy I can imagine in my life is losing you. There, I said it. It's like the man in the parable who finds the treasure in the field, Tracy, and after that nothing else is the same. The treasure makes everything else different. He feels this extraordinary joy, and he goes and sells all he has and buys the field with the treasure in it. Lucky him! I can't buy you! I can only hope.

"I can hear you saying, 'Don't idealize me.' But what I know is that you are the treasure for me, and all that other stuff about God, like Sainte Chapelle and Chartres and even *Cry, The Beloved Country,* is somehow related to you. I should do all that other stuff for its own sake, I know that, but still what I know in my heart— remember Pascal—'the heart has its reasons'—is that all these things are better, more beautiful, more meaningful when they are connected to you.

"So, if I have to live without you, I can. But I don't have to like it, and maybe there would be someone else down the road who is just as wonderful, but I don't believe that, and so I will dare to hope that you will be standing there at the Pier waving to me, and that even if you are not there in the body, your spirit will be there, and I will stand on the deck and watch for you."

Anthony S. Abbott

On Friday morning, August 2, 1953, the Queen Mary sailed into New York, and David stood on the deck, as he said he would. He could see Ellis Island, where the immigrants had come in, and the Statue of Liberty with her torch upraised, and he felt the pang of being an American and coming home. He wondered what it must have looked like to those immigrants who had come here seeking freedom. He thought of the end of *The Great Gatsby*. How did it go? He remembered. ". . .I became aware of the old island here that flowered once for Dutch sailors' eyes—a fresh green breast of the new world. . . for a transitory enchanted moment, man must have held his breath in the presence of this continent. . .face to face. . .with something commensurate to his capacity for wonder." He liked that. He felt it, too, and he was glad to be home.

As the great ship slowly made its way up the Hudson River past the financial district toward midtown, he could see his favorite landmarks, the Empire State Building, the Chrysler Building, and the RCA Building in Rockefeller Center. He thought of the subway line running all the way up to the tip of Manhattan and to the Bronx, and wondered if he would ever take the D train again up to 167th Street. Of course, he would go to the Stadium and see his beloved Yankees, or he would call Billy DuPont and they would go to the Polo Grounds and see the Giants.

Or maybe Tracy would be there, and they would take a yellow cab to Grand Central and get on the train to Greenwich and count all the stations from New York to her house, as they had before, and as he had when he went off to Lowell School so many years ago. He imagined himself sitting next to her on the train, their arms and shoulders touching, her right hand clasped in his left, her silver bracelet glistening, but a little cold against his wrist, Tracy in her red bandana and her yellow shirt glowing like gold, and the love in her eyes holding him, welcoming him home.

About the Author

ANTHONY S. ABBOTT was born in San Francisco and educated at the Fay School, Southborough, Mass., and at the Kent School in Connecticut. He received his A.B. from Princeton University, Magna cum laude, in 1957. With the support of a Danforth Fellowship he received his A.M. from Harvard University in 1960 and his Ph.D. in 1962.

From 1961 to 1964 he was Instructor in English at Bates College. In 1964 he became Assistant Professor of English at Davidson College in North Carolina. He was promoted to Associate Professor in 1967 and Full Professor in 1979. In 1990 he was named Charles A. Dana Professor of English. He served as Chair of the Department from 1989 to 1996. He was honored for his teaching with the Thomas Jefferson Award in 1969 and the Hunter-Hamilton Love of Teaching Award in 1997.

His first book of poems, *The Girl in the Yellow Raincoat*, was published by St. Andrews Press in 1989 and was nominated for the Pulitzer Prize. His second poetry collection, *A Small Thing Like A Breath*, was published by St. Andrews Press in 1993, and his third, *The Search for Wonder in the Cradle of the World* in 2000. In 2003 his first novel, *Leaving Maggie Hope*, won the Novello Award and was published by Novello Festival Press. The novel won the "Gold Award" from ForeWord Magazine in the literary fiction category. His fourth collection of poems, *The Man Who*, published in 2005 by Main Street Rag Publishing Co. of Charlotte, won the Oscar Arnold Young Award of the N.C. Poetry Council for the best book of poems by a North Carolinian in 2005.

He is past president of the Charlotte Writers Club and the North Carolina Writers Network and also past Chairman of the North Carolina Writers Conference. He has won the Thomas H. McDill Award of the North Carolina Poetry Society three times. Between 1985 and 1992 he served on the Governor's Committee on the North Carolina Awards. In 1996 he was honored by St. Andrews College with the Sam Ragan Award for his writing and his service to the literary community of North Carolina.

He is married to the former Susan Dudley of South Orange, NJ. They have three sons, David, Stephen, and Andrew, and seven grandchildren, James, Robert, Clara, Elliot, Henry, Josephine and John.